REDOUBT

MERCEDES LACKEY

THORNDIKE PRESS
A part of Gale, Cengage Learning

Detroit • New York • San Francisco • New Haven, Conn • Waterville, Maine • London

GALE
CENGAGE Learning®

LIBRARY OF CONGRESS CATALOGING-IN-PUBLICATION DATA

Lackey, Mercedes.
    Redoubt / by Mercedes Lackey. — Large Print edition.
       pages cm. — (The Collegium Chronicles ; Book Four) (Thorndike Press
    Large Print Basic)
    ISBN-13: 978-1-4104-5632-8 (hardcover)
    ISBN-10: 1-4104-5632-3 (hardcover)
    1. Orphans—Fiction. 2. Valdemar (Imaginary place)—Fiction. 3. Large type
books. I. Title.
PS3562.A246R43 2013
813'.54—dc23   2012044213

Published in 2013 by arrangement with DAW Books

Printed in the United States of America
1 2 3 4 5 6 7 17 16 15 14 13

Dedicated to the memory of
Anne McCaffrey.
No one could have had a better
inspiration or role model.

1

Herald Trainee Mags and his Companion Dallen stood so quietly in the blue dusk that they might have been an equestrian statue. The last light of the sun burned a rim of muted rose against the trees and the wall around the western side of the Palace. Overhead, stars gleamed in a sky gone a blue so dark it was just barely a color. Mags knew there would be only a sliver of new moon tonight, nothing to drown the splendor of the stars. The scent of newly cut grass surrounded them, but the gentlest of breezes at their backs brought whiffs of the mingled perfumes of roses, lilacs, honeysuckle, and lilies. The stars seemed near enough to touch, blazing jewels strewn across velvet.

Dallen dipped his head a little, and Mags absently patted his Companion's neck. Dallen was attired in unusual splendor, in his full formal gear, with blue leather saddle and bitless bridle, the bridle adorned with silver-plated bridle bells, brow-band with his name tooled into it, and blue-and-white barding embroidered with silver. Mags had spent hours grooming him, and it showed; there was not a hair that didn't gleam like the finest satin. Mags had even polished his silver-gray hooves until they looked almost like real silver.

Mags was clothed to match in a set of formal Grays in a velvet as light as a cobweb and linen fine enough to use in a Temple. And for once, these weren't hand-me-downs from some other, wealthier Trainee; no, this was a very special occasion that warranted a very special outlay by the Crown itself. Every Trainee at the Collegium had an identical set of splendid new Grays, or the dull Scarlets and Greens of the Bard and Healer Trainees — and every Herald, Bard, and Healer here who didn't already own a sumptuous uniform or set of robes of his or her own had been supplied with dress uniforms that had left some people gaping.

Mags wasn't thinking about his new uniform. He was putting himself into the quietest state of mind he could manage. What he and the others were about to do required that every Herald and Trainee sur-render himself to a kind of common pool of *doing*. It wasn't unlike Kirball in that way, actually, and the more he thought about it in that fashion, the calmer he felt himself becoming. Finally he felt that last little bit of tension ease out of his shoulders, and Dallen shook his head gently.

:It's time, Chosen.:

Mags took the blue-glass lantern hanging from the saddle horn, found the fire-striker in his belt pouch without even thinking about it, and set the wick alight. Then Dallen turned, and they moved down toward the chapel in Companion's Field, joining one of half a dozen processions of Heralds and Trainees, all carrying identical lit lanterns in one hand, coming from all parts of the Collegium and moving as if they were all directed by the same will. Dallen moved smoothly under him, not like a horse at all — the few times Mags had ridden one of the Kirball horses had left him with a hearty sympathy for the Riders.

The lanterns provided the only light anywhere up on the Hill. Not a single light of any sort shone from the Palace or the Collegia. As dark as it was, they all might as well have been riding through a forest somewhere in the wilderness rather than through Companion's Field. Within a few moments, Mags was at the head of the farthest left of the six lines, and he sensed, rather than saw, that King's Own Nikolas was at the head of the farthest right. All the lines stopped. And in that same moment, with one accord, the Companions took up the curiously slow, graceful, and beautiful gait that was known as "Companion Dancing."

The only sound was that of the rhythmic chiming of the bridle bells as all six lines halted in place, Companions still pacing. Then Mags and Nickolas led their lines out, while the inner four remained pacing in place. When they were six lengths in front of the rest, Mags and Nikolas turned toward each other. The lanterns seemed to make graceful arcs in the darkness as they moved, with the blue light reflecting off the snowy coats of the Companions and the white and gray uniforms. The next two lines began to move forward, as the outermost lines curved toward each other, met, and passed. Then the innermost lines moved up, until the entire path to the chapel had become an interlacing of dancing Companions, coats throwing back the blue light of the lanterns, bridle bells making the only music needed for this dance. From any distance, it would all blur into a moving, weaving, and reweaving braid of light whose goal was clearly the chapel.

Mags found himself in a kind of pleasant half-trance, aware of every Companion and every Herald and Trainee around him, aware of exactly where they were in the procession, somehow conveying minute corrections to the others so that the distances between the riders never varied, and every hoof was precisely placed.

He and Nikolas arrived at the chapel, again at the heads of the two outermost lines, and Dallen and Rolan pivoted so that they faced one another with a broad stretch of the path between them. As the rest arrived, they too lined up, and only when the last of them were in place did the Companions cease to dance.

But there was still the sound of bridle bells, for coming down the path they had left was a single Companion with two riders, followed by another, followed by a very select group of witnesses.

The first riders were, of course, the Heir, Prince Sedric, and his bride, Master Soren's niece Lydia, and as they reached the chapel, the door opened, spilling out a carpet of soft, warm light, although there was no other light visible. Lydia was radiant, her green eyes shining with happiness, her tumble of red curls pinned up under a wreath of white flowers. Mags knew more about cloth and dresses than most young men, since such knowledge was part of the training he had as what was essentially a spy for the Crown. Her white gown, trimmed in silver, was rich but not ostentatious — quite good enough for a princess, but it said without words that this was a lady who would not break the Treasury for the sake of a dress. Sedric, of course, looked every inch the Prince and Herald and very much his father's son, dark as his father was and with his father's chiseled features. And very, very happy.

The Prince dismounted, and his lady slid down into his arms; the King and Queen followed suit, and the wedding party proceeded into the chapel to the sound of a harp from somewhere inside. The door closed, leaving everyone outside with only the blue light of the lanterns illuminating them all.

It was a very small wedding party. The chapel wasn't very large and they all fit inside handily, with room to spare. Faced with an ever-increasing guest list, the princess-to-be had finally put her foot down, gently, but firmly. "Every time we meet, there is someone else who cannot be left out without offending them," Lydia had said, with the aplomb of someone who had spent all her life watching the factions and movements in the Court. "Very well. We will offend *everyone*. I want no one at the ceremony but our immediate families."

The Council had been horrified. But Lydia was both firm and charming in a way that made some suspect some sort of Gift at work. Or, as Nikolas had said, in tones of admiration, "She can tell you to go to hell in a way that will send you running off to pack your bags." Lydia had gotten her way.

Of course, no one was going to be offended. The vast mobs of people who could not possibly have been accommodated in any temple or cathedral in all of Valdemar could certainly fit into the Palace grounds, and as soon as the two were declared officially wed, the celebration would begin. And meanwhile —

Nikolas nodded at Mags, who dropped back into his trance. Rolan and Dallen pawed the ground three times in perfect synchronization, and the Heralds and Trainees raised their lanterns again on the third beat as the Companions resumed their dance.

This time it was only two lines, crossing and recrossing, weaving and reweaving, to the sound of the bridle bells. When the King signaled from within the chapel that the

13

ceremony had concluded, they needed to be back in their places for the recessional within four beats of the dance. But it was certainly a fine display up there on the hill, and it was making those who had been shut out of the ceremony feel as if they were part of it. Or that was the theory, anyway.

As if someone had conjured it to make the entire scene perfect, a flower-scented breeze came up from somewhere deep in the Field, wafting up to the top of the hill where the silent onlookers waited.

:Now,: Mags heard in his mind, and within the allotted four beats, they were all back in place.

:Ready,: Nikolas replied to the King, and the entire chapel suddenly blazed with light. Light poured from every window. Light streamed from the Bell Tower. And that, of course, was the signal for the Palace and gardens to answer with their own blaze of glory, as the chapel doors opened, and the wedding party came out.

From up on the hill, it was the Bards' turn to contribute, as the massed musicians of the Collegium and every other Bard who could possibly get here broke into a processional march especially composed for the occasion. The Prince mounted his Companion; Nikolas, who had dismounted, lifted

14

the new Princess up onto the pillion pad behind him. Then the King mounted, and Nikolas then did the same for the Queen. Then with the Prince leading Mags' row, and the King leading Nikolas', they made their way in two long lines back up to the Palace. The breeze seemed to accompany them like an invisible train of flowers, and the music came down to them like a blessing.

The onlookers withheld their applause until the royal party reached the half-circle of splendidly clad Guardsmen awaiting them, and the Companions stopped just as the recessional ended. Then the clapping and shouting began.

The two rows of Heralds and Trainees passed by a pair of tables, where a couple of servants took their lanterns from them.

Mags was mightily glad to be rid of that lantern when he got to that edge of the grounds and the people waiting to relieve the honor guard of their glowing burdens. It might not have been very heavy, but they were awkward to carry, and you couldn't just hang a lit lantern on your saddle-bow. The lanterns were going to be gifts to all those people who dared not be offended; he was pretty certain they'd be satisfied enough with them. If you couldn't be at the cer-

15

emony itself, it certainly would not displease anyone to have a pretty thing like the silver-plated lantern to show you had been to the event.

The lanterns were placed on a table next to the King and Queen to be distributed (after which they became the problem of their new owners!), and a long reception line began to form to tender congratulations.

Not, however, to the bride and groom.

No, the Prince waited until all the Companions were back up at the gardens and all the lanterns collected and blown out. Then with a general wave and an exuberant whoop, he and his bride galloped back down to Companion's Field and their own secluded little wedding bower somewhere in it. There they would be guarded by all the unpartnered Companions, and heaven help anyone who tried to disturb them. That had been the Prince's demand, and who could blame him? He'd had to wait two years for Lydia already. The festivities were scheduled for three days; they'd come out for some things, and at the end of the third day, he and the Princess would return to the Palace and take their congratulations at a formal reception as the invitees left.

The gardens had been illuminated not

only with their usual lamps but also with scented lanterns and torches. Tables with drink and refreshments — drink, mostly, Mags suspected–were scattered about. The guests had been feasting all afternoon, unlike the Trainees.

Mags was scanning the crowd for another face entirely, and he felt his heart lift as he spotted Amily slowly, and with great determination, making her way toward him. You had to be watching for her to see her; as always, she was dressed to blend in, rather than stand out. Among all of the jewels and extravagant costumes, she was like a sparrow among scarlet jays.

He did not urge Dallen to her, for he knew she was exceedingly proud of how strong she was growing, and he was not going to undermine that by offering more help than she wanted. But by the time she had reached him, Nikolas had pulled up beside him and dismounted, and he boosted her up behind Mags exactly as he had helped the Princess and Queen.

Amily was very like her father; you had to look at her closely to realize she was pretty, and you had to really know her to understand she wasn't merely pretty but had a quiet beauty that was so self-contained that very little of it escaped. Like her father, she had soft brown hair and brown eyes, and something about her made the eye tend to slide over her. In his case, Mags suspected that the ability to make people overlook Nikolas was entirely training. In Amily's case, it was something more subtle than training; it had been, at least in part, the desire to draw no attention to herself and her disability. A disability that, thanks to Bear, no longer existed. She had learned all the ways she could distract attention from herself by sending it to someone, or something, more interesting.

"How did we look?" Mags asked her, as her father remounted and he and Rolan trotted off elsewhere. The breeze lifted her soft hair and teased it into gentle curls. He had to crane his neck around to see her.

"Magnificent," she told him, with a touch of pride. "The bridle bells were quite clear up here as well. Everyone was really impressed. They would probably have been even more impressed if they could have seen the dancing clearly, but the light reflected off of all of you and turned the whole thing into ribbons of glowing blue."

"Good," Mags sighed. "I was hopin' it was going to be worth it. I swear to you, that poxy dancin' took more working out and practice than Kirball." He'd lost a great deal of his thick, rural accent by dint of a lot of practice. It still slipped out a little when he was relaxed and among friends, but he was as proud of his speech as Amily was of her ability to walk.

Of course, when he was *really* playing a part, his concentration on his speech ensured nothing would slip.

Amily laughed and patted his shoulder. "It was more than worth it if all the oohs and ahs I heard were any indication. Well, where do we go tonight?" she asked. "The gardens and the official celebration?"

Mags made a face that she, of course, could not see, since she was behind him. "Thank you very much, no. I'm not interested in being feted because I can bung a ball through a goal."

"Surely not everyone here is a Kirball fanatic," she teased. "I'm sure one or two people have heard of you as something other than the neck-or-nothing player. You actually *have* done one or two things besides that."

"Oh, no," he replied firmly, as Dallen waited patiently for the path before them to clear. "I've even less interest in talkin' about what happened when those fiends took you."

He felt her shiver, but she said, quite

bravely, "Mags, you *were* a hero . . . and there are people who know that." He could not imagine how she must have felt — drugged, terrified, in the hands of a couple of known murderers, and fully aware that even if she managed to throw off the effects of the drugs they had poured into her, she would never be able to escape from them on her own. Not a day went by that he didn't berate himself for not being there when she had been kidnapped. Because of his Gift, he would have *known* that the carriage sent for her was not the right one. He would never have let her get into it.

Just as bad was the fact that he had been within inches of catching the carriage, and he and Dallen had been neatly knocked senseless.

It had been the worst day of his life.

"The fewer people who think I'm some kind of hero when I ain't, the better," he said shortly. "I'm just Mags. Let's leave it at that. No, the Trainees are havin' a stable party. I thought we'd go there."

"Oh!" she exclaimed happily. "I love stable parties!"

"It's going to be in the hayloft," he told her, as people managed to clear away from the way they wanted to go, and Dallen turned his head and ambled in that direction. It was almost as bright as day up here, but down at the stable, things were a little more subdued, at least from this side. It *was* lit up, but it looked no different from any other early evening. "Stablemaster took the opportunity to clear the place out down to the bare floor, since we were going to have to feed all the visitors' mounts anyway. Once they're gone, he'll bring in the first of this year's cutting."

He didn't ask Amily if she could climb to the loft; he knew she would, or die trying. But he had something else in mind for her.

There were more doors in the stable now — one for every stall, in fact — and all of them stood wide open. The ground floor was mostly empty except for a few bales of straw and some Trainees and stable hands taking advantage of the quiet places to sit, for there were not a lot of those available with so many people on the Palace and Collegia grounds. Only the two night lamps, one on each wall, were lit. Mags had a notion that in some of the darker corners people were taking advantage of the quiet places to do more than just sit, but that wasn't any of his business. Dallen went around to the hoist side of the stables, where four or five young ladies in lovely gowns were waiting with varying degrees of impatience and varying degrees of giddiness.

The hay hoist was made for one man to haul up a pallet of several hay bales at once, so the weight of one young lady was hardly likely to strain its capacity. A comfortable canvas sling, stolen from one of the tree swings down by the river, had been fitted to the hoist. Anyone who wanted to ride up to the loft rather than climb the steep, ladderlike stair would be able to take this somewhat more exciting route up. The trick, however, was that the man at the top of the hoist would use a hay hook to snag the rope and haul the pallet in through the open door at the top. Rather than flailing about in the dark with the heavy hay hook, the young ladies were being encouraged to *swing* their way to the door and be caught by their escorts. There were a lot of squeals and giggles. And every so often, one of the lads appropriated the swing so he could show off by swinging and jumping in through the door at the apex of his swing.

If the teachers and other elders had known about this, Mags reflected, they would probably have had a proper fit over it. But they didn't, and he was pretty sure that with all the Gifts scattered among the crowd, no one was going to get seriously hurt.

His thought was confirmed when he spotted First-Year Trainee Finny standing just inside the hayloft door, out of the way of the swingers but well in line-of-sight. This was important, because young Finny's Gift was a particularly powerful one, a kind of Fetching that allowed her to lift or catch objects with her mind that could weigh as much as a Companion. Finny would not allow anyone to fall.

"Well," he said over his shoulder to Amily, "Care to try? Finny's up above, so it's safe as houses."

He could just see Amily's face by craning his neck, and she looked both excited and a little bit anxious as she watched one of the Bardic Trainees fling herself into the waiting arms of another.

"If you're going to catch me, and Finny's there . . . I think so. But you won't think badly of me if I get scared and ask to be put down on the ground again, will you?" She bit her lip a little.

He wanted to kiss her. "Nay, I'll just reckon you have more sense than the rest of us." He swung his leg over Dallen's saddle horn and dropped down to the ground, then lifted Amily down. And, feeling emboldened, he led her into the line while Dallen ambled off to be divested of his regalia and join the other Companions in the Field.

:Don't get yourself knocked silly-sideways,: Dallen said mildly as he vanished into the darkness.

:Eh, this is nothing compared to m'roof-running,: Mags assured him, as he took his place in the sling and waited to be hauled aloft. And really, it wasn't. He'd done *much* more perilous leaps on the nighttime roof-tops, and the loft was very well lit. The absence of hay meant people could bring up as many lanterns as they chose, and they did. A couple of good pumps of his legs got him the height and momentum he wanted, and he capped his jump by turning it into a somersaulting tumble through the air, rolling to his feet, that left him standing again with his arms spread, taking a little, mocking bow.

"Allo, Finny," he said, nodding to the short, shy girl who must have changed out of her Formal Grays into something more comfortable as soon as she got the chance. *I should've done that. Oh, well, too late now. These'll need a wash.* "Glad to see you're here to keep us from breaking our necks."

Finny blushed with pleased confusion. "Really . . . I couldn't . . . I mean . . ."

Mags beamed at her. "Damn shame with a Gift like yours they won't let you on the

24

Kirball teams. Did you think about volunteering for the Healers' squad? Be *really* useful to have someone that could lift a person with a busted bone without moving anything."

She flushed even redder. "Do you think . . . would you . . ."

"I'll talk to the Captains and Bear as soon as all this wedding flummery is over," he promised. "Bet they'll all be falling all over each other to ask you first."

"Oh!" she said, deep pink with pleasure. He gave her shoulders a friendly squeeze. Sometimes being "Mags the Kirball champion" and "Mags the hero" was nice. When he could make someone as shy and anxious as Finny feel wanted and good — that was when it stopped being annoying.

She was so happy now her eyes just shone behind her glass lenses. He grinned again. "Thenkee, Finny," he just said, with all the gratitude he could put in his voice. "Now, it'll be Amily coming up next, so let's make sure she comes in just as soft as a feather." He looked over the edge of the loft door. Amily was just getting into the swing; she glanced up and spotted him, lamplight falling softly on her face, and she saw Finny's close-cropped head beside his. She waved, looking relieved.

"All right, boys, it's Amily, give her a smooth ride!" cried a young Guard Trainee who was helping the girls into the swing down below. Mags looked over to see a cheerful-faced young giant of a Guard Trainee on the rope and nodded to him. The youngster nodded back and began hauling the rope, slowly, carefully, and very smoothly. At one point, only her friends had known Amily was the King's Own's daughter, and most people up here on the Hill were not aware she existed. But after the first attempted abduction, *everyone* became aware of her, and after the second, successful kidnapping, she suddenly acquired a veritable army of protectors.

Finny remained poised at the edge of the loft door, practically quivering with concentration. When Amily came into view, Finny waved at her.

"I can . . . I . . . I can give you a little push . . . if you want," Finny said hesitantly. "If that would help . . ."

"Oh, would you?" Amily begged. "It looks a *lot* higher from here than I thought!"

On hearing that, Finny did a lot more than give Amily a "little push." With her face set in a grimace of concentration, Finny stared at Amily, and without Amily having to move her legs at all, she began swinging in a gentle, highly controlled arc, until she was close enough for Mags to catch. And as he reached for her, he could *feel* Finny helping to steady her, so bringing her into the loft was no more difficult, and no more dangerous, than lifting her down from Dallen's back.

She felt it too, and she beamed as she thanked the Trainee. Finny went an even deeper pink but managed to accept the thanks graciously.

Another girl was already coming up, though, and Finny quickly turned her attention back to making sure she did so safely. Mags and Amily moved out of the way and scanned the hayloft.

There were dozens of lanterns hanging from the rafters, and since the loft was meant to store hay and straw through the winter for a great many Companions, these upper walls with their black timbers and white-plastered noggin between were a full story tall, with the roof and rafters above that. Without the hay, it looked like a rustic hall, and not part of a stable. There was plenty of room for whatever anyone wanted to do, even though there must have been more than fifty people up here. Mags had been part of the contingent helping to get food up during the day, so he had a pretty good idea of what was on the crowded tables down at the north end of the loft. "Are you hungry?" he asked.

He certainly was. There had been an awful lot of running around today and not a lot of time to eat.

"Starving," Amily replied, her eyes warming with her smile.

The south half of the loft was where the gathering of musicians had set up, so it wasn't too hard to weave their way through the crowd to get to the food. It was every bit as good as a Midwinter spread at Master Soren's. There were pocket pies, both meat and fruit, and tiny egg pies and fruit tarts. There were cheeses — sharp and yellow, mild and white, pungent with veins of blue running through them. There was white and rye and barley bread and even an oat bread that Mags was rather partial to. There were hard-boiled eggs and everything pickled that could be pickled. There was thin-sliced hard sausage and sausage in pastry. There were cookies, candied nuts, hard-boiled sweets, and plenty of fruit, but for once, there was only one sort of cake — the wedding cake, which Mags expected would be good enough that no one would miss any other sort. Mags was pleased to see that his favorites and Amily's were still available.

There weren't any plates, probably because everything that even *looked* like a plate was in service up at the Palace, but knowing that this was coming, some enterprising soul had bought up the entire output of Haven's apprentice basket-weavers to use instead. The work was terrible and would ordinarily have been burned, but it was certainly good enough to hold food for the night. Mags secured something that looked as if it had been intended as a sieve and something else that might have been a lid, and he filled them with little meat and fruit pies, cheese chunks, bread, grapes, and slices of the wedding cake, which was a rich, dark creation scented with spice and honey, bursting with chopped nuts. There was quite a crowd at the food tables and not so much at the drink tables, so with unspoken accord, Amily had gone to get drink for both of them.

Although there was a light spiced honey wine available, Amily had gotten them both cups cleverly made of molded and waxed paper pulp full of spiced cider instead. "Oh, good choice," Mags told her, when he managed to make his way to her.

"Well, you're playing a game tomorrow, and I don't want you to have to do so with a mead head," she laughed.

He rolled his eyes ruefully. "I hope the

others remember that," he replied. The Kirball match was going to be an exhibition game, the Prince's team against the King's, with the members of each picked by their respective patron. Mags was on the Prince's team, which pleased him quite a bit. If nothing else, that would put to rest the last unease about his loyalty and how Prince Sedric felt about it.

The loft might have been cleared of straw and hay, but there were plenty of other things to sit on. The bedrolls everyone was supposed to make and keep available at all times, in case there was a sudden need to put everyone in the Field (or take a survival test), made perfectly good seating, some people had hauled up benches from the stable below, and others had brought up the folding cots some preferred over bedrolls, and which Mags did not trust at all. He had brought up his own bedroll and a couple of old cushions, and he got them out of the corner and spread out in no time at all. Amily needed a little help to get down to the floor, but once there, she seemed quite comfortable.

It was rather like having a picnic indoors. All the loft doors were open, and a good breeze was coming through; all the musicians were clustered around the door at this end with people disposed on their various seats around them, too busy eating and drinking to talk.

"Where's the dancing?" Amily wanted to know.

"Down below," Mags told her. "There're too many to fit up here *and* have dancing, so we all agreed the dancers would be outside, and people who just wanted to get together would be up here. That's why the musicians are at the door there. Look! There're Bear and Lena!" He waved at their friends, who had several more of their usual circle in tow, and before long there was a cluster of Kirball team members, a couple more Bardic Trainees besides Lena, and two more shy and very young-looking Healer Trainees. Mags remembered when Lena was as shy as that, a thin, delicate, dark-haired thing with sad brown eyes. Now although she was still thin, she gave the impression of strength along with delicacy, and her eyes were seldom sad. Bear, of course was Bear, still. Still peering from behind his lenses, still looking like a sleepy, affable bear full of honey and good nature. Not so round anymore — he'd grown into some good muscles of late. But it was no surprise that he'd rounded up the Healer Trainees — he was always one for picking up strays. Rather like Mags.

Bear introduced them, but they seemed very much overawed by the company they were in, and they just sat there with round eyes, occasionally remembering to eat and drink. The rest of them, however, were as famished as Mags was, which was not surprising, really. Every free hand had been needed right up until the beginning of the ceremony, and what meals had been snatched had often been eaten on the run.

The cooks had clearly rewarded their diligence, however. This was not cast-offs from the tables meant for the nobles.

When he and Amily had sat down, the musicians had been a tambour drummer, a girl with a gittern, another with a hautboy, and someone Mags couldn't quite see with a set of small-pipes. By the time Bear's group settled, the hautboy player and the tambour drummer had been replaced by someone with a set of bones and someone with a shepherd's flute. It was clear that the musicians — not all of whom were in Trainee Red — were rotating in and out as people got tired of playing or were ready to eat. Right now the music was all lively country dances, things most musicians knew very well. And from the sound of whooping and laughter outside, the dancing was going on apace. The breeze outside had strengthened, which was a good thing; it kept the air moving through the loft.

"Are you planning on playing later?" Amily asked Lena, who nodded.

"We brought up practice instruments and left them here to share," she explained. "That way nobody needs to worry about his personal instruments tonight. Accidents do happen after all. No one wants to have a foot put through his prize gittern."

One of the other Bardic trainees shuddered and ate a big piece of cake to comfort himself. "That happened to me over Midwinter," he explained. "Family gather got rowdy. I was like to die."

He ate another piece of cake to comfort himself. "Did all right out of it I s'pose," he said, after a while. "Family took up collection, Master Martin, the luthier in Haven, took pity on me, and I got a nice gittern out of it, I guess . . ."

"But no instrument is like the first *good* one you ever get," said Lena sympathetically. "That one is special."

The other lad nodded glumly.

"Write a song about it," Lena suggested. "It probably won't make you feel better, but it's good to get things like that out in the open. You know what the teachers say, strong emotions make strong music."

"Huh. Maybe I will," the other Trainee said after a moment, then turned his attention back to his food.

Amily got up and slowly made her way to the open door, smiling a little at the musicians as they made room for her. She settled down where she could look down at the dancers. Mags picked up the cushions and brought them to her.

Down below, the crowd was egging on two young men who were particularly good at some sort of rather acrobatic endeavor that involved a lot of jumping and kicking and tumbling. It didn't look like any dance he was familiar with, but, then, he wasn't familiar with a lot of dances.

"I'll dance at Midwinter," Amily said, softly, out of the blue. "I will."

Mags felt as if he were going to burst with pride. "Yes," he said simply, and sat down beside her. "You will."

He had been afraid that watching the dancers would just make her more aware of what she still couldn't do, but instead, it seemed to be making her more determined. She'd never wanted to watch dancing before —

Dallen put in his two coppers' worth of observation. :*Maybe that was because before, she'd been defined, at least in her own mind, by everything she wasn't.:*

:You think?: Mags asked.

:Use that clever magpie mind of yours. How many things did she have that she was?:

Dallen was right, as Dallen usually was. The more he thought about it, the more he could see all the "nots" that had been in Amily's life, and fair few positives. She wasn't able to walk without help, which automatically made her someone who had to be aided rather than someone who could aid. All that could have been worked around if she had qualified for any of the Collegia, but she had no Gifts and obviously no Companion. She wasn't a courtier, she didn't have her father's ability to seduce information out of people without them knowing it, she wasn't — well, so very many things. But Bear had changed all that. One thing that had been impossible, that she should ever be like everyone else in the most basic of ways, suddenly became not only possible but actually *happened.* And if one impossible thing had happened, how many more could? She could dance, she could learn to ride, herself, and on a horse, not a Companion, she could —

"And I am going to ask the Weapons-master to help me," she went on, as the two young men finally exhausted each other. She turned to look at him, her chin set stubbornly. "After all, Lydia and Saski and some of the other girls all know how to fight as well as any of you Herald Trainees. I want to be able to fight back if I need to. I don't want to be the weak point anymore. I don't want to be the one everyone has to worry about. And if something happens again, if there's another attempt . . ." for a moment, her eyes flashed steel ". . . I want to give anyone who thinks they can hurt Father through me the surprise of their lives."

:Well good for her,: said Dallen. *:I expected something of the sort from her, but not quite so soon.:*

"That sounds like a good plan to me," he agreed. "It can't help but strengthen you more, faster. Bet Bear'll agree. The Weaponsmaster knows all sorts of tricks, all kinds of — well — dirty-fighting ways. Sounds like something worth doing."

Her expression softened, as if she had been bracing herself for him to object. "I'm *glad* you think so."

"I'm glad you're glad." He chuckled. "An' if we're done bein' all serious and everything, I reckon I could use some pocket pies."

■ ■ ■ ■

Amily got tired sooner than everyone else, of course. She was still recovering from what had been a harrowing piece of Healing, and everything she did was still twice as difficult for her and took twice as much energy as it did for anyone else. Long before Mags was even thinking about sleeping, she was ready to rest.

She came down out of the loft the same way she had gone up, and with the same care — but this time with greater enjoyment. "Would you like me to get Dallen?" he asked, when she was safely on the ground again.

She shook her head. "I'd rather walk. Besides, being on Dallen would make me a bit obvious once we get nearer the Palace, and I'd rather not be obvious."

Mags paused a moment to let his mind drift to what Dallen was up to. "Seems he's found some talk he wants to eavesdrop on, so he'll thank you for that anyway," he said thoughtfully. "Wouldn't you think people could stop with the politicking and all for just one day?"

The breeze lingered around them, stirring her skirts. "Court politics *is* all some people have in their lives," she replied, then shrugged. "But since Dallen has so kindly decided to deal with this particular bit of it, we can probably let ourselves enjoy the evening without worrying about it. Dallen is as good at not being noticed as you."

:Wise woman,: Dallen commented, then went back to eavesdropping.

It wasn't a quiet walk nor a private one, what with all of the celebrants swirling about the grounds. Judging from the amount of reeling some of them were doing, not to mention what Mags could only think of as "drunken shenanigans," there were going to be many, many sore heads in the morning. But as he held Amily's hand, and they walked slowly toward the Herald's Wing, he felt oddly as if they were somehow apart from all of that. It was a feeling he liked, as if the two of them were enclosed in a magical bubble through which they could watch what was going on if they chose, and yet were in a world away from it.

They entered the Herald's Wing, and the noise dropped precipitously as soon as they closed the door. There was no sign of anyone in the long, wood-paneled corridor, and the sound of their footsteps echoing down the hall was louder than the music and voices outside.

When they got to the door of the quarters she shared with her father, however, things got a little . . . awkward. Just to begin with, there was her father. Nikolas was not only a Herald, and thus would certainly find out if they got up to any shenanigans of their own, but he was the King's Own Herald, which meant he would probably find out about it from multiple sources.

This did put a bit of a damper on romance. It was altogether awkward, in fact, since both of them were aware of it.

At least the hallway was empty; in fact, it felt to Mags as though most of the wing was empty. So when they reached the door, he leaned over without warning to steal a kiss, and Amily wasn't shy of reciprocating. He put both his arms around her when she did, pulling her closer, and felt her arms around his waist.

"I don't think there would be any harm if you came in," she said huskily.

"It'd probably be better than standin' about in the hall," he agreed.

The little sitting room had been laid ready for the evening, though it wasn't likely that Nikolas would set foot here before dawn. Two lanterns were lit in the sitting room, and the windows had been left open to the breeze, although the curtains had been drawn before them. They both sat down on the couch before the cold fireplace and listened to the distant sounds of celebration coming in through the open window.

All right, Mags. Do manage to make some kind of talk, won't you? He seized on the last thing she'd mentioned in the loft.

"I might be able to help you with weapons'-work and all," he said, "I've got some weapons I think'd suit you," then blushed as she giggled. "I don't think that came out right."

"Oh, you probably have a lot of weapons that would suit me, but we should confine ourselves to the ones my father would approve of," she flirted, making him blush even more. But he liked this new side of her; she was so much more *alive.*

They flirted a little more and kissed a little more, but eventually the fact that she was tired and the fact that Nikolas was very much a presence even though he was occupied elsewhere made him take his leave of her.

He was by no means ready to call an end to the evening, which was still going strong in the gardens. By the time he got back to the stable loft, however, Bear and Lena were nowhere to be seen.

:Don't go looking for them,: Dallen advised.

:And for Haven's sake, don't go knocking on Bear's door for a nightcap!:

Oh, so *that* was the way the wind blew . . . he'd had his suspicions for quite some time, but this was the first Dallen had confirmed them. He felt a flash of envy. Lena's father was in no position to dictate anything to her, given that he was utterly in disgrace, and Mags rather doubted that her teachers would disapprove either of Bear as something more than a friend or of anything that would give her a little distraction from her studies. If anything, her teachers at Bardic Collegium had difficulty in getting her to think about anything other than music. Being in love would certainly give her perspective on love songs. And as for Bear himself, well, his parents were already so furious about his defiance of their wishes (with the help of Healer's Collegium) that it was difficult to imagine how anything he would do short of murder would change their opinion for the worse. Bear already had the responsibilities of a full Healer in many areas, and even his teachers tended to regard and treat him as a full adult and peer.

:Well,: Dallen said, commenting on his thoughts, *:your case is a bit more complicated.:*

:It always is,: he sighed. *:It's bad enough*

*that Amily has been a cripple for so long and
all her friends feel protective of her. It's worse
her father is a Herald, so the chances of us
actually keeping anything to ourselves is
pretty low. But given that Nikolas is the King's
Own Herald . . . sometimes it feels as if every
single person in Whites and half of the Companions thinks themselves her substitute
parents. Awkward don't begin to describe it.:*

:It could be worse,: Dallen observed. *:You
could be the Prince. No matter what he does,
someone is bound to disapprove.:*

Mags snorted. But that was entirely too
true.

He nibbled a little more, drank a little
more, mingled with his fellow Trainees and
some of the younger Guard recruits who
had managed to find the party, and finally
decided to try his hand at dancing. If Amily
was determined to dance by Midwinter,
he'd better be ready to dance with her. On
a night like tonight, the girls would forgive
his mistakes, he reckoned.

And so it proved. He danced a great deal,
even if he didn't dance well; he drank a
little, and when Dallen turned up to shove
him into his own room in the stable, he was
tired enough and just light-headed enough,
not to resist.

2

The morning was cool and the breeze still persisted, which was a good sign for the game that afternoon. Mags got himself an early wash, courtesy of the stable pump, knowing he was going to be wanting another before the day was over. The air was clear, the sky cloudless as he walked up to the dining hall that was shared by all three Collegia. He enjoyed the solitary walk; in a few hours, he wasn't going to find anywhere but Companion's Field that didn't have a crowd.

Breakfast — and, for that matter, lunch and dinner — for these three days was going to be a free-form affair, at least at the Collegia. He wasn't sure how it would be managed at the Palace, and, of course, it would probably be just another day at the manors around the Palace, so far as the servants of the highborn were concerned. But here, since every possible hand was needed, the Collegia servants had been somewhat conscripted. So at most of the meals during the wedding, cold food was laid out on the tables, and you were expected to help yourself.

These were holidays for everyone except the servants. Amily had told Mags that there was going to be a separate set of holidays for the servants still on duty, some of them getting three days leave before the wedding and some getting three days leave after, which only seemed fair to him.

And, of course, a great many things — even food — had been prepared in advance, so *all* the work wasn't being done in these three days. But with so many visitors, and so much to be done on the festal days themselves, there were still not quite enough hands to cover all the work.

There was, of course, a solution for that here at the Collegia. Not a bad thing if you asked him; after all, even the highborn Heralds, Bards, and Healers were going to, one day, be in positions and places where they had to do their own cooking and cleaning. Out in the Field alone, there were plenty of times a Herald would be living in a Waystation and not at an inn or a Guardpost. From the way Amily had talked, it looked as if the Deans had decided that they all might as well start learning how to tend to such common chores now. All the Trainees were taking a turn in the kitchen on cleaning duty, for instance; he had been on breakfast and dinner duty yesterday; they were letting him off today because of the game, and he had dinner duty tomorrow.

He seemed to be one of the few up and awake this early. There was a Bardic Trainee who looked as if he hadn't gotten to bed yet, another who seemed to be nursing a hangover, and a couple of Healers chattering away brightly enough to make the stricken Bardic Trainee wince. Mags went over to the food tables to see what had been laid out.

After all that food last night and with a practice and a game ahead of him today, he left the sweet stuff alone and ate lightly: some fruit, a couple of hard-boiled eggs, a little bread and butter, tea. While he ate, he considered what the game this afternoon was going to be like.

Gennie and Pip were the only Trainees from South Team on the Prince's Choice, and Jeffers was the only horse-mounted player, or Rider. The rest were all people he had played *against*, never with, and a good solid practice was definitely in order before they went out against the King's Choice.

The two Bardic Trainees staggered out the door, leaving him and the Healers alone. The sun outside the windows suggested it could get very warm. That could be an issue. He knew how Gennie, Pip, and Jeffers reacted to heat, but not the others.

Then there was strategy to think about. Mixing members from all four teams meant that strategies that had been worked out in the past were now flying completely out the window. The things that had worked for Gennie on their own team *might* work for this one . . .

Of course, over on King's Choice were Halleck, Meled, and Lord Wess, and Corwin and Beales of the South Foot.

Both sides would have a good notion of the other side's potential strategy. Unless both sides came up with something brand new, there would be no surprises, strategically. Provided nothing went pear-shaped, this would either be a lot of stalemate, or a very interesting game.

The Healer Trainees left, and two more and a much more alert-looking Bardic Trainee came in. They applied themselves to food without much conversation.

Mags, as was his nature, continued to worry at the possibilities ahead of him. When the picks had been made, everyone

looking for signs that someone had been lurking about who shouldn't have been there. After all the assassination and kidnapping attempts, no one was taking any chances that someone had gotten onto the grounds amid all the comings and goings of guests. Just because the assassins had vanished again, it didn't follow they had given up. On the contrary, if past history was anything to go by, they were definitely still out there, and defeat only meant they were going to come back with someone more skilled.

He and Dallen were early; only Gennie and Jeffers were waiting, with none of the King's team in sight. He didn't even need the nod from her to begin warming up; he and Dallen followed her over the course, going over the obstacles in a pattern they had established months ago. First at a gentle jog, then at increasingly greater speeds, and gradually the others joined them, catching up once they had warmed up their own muscles. Eventually Gennie was leading the entire team at a canter in single file. When everyone had turned up and gotten warmed up — and so had the other team — Gennie gathered them all in front of their own goal.

They stood in a rough circle, with Gennie in the center, all dismounted, with the

Trainees and Riders standing beside their mounts' heads. Mags was very glad there was still a good breeze; there was no shade on the Kirball field at all, and the sun had gotten high enough to make itself felt. He rested his hand on Dallen's neck, surrounded by the not-unpleasant smell of warm horse. Leather creaked as horses and Companions shifted their weight; a couple of the horses snorted their suspicion of one another. "Right, then," Gennie said, when she had their complete attention. "Here's the situation. As I am sure you already figured out, the Prince and the King are pretty shrewd judges of us players. We're evenly matched in strength and speed, and I suspect it's going to amount to the best use of skills and how well we manage coordination. No Fetchers on either side, and both sides have strong Mindspeakers. So it's going to come down to playing the game."

And the heat. And accidents, Mags thought, but they all knew that.

"What are their horses like?" Jeffers wanted to know.

"Ah." Gennie smiled with satisfaction. "Now *that* is where we are not evenly matched. Have a glance over there." She jerked her head in the direction of the other

50

team, who had lined up, rather than huddling up, in front of their Captain. "The four Horse that the King picked are all mounted on light cavalry. Which makes sense when you think about it; light cavalry is what the King handled when he did his stint in the field. But the Prince commanded the Scouts, down in the hills on the southern Border. He knows our sorts of ponies."

Jeffers looked at his three fellow Horse, who all rode tough, smallish beasts, as he did. "Well, the Prince knows light cavalry too," he pointed out, looking more cheerful than he had a moment before. "And he picked us."

One of the others nodded. "We've all faced those four in the game, but you Trainees might not remember them well. Us Guards though, we all train with 'em apart from the game, and if there's one thing the Lights hate, it's being crowded by things other than horses. Especially things they aren't allowed to jump over. Good in the scrum, but they'll shy from the fence."

All four of the Horse looked expectantly at Gennie. "Obviously we can use that," she said. "But they know it, and they probably know we know, so they'll do their best to keep off the fence."

"They'll have no choice if they can't keep the ball off the fence," Jeffers pointed out. "And we're closer to the ground and the ball than they are."

"Which is good on the fence," said another of the Horse. "Only problem is that those beasts are taller than ours, with longer legs, so they'll outrun us on the flat."

"So that's the first part of our strategy, then," Gennie said. "No races if we can help it. *We* don't mind the scrum, I know your mounts can keep their tempers, and they don't think twice about a fence. So we run to the fence as often as possible, and if we can scrum against it, all the better."

"Their Foot are good, though," one of the others said doubtfully. "They're all sneaky beggars."

Gennie shrugged. "They should be. I think they must have voted Corwin as their leader. We don't dare let their Foot get a chance at the ball, or there will be no way of getting it away from them short of hurting someone."

One of the Riders scratched his head as a horse pawed the ground restlessly, and another let out his breath in an impatient snort. "That leaves us thin on the ground for strategy, Captain."

Gennie shrugged. "It's what we've got,

until we know how they work together."

"Keep away from the Foot, get the Riders to the fences and scrum there?" Jeffers shook his head. "That'll make for a slow game."

She made a wry face. "It's not a demonstration, we aren't trying to impress anyone, and most of the people here are likely to drift in and out of watching the game. The ones that care about Kirball love a good scrum, so we won't disappoint anyone who cares. For the rest? We're just one of the entertainments. It won't matter if it's slow; they've got plenty of other things to go watch and listen to. The thing is this — I really want to avoid having an injury. Some people would take that for a bad omen, and I know the Royals would be upset."

Mags didn't like to think about that. He'd had his fill of omens and what people made of them. He didn't want any omens marring Sedric and Lydia's wedding. He knew at first hand how people could blow such things up and twist them around.

One of their own Foot raised a finger. Gennie nodded at him. "You know, there's something nobody's tried for a while," he said. "Taking the flag while everyone's tied up with a long scrum."

"Nobody's tried it 'cause nobody ever leaves the goal unguarded even in a long scrum," Jeffers objected. Which was true; although it was, theoretically, still a viable strategy, in practice it was impossible to pull off.

"Aye, but that was when the Mindspeakers were only chatting to their own teams." The fellow looked straight at Mags. "But what if our Mindspeaker was to make a mistake and let slip something to both teams?"

It took Mags a moment to get the gist of what the fellow was suggesting.

Gennie gazed at him in undisguised admiration. "You sneaky beggar!" she exclaimed. "Mags, what do you think?"

"That it'd be nothing to slip control and let both sides hear what I was telling you all," he confirmed. "It's a lot harder to keep things confined, and no one would think twice about it in the middle of the game."

"Narvil can't do that," offered one of the other Riders. "He has to head-talk one person at a time."

"The only problem I can see is it's awful hard for one Mindspeaker to lie to another," he pointed out. "The truth tends to leak through, no matter what you try."

"It'll be in the heat of a scrum," Pip put in thoughtfully. "The Horse and Foot don't have Gifts, and they won't know it's a lie. All we really need is confusion for a moment; we don't really need to convince anyone of anything for very long."

The Companions nodded or otherwise indicated their agreement, as Mags sensed that they approved of this. That made him feel a good bit better about it. If the Companions felt he could do this, then he'd give it the best try he could.

"I like this plan more and more," Gennie said with glee. "But we can't use it more than once, so we'll have to pick our time carefully." She considered the Foot thoughtfully. "You know, we could do something else, if you lads are game for it. All *four* of you make for the flag, then when one of you has it, hide it, split up, and run like billy-oh for our side. When they realize one of you has it, they won't know *which* one, and that will force them to split up too. And meanwhile, they'll still have to watch the ball, or we'll take it over and keep them away from it. We might even get a chance at a goal."

"What about our goal?" Pip wanted to know.

Gennie looked penetratingly at Mags. "Think you and Dallen can hold it alone?"

Mags thought for a moment and then got an idea. "Nothing in the rules about me being dismounted, is there?" he asked. "That'd make two guards instead of one. I can run pretty fast, an' Dallen moves like a scared cat."

:I like that plan.:

"Nothing in the rules," Gennie said cheerfully. "And there's plenty of times in a real fight you'll be going dismounted, so I doubt very much anyone is going to object. At least not for this particular game."

This was sounding better and better.

"And nothing in the rules says that you have to hit the ball with the stick." He grinned. "Plenty of times in the scrum Companions've been kicking the ball around, right? Well, Dallen and I have been working on something, something you have to be in the open to do. I lob the ball to him, he kicks it to the sky. More *up* than straight, and no direction to speak of, but that's good 'cause they'll have to figure out where it's coming down. If they come at the goal when we're there, taking a chance on the Foot not getting through, that's what we'll do. Bet they'll be so busy skywatching they won't see the flag stealer till it's too late."

It was obvious from the now eager expressions on his teammates' faces that everyone liked this plan. Even the horses seemed to catch the excitement and brought their heads up, looking alert and ready to play.

"I like it," Gennie said firmly. "Right, then. Everyone mount up, and let's go through the usual drills. The sooner we turn ourselves into a team, the better. Mags, you and Dallen sort out whose heads you're supposed to be in, and make that your priority. Now let's get working. We only have until lunch to turn ourselves into the team worthy to be called the Prince's Choice."

Mags rather liked the look of the new armor. Rather than repainting the old, two teams'-worth had been made in their specific team colors, and basic tunic and trews in matching colors were passed out along with it. That was a lot of work and quite a bit of money, and that made him wonder if Nikolas and the King had some notion of creating Kirball teams for the adults once enough players had gotten out of Grays to form two sets of four. It might be a good idea . . . it would certainly be something to look forward to. But realistically, how often would they actually get to play? Once Heralds went into Whites, they generally spent the majority of their time in the field. The odds of actually getting eight players at the Collegium long enough to practice and play on a team were fairly long.

Or maybe the King was thinking about making this sort of match an annual or semiannual affair. The sort of thing that could be played down in the city, for instance. . . .

He thought about that with some glee. What if there were an abbreviated version of Kirball, something that used only eight Trainees, maybe with a simple goal instead of the goal and the flag, and played on a plain, flat field? Would people like to watch that? He knew he would enjoy playing it. Any time he got to play a game on Dallen's back was —

:Wake up, dreamer. Game time.:

He blinked and put his mind firmly back in the present. And, predictably, the nerves started.

He *always* had nerves before a game. He had too cursed good an imagination. He could picture all sorts of things going wrong, anything from messing up so badly he looked an utter fool and was asked to never play again, to causing some sort of hideous accident. And no matter how many games he played, he never got over having the nerves. It made him feel keyed up, muscles tense, and just a little bit sick. Gennie and Pip always looked so relaxed at this point, and he could never imagine how they managed it.

He comforted himself with the fact that once the game started, he would be far too busy for nerves.

And if he hadn't been picked for either team, he would not be getting any sort of holiday today; like Nikolas, he would be working. He would probably be in a servant's uniform or a page's tabard, moving among the audience, observing and listening. If the nerves he was experiencing now were bad, the nerves he would be experiencing out there would be much, much worse. The last time he had been watching a crowd, Amily had nearly been kidnapped. Every time he thought about that, he got a sick, horrible feeling, thinking about what could have happened to her.

The assassins had intended to use her as a way for the Karsites to ruin her father, the King's Own, and utterly discredit the Heralds for being unable to properly protect one of their own. They'd nearly managed it, too.

No, no one, least of all Mags, had forgotten for a moment that there was still a set of skilled, determined, and unknown assassins out there, hired by Karse. They had not fulfilled their contract, and without knowing whether Karse had dismissed them or they had forfeited, there was no choice but to assume that they were still bound to that contract.

That, in truth, was why the newlyweds were spending their wedding nights in Companion's Field rather than some other romantic and secluded venue. The last several monarchs, for instance, had used a royal hunting lodge, but that was quite out of the question at this point. Nothing and no one was going to get past the ring of determined Companions that surrounded them while they were there. Even the food and drink brought to them was left well away from their pavilion and brought to them by the Prince's Companion or one of the four trusted — and tested — servants that were with them. Short of dropping down out of the sky, there was no way to approach them, which was exactly how everyone wanted it.

:Hello? Game?:

Mags shook his head a little. He really *was* going to have to do something about the way his mind wandered.

As Mags lined up with his team, the Prince and Princess arrived to a fanfare, galloping up to the viewing stand with an escort of Companions. It made a very pretty sight, but Mags had other things to watch than the Heir, who at this point was probably the safest person up here on the Hill, what with Guards and Companions and Heralds all on alert for danger.

He resolutely put his mind back in the game, sizing up their opponents on the White team.

He worried less about the ones he hadn't worked with than his former teammates; he'd faced all of them over the ball many times already. He reckoned that being from different teams would matter less to the Foot and the Riders than it would to the Herald Trainees. And the four Trainees on the White team were all from different Kirball teams, which might give them just a moment or two of hesitancy that Mags, Gennie, and Pip wouldn't have. But the Foot and Riders from Gennie's original team knew her style and knew how the Reds tended to come up with unexpected strategies; they might not be fooled when Mags "accidentally" Mindspoke to all of them.

The sun was high overhead now. The Prince had timed his wedding well, insofar as it did not interfere with the lives of his subjects. This was the end of summer. It was not yet harvest time, yet harvest time was near enough that not even Karse would be insane enough to attack with an army that would pull men away from the fields near the time they would be most needed. Foods that were not harvested in the fall were abundant, it had been easy to transport them here, this was right in the middle of trading season, so traders were perfectly happy to have excuses to set up fairs alongside all the wedding celebrations taking place all over the country. The weather was absolutely splendid — dry, warm, perfect for outdoor celebrations.

Unless, of course, you were wearing half your own weight in Kirball armor.

Mags was already sweating, and he was grateful for the breeze that was making the pennants at the grandstand snap and pop.

:Whether or not our old teammates believe your "slip" won't matter as long as the rest are fooled,: Dallen pointed out, swishing his tail slightly as the wind played with his mane and forelock. *:It will take their Mindspeaker longer to sort that out and tell them than it would you. That will translate into a lot of distance for the Foot with the flag.:*

The referee was coming out with the ball, and time for woolgathering was over.

The two teams got into place. The Foot went to the blue and white goals, the Riders and Trainees gathered around the referee.

Mags leaned forward over Dallen's neck, feeling the Companion's muscles tensing under his legs.

He was amazed the ball didn't burst into flames from the intensity of the glares on it.

The ball went up in the air, and the referee scrambled for cover. As the team had anticipated, the moment the ball hit the ground, the scrum was on.

Mags was pressed on both sides by tall cavalry horses, but Dallen was just as tall, and heavier, and not at all averse to shoving back. He had no idea where the ball was, and neither did his Companion. They milled with the others in a tight mob. There was no need to put on a showy exhibition for the crowd this time; those who were watching were here to ogle the new Princess, to be seen themselves, or to watch the game. For the first two groups, it wouldn't matter what happened on the field, and for the last, *everything* that happened on the field was of intense interest.

:Aha. The ball's under the feet of that tall roan!:

:Under the roan!: Mags "shouted" to his teammates.

Those wicked little ponies on the Blue side went straight to work, and Jeffers got control of the ball, but they were matched by mounts and Riders on White who loved a good dust-up. Mags backed a little out of the scrum, just enough that he could see the ball among all the hooves, and kept them all aware of where the ball was; but it was going to take an accident, a misstep, or a lucky move to get it out from under the ponies' hooves and noses.

:I told you it would be easier to keep track of your teammates than you thought,: Dallen pointed out as he warned one of the Riders that they were about to lose the ball.

:Huh. Practice?:

:Generally makes perfect, yes. Or at least "much better.":

The scrum moved slowly up and down the field without getting far from the center until just that lucky move on the part of a White — a daring and accurate hit with the stick — sent it skittering out of the scrum and toward the Blue goal.

Off went the Riders and half of the Trainees, following it like a cat after a mouse. Gennie and Mags stayed behind a little, in case someone got the ball away from the Whites, and he finally got a lungful of air that wasn't full of churned-up dust. *Quartertime can't come too soon.* They were barely into the game, and already his throat was parched. and he desperately wanted a drink.

After drilling all morning, Gennie was confident in the ability of their own Foot to keep anyone from scoring on them. The Prince had chosen shrewdly, picking people who were agile, quick, and utterly fearless in the face of risk — people who, in fact, were being trained as battlefield messengers.

Even as Mags thought that, one of the Whites bunged the ball toward the goal, and one of their own literally leaped for it, intercepted it with his body with an audible impact, rolled around it, tumbled, rolled to his feet —

Coming at you, Mags! he heard the thought in his mind and was ready when the Blue whirled and flung the thing at him like a woolsack. He forgot all about his dry mouth, the persistent tickle in the back of his throat, and the sweat pouring down the back of his neck and gave the ball a *whack* with his stick, sending it to Gennie who was closer to the goal. She took a chance and gave it another smack, sending it toward the dead center of the goal, but she wasn't really expecting to get it in, so the team was ready when the White Foot intercepted it and bunged it back to their own Rider.

That was when the Blue Riders and Trainees rushed him and forced him into a scrum on the fence. He was almost bowled over by the avalanche of Companions and horse-flesh; desperately trying to control the ball, he was carried along in the direction *they* wanted to go.

The White Trainees were good, but the Riders were fighting their horses to get in close. Blue kept the scrum right up against the fence for the rest of the quarter, as Mags warned them every time it looked as if the ball was going to escape into the open, and it ended without either team managing to score.

The team huddled up to consider the strategy for the next quarter.

Mags pulled off his helmet and poured water over his head, then poured more over Dallen's. The sun was punishingly hot out here; only that stiff breeze was keeping things bearable.

"It would be awfully nice to actually get a goal," Jeffers said wistfully.

"We might want to consider the politics at this point," put in another of the Blue Trainees, thoughtfully, as he paused in drinking down about half a pitcher of water. He was one of the older lot; Mags knew him only as Byren, and not much else about him, except that he was highborn. He passed the pitcher to Gennie, who drained it and handed it back down to the bearer.

"How so?" Gennie asked. "You've more of a head for court politics than I do, Byren. How can the game make any difference?" She eyed him with speculation, not skepticism. Mags figured at that point that this Byren probably knew what he was talking about and might be another person to add to his personal circle of helpers. It would help to have someone besides Amily around who know about court politics.

"Well, there's the thing. Is it better for the Blues or the Whites to win? Better to keep balance in the Court," he said, then elaborated. "What sort of message will the rest of the Court read into a victory for either side? Because they will, it's inevitable; no matter what happens, they are going to read *something* into it. If the Blues win, will they read that as Sedric getting impatient for the Throne? If the Whites win, will they read it as Sedric not being experienced enough?" Byren's Companion shuffled uneasily beneath him, as if this sort of talk made him uncomfortable. "I'm the last one to suggest that either side throw the match, but I'd like to know if there are going to be any possible ramifications for a win. If there are, well, we need to consider that as much as how we play the game."

:He might not be aware of the actual flow of

politics, but he knows to think ahead about them, and he knows how to spot a potential spot for a bit of trouble. It might only be that he's just not privy to a lot of the information yet. I'd bet one or both of his parents are. And I'd bet they'll coach him in Court politics more as he gets older. I'd consider him for the future. I'll remind you to ask Nikolas about him.: Dallen was already on top of that idea, which pleased Mags. It was good to know that *he* was getting good at figuring out people who had the potential to help him in the future.

Gennie blinked, then turned to Mags. Mags was already Mindspeaking Nikolas, because Byren had put his finger on that potential problem, and only Nikolas was likely to have an answer. Fortunately, Nikolas had anticipated Byren's concern and must have been keeping his ear to the ground for the last couple of days. "Nikolas says no worries," he replied with relief. "The Prince is the . . . ah . . . Nikolas says, *sentimental* favorite, 'cause of the wedding. An' he and the King have already worked out that if the Whites win, the King'll present the prize to Lydia, an' if the Blues win, the Prince'll present the prize to the Queen."

"Ah, well then, sorted!" Byren replied with

relief. "I'd much rather play the game without worrying about politics. So, about getting that goal!"

"Anybody see any obvious weak points aside from the Riders and the fence?" Gennie asked.

"Not a weak point, but there's something we might be able to use in the terrain," said Pip. "Our side, just at the boundary line, left, there's a clump of bushes with a pocket at the base. Looks like it just grew that way over the summer. If we popped the ball in there, then tore off for the fence with the Trainees, we *might* trick them into thinking the Trainees had the ball, and while they're confused, the Riders can kick the ball out and make a run for the goal."

Gennie nodded. "That would be the time for you to *accidentally* tell both sides Pip had the ball, Mags. It's earlier than I thought we'd use that trick, but it would be a good time for it."

He nodded.

"Right then, it's set," Gennie said. "Let's play it."

But White got the ball first, and the players were determined to keep it away from the fence. They'd learned from the first quarter, and it was a fierce fight up and down the field as they looked for a weak point in the Blue defense. Finally Blue was able to force them into another scrum, but in the middle of the field and not nearly close enough to that clump of bushes to do any good.

:Where's the ball?: Mags asked desperately, as the dust from the churned-up ground rose about them all in a cloud.

:Under my tail,: said Companion Dustin. *:And that wretched White horse knows it, he's kicking at my hocks! Ow!:*

Dallen crabbed sideways and gave the offending mount a good shoulder-shove. Dallen's weight prevailed; the horse went down on his haunches for a moment and gave Mags a chance to lean down in the saddle while Dustin held *very* still for just a heartbeat, and Mags bunged the ball out of the scrum and toward the bushes.

Away the whole pack went after it, but the Blues got there first and wedged it in, then kicked up enough dust to hide what they'd done before the Whites got there. The lot of them milled in confusion as the dust rose in clouds about them and coated their armor in a white film.

:Pip's got the ball!: Mags shouted to every familiar mind — which, of course, included their former teammates on the White side. Pip shot out of the pack like a bullet from a

sling, followed by the Blue Trainees, all heading for the fence on the grandstand side. And enough of the Whites peeled off after him to let the Blue Riders kick the ball out of its hiding place and bung it down the field toward the White goal.

The Whites caught on to the ruse immediately, but the Blue Riders had distance on them, and even their long-legged cavalry horses couldn't make it up. There was some fast ball-passing at the goal, with the White Foot trying to be in six places at once, then three attempts at the goal, and the last one got in to tumultuous cheers from the crowd. And just then, the signal sounded for the end of the quarter and a change of horses for the Riders.

"They're going to be hopping mad now," Gennie observed, as they huddled up for the third quarter. The water carriers had brought out damp rags for washing the dust off armor; Mags opted to upend an entire bucket of water over his head instead. This was excellent preharvest weather, nice and dry, allowing crops to ripen and not rot, but it made the Kirball field dusty. He coughed, hard, trying to clear his throat, then took off his helmet, wrapped one of those damp rags around his nose and mouth, and put the helmet back on. He didn't need to talk, anyway.

"They'll get a goal on us," Pip predicted. "I can't see them letting this go."

"Maybe we can use that. We let them have a goal, then we try our Foot for the flag." Gennie grabbed an offered bucket of water from one of the water carriers, took a drink from it, and poured the rest over her Companion's head. "That will give us a lively fourth quarter if we pull it off, which wouldn't be a bad thing. And if we don't, we can try it in the fourth anyway."

But the Whites were incensed at the Blue's deception, and nothing in the third quarter went as it should. To begin with, the Whites got hold of the ball, and the Trainees kept it in the air with some brilliant stick play. They all were so busy keeping watch on the ball that they never noticed when one of the Riders broke away from the fight, and Mags knew something was up only when he heard a desperate mental howl from their own Foot. The Rider was managing to keep them encircled with his wickedly fast cavalry horse, and there was nothing they could do about it.

:*The Foot!*: Mags "shouted," but by then it was too late. The White Trainees shot the ball toward the goal and screamed after it, and one of their Riders smacked it right from underneath the nose of Gennie's Companion and into the goal. And that was the end of the third.

"Now or never," was all Gennie said, as the Riders changed horses. They all nodded. "And they'll be expecting something from us."

"Whatever happens, no one can say we didn't play the game," said Alton, one of the Foot, with some satisfaction. "Take a look over at the rails."

They all did. And there was not a face out there that was not turned toward them.

"I'd call that a job well done," Gennie said with some satisfaction. "All right then. Win or lose, well played, Blues. Let's give them the best quarter of the game."

When the ball was in play, a White Rider immediately headed for their Foot. *:Get on him, Mags!:* Gennie called, as the pack fought for the ball. *:We'll hold them off if we can!:*

Mags and Dallen charged after the Rider, full speed. He'd already started his encircling strategy when they ploughed into him. They were matched for size and weight, and Dallen made no attempt to check his speed at the last minute; Dallen had never made a full-out body-slamming charge before in this game, and no one expected it of him.

:Get ready to jump!: Dallen told him, just before they hit.

Both Rider and Dallen went down on their haunches, and Dallen went right over, but Mags was ready and had jumped out of the saddle before Dallen went down. Mags was on fire with anxiety, even though he hadn't *felt* anything from Dallen

:I'm fine!: Dallen said, scrambling to his feet.

The same could not be said for the Rider's horse, who got himself up but with a bad limp. The referees whistled for a halt, and play stopped while the rider got himself another mount.

:Stay down, Mags,: Gennie ordered. *:Tell our Foot if they get a chance to go for the flag, but otherwise, I want you and Dallen down there to keep them off our goal.:*

He and Dallen arranged themselves at either end of the goal area, and a good bit ahead of the Foot, ready to move at any instant. It was a little disappointing, not to be able to get right in the fight, but on the other hand, it would be a lot more disappointing to see the Whites score on them. He noticed the referees watching them and conferring with each other; he figured that they must be trying to work out whether being on foot was against the rules. But a few moments later, they broke apart, without anything happening, so he reckoned that they were going to let it pass.

Despite being a Trainee short, the Blues managed to fight the ball down the fence well into goal-range on the White side. From where Mags stood they were just a tangle of limbs and dust; he was peering after them when something caught the corner of his eye.

:Ware the flag!: he yelped to his own side, just as Dallen rushed the Trainee who had dismounted and snuck up within snatching distance of the flag. *:Halleck, you sneaky git!:* he growled, and was rewarded with Halleck's chuckle as the Trainee's Companion materialized out of nowhere and Halleck remounted at a run.

:Sneaky is as sneaky does,: Halleck mocked, and suddenly the scrum broke away from the fence and headed their way at a gallop.

Mags saw the ball speeding straight for him. He didn't even think. He stood right in its path with his stick in both hands, braced for impact. The ball hit him hard enough to drop him on his behind in the dirt, but the ball went up, and Dallen somehow managed to get under it, and with a mighty kick, sent it soaring.

All eyes followed it. It seemed to hang in the air forever, a tiny speck you had to squint to see. *:Flag!:* he shouted into the minds of the Blue Foot, who split up and began using the tactics they had been taught as battlefield messengers to sprint from bit of cover to bit of cover, leaving him alone at the goal.

But everyone else was after the ball.

And for one mad moment, Mags thought the ploy just might work.

But the one thing that no one had reckoned on was that the time ran out on the quarter, and just as the first of their Foot reached the White flag — in fact, as he got his *hand* on it — the whistle blew, signaling the end of the game.

The end, and a dead tie.

The bathing room was noisy with good-natured complaints. Really, no one was unhappy with a tie. No one could claim that either side had given away anything. Both sides had proven themselves. Everyone agreed that both teams were made up of the best of the best. "The only ones who lost were the people making bets," Corwin observed from somewhere in the steam.

Mags had managed to lay claim to his

favorite tub and was lying in the hot water with his eyes closed, soaking his sore muscles.

"Well the more fools they," snorted Lord Wess. "That maneuver with your Foot, Mags, was brilliant. Too bad the time ran out. Was that yours or Gennie's?"

"Gennie's," he replied, scooting down up to his chin in hot water, nursing his bruised chest and content knowing that Dallen was getting the expert attention for that tumble that he deserved. "But the kick was me an' Dallen."

"Another good move. We should practice that."

:Not today,: Dallen said firmly.

"Without th' standin' there and blockin' the ball," he said, firmly.

"Whatever demon suggested you just *stand* there and let the ball come at you like that?" Corwin asked.

"Prolly the same one that told you to pull the stunt that got your arm broke," Mags retorted. The hot water felt very good, but he didn't think he would be trying that particular trick any time soon. When he'd taken his armor off, his chest had a most interesting black and blue bar right across it. Not much by the standards of his injuries at the hands of the Karsite agents, but enough to make breathing a bit achy.

"I think we need to stop listening to demons," Corwin muttered. The steam was as thick as a pea-soup fog. It was easing the cough in Mags' chest and the scratchiness of his throat. But he had a notion he would be coughing up nasty dust for days.

"I think you should listen to them more," Halleck said cheerfully. "Those were brilliant moves. You just go right on listening to them, I'll watch and applaud."

The sound of a sponge hitting someone in the head — probably Halleck — ended that particular line of thinking.

Mags let the heat lull him into a pleasant stupor until the water began to cool, then reluctantly pulled himself out of the tub. Back in clean Grays, he gingerly made his way out of the Collegium. *:Need me, sir?:* he asked Nikolas, tentatively.

:As a matter of fact, yes,: came the reply. Mags stifled a moment of disappointment; he really would have liked to track down Amily and get some much deserved sympathy for his bruises. *:Would you come over to the south side of the rose garden, please, and let yourself be fussed over? Yes, for once I want you to be conspicuous.:*

Mags sighed again but obeyed, slipping through the crowd as best he could with his

78

head down to avoid being intercepted. When he got to the appointed spot, it was pretty obvious who Nikolas wanted him to distract. A knot of people in extremely expensive clothing were arguing heatedly, with a lot of energetic gestures.

One of them spotted him. "Ah, look, just the person we need to settle this!" the man exclaimed. "You're Mags, yes?" He waved at Mags, indicating that he wanted the Trainee to join his group.

Mags immediately went into his "good natured but slightly dim" persona, the one he cultivated when being feted for his Kirball prowess. "Aye, milord," he said with a sheepish smile. "At your service."

"Did you collude to have a tie?" demanded another man, a balding, strongly built noble who looked as if he spent a lot of time under armor. He spoke angrily, without so much as an introduction.

Mags made his eyes go big and round. "What?" he exclaimed. "No!" He rubbed his ribs ruefully, and winced. "Milord, if there'd been any colludin' about, I wouldn' be standin' here with a bruise like I'd been beat with a broom acrost my ribs." He shook his head. "Jest how it come out, is all, an' we'd have won, if the time hadn't run out on us. We had that flag-stealin' move planned from this mornin' when we trained up t'gether." Now he sighed with unfeigned regret. "Wish't the time hadn't run out. Feels like I got beat up for nothin'."

"There, see?" the one who had accosted Mags said in triumph. "I told you. Nothing more sinister than two evenly matched teams."

"An' we knowed each other's main strategy, milord," Mags pointed out. "There was people from all four Kirball teams on both the Blues an' the Whites. I reckon the two best strategists were the captains; I know I'd put Gennie again' anyone else. We could all pretty well predict what'd happen, what th' other side'd do. Coulda been a stalemate. Coulda spent all four quarters scrummin' up an' down the field. But we all *play* th' game, so we come up with some new stuff. Some worked, some didn', an some, the time ran out on."

The first man nodded with understanding; reluctantly, so did the second. Then the entire group began an intense questioning of him that went over every point of the game. Mags wasn't sure what Nikolas was getting out of this, other than the fact that these men were positively Kirball fanatics, but it must be something.

Once they were all convinced he was telling them every bit of the truth, they became more affable, if just a tiny bit sour over no one winning any bets. They waved a page over, ordered Mags to ask for whatever he wanted, and moved to where he could sit down, and gave him permission to do so. Which was no small consideration, among the highborn; he might be a Heraldic Trainee, but he was still only a Trainee, and his birth was the lowest of the low. For them to insist on his being seated in their presence was quite the mark of conciliation. And . . . quite the mark of politeness, when it was all said and done.

When they finally let him go, he felt as if they had turned his brain inside out like a bag and shook it to make sure there were no crumbs of information remaining.

But Nikolas was clearly pleased. *:Well done, Mags,:* his mentor said warmly. *:Now, there's another group over by the rose trees . . . :*

Mags resigned himself. It looked as if he would be talking Kirball until he ran out of wedding guests or ran out of voice. Whichever came first.

It wasn't that he didn't *like* talking Kirball. He could probably talk about it for days. But he'd rather talk about it with the other players, not people who thought they knew what Foot, Riders, and Trainees should be doing (as opposed to what they were actually doing). Some of their ideas were reasonable, but most ranged from silly to dangerous. Silly, he didn't mind, but dangerous?

Reckon ye kin keep yer ideas to yerself, unless you *be the one ready to try it first,* he thought as he approached another gesticulating group. *Then, mebbe we'll talk!*

3

Nikolas — apologetically — kept Mags "working" until he was quite ready to pack it in. It wasn't all Kirball talk; once the evening really started and the drink began to flow, he was welcome as a sort of ornament to knots of guests, rather than as an active participant in conversation. Once that started to happen, rather than being conspicuous, Nikolas asked him to merely stand in the background and listen. This was where he was more than grateful for Dallen's help, "listening" through Mags; though a bit sore himself, Dallen was more than willing to filter what Mags overheard for useful bits and relay only those useful bits on to Rolan and Nikolas. He was somewhat relieved to discover that her father had set Amily at the same task; they crossed paths several times during the evening and were able to steal a kiss or two before going their separate ways. At least she wouldn't feel slighted, thinking he didn't want her company. And although this wasn't *quite* the holiday he'd had in mind when the wedding was announced, he was still getting a break from classes and training, eating some amazing food, and getting to spend more time with Amily and his friends than his schedule usually allowed.

He was beginning to get the shape of what Nikolas was looking for a couple of candlemarks before he began to get so tired he was having a little trouble keeping track of who was saying what. It wasn't that Nikolas was interested so much in what was said, as in who was saying what to whom. He figured that out after Nikolas asked him to follow a couple of people from group to group. That was when he ran across a couple of instances where a particular courtier expressed one opinion to one group of people and the contradictory — or at least, differently slanted — opinion to another. Alliances within the Court were always shifting, and Nikolas was keeping track of just how they were shifting. And it wasn't that anyone was actually up to any mischief — at least, not overtly. But it definitely was that the wedding was shifting the power within the Court, people were looking for opportunities, and this was like putting dye in the water to see where the currents were going.

And people were being considerate of him, especially after he started walking with a slight limp. They let him sit, even though all of them could have insisted that he stand in their presence. They made sure that the pages waiting on them brought him cooling drinks. One old lady even insisted he try her "special" mint cordial; he did so out of politeness, but he found it so delicious that he had to restrain himself from asking for more. The gardens had been specifically constructed to funnel breezes around, so they were cool and comfortable despite the crowding. And he had to admit the music was much, much better, plus there was a conjurer who performed clever tricks, a little performing dog, and some acrobats to watch — and some *professional* dancers, who made all the dancers that he had ever seen look like the mine kiddies capering.

Once he knew what he was supposed to be doing for Nikolas, he also knew that Amily, of course, was already aware of what her father was looking for; she didn't need Mindspeech to relay everything she heard because she could just drift over to where he was, drop a few pertinent remarks, and drift away again. But that was due to her own experience in and around the Court, working with Lydia's friends under the supervision of Master Soren as well as with her father. Although Nikolas cherished his daughter, he didn't overprotect her, and Mags knew he discussed nearly everything that wasn't a secret with her. Since her abduction, that had been more of a priority rather than less. Keeping secrets from her hadn't saved her; knowledge, and forewarning, might.

But it had been a very, very long day. Even though he wasn't drinking very much with spirits in it, he was beginning to find it hard to stroll around and even harder to focus his attention on conversations that didn't explicitly include him. Not even the cooling breezes were helping, nor the mint cakes. When Nikolas finally noticed he was becoming muzzy headed, he ordered Mags to bed.

:I'm sending Amily in too,: the King's Own added, as a subtle way of letting him know that Amily wouldn't be free to take off to the stable party. *:She wasn't playing Kirball, but she was with Lydia in the stands, and it got rather hot there.:*

Poor Amily! She wasn't getting much of a holiday either.

:That's the hazard of being the offspring or spouse of the King's Own,: Dallen said,

sounding a bit sleepy himself. :*When you are the King's Own, you have to be willing to use everyone if you have to.*:

Mags thought about that, and countered, :*Well, it ain't using if we* want *t'be used, is it?*: Because he couldn't imagine Amily — especially not the Amily of late — not wanting to help if she could.

Dallen chuckled a little. :*Point taken; no, it is not.*:

So Mags just bade Nikolas goodnight and made his way down to the stable. He was very glad to see his bed again; he stripped off his clothing, threw the windows wide open to the breeze regardless of the noise outside and not even the party going on in the loft over his stable room kept him awake once his head hit the pillow. It had been a very long day, and he hoped that Nikolas would let him off easy on the morrow.

Breakfast the next day was looking barren of people when he ambled up to the Collegium dining hall. If anything, it appeared that people were sleeping later this morning than they had yesterday. There wasn't even a sign of whoever had laid out all the food on the tables. He resigned himself to eating alone, when, to his pleasure, Bear appeared.

He didn't have to wave, since there were only the two of them. Bear seemed just as happy to see him and sauntered over to stand next to him. They both examined the offerings on the laden tables thoughtfully before making their selections.

"Where were you last night?" Bear asked, as they looked over the fruit. "Everybody was asking for you. They were a bit worried about that whack you got from the ball, and since I didn't look you over, I couldn't say one way or another, just that you weren't in the infirmary or in your bed, 'cause I checked."

"Nikolas," Mags sighed. Bear was part of his own little circle of support, so he didn't have to say anything more.

"Well, damn. Seems a shame to have to work when everybody else is having fun." The Healer Trainee shook his head.

"Well, I got to snatch what the highborn were eatin', at least," Mags admitted. "There's some advantage. An' there was a conjurer an' acrobats."

"Huh. I'm jealous. I'd smack you, but I saw that hit you took, and I bet you're bruised." Bear mimed a cuff at his head anyway. "Let's just take stuff that's not sloppy and take over the Royal gardens before those the gardens are meant for wake up with hangovers. At least you can actually *eat* this morning, since you aren't gonna be

Kirballing right away."

That sounded like a fine idea to Mags, so they both loaded up with pies and other portable foodstuffs and headed for one of their favorite spots. But finding it already occupied, they changed their goal to another spot by the river, near the grotto that was always cool, if a little damp.

"Somethin' on your mind, Bear?" Mags asked, as the two of them threw themselves down on the turf to enjoy their food. They'd each taken a napkin and tied food up in them; now they untied their loot and spread the napkins out to share. He knew Bear very well, and could feel how his friend was trying to find some way of broaching something. There was unease, which Mags put down to Bear not knowing how Mags was going to react to what Bear said.

"Well . . ." Bear picked at a bread roll for a moment. "Aye. Been something on my mind for a good long while, actually. If I can't trust you, I might as well just throw myself in the river and have done. Lena and me, we've been talking. We're thinking we ought to go talk to our Deans and see if they'll let us get married."

For a moment, Mags was not sure he'd heard Bear correctly. "Wait, what? Married? Wouldn't that — what about your studies and all?" There weren't any *married* Trainees at any of the Collegia. Would the two of them be told they'd have to leave? "I mean . . . I ain't never heard of that. I heard of people older than us, who came here as Trainees, an' they had t' leave their families behind until they was in Greens or Reds." Not Whites, of course. He'd never heard of an adult with a family being Chosen.

"But they weren't *both* Trainees, the husband and wife, that is. We're both Trainees. And if you choose to get your Healing training at one of the Houses outside of the Collegium, you can keep your family with you. I mean, that's what my own father did. Aside from that, Lena can leave her room at Bardic, and my space is pretty big and private," Bear pointed out. "More than big enough for two."

Mags nodded; Bear was in charge of the greenhouse, and his quarters, unlike those of the rest of the Healer Trainees, were those of the original greenhouse tender, who had been a full Healer. They had been meant for someone like one of the instructors permanently assigned to Haven, a Senior Healer who might very well have had a family, so they were actually more spacious than the quarters housing the King's Own, making up in space what they probably lacked in luxury. Bear was there because Bear knew more about herbs and how to tend them than anyone at the Collegium, and he had been entrusted with the greenhouse almost since the time he had arrived here. He had a bedroom, a sitting room, another room he just used for storage, *plus* the greenhouse and a stillroom. There was plenty of privacy, and Lena could practice without bothering any of the other Healers or Healer Trainees.

"Aye, but . . . will they let you keep studyin'?" That was the question. Would they insist that the distraction of being together could not possibly allow for concentration on work? That was ridiculous if you knew Bear and Lena; they'd likely be less distracted, if anything, but there was always going to be someone who would find something to object to.

"Lena's looking into that, seeing in the archives if there have *ever* been any Trainees that kept their families here, or at least, nearby." Bear let out a breath, as if he had been afraid Mags would oppose the very idea. Mags didn't, not outright . . . where he came from, among the virtual slaves at the mine, those who had energy left over at the end of the day for anything other than scrambling for a little more food just went ahead and did what they were going to do without thought of marriage. And his masters were perfectly prepared to marry off their youngsters in the cradle if that would get them some kind of advantage.

On the other hand, here, Trainees were not exactly encouraged to think about things like getting married. After all, there was a lot of schooling to get through before they would go into full Reds, Greens, or Whites. Some of them had, in fact, used the very opportunity of being selected for the Collegia to avoid an unwelcome marriage.

Mags considered all of this. "They're gonna say you're too young. You're gonna say your pa was gonna marry you off regardless. They're gonna say how can Lena go off on 'er Journeyman round, and *you'll* say you'll go with 'er an' teach people how t' use your kit. Or you'll say, why can't she do her Journeyman round in Haven, an' you can stay here an' teach and show the midwives and all down in Haven how t' use yer kit." Bear had developed a kit of herbs and instructions that people who had some medical knowledge, like midwives and herbalists, could use if there was no true Healer nearby. The Healers' Collegium and Healers' Circle were, for the most part, excited and supportive of this idea. There were never enough Healers, and always people who could have been saved by such knowledge.

Bear's father and brothers, however, who were the Senior Healers at their local House, were adamantly against it. Then again, Mags had the suspicion that if Bear said the sky was blue, his father and siblings would insist it was some other color.

"I hadn't thought of that argument!" Bear said, looking a little more cheerful. Cheerful enough to stuff the rest of the roll into his mouth.

"Aye, but . . . Bear, are you *sure?*" Mags chewed his lower lip. "I mean both of you . . . 'tis easy enough t' *get* married, but once in, harder out . . ."

"I . . . if it was anyone other than you saying that, Mags, I'd be mad," Bear replied after a moment. "And I know what you're saying. But people younger than us get married all the time, all over the Kingdom. *Most* people get married as young as we are, if they aren't wealthy or highborn. The earlier you can start on a family, if you've got a farm, the better. Even the highborn marry off their youngsters if there's a political advantage. I can't imagine living my life with anyone but Lena, and she feels the same way. And if we don't do this," he continued, in tones of desperation, "my father is just going to *keep* trying to get me married off to go breed 'proper' Healers with a Gift, and . . ." he waved his hands around a little in a gesture of despair. "What if some day the Collegium says he's right? Right now, there's no reason to give in to his bullying, but you never know what is going to happen with power and politics, and my father is damned good at getting his own way. He's just as good at figuring out advantages. But if I'm married, he can't keep playing that game."

"He'll prolly disown you," Mags observed thoughtfully, and salted and ate a hard-boiled egg. "That wouldn't be a bad thing."

"There's only one thing I would regret about that, and it's that it would make my mother very unhappy. I'd hate to upset my mother that way, but . . ." Bear sighed. "I figured, with the Prince's marriage and all, and how my father hired Cuburn to mess things up and Cuburn ended up helping those assassins because he was an idiot real fresh in everyone's mind, if we asked now, we'd be more likely to get a 'yes.' I just can't keep waiting for my father to drop some other rock on me. If I were married, legally, he'd have no more say in what I do. Lena looked that up. Once people are married, no matter how young they are, they can't

was an angry pa with a daughter lookin' fer 'em that you could 'scape in the stampede."

Bear had to laugh at that.

By the time they finished, the Palace servants had begun setting up for the last day's entertainments, and people had begun to appear from the Palace to enjoy those festivities. Some of the servants were making their way down to the riverbank, laden with what looked like pavilions and with purposeful energy in their steps. Some of them stopped right outside the grotto . . . and it occurred to Mags that if there was one place beside the river that was clearly suited for keeping cool drinks cool, it was where the two of them happened to be sprawled. "Ain't there supposed to be boat races today?" Mags asked, noting a look in the eyes of the nearest that said *It would be very nice if you weren't here right now.* Of course, no Palace servant was going to be so rude as to shoo off a Trainee, but if they were in the way —

"Oh, pox. Aye." Bear got to his feet and dusted himself off. "Here, let me give you a hand. They'll want us to clear off so they can set up."

The two of them cleaned up what was left of their impromptu picnic, to the unspoken gratitude of the servants. No sooner had the two of them gotten out of the way than a pavilion was set up on practically the same spot they had occupied a moment before, and servants began bringing baskets of bottles and jugs to store in the back of the grotto.

"Where's Lena?" Mags asked belatedly, as they moved back toward the Palace.

"Busy all day," Bear sighed. "Just like yesterday and the first day. Don't get to see her until tonight. Since I figured way ahead of time that people were going to mostly need hangover tea and remedies for overeating, and made up pounds of both for the past couple months, I haven't had anything to do with the visitors. They wouldn't want to see a Trainee anyway; they wouldn't trust anything less than a full Healer."

"Go talk to Trainee Finny," Mags suggested. "She's a Fetcher, an' she'd be real useful with the Healers doin' the Kirball matches. She can pick up an' hold a whole person. If somethin' bad happened, she could lift a person into a stretcher without hurtin' 'im more." Out of the corner of his eye he'd just caught some motion in the Kirball field and spotted a few of the Kirball players over on the course, playing the version of the game that was just for fun and didn't need helmets or padding. That is what had reminded him of his promise to Finny — but once he'd told Bear, he found himself wondering if there was room for him on either team.

:*I saw that too,*: Dallen said with interest. :*Want to join?*:

:*You really need to ask?*: he retorted.

:*Meet you there.*:

Bear had seen the direction he was looking and laughed good-naturedly. He knew Mags altogether too well, it seemed. "You never get enough of that, do you?"

He grinned sheepishly. "Well . . . I . . ."

"No, no, you don't need to explain," Bear chuckled. "Don't have to explain that you just like to do something. I'll go listen to Lena play, she always likes it when there's friendly faces in her audience. When she's done, I'll go have a chat with your Finny. If you say she'd be useful, then there's no doubt she would be."

Relieved, Mags trotted down to the Kirball field, glad that it was only midmorning and the field hadn't heated up yet. That blessed breeze was still holding steady, and he was mortally glad of it. The "easy" version of Kirball was played entirely by Trainees, teams could be anywhere from one to eight players, the ball was never supposed to be hit hard and never supposed to leave the ground. By the standards of one of the regular players, this was just a sort of warm-up, but that didn't mean that it wasn't fun. Mags couldn't have said that he preferred the "real" version or the "easy" version better. The easy version was just simple-hearted fun, the real version was a challenge, and he loved both.

Dallen cantered up the moment after he arrived, and since Pip had been sitting out until that point, they were both welcomed to the teams, making both sides six players.

Mags declined the offer to be team Captain, Pip accepted it. There was a lot of whooping and laughing as the game restarted. No Gifts were allowed, not even Mindspeech, so instructions had to be shouted for anyone to hear. It was chaotic good fun. They soon got into a scrum, but Dallen solved that by kicking the ball halfway down the field as soon as it got under his tail. The fun version was certainly a lot more mobile than the real version.

Without the armor, without helmets, without the padding, this was just a romp. The breeze blew over them, keeping them cool, they could actually see an unrestricted view, they could move more freely. And without the competitive pressure of an actual game, everything was much more relaxed.

Not that actual games weren't fun in their way . . . but you couldn't call them relaxed, not by any stretch of the imagination.

:Yer getting right good at that,: Mags noted, as the entire pack galloped off after the ball.

:Thanks. No idea what earthly use the skill could be in combat though.: Pip had got there ahead of the others and bunged the ball toward the single goaltender.

:Kick out someone's knee, maybe,: he replied, as the goaltender intercepted the ball and smacked it back at them.

Mags got it and sent it back at the goal, with Dallen pounding after it. Pip shouted at the others to swarm the goaltender and keep him off the ball. They managed to do so while Mags and Dallen chased the ball right into the goal, with Dallen pulling up at the very last minute to avoid getting into the goal itself. Which would have been unpleasant, since the door to the goal was the size of an average human door, and not exactly fit for a Trainee-on-Companion. He practically sat down on his tail to keep from getting into trouble, but that was where Mags' ability as a rider came in. Dallen got right back up, shook the dust from his coat, and they trotted off while the referee got the ball.

Corwin, serving as sole referee, got the ball out and took it back to the center of the field, and they began all over again. No one was really keeping track of the goals, and no one but other Trainees were really watching. Since it wasn't a "proper" game, the real aficionados of the sport couldn't be bothered with taking their attention away from all of the other entertainments. But the rest of the Trainees, who were somewhat intimidated by the skill level required to play the full-on game were encouraged by this "gentler" version, and when a player got tired and was ready to drop out, there were others queuing up to take his or her place. Mags played most of the morning, but by the time his stomach told him that breakfast had been several candlemarks ago, he was ready to stop, and so was Dallen. They rode over to the stable, where Mags unsaddled and rubbed him down himself, making sure to clean the tack before putting it up.

Horse aroma was not the best of perfumes, so a quick wash at the stable pump was in order before he went to find himself some lunch. And, predictably, his conscience nagged at him. Nikolas was working. Should he be? Shouldn't he at least make sure Nikolas didn't want or need him?

As he pulled on a fresh uniform, he gently nudged Nikolas' mind without trying to read anything. Nikolas responded immediately.

:Enjoy yourself. Nothing for you right now; perhaps tonight, when drink makes tongues loosen again. Oh, I thought I saw Amily heading for the lunch tables at the Collegium.:

Nikolas went back to whatever it was that was occupying him; Mags grinned. Until after dinner, then, when he'd be helping clean up, his time was free. He felt almost giddy at this point; this was his third day with no classes and little work of any kind except for last night. Really, that hadn't been so bad, other than having to talk Kirball with a lot of highborns who thought they knew the game and probably would not take well to being corrected. Even on Midwinter holiday he'd been working at Master Soren's get-togethers, at least, to an extent.

He wondered what Master Soren would do this year, with Lydia being the Princess and all. He couldn't imagine Soren *not* hosting his open house, and yet, it could hardly be the same again, could it? There would be more guards, and maybe the "open" part of the open house would have to end. Or maybe Lydia would only be able to come to part of it. She certainly couldn't attend the Midwinter Night vigil with her uncle; she would *have* to take her vigil with her husband and her new household. Anything else would be unthinkable.

Ah, worry about that at Midwinter.

He hurried up to the Collegium, hoping to catch Amily there. If Nikolas didn't have any work for *him* this afternoon, surely he wouldn't have any for Amily. Of course, there was always the possibility that Amily had plans with her other friends, Lydia's own personal circle, but since they were also *his* friends, surely they wouldn't mind him coming along.

He actually caught her just finishing her lunch, but she was happy to join him, since a fresh set of sweets had just been brought out. They soon had a chattering group around them, discussing the rest of the entertainment planned for the afternoon and evening.

A great deal of the entertainment was for the highborn only, being set in the Great Hall, the Audience Chamber, the Lesser Audience Chamber, the Throne Room. There were small plays, more professional dancers, some very exotic entertainers rumored to come all the way from Katashin'a'in, the conjurer from last night, more Bards than one could count, of course — all of these were for select audiences who would be able to disport themselves in the cool, shaded rooms, with breezes blowing through the windows and cool drinks available at the lift of a finger.

But for those who were not so elect, the grounds had their own entertainments, which would culminate tonight with the illuminated procession of barges.

"Fire juggling," Pip said with relish. "Only ever saw a fellow do that once. And it was just him by himself, but this time there's supposed to be a team of four jugglers who work together. And a lot of acrobats, and a ropewalker this afternoon!"

"And a play in the Great Hall in the afternoon and early, and they'll do it twice to fit everyone in," Gennie reminded them. "It's a comedy, and that's all I know, but it's that troupe from down in Haven that plays all the time in that inn." She made a face. "The ones *we* never get to see because the plays are always over after Lights Out."

Mags knew exactly what troupe she was talking about and was relieved, because these were people Nikolas worked with all the time. That meant that the entire troupe was "safe" to be up here. In fact, the inn in question was one of the ones where he could hide Rolan and Dallen when he and Mags went down into Haven in disguise. He didn't know anything about the plays themselves, since he had never been there long enough to see much of one, except for once. He'd enjoyed that, but it had been a tragedy, with practically everyone dead at the end. Not the sort of subject for a wedding festival.

It appeared that there was a great deal of entertainment planned, ending with that lighted parade of tableaus on barges going down the river; but there was a detail new to him: an ensemble of musicians playing on the bridge. His mind rather reeled at the idea of everything going on this final day. The jugglers and acrobats in the gardens, the ropewalkers in the courtyard at the front of the Palace, the plays in the Great Hall, three different small stages where Bards would be performing, the play, and the barge parade — anyone who complained there was nothing to do had to be very jaded or ridiculously picky. And that didn't even count all the things that had been going on this morning while he and his friends had been at their game.

He just wondered how much he would be able to watch . . . depending on whether Nikolas wanted him and Amily to "work."

Well, at least there was plenty to do this afternoon.

As they left the Collegium, Dallen was waiting for them. The Companion presented himself broadside to them and gave them both a *look*. Mags didn't even need to Mindspeak to know what he meant, and it was pretty clear to Amily too, who laughed. "Thank you, Dallen," she said, with a little mock curtsy. "Since you are going to insist that I ride instead of walk and stand, who am I to thwart the will of a Companion? If we are going to watch the tumblers and acrobats, I don't mind having a seat up higher than anyone else."

Mags boosted her up onto Dallen's back; she was wearing a split skirt today, perhaps in vague anticipation of riding at some point, so there was no question of her having to try to ride aside *and* bareback. Not that Dallen would ever let her fall.

"Ropewalkers or acrobats?" he asked. "Though the acrobats might turn up too."

"Ropewalkers," she said instantly, and they made their way through to the court-yard at the front of the Palace. It was a side of the complex that Mags had only rarely seen, since he usually came and went through one of the back or side gates. The entire area was paved over, with trees set in stone boxes along the edge. Today a net had been strung from one side of the courtyard to the other at about head height from the trunks of those trees, and at about the same distance above it was a single rope strung between two small platforms. A young lady in a very short outfit of colorful stockings and breeches and a tight tunic was posed on one of the platforms, looking as calm as if she were standing on the ground. She looked as though a rainbow had been cut up and made into her clothing. Her hair had been wound up into a fanciful heap on the top of her head, ornamented with feathers and artificial flowers.

Mags watched her with professional admiration. Most people, even Heralds, would not be able to stand so far above the ground on such a small space. And even he would not dare to do what she was about to, without an awful lot of practice. Rooftop-running, fine. Walking along a rope? Even with a net for safety beneath you?

Not without a damn lot of practice, thenkee. Not only is it narrow, it's gonna be moving. Moving more even than a tree branch.

When the crowd had quieted, she stepped out. She kept both arms outstretched for balance, but moved like a dancer along the swaying rope, walking toe-heel, but lightly and quickly. She walked all the way to the other platform, back to the first, and paused for applause.

She got it and bowed, but her face was an expressionless mask of concentration. She set out again, this time going out to the middle, where she turned in place on one foot, not as fast as a dancer but not so slowly that she was likely to lose her balance over it. Then she eased herself down as the crowd went silent. The rope trembled under her. She got all the way down to a knee and knelt.

She didn't pause for applause this time. She rose, turned, and lowered herself again, this time with her weight centered farther back and one leg stretching out in front of her. Mags understood what she was doing probably before the rest of the crowd did, as she sat on the rope, that outstretched leg lying along it. He could tell she was pausing for breath before she got up again, turned, ran down to the other platform, and bowed.

Mags found a part of his mind suddenly springing into action, watching and taking notes on her performance. He noted her shoes — thin things, with soles of very flexible leather, with a split between the big toe and the rest. She could probably feel the rope through those soles, and the split allowed her to grip the rope between her toes, although normally she walked with the rope along diagonally along the sole of her foot, just as he would walk a rooftree. He watched how she balanced, how she was making it look more difficult for her than it really was, exaggerating her balancing movements. He saw how she kept her center of balance directly over her feet, no matter what her posture was. He noted the rope itself — how thick it was, how stiff it was, how slack it was.

He wondered in that analytical part of his mind how this could be of any use to him . . . surely, if he found himself in a situation where he had to cross by rope, it would be both more secure and more efficient to hang under it and pull himself along . . .

But wait . . . what if it was fastened to something in such a way that if he got to the other end, he'd find himself faced with a blank wall, no way to pull himself up, and nothing he could lower himself down to? In that case, assuming there was a roof or a ledge he could reach by standing on the rope, it would make much more sense to cross it standing than upside down. Or practice until he could get himself to a standing position without anything to pull himself up by.

Well, that could be tricky. It could be done, though. It would take a very strong body, but it could be done. If he could get himself lying flat and balanced on the rope, he could then get himself into a seated position, and, as this girl was doing, from seated he could get to his feet.

She waited for the applause to die, then went out to the center again, this time carrying a child's skipping rope. Mags could scarcely believe his eyes, nor, from the sound of the intake of collective breath, could anyone else. But she did it. She swung the rope in her hands over her head and did three skips, and how she managed to keep from being flung off the rope, he had no idea.

At least, not at first. Then he realized that the trick was that she kept her feet so close to the rope that there was barely enough room for the skip rope to pass beneath them. The rope was stiff enough it didn't move that much, and she had kept her knees so flexed that she didn't bounce it much. Not much use to him. He couldn't imagine a need for being able to skip rope while standing on a rope . . . but it certainly was a pure marvel to watch, and he was more than prepared to applaud her wildly when she returned to her platform.

Back to the first platform she went and then back out to the middle of the rope. This time when she went out to the center, she paused and balanced on one foot, with the other behind her rather than in front of her. Slowly, slowly, she brought that foot up behind her, reached around behind her head with both hands and seized it, and stretched that foot and leg up over her head, while the rope trembled and swayed under her. She held that pose for as long as ten heartbeats before releasing her foot, bringing her leg back down, and running back to the second platform.

All righty, then. Not only is that little thing all sinew and muscle, I think she's just a tad crazy, too.

This time the applause made the very stones tremble. But it appeared that she wasn't done yet.

Now she went out to the center, posed there for a moment, and began bouncing on the rope. When it was moving at an alarming rate, she suddenly let her feet go from underneath her, and bounced her rear on the rope, bounced back up again, and got her feet underneath her. Then she did it again. Then she twirled at the top of a bounce, making a full rotation before she

112

landed on the rope again.

He couldn't think how he would use this either, until it occurred to him that if the rope started to get out from underneath him, he could probably manage to use this to get things back under control.

She ran back to her platform and posed with one arm flung up, for applause.

He thought that surely, surely now she was done. But no!

A tiny little girl swarmed up the little ladder leading to the platform and stood beside her. They were dressed identically and even had their brown hair done in the same fanciful way, with feathers and flowers on the side and a kind of pad of hair on the top. The first girl knelt down, and the little one climbed up onto her shoulders. Now with the little girl balanced there, the two of them went out on the rope together. They paused in the middle, then the little girl put both her hands on the top of the older girl's head.

Now Mags understood that hairstyle. The feathers and flowers hid what must have been a headband, which held the pad in place securely so that it wouldn't move. The pad gave the little girl something to balance on rather than slippery hair.

He thought he knew what she was going

to do, but he could still scarcely believe it when she inched her way up into a handstand, then inched her way back down again as the crowd held its collective breath. With the tiny thing perched on her shoulders, the older girl executed several deft turns, then balanced with one leg outstretched in front of her, turned, and then balanced with one leg behind her, as the little girl took the same pose, but kneeling on her shoulders rather than standing.

So . . . it was possible to carry a weight on your shoulders and keep balanced. That was useful to know, too.

Then the older girl held out her hands, and the little one put both feet into them. With a quick toss, the little girl went up into the air and down into the net. As soon as she had rolled off the edge and dropped to safety, the older girl jumped down into the net herself. Then both of them raced up the ladders to the two platforms and posed there, one hand on the support, leaning precariously out with the other hand waving, collecting their well-deserved applause.

A moment later, a set of tumblers in bright yellow tunics and trews came rollicking through the crowd, which cleared away from the center of the courtyard to give them room. They had brought with them a drummer, whose rapid beats set the rhythm of their performance. Mags noticed there was a strong family resemblance among them, and between them and the ropewalkers.

They leaped over one another, somersaulted through the air, cartwheeled, and threw one another about as if they weighed no more than balls of feathers. The two girls joined them, to be flung about, balanced on shoulders, turned into the tops of stacks and pyramids of people, and balanced on a single hand by one foot. Mags could only stare at them and marvel. He knew they must have been training since they were mere babes to achieve what he was seeing, and he couldn't help but think that if he'd been born into any other body, he'd like to have been in one of theirs.

What a wonderful life they must have! To be able to travel wherever they wished and to get paid for making people gasp and applaud! And to be able to do the feats of skill and strength they were doing now! Of course, he was under no illusion that any of this was easy; he knew from his own training how hard it was. But his skills were used in terribly serious ways, and it would have been so liberating to be able to use them just to make people smile. For a moment he imagined himself doing just that, with no more cares in the world than to have to think of and train in some new trick to amaze the audience.

But even before he heard Dallen's chuckle in his head, he knew that this dream was rather silly — because he would never be happy living such a shallow life, and he would always be getting himself into trouble trying to help other people. At least as a Trainee helping other people was what he was supposed to be doing, and if he got into trouble, there were plenty of people who would help him out of it again.

But such a strange life he had now . . . one he could never have imagined when he had been a mine-slave. Strange to think that once he had spent most of his life crawling through claustrophobic, dangerous tunnels under the ground, seldom seeing daylight, only to now be studying the techniques of these creatures who seemed to live in and move on the air.

:They really are awfully good,: Dallen observed. *:Perhaps we can get them to train you. I'll mention it to Rolan. I assume if they are performing here, they are certainly to be trusted.:*

When they finished and ran off, they were succeeded by two fellows who made a succession of small balls do quite amazing things. Amily watched them in delight, but Mags paid only half his attention to them. That was another odd thing about this life of his — at least of late. Unless it was something that could be of use to him, he was never able to devote all of his attention to just *watching* something anymore, nor just to be simply entertained. Half of him might be absorbing the entertainment, but the other half was like a watchful cat, keeping track of everything else that was going on around him.

I guess nearly getting killed a few times does that to you, was all that he could think. Not an entirely comfortable way to live . . . but it certainly beat the alternative: being caught unprepared and unaware.

He snorted to himself when he realized that in the back of his mind he had actually been wondering if those colored balls could be used as weapons. It was only when the jugglers were finished that the afternoon performances seemed to be at an end, and a small group of musicians who had gathered there unnoticed by everyone except Mags began playing on the steps of the Palace. Some folk who were not dressed in very fine clothing began to sort themselves into a contra-dance, but this seemed to be not to the taste of the more refined, who drifted back to the gardens.

While they had been watching, Mags had also been debating with himself about revealing Bear's plan to Amily. She was, after all, one of the cleverest people he knew. But on the other hand, would she consider herself bound to tell her father?

:What do you think?: he asked Dallen, as they moved out of the courtyard and back toward the trees and some shade. *:Should I talk to her about it? Or not?:*

:Bear didn't specifically ask you to keep it in confidence,: Dallen observed. *:But I am not at all sure that he would want you to tell anyone else, either. He seemed reluctant even to discuss it with you, and I got the impression he hadn't talked with anyone else. Thinking about it, I don't think you should, until you can ask him whether he wants you to keep it quiet.:*

That squared with Mags' own thoughts on the matter. *:But what do you think?:* he asked Dallen, as the three of them walked toward Companion's Field, which seemed like a good place to go for now. *:I mean, you've got a lot of experience, and you've never been backward about giving me an opinion before.:*

:About Bear and Lena? I am impressed they

have been thinking about their situation. I approve of being proactive. It's a solution, this idea of getting married. I simply haven't yet made up my mind about whether it is a good solution or not.:

Mags felt a little anxious. *:You think it's not?:* If Dallen didn't like it — well, he might go talking to Rolan about it, and then there was no telling what would happen.

But Dallen's reply both surprised and pleased him a little. *:Actually I think it is, I just want to make sure I have uncovered all the possible negatives before I say so.:*

"A copper for your thoughts," Amily said cheerfully. "Because if I were a jealous sort of person I would want to know why they weren't centered on me."

He laughed. "Nothin' interesting. I was thinkin' about that rope dancer, wonderin' how long it'd take me t'learn that sort of thing, an' if I would ever need to run out on a rope that way myself."

"Knowing you?" She made a face. "Probably."

They bantered a bit more, with part of Mags' mind still thinking about how the rope dancer had performed her tricks and part of his mind mulling over Bear and Lena. And still another part of him thinking about how strange it seemed; once he had only ever been able to think of one thing at a time, and now he could think about two — *three* if you counted thinking about thinking about things — different subjects at once and still hold a good conversation with Amily.

"Your Pa likely to want us to work again tonight?" he asked, finally. " 'Cause I gotta help in the kitchen after dinner."

"He probably won't know until then," she told him, and shrugged, looking down at him from Dallen's back. "If not, I want to see the fire jugglers and the barges. And if so, I still want to see them, if it can be managed."

"Wonder if Lena could wangle a place for us on the bridge with the musicians," he said thoughtfully. "That would sure be a good place to watch. . . ."

"What about *under* the bridge? Do you think anyone would think of that? The banks are sure to be crowded." She patted Dallen's neck. "It's too bad you wouldn't fit under there."

"Given that's one'a Corwin's favorite spots t' hide when he reckons t' get outa barracks cleanin'?" Mags chuckled. "I expect he's already got his place staked out."

:I wonder,: Dallen said suddenly, breaking his mental silence, *:if it wouldn't be better for*

120

Lena and Bear to just find an accommodating priest and get married without asking permission first.:

Mags blinked with surprise. That was the sort of thing he'd expect out of — well, someone like Pip. Not Dallen. *:Well,:* he said. *:That's the last thing I would've expected you t'say.:*

:Really?: Dallen sounded mildly surprised.

:I thought you was all about playin' by the rules!: he responded.

:There are no rules about Trainees getting married,: Dallen replied smoothly. *:And it's often easier to ask forgiveness than beg permission. I've been thinking about it, and every single one of the drawbacks to their idea has two or three points countering it, in favor. They are very responsible. Bear is already being treated as a peer and an adult by the rest of the Healers. He's right about his father, and I see no good solution to that problem as long as he is still technically a dependent. It's always possible — not likely, mind you, but possible — that some situation would require the King and the Collegium to withdraw their protection from him. And I thought of another thing. Lena is still a Trainee and has not yet begun to make a name for herself — but when she does, I rather doubt at this point that she would care to be associated with the name*

"Marchand." However, "Bard Lena Tyrall" has a rather nice ring to it, wouldn't you say?.:

Mags refrained from chuckling, because Amily would ask *why,* but he was highly amused at that. And Dallen was right.

:Of course I am. I generally am. Right, that is. But it is nice of you to agree.:

:And so modest, too,: Mags jibed.

Dallen just curved his neck and posed.

In the end, the question of whether Nikolas was going to ask the two of them to continue their eavesdropping was solved by the new Princess. They had just settled in to listen to a consort of lutenists in a riverside pavilion, when a page found them and delivered invitations to both of them from Lydia. She wanted her old friends about her for the barge viewing, and he and Amily were being invited to share her viewing stand.

Mags had to laugh at that. "That's better'n the mudbank under the bridge, I'd say," he said cheerfully.

But Amily looked thoughtful. "I think there's a little more to this than is on the surface. I think we should talk to Father."

Before Mags could suggest it, Dallen was Mindspeaking with Rolan, and he came back with a reply

:Oh, I may faint with surprise. He's actually not busy. Rolan suggests we all join him for some dinner, then you can take care of your dinner duties before the barge procession.:

"Yer Pa says we should come join him for dinner, Dallen says," Mags relayed, looking at her for her reaction.

He was relieved when she smiled. "My instincts are still good, then! He'll have gotten something brought to our rooms, they are the only place you can find privacy at a time like this. Well, shall we?"

Dallen had drifted off somewhere, not being interested in the lute playing, so the two of them made their way slowly to the King's Own's quarters, under Amily's own power. Under other circumstances, Mags might have been impatient, but their path was so impeded by other people that there was no way they could move other than slowly.

Amily had been right; though people streamed and thronged everywhere in the grounds and even the Collegia, as soon as they opened the door to the Heralds' Wing, they were met with an empty corridor and relative silence. Mags let out a sigh, not realizing until this moment how the crowds had begun to wear on him.

"It's been fun and exciting, but it's time for everyone to be gone," Amily said firmly, as if she had read his mind. "It's just as well that people are getting tired of being crowded into shared rooms here and in the Great Houses on the hill."

The celebrations would be continuing for the rest of the week down in Haven, Mags knew — but that sort of thing would not interest most of the highborn and wealthy. There would probably be private fetes and parties, but those would be held in the Great Houses, and the Great Houses would be taking in select guests. Tomorrow would see the clearing out of everyone who didn't actually have ongoing business with the Crown or Collegia. And he would not be unhappy to see them all go. Although he had gotten much, much better with his shields, the press of so many people's thoughts against them was just a trifle wearing.

They walked quietly down the corridor to Nikolas' quarters. Amily tapped on the door, then opened it. Nikolas was seated already, waiting for them, with food laid out on a small table. "I thought by now you'd be sick of the wedding fare," he said, indicating what he'd had brought. "I asked for something a bit less fancy. You should have seen the cook's face when I requested what *they* were eating."

Mags examined the food with approval as he helped Amily to her favorite chair and took one himself. Salad, some nice crusty bread, hard-boiled eggs, some soup, and fruit. "Never thought I'd say I was tired of pocket pies, but I'm weary of pocket pies," he admitted. "Even Dallen is tired of pocket pies."

Amily made a face and helped herself to salad, bread, and a bowl of soup. "I'm tired of all the sweets. There really *is* such a thing as too much of a good thing. So, Father, I assume you know Lydia has invited us to sit in her gallery for the barge procession?"

"I should be, since she consulted me about it." He waited while they helped themselves, then waved his fork at them. "It occurred to me that this would be a good chance for Mags to take the temper of her new ladies and their parents."

The curtains at the windows blew in the continuing breeze. Somehow — perhaps because of the plantings outside the window — all the noise was muffled to a pleasant murmur.

He nodded. "Any trouble?"

"Not that we've foreseen, but it's not going to harm anything to be sure," Nikolas replied. "This is more a matter of information gathering, Mags. Unfortunately, she has a limited number of friends who can serve as her ladies-in-waiting. Most of the ones in the running for the position are the daughters of the nobly born; she does not personally know most of them, and all of them will be sitting in the stands tonight. I would very much like you two to observe them so we can at least eliminate the ones she absolutely will not want. Most of them know each other. Lydia is going to surround herself with her oldest friends just for tonight — but I want you two to sit down at the back and center of her stand so you can listen and observe."

By "listen," of course, Nikolas also meant that Mags should keep his attention open for strong and malicious thoughts. Not overtly *read* minds, but if something should happen to be strong enough that it got past his primary shields . . .

"Isn't it possible there will be some sniping just because a couple of Lydia's old friends are . . . well . . . rather common?" Amily asked, doubtfully. "That alone could give her some problems. There are some otherwise reasonable girls who are awfully snobbish."

"They won't know." Nikolas offered. "We've taken care to supply clothing for those who don't have it. These are all outfits that are at least the equivalent of those that the potential ladies-in-waiting will be wearing," Nikolas assured her. "And everyone knows to be suitably vague about their backgrounds tonight." He smiled a little. "The only one who might give himself away with his speech and language is Mags, and since he is the Kirball hero — not to mention the hero of Amily's rescue —"

Mags made a face. "I could jammer like a mine-kid an' they'd just giggle an' say how charmin' it was," he said.

Nikolas nodded. "I couldn't have managed to contrive a better opportunity for you if I'd tried," he said. "While this is not critically important, you'll be getting the chance to do what I do all the time in the Court, and do Lydia a favor at the same time. And there is nothing vital hanging on the information you gather. Lydia has been playing at politics for a very long time, thanks to her association with Master Soren, and I very much doubt there is a young woman in the entire Court she couldn't handle on her own. But it would be a good thing for her — quite the favor, in fact — if you could help her find the ones that are going to give her the least trouble."

Amily nodded. "We'll leave it up to you and her to work out what sort of reasons you are going to give to the ones you reject," she said cheerfully. "The rest, I think, we can manage."

Mags had to chuckle a little at that. "I don't suppose Bear and Lena'll be included?" he asked.

"You suppose incorrectly," Nikolas replied, with an arched brow. "After all, Lena is the most promising student in Bardic, and even if her father is in disgrace now, he is still one of the most prolific and prominent Bards in the Circle. No one doubts Lena's Gifts. And as for Bear, he has, as a mere Trainee, successfully planned and supervised a most difficult and complicated medical procedure on the daughter of the King's Own. Lydia would be a fool not to want to include such a prodigy in her circle of friends, and I assure you, she is no fool. All the ladies will be eyeing Bear as well, wondering if they should be making overtures to him to secure him as a Healer should they need something that doesn't require a Gift."

"Well, then," said Mags, feeling a bit more comfortable with the situation, "We surely can't turn down the chance at a bunch o' good seats for the procession now, can we?"

A bell rang, reminding Mags that he might be a Royal Guest tonight, but at the moment he was a kitchen boy. He excused himself, leaving Amily and her father to continue to discuss whatever it was he wanted *her* to be on the watch for, and ran down to the kitchen to take his place at a sink.

He reflected, as he scrubbed away, on all the times he had longed to be one of the kitchen drudges at the mine. Until he was old enough to actually work in the mine, he'd been put to work in the kitchen, under the care of one of the other drudges. He remembered her as being an old lady . . . but who knew? She could have been as young as twenty, but wizened and aged before her time by the endless hard work and constant hunger. He only remembered she had been as kind to him as she dared, and she curled up around him at night to protect him. Life in the kitchen had been hard, but nothing as hard as the mine. In the kitchen there was always the chance of snatching a little extra food, and it was warm in winter at least. The master was so stingy that he never wasted a twig of wood if he could help it, so the kitchen never got punishing hot in summer, because all the baking was done in a clay oven in the yard rather than in the oven built into the side of the hearth, which made very efficient use of the wood, and kept the heat out of the house.

His first memory of the kitchen was from before he could walk; a bundle of rags would be tied around him, and he would sweep up the kitchen as he crawled. No matter how young you were at the mine, you were working, whether you were aware of the fact or not.

Often he had cried himself to sleep, unable to understand why he could not have the food he smelled, or tired and worn out with work he was barely strong enough to perform. But once he had been banished from the kitchen to the mine itself, and a hammer and handpick put in his little hands, he dimly began to think of the kitchen as paradise. The older he got, the more like paradise it seemed. When he and the others sluiced the gravel in winter with water just barely above freezing, he would think bitterly of the relative pleasure of scrubbing crusted pots in water that was at least *warm.* When he and the others huddled together under the barn floor in their sleeping pit, fighting over scraps of blanket, he would remember how he could press his back against the bricks of the hearth and be comfortable all night. When he managed to steal burned bread or otherwise ruined food from the pig buckets before they went into the trough, he would think of how his caretaker had picked the least-burned bits out of the husk and fed them alternately to herself and him.

So, all things considered . . . he found himself quite content to scrub dishes here in the Collegium kitchens, in good, hot water, with plenty of soap, conscious of a full stomach and the cheerful chatter of his fellow Trainees. Knowing that when he went to bed tonight it would be in a real bed, and he would sleep without being kicked awake, and . . . he just found himself marveling all over again at the change in his life.

There were not as many dishes to be washed as he had anticipated, although there were plenty to keep him and the other Trainees busy until sunset. He was freed just in time to run down to the stables and change into his *other* Trainee "best."

When he had first started coming out of his shell here at the Collegium, he had made the accidental acquaintance of Master Soren, advising him that a gem he intended to buy for his niece Lydia was flawed. Soren had invited Mags to his Midwinter open house, and when Dean Caelen was advised of this, the Dean had known he had noth-

131

ing in the way of clothing that would pass muster on such an occasion.

Fortunately, there were easy remedies for this.

All Trainees were supposed to wear the same uniform. But, of course, there were Trainees who were highborn, and wearing the common uniform at something outside the Collegium could make them stand out in a way that was flattering neither to them nor to the Collegium. So wealthy or highborn Trainees were permitted to have uniforms made of finer materials, to be worn only outside of the Collegia — provided that those uniforms went into the common pool once they were outgrown.

So Mags had been given one of those. He had more than one set now, a couple for winter that were made of heavier velvet and fine wool, and some of lightweight and supple leather and fine linen for warmer weather.

And, of course, thanks to the wedding, now every Trainee had one especially good outfit of formal Grays that were the equivalent of formal Whites — but Mags' new wedding gear was very much in need of cleaning, so his second set would have to do. Any deficiencies in it would be covered by the fact that it would only be seen by lantern and torchlight.

:Go get Amily, would you?: he begged Dallen, as he cleaned up and changed. *:I don' want her tired out, and she's done a mort of walkin' these past three days.:*

:Not only will I do that, I'll make sure that her father insists she ride me,: Dallen replied. *:We'll meet you at the stands.:*

Several grandstands had been set up beside the river for this procession, but, of course, the best were in the middle and were reserved for the King, Queen, Heir, and Princess, and their respective entourages. Mags had only just learned that the term "Court" did not actually refer to what he had *thought* it did — the collection of highborn and wealthy folks who thronged the rooms of the Palace by day, some of whom actually lived in the Palace, some of whom lived in their great manors outside the walls of the Palace and Collegium up here on the Hill, and some of whom lived far from Haven and only put in an appearance in winter, when the business of running their estates was fundamentally over.

Most people used "Court" to mean all those people, but it was not entirely accurate. There were — or would be — *four* Courts now. There had been two. The King's was composed of his gentlemen, his advisors, and his officials. It was almost entirely male. The Queen had her own Court, much smaller, consisting of her ladies-in-waiting. Now that he was back in Haven and taking his place at the King's side, the Heir had his as well, consisting of his gentlemen and friends, although he himself actually belonged to the King's Court. And now the new Princess would have a Court of her own, smaller than the Queen's, though she was also part of the Queen's Court. Of all these four Courts, the Prince's was the one that was most under the control of its head; no one expected the Prince to have anyone in his Court except his particular friends. In fact, it would have been shocking to discover that Kingdom business of any sort might be negotiated with the Prince. He was supposed to remain his father's subordinate until the King died or handed over the reins. The other three Courts, however, were very much subject, not to the wills of the King, Queen, or Princess, but to politics.

Court also meant the formal session held every day during which the King made pronouncements and held judgment on matters of state and between his courtiers.

Mags had never quite realized it before, but most of the people who hung about the

Palace were male; although the ladies-in-waiting might have their entire families here if their husbands were part of the King's Court, that was rare, and the Gentlemen of the King's Court and the Prince's Court generally were on their own or had only their eldest sons with them. This made the place a very desirable hunting ground for any mother hoping to marry off daughters and for daughters wishing to marry well. So positions in the Queen's Court, and in the new Princess' Court, were greatly desired.

All of this had gone right past him. Maybe it had just been because he was male, and males (even the ones in Court!) were often oblivious to such things. It was Amily who had introduced him to these realities in the weeks before the wedding, while she was recovering from her surgery. It had made his head reel, to think of all of this white-hot jousting and jockeying that had been going on under his nose without him ever being aware of it.

"The Courts are like a swan," she had said with a chuckle. *"Serene on the surface, with furious activity below."*

So tonight he and Amily were going to be actually useful to Lydia. There would be twice as many young ladies in the stands around the Princess than there were places in her Court — quite literally, because they would all have rooms in her section of the Palace, and there were only so many rooms to be had. It was true that there were young ladies who would be *part* of her Court who would be living in their parents' stately mansions outside the walls, but they would not be her actual ladies-in-waiting. It was the ones who would be living together in the close confines of the Palace walls, sharing rooms, that were the concern. He and Amily were going to have to try to help Lydia choose a set of ladies-in-waiting who were unlikely to ignite a firestorm of infighting.

Thank goodness that breeze was still blowing. At least he wouldn't have to try to decide if a flare of temper was due to being overheated and overstimulated, or due to genuine ill will.

He arrived at dusk as the lanterns and torches were being lit. There were pages at the ends of the grandstands to show the guests to their proper seats. One of them caught his eye and motioned to him; Mags went to the boy. "Amily'll be along — ah, she's here," he said, catching a glimpse of Dallen coming through the crowd, which parted to let a Companion through. He lifted her down off Dallen's back, rather than cause her to crease her gown, which suited her admirably. For once, she wasn't dressed to hide, she was dressed to fit in. In this case, to fit in with Lydia's potential ladies. Her gown was of the finest linen, soft and supple and, as he was aware, an extremely expensive fabric. It was hard to tell exactly what color it was in the torchlight, which made everything look yellowish, but he thought it was a dark gold. It had been trimmed in woven bands in a geometric pattern, and a wider version of the same served her as a belt that passed twice around her waist with two lengths depending from a knot in front.

She had a flower wreath with ribbons at the back around her dark hair instead of a jeweled filet, as did many of the ladies, and Mags thought she looked wonderful.

The page took them to their place, at the back and top of the grandstand. Lydia was at the front, of course, with some of the more important of her guests and potential ladies, but also with some of her closest friends. From the back Mags and Amily had a fine view not only of the river but also of everyone in front of them.

He relaxed and eased his shields down just slightly. Not enough to be bombarded by thoughts, just enough to get telling, strong fragments.

As the stands filled, he and Amily watched the young ladies below them while appearing to be engrossed in each other. Most of the young ladies were, in fact, watching the young men in the Prince's entourage rather than each other. A few were actually eyeing some of the older men in the King's train with some covert avidity. One of them, somewhat to his amazement, was openly trying to flirt with one of the Guild-masters, who was easily old enough to be her grandfather.

:*She knows what she's doing,*: Dallen said dryly. :*Large title, small fortune, and her brother will get all of it. She reckons to be a young, wealthy widow, and she supposes a few years of serving an old man is a small price to pay.*:

Well, that made sense, he supposed, especially since very few marriages at this level of wealth or title were love matches. And it wasn't his job — thanks be to the gods — to pick out who was and was not suitable to be one of Lydia's ladies. It was only his job to observe and report.

Amily knew them all by name and was making careful notes, covertly, in a little book that hung from her belt. Mags, who did not know them at all (except for Lydia's friends), murmured his observations to her.

And somehow in all of this, they even managed to enjoy the lighted tableaus on the barges and the music coming from the bridge. Some were scenes from legend or history, others were just general "scenes" — like a pair of shepherd and shepherdess lovers and their sheep, or gods among clouds. The barges probably looked tawdry in daylight and up close, but at night and lit only by their lanterns, they looked magical.

And the music was certainly wonderful, with a special short piece for each tableau.

It was, however, a very long pageant, and it came at the end of three very long and (for Mags at least) very active days. By the time it was over, he knew he was not going to be among those who were having one last loft party — and Amily herself was yawning.

"I think ye'd better go back by Dallen," he whispered to her, and she was so tired she just nodded.

"I think I am going to be able to stay awake just long enough to write down my notes in a way that someone other than myself can read them," she confessed.

He stole a kiss under cover of getting her on Dallen's back, and a second when she leaned down to bid him good night. The second kiss was quite long, and rather warm, and kept him in a pleasant state of satisfaction right until he opened his windows for the night breeze, lay down, and closed his eyes.

And when he opened them again — it was morning.

Morning and, he realized with a touch of regret as he rousted himself out of bed, back to classes and the regular schedule of the Collegium.

"Well," Bear said three days later at luncheon, leaning over the table in a conspiratorial manner as the others helped themselves to fruit mixed with a little beaten cream. "You've had time to think about it. So?"

Mags didn't have to ask what Bear meant. And Bear was right, he *had* had time to think about it. He'd even asked Dallen's opinion a second time. And he thought he had an answer.

"Ye're still set on this, aye?" he asked.

Bear nodded.

"Elope."

If he hadn't been trying so hard to keep his face sober, he'd have laughed aloud at the expression on Bear's. He looked as utterly dumbfounded as if he had been presented with a singing pig. "What?" Bear stammered, finally.

"Elope," Mags repeated. "Dallen says 'tis easier t'ask fergiveness than permission. Ye know that priest down in Haven what tends to the poor folk — ye help him all th' time. Ye know he'll help ye in turn. You an' Lena just go down there an' ask him t'marry ye, an' I bet he will, without much question. Then ye come back up here an' tell the Deans ye're married, an' what ye intend t'do with yerselves. They'll see ye thought it all out, an' it's mortal hard t' unmarry someone that's been priest-married if they don' want t'be unmarried. So there. Elope. Then ask fergiveness."

He sat back. Bear remained where he was, blinking blankly for a good long time.

Then he got up without a word and went out.

"I need you to come with me."

Mags looked up from the book he was studying and blinked in surprise to see Bear standing next to him as he sat at his table, trying to puzzle out some sort of complicated etiquette.

How had Bear managed to sneak up on him?

Granted, he had all the windows and the

door to his room wide open for the breeze, and granted, there was plenty of sound from both outside and inside the stable to cover any footsteps. But —

:Don't concern yourself. First of all, you know I am right outside your door. Second, you sensed someone coming, recognized the mind as Bear's, and didn't even break your concentration,: Dallen advised him. *:Don't worry, your instincts are just as sharp as ever.:*

Oh. Well, all —

"I *need* you to come with me," Bear insisted again, oblivious to the silent dialogue going on between Mags and Dallen. "Right now, please." He fidgeted a little, shifting his weight from one foot to the other. Mags was using a single candle with a clever reflector that concentrated all the light on his book, so the peculiar lighting actually made Bear look a little sinister.

"Might help if ye told me why," Mags replied mildly, shutting his book. "I do got studyin', unlike some folks that's got no problem with book stuff."

"Lena and I . . . we're trying to do what you said to do, but Father Poul wants to talk to *you,*" Bear said, a bit desperately.

Mags sighed and shoved his book aside. "Now? Really? I don't got leave t'be down in the city late tonight." It wasn't late yet . . .

the sun was barely down. But if he had to spend any time at all down in Haven, it *would* be late when he got back, and it might be after the time when Trainees were supposed to be abed. "And I don't reckon ye want me to go to Nikolas or Caelen an 'splain *why* I wanta be down in Haven tonight. It's all right fer *you,* you got leave to be down there any time," he added, a little crossly. Granted, he had an extraordinary amount of freedom now, but he was, by nature, still cautious about everything. When there wasn't immediate danger, or when he wasn't acting directly on Nikolas' orders, he just didn't want to chance getting into trouble. His body remembered what "trouble" meant, all too well, and even if he knew in his head that no one was going to beat him half to death here for an infraction, his instincts were still set by his life in the mines.

:*I'll tell Rolan that Father Poul sent Bear for you,*: Dallen said unexpectedly. And at Mags' start of surprise, the Companion added :*What? It's not a lie. It's just not the entire truth.*:

Well . . . that was interesting. So . . . a Companion was willing to occasionally tell a partial truth?

Then again, Dallen didn't seem to be the

run-of-the-mill sort of Companion, if there was such a thing.

:Are you going with me?: Mags asked. A good question, since having Dallen along would make it easier to pass the Gate Guards without question. Since the night that the assassin had tried to burn down the Companions' stable with all of them in it, an insect couldn't get over the walls without a challenge, so sneaking in and out was completely out of the question.

A mental snort of disdain. *:Of course I am, otherwise it will take you all night. Father Poul won't think twice about keeping a boy as long as he likes, even a Herald Trainee, if Poul thinks he needs to question him in detail. He will think twice about keeping you if I am there to insist it is time to go back. Remember, he is used to impulsive younglings colluding with each other to do something foolish. Normally he would trust Bear and Lena, and he'd trust you, but in his eyes, this probably looks very foolish indeed and could potentially bring a great deal of trouble on all of you.:*

Mags sighed again. "All right," he said reluctantly. "But if you wasn't my best friend . . ."

Bear didn't let him finish that statement, hustling him up out of his chair and out the door. Mags didn't bother with tack on

144

Dallen, not for a little jaunt like this. He mounted Dallen's back without any effort at all, just putting his hands on Dallen's shoulders and rump, hopping up, and swinging his leg over, then leaned down and offered Bear a hand, pulling his friend up to sit behind him. Bear took a double handful of Mags' short-sleeved tunic to steady himself. Mags glanced back to make sure he was secure.

Bear's dumbfounded expression made him pause. "What?" he asked.

"You've gotten strong . . ." Bear said slowly. "You still look like anybody could take you, but you've gotten *strong.*"

Mags just shook his head, twined his left hand loosely in Dallen's mane, and patted Dallen's neck as they cantered out of the gates and down the road that would take them into Haven. "All the Kirball, all the roof-runnin', an' yer just *now* noticin'? Bear, all this business with yer Pa an' Lena's has made yer mind go soft."

Bear let go of his tunic long enough to smack him lightly in the back of the head.

It was well after lamp-lighting that they reached Father Poul's little temple. It was a walled area in one of the poorest areas of the town, with a front courtyard that was open at all hours to all comers. Mags was

not entirely certain which gods Poul repre-
sented, since after a while they all seemed
to blur together to him. The important thing
was that he and his brother priests adminis-
tered to some of the most poverty-stricken
and desperate people in Haven — and that
Bear often came down here to help them.

The wall about the place was plain rough
stone. It was there largely to give the priests
and acolytes some semblance of peace and
privacy rather than to safeguard much of
anything. The building within the wall was
made of similar rough stone, with plain
wooden doors and windows with wooden
shutters for harsh weather. There was no
way that turf would survive all the traffic, so
it had been filled with river gravel and sand.
There were benches made of salvaged wood
to sit or lie on, and a much-patched swath
of canvas had been affixed across the area
for shade in the day.

Although it was after lamp-lighting, the
courtyard was still playing host to people
who were looking for help, either spiritual
or physical. The poor folk didn't have much
choice about when they could come to a
place like this for help. They were limited to
those few hours they had between finishing
their work for the day and falling into a
weary sleep, so there was actually more

activity here in the evening than there was in the day.

The arrival of a Companion caused a bit of a stir and brought one of the Temple acolytes out to find out what was going on before Mags had even dismounted.

"Father Poul asked t'see Mags," Bear told the brown-robed acolyte shortly. The young man nodded and disappeared back inside the Temple. As with most such places in Haven, Mags was unsurprised to see that the courtyard was in use for many purposes. Some, too poor to afford lamps, candles, or even tallow dips, came here to read or to learn to read or figure. They had their own place, under one of the two courtyard lanterns. The sick and injured waited patiently off on the quietest, darkest side of the yard, and those who were here for reasons not obvious sat on benches in the middle.

Father Poul came out after a bit of a wait; Mags knew him well enough, since he had come down here a time or two in order to give Bear a hand. He was short, slight, and harried. The thinning of his hair might have had more to do with his habit of seizing a handful of it at the scalp when vexed than to balding. Like all the denizens here, he wore a simple brown divided robe. The priest gestured them to a side door in the wall, that looked to lead into a garden. Since his gesture had included Dallen, and the door was big enough to accommodate him, the Companion came too.

It was, indeed, a garden — a very neat and efficiently planned herb and vegetable garden, lit with a single small lantern. That was probably a necessity — if someone came in over the wall, whoever came to investigate would need *some* light to see by. It didn't afford any seating to speak of, but it did seem to offer some privacy. Dallen politely backed himself into a space where he wouldn't trample anything.

Father Poul didn't waste any time with polite niceties; he came straight to the point. "If what Bear has told me is the truth, you already know why I want to talk to you," the short, slight priest said firmly. He planted both hands on his hips, in an "I will not tolerate any nonsense" pose.

Mags sighed, wishing he could see the priest's expression in the gloom. "They want t' get married. They think it'll solve some of their prollems. I tol' 'em that Dallen tol' me that they prolly ought to, an' that it'd be easier t' do it and let things sort themselves out than try an' get permission. I dunno if it's gonna solve much, but I trust my Companion, an' it'll at least stop Bear's Pa from tryin' t' treat him like a prize breeder. That pretty much what they told you?"

"Your *Companion* told you this." Poul made it a statement rather than a question, but Mags answered as if it had been a question.

"Aye. He don't seem t'mind bendin' rules, does Dallen," Mags sighed. "I s'pose since he's a Companion, people won't think so bad of him for it."

Dallen bobbed his head emphatically and pawed the bare dirt with a hoof.

Father Poul huffed out his breath, sounding a little annoyed in the darkness. "I've never known a Herald or a Trainee to lie about what their Companion told them —"

Dallen snorted indignantly, and before Mags could stop him, he nipped the priest's sleeve in his strong teeth and gave the sleeve, arm and all, an admonishing shake.

"Here now! I wasn't saying he was lying *now,*" Poul snapped, pulling his sleeve back. Dallen let him have it. He rubbed his hand over his head, seized a handful of hair, and then let it go. "Well, now you've presented me with a pretty problem. A Companion advised this. And if they were just a little older, I wouldn't hesitate. But —"

"You reckon why a *Companion* would say to do something, eh?" Mags retorted. "Prolly a good reason he can see that we can't. I reckon I'd listen to 'im if I was you. I tol' ye, he don' seem t'mind bendin' the rules, 'cept Lena's been checkin', an' there ain't no rules 'bout Trainees gettin' married. I s'pose there's rules about young'uns gettin' married outside of what their folks arrange, but . . ." He shrugged. "Near as I can tell, rules 'bout Trainees not bein' *forced* t'get married is the only thing goin'."

Dallen stamped a hoof to emphasize Mags' words.

"I can see that I'm not going to shake either of you on this, anyway," Father Poul said, a little crossly. "I thought perhaps it might have been Bear that persuaded you, on the strength of your friendship, but I can see I was mistaken."

"Aye," Mags said shortly. Then added, belatedly, "Sir. An' it's gettin' late, an' I don' wanta break the rules about bein' down in Haven late."

Dallen shook himself all over and looked pointedly at the door.

"All right, all right, you can go," said the priest, waving dismissively. "I'll have to rethink this — *you* stay," he added to Bear. "You and I are not done yet. I'll make it right with your superiors if need be." He shook his head and muttered, "Even if I have to lie about it."

Mags made his escape, and while under other circumstances he might have been reluctant to leave Bear in Father Poul's hands . . . well . . .

In this case, Bear had put himself there.

Mags was not at all surprised two days later to come into an uproar at dinner and discover that Bear and Lena had done exactly as he advised. The word was all over all three Collegia; gossip was that the two of them had gone straight down to Haven after luncheon and come back a couple of candlemarks later to present themselves as a couple to the Deans. They had been closeted with the heads of the Collegia ever since, and there was a lot of speculation as to what was likely to happen to them.

Mags just held his peace. As he had said, it was very difficult to force a lawfully married couple apart if they didn't *want* to be forced apart. Add to that Bear's situation, and Lena's, and the fact that Mags knew they would present themselves with a well-thought-out plan for the future, and he figured the conclusion — once everyone exhausted all the shouting and scolding they

151

would feel themselves bound to do — was forgone.

And so it was. Near the end of supper, the two appeared in the dining hall, hand in hand, looking tired but satisfied.

No one had left, of course; everyone knew that the first place they would come would be here, and by this time everyone who could fit inside was in there waiting, including Amily, who was just a little, tiny bit put out with him for *not* telling her what he had known before this happened.

"You might have said *something,*" she whispered for the third time, as the buzz of conversation made the room feel much too small.

Finally, he told her the truth. After all, she really deserved the truth, didn't she? "I didn't say nothin', on account of I didn't have Bear's leave, and I figgered you'd feel obliged to tell yer pa."

She opened her mouth to object, her pretty face betraying her obvious irritation, then stopped. She closed her mouth, opened it again, then closed it. The irritation was replaced by thoughtfulness.

Finally she spoke. "I'm still *annoyed,*" she said. "I see your points, but I am still annoyed."

"Aye, and I still didn't have Bear's leave,"

he countered.

"Did you even ask for it?" Irritation again.

"I figgered if he wanted ye to know, he'd'a tol' ye himself." That did seem, at least to *him,* to be irrefutable logic. "It's not like he isn't seein' ye once every couple of days, aye?"

The irritation was replaced with frustration, because she knew very well he was right. The meetings were even in private, since he was making sure her leg was continuing to heal correctly.

"An' *wouldn't* you have felt obliged t'tell yer pa?" he continued —

:You really are pressing your luck, you know,: Dallen interjected. *:You might win the argument, but you might not like the results of winning.:*

Fortunately, the arrival of Bear and Lena saved her from having to answer and him from the consequences of that answer.

When they came in, hand in hand, looking triumphant but exhausted, they were swarmed. Mags didn't even try to get near them, and finally someone took charge of the chaos.

A horn blast from one of the Bardic Trainees (why had he brought a *horn* to dinner?) brought momentary silence, and into that silence came a bellow in a quite familiar voice.

"Everyone just *shut up,*" shouted Gennie. In the ensuing quiet there was only the shuffling of feet. "Good. Bear, Lena, would you mind telling us all what the *hell* you were thinking, running off like that? And what happened today when you got back?"

They looked at each other. Everyone looked at them. Finally Bear coughed. "We were thinking, it's easier to ask forgiveness than get permission," he said, quoting Mags and Dallen directly. "You all know what my father keeps trying to do. Lena and I, well, we don't want anyone else, never have. Where I come from, people younger than me get married off all the time — probably that's the same for most of you, too. Father Poul down in Haven's spent the last couple of days pretty much talking us to death, and he reckoned we knew what we were doing, so he married us today, we came up and 'fessed up to the Deans. And that's it, really."

"Well, other than that I won't be Lena Marchand anymore, I'll be Lena Tyrall," said Lena when he had finished. "And when I go into Scarlets, I'll be *Bard* Tyrall. Which . . . is kind of important to me, even if it doesn't mean anything to anyone else."

But there were nods, especially from the Bardic Trainees. Mags didn't quite get it, but after some whispered explanation from Amily, he began to understand. After all, there already was a "Bard Marchand," Lena's now-disgraced father. Even if he had not fallen into disgrace, she would still be forced to compete with him as the "other" Bard Marchand. Not all of his compositions had been stolen from his protégés, and he had a formidable body of work that hers would always be compared to.

Now, she wasn't competing with him, and except for those who knew who her father was already (not many, relatively speaking), she was not going to be compared more with him than with any other Bard. And now, no one would be associating her name with infamy. This probably would have been less than successful if she had changed her name after she had attained the title of "Bard," because her Masterwork would have been, perforce, done under her old name.

"As for what happened when we got back, Father Poul came with us, and . . . let's just say we went through the last couple of days all over again." Bear sighed, and he squeezed Lena's hand. "Deans of all *three* Collegia, and the heads of all three Circles. *And* the

King's Own *and* Prince Sedric and Princess Lydia. But it's all right. They reckon we didn't run off and do something stupid, we'll be living in my quarters still, and we're still Trainees. And let me just say, if that's how they question a couple of folks who just went off an' got married, I wouldn't want to be caught stealin' so much as a pocket pie."

That got a laugh. Bear's fellow trainees had been zealously guarding some dinner for him and Lena, and the two of them were allowed to eat in relative peace, while smaller groups asked them questions. Mags and Amily waited until pretty much everyone else had been satisfied, and Mags brought them over some custard tarts and a pitcher of tea after most of the mob had cleared out.

"Thanks for keeping quiet," Bear said, when they sat down across from him and Lena. "Nikolas was kinda irritated you hadn't talked to him, but —" he shrugged. "— even he admitted he'd've tried to stop us if he'd known."

Mags did *not* say "I told you so" to Amily. He didn't need Dallen telling him what a bad idea *that* was.

"Ye know, this ain't the end of trouble," he said instead.

"Oh, we know," Lena replied, since Bear had a mouthful of tart. "We fully expect the fury of hell itself to descend when Bear's father finds out." She smiled slyly. "But let's just say we have a very unexpected weapon on our side."

4

With all of the wedding business out of the way, Nikolas decided that it was time to reopen the shop down in Haven. He had no doubt that with all of the visitors that had been packed into Haven, it had been a glorious time for thieves, and if there is one thing that thieves require, it is someone who can turn what they stole into money. Nikolas, in the persona of Willy Weasel, already had the reputation for taking in unusual objects no one else would touch because his mute "nephew" could evaluate stones, allowing him to pry them out of settings and sell them without the concern of a piece being recognized. "Unusual jewelry" was how they had caught the assassins before. There was always the hope that the men had neither realized this nor reported it, and this would be an effective way of uncovering more of them.

At this point, Nikolas had decided that it

was time for Willy to show some evidence of prosperity in the form of employees. Where Nikolas had found these fellows, Mags had not been able to guess, but they certainly looked villainous enough. When Nikolas had taken him down to the shop before the wedding, he'd blinked at the sight of them; big, grizzled, scowling, they were twins for some of the mine guards.

"Are ye sure you can trust 'em?" he'd asked Nikolas, aghast. That was when Nikolas had laughed and told him that they were actor friends of his, retired now from their profession, but more than willing to put in "short performances" at night at the shop.

That had eased Mags' mind a great deal. Nikolas had never once made a mistake with his actors, and Mags very much doubted he had this time, either.

They knew exactly what to say when something that looked important came in the shop door. "Willy" would not give them the authority to buy more than the most trivial of goods, however, nor purchase information, and no one would be surprised at that. Anyone with any sense would probably figure that "Willy" kept most of the shop money locked up somewhere and only doled out the little they needed to run the place in his absence. This meant anyone with anything of note to sell would have to wait until Willy and his nephew turned up.

This was a profound relief to Mags; it meant he and Nikolas only needed to put in an appearance for a few candlemarks every few days and not spend every night down at the shop. That had been exhausting, even with all of Mags' instructors doing their best to accommodate his schedule.

It also meant that instead of waiting for those potential clues to come in, he and Nikolas could have them turning up when *they* wanted. So if there was any appearance of danger, well . . . they could arrange for the danger to have a terrible surprise.

Mags didn't expect any suspicion to arise from this change in the shop schedule. It was entirely within the realm of believability that the Weasel had managed to make a big score. No one would be in the least surprised at the Weasel delegating the running of his shop, if he had managed to come into money. The Weasel was known for his sharp dealings, not for being so miserly that he begrudged the spending of so much as a pin more than he needed to. Nikolas had carefully manufactured a persona of a man who did not begrudge himself small luxuries or indulgences.

Being able to do something other than stand behind the protected counter of his own shop every night was one of those things every shopkeeper hoped for, one day.

Mags was not altogether certain he was looking forward to their first foray down in Haven again, however. He had the feeling that Nikolas had a few things to say to him about Lena and Bear.

"I have a few things I would like to discuss with you about Lena and Bear, Mags."

The shop was quiet, which was not at all surprising. The first lot of people with something valuable to get rid of had *almost* been lining up at the door, waiting for the Weasel. Almost, because they had trickled in slowly over the first couple of candlemarks, probably scouting first to make sure no one was lying in wait, hoping to ambush a fellow thief while he was carrying something good.

And the wedding had, indeed, brought a wealth of small, valuable items into Haven, if what had been spread out for the Weasel's perusal was anything to judge by. Nothing that would impress a highborn, of course; no one who came to the Weasel was *that* good or lucky a thief. But there was a lot of real silver and real semiprecious or poorly cut precious gems.

When anything had gems in it, the Weasel passed it over to his mute "nephew" for grading. Mags passed a practiced eye over it, graded the stones, scribbled the grade on a bit of slate and passed both back. The Weasel never paid jewelry value, of course, only metal and stone — because if he really had been a pawnbroker and a fence, he would never have kept any of it intact; he would pry the stones out, melt the piece down, and dispose of the things that way.

In fact the pieces were going to the City Constables; if there were recognizable theft claims on any of it, the jewelry would go back to its owners. If not, it would be held for a year, then disposed of, and the proceeds would go to the families of Constables who had died to help them out.

But now the shop was quiet, he didn't have to pretend to be mute. And Nikolas, who hadn't had a chance to speak with him privately before this — exactly as Mags had wanted it — now was going to get his chance.

Now I'm for it.

"I understand, I think, why you didn't consult with me about their plans," Nikolas said slowly. "I'm . . . annoyed, however. Did it occur to you just to say 'I have something

I would like you to keep in confidence, and if you can't do that, just say so'? The King's Own keeps many secrets, even from the King."

"Uh . . ." Mags replied, feeling stupid. "No."

Nikolas nodded. "All right, then. Now I am a bit less annoyed. I might very well have said no, depending on what Rolan and Dallen said to me, but at least then we would have known where we stood, I would have known that you younglings were up to something private, and I would have looked less foolish when Bear and Lena turned up married."

"Well . . . Dallen said 'e didn't think I should tell nobody about it," Mags ventured. " 'Cause Bear hadn't given me leave."

"But you didn't ask Bear for leave?" Nikolas was pitiless.

"I reckoned if he wanted t'give me leave, he would've." It was weak, and it sounded weak, and he knew it.

"Hmm." Nikolas wasn't convinced.

:I didn't see any way it could cause any harm at this point in time.:

Mags knew exactly what Dallen meant. "Dallen says he didn' think *right this moment* them gettin' married'd cause problems," he relayed, then elaborated. "Lena's

163

Pa's in disgrace. Bear's Pa's in bad with the Healer's Circle an' the Collegium, on account of how he was actin'. He's in worse, 'cause he sent Cuburn t'spy on Bear in the first place, and Cuburn near got Amily killed in the second. So right now, pretty much anythin' that might spite him is all right with everybody. But . . . ye just never know 'round here. By Midwinter, maybe somehow Bear's Pa manages t' save somebody important, an' all of a sudden he ain't in bad no more, 'cause nobody dares counter his backer. Or maybe Bear makes some mistake, an' everybody decides maybe his Pa was stupid, but right." He shrugged. "Y'see? Right this moment might be th' only time they could do it without stirrin' up trouble for more people than just themselves."

Slowly, Nikolas nodded. "So you did think this through."

"As much's I could, since it ain't my call t'make. 'Twas Bear an' Lena's, an' that's that." That seemed to him to be the real argument here.

Nikolas pinched the bridge of his nose, squeezing his eyes shut for a moment. "All right. I still don't like it. As the King's Own, I am still slightly offended that the person I am teaching and responsible for did not come to me with this information. *However,* you are correct in that at this point in time, the information really was of no importance to anyone except Bear and Lena, and there were no possible ramifications."

Mags let out the breath he had been holding in.

But Nikolas wasn't finished. "Nevertheless. Mags — *and* Dallen — you both forget that I am privy to absolutely everything regarding this Kingdom, and it was entirely likely that I would know something that would reveal that yes, there *were* possible ramifications. I do not wish to have to repeat this lecture again. *Ever.*"

"Yessir," Mags said immediately.

:Hmph.: That was all Dallen said. Mags very much feared that his Companion was not impressed.

"Now, of everything that came in tonight, what was the thing that didn't fit?" Nikolas asked.

Mags shook his head, and Nikolas held out his hand. In it were three rectangular pieces of finely finished metal. They looked bronze; they also looked as if they should have been pendants, except there were no holes in them for stringing on a necklace.

All three were of the same design: flowers, or what appeared to be flowers, on one side, and some sort of cursive pattern on the other.

Mags cocked his head to the side. "They ain't all that valuable."

"Not in and of themselves, no." Nikolas turned them over in his hand with a finger. "The thing is, they aren't anything I have ever seen before. I think this is writing, but it's no language either I or Rolan is familiar with. It's not the same language as the one book our mysterious assassins left behind is written in. So I am sorely puzzled. Are they coins? I've never seen a rectangular coin, it's possible. Are they talismans? There don't appear to be any images of gods. Are they gaming pieces? If so, whoever owned them must be very wealthy, and you would *think* that a wealthy person who has lost some pieces to his game would be going to jewelers to have them replaced so he can continue to play — and believe me, if that had happened, I would have been told about it. The jewelers in Haven know *very* well to come to one of the Guard or a Guard agent, or a Constable if something turns up that they just don't recognize."

Mags nodded. He'd actually relayed a few of those messages, which had all but one turned out to be false alarms — some bits and pieces from the Shin'a'in and from

Rethwellan. The one that had not been a false alarm had sorely puzzled them all until someone found a half-obliterated hallmark on it, and had realized the piece was a botched attempt at melting down a more intricate object, and what had been a delicate tracery of leaves and vines had ended up looking like an unknown script.

But these pieces were clean, not shiny, but still, with no wear and very little patina on them. Even though Mags could not have told what sort of flowers were on the front — if it was the front — he had no doubt that they would be perfectly recognizable to someone who knew their type.

Nikolas closed his hand on them. "They'll go to the Guard Archivist. If there's a record of anything like this, he'll have it." He put the pieces in a secure pocket of his belt pouch. "I'd like you to run the rest of this over to the Constables," he continued, handing over a heavy, if tidy little bundle. "Get back here as soon as you can. The lull won't last forever, just until the most cautious of our clients decide that it is late enough they can take the chance on catching the Weasel before he goes home for the night."

Mags took the bundle and secured it inside his tunic, in a pocket he'd sewn there himself, with heavy, double-stitched seams. Then he pulled down the ladder that accessed the attic and the roof and scrambled up it, pulling it up after himself once he reached the top.

Obviously, he was *not* going to travel on the open streets with this much silver on him. And equally obviously, he had no intention of allowing anyone to see that the Weasel's nephew was visiting the Constables.

As he came out on the roof and sniffed, he thought he caught a hint of ripening hay in the air. It was possible; there were hayfields just outside of Haven's walls. Well if the last hay harvest had begun, then the grain harvests would not be far behind, and that meant autumn was definitely on the way.

:Ah, Kirball matches without fainting from the heat. I favor that.:

Mags grinned as he paced across the roof tiles and poised at the edge, then made the leap to the next roof to land as softly as a cat. *:I'm with ye there, but I'm not lookin' forward t' roof-runnin' in the cold.:*

:Then let's hope you don't have to,: came the entirely practical answer.

The good thing about this part of Haven was that the houses were crowded so closely together that even when crossing streets he still didn't have to descend to the ground. And he knew his way to the Constable's station so well that he could easily have made the run half asleep. It took him a quarter candlemark, and it wouldn't have taken him that long if he hadn't had to wait a few moments for a patrol of Constables to pass. They wouldn't know who the shadow flitting over the rooftops was, and they would raise the alarm. Then he would have to lose them. They'd probably recognize him if they caught him, but then they would have to go through the charade of taking him in, and . . . well it could turn into an all-night debacle before he got turned loose, and he was really hoping to be back in bed a bit after midnight.

Better not to be seen.

He got to the Constabulary roof, found his special access hatch, and tripped the hidden catch. Once he was down in their attic storage, he could breathe easier.

There was a proper set of stairs down into the readying room, and he came down them just as the patrol he had spotted came in to get rid of their gear and get a little rest before going out again.

"Well, if it ain't the lad!" exclaimed Constable Baltis, a grin splitting his homely face. "We thought you and the Weasel'd come into a pile of money, packed up and left us!"

The men here did not know that the Weasel and his nephew were King's Own Nikolas and Trainee Mags — but they *did* know that the Weasel and his nephew were agents for the Crown.

They also knew the nephew wasn't mute.

"Brought you lads loot," Mags said, pulling the bag out of his tunic and hefting it. "The bad lot's been busy over the wedding. Which one of you wants to take it to the Sergeant?"

"I will," Baltis volunteered. "Is it tagged?"

"As usual. You know the Weasel is as fussy as an old hen about that," Mags said, getting a laugh. Nikolas always tagged every piece he turned over to the Constables with the name of the thief that had sold it on the paper it was folded into. The Constables as a whole thought this was overdoing it a bit. They *knew* who the thieves were, that wasn't the problem. The problem was catching them in the act, or at least with the goods on them. Once Nikolas had a piece of stolen goods, it was too late. They couldn't arrest the thief without revealing that Nikolas was an agent.

"Water?" suggested one of the others,

holding up a dipperful. "It's still hot enough out there —"

"Aye, thenkee." Mags took the dipper from him and drank, filling it twice from the little pottery barrel they all got their drinking water from — thoroughly boiled, for the water from the pumps in this part of town was not safe to drink without boiling first. The barrel was damp on the outside; a little of the water worked its way to the surface and evaporated, keeping the water still in there cool.

Baltis came back with a slip of paper from the Sergeant, which was all Mags needed. "Be careful out there," he said, giving them a sketchy salute as he turned to go up the stairs.

"You too!" Baltis called after him, as he passed into the attic and felt for the release for the hatch. "Don't want to pick you up with a broken neck come morning!"

He paused with one hand on the Constabulary chimney and looked up at the stars. This fall he was supposed to learn how to navigate by them. That was something he never would have *dreamed* of in the mine. He was on the day shift, and night was time for sleeping — the mine kiddies lived in a perpetual state of hunger and exhaustion, and in winter, you could add "cold" to that.

He couldn't remember more than one or two times he'd even bothered looking up at the sky at night — at least, not when it was clear, as it was tonight. The stars did nothing for you; they wouldn't feed or warm you, they wouldn't help you find food, they were just incomprehensible bits of light in uncaring darkness.

Had *anyone* at the mine paid any attention to the stars? Not that he remembered.

:Does a dog?: Dallen asked, unexpectedly. *:You were treated like abused animals, small wonder you hadn't any energy to spare for thinking past mere survival. Oddly enough, your early life might turn out useful one day. If you are ever in the regrettable position where you* must *concentrate on mere survival, well, you've had practice in it. And you've had practice in concentrating all your effort on it.:*

Well, now he had to concentrate all his effort on getting safely back to the shop. This was going to be an easier proposition than getting out to the Constabulary, however. He wasn't going to have to roof-run the entire way, just get over *there,* to a house actually owned by the Crown and used by Nikolas and his agents for a variety of purposes. Just now it stood empty, but even if someone had been staying there, it would still serve Mags.

The route off the roof of the Constabulary was a bit tricky and involved the longest leap of the night. The good thing was that the roof he was to land on had a nice flat bit that fetched up against a cornice, so he could tumble his landing and end up tucked against a bit of flat wall. After that, it was clear running; from this roof to a taller one with a steep pitch — but it was wood shingles rather than stone slates, and not at all slippery, The challenge was to get across it crabwise, but since he wasn't actually running, it was only that, a bit of a challenge. The next roof was hardly more than a hop, and the next only a bit farther away than that. The one after that was the roof of the house he wanted, only he didn't want to get into it tonight. He went to the edge on the darkest side, felt for the drainpipe at the corner, and hung by his hands over the edge until he found the place where it was strongly fastened to the house with his feet. Then he transferred his grip to the pipe and let himself down hand-over-hand until his feet touched the barrel at the bottom. He positioned his feet on either side of the barrel, balanced there for a moment, then jumped off.

He slipped around the corner of the house to the street side and peered about to make sure no one was within sight of him. Then he walked out into the street as if he had been walking along there for some time.

Well, "walked" was relative. No one here acted as if they were walking the street in broad daylight — poor as the neighborhood was, anyone making trouble during the day would probably find himself piled on by everyone in the area. There was strength in numbers, and if you wanted to be able to count on people coming to your rescue, the folks here knew they had better just come to anyone's rescue. There was a reason why the Constables patrolled constantly at night, and even so, they were well aware that what they mostly did was keep the criminals moving. So what he was really doing was moving at a brisk pace and making it clear he was watching all around him. Between that — which told thieves he was not going to be caught unaware — and his shabby clothing, he didn't look like a very good target.

He got back to the shop without any incident and presented Nikolas with the receipt. Nikolas pocketed it without a word, then went to the door and took a brief look up and down the street, then grunted audibly as if in disgust.

Mags knew what he was up to. The Weasel was now a man who no longer needed to keep his shop open at all hours if he didn't care to. If there was anyone lingering out there, trying to make up his mind whether or not to pay a visit, this would signal that he'd better do so quickly, because the Weasel was tired and wanted to go home.

They waited a little while longer in the crowded, narrow shop, but the little bell over the door didn't so much as vibrate.

"That's enough for one night," Nikolas said, finally. "We'll try again . . . oh, say in two nights." He left a note to that effect for his two "assistants" in the lockbox in the floor where the shop cash was kept. If anyone turned up with something special, they would pass the word when the Weasel himself would be keeping behind the counter.

"It is too bloody hot to be in that box," Nikolas said aloud as he locked up. Mags figured he was doing so for the presumed benefit of anyone who might be watching. Then again, he could just have been doing it to stay in character, since the Weasel continued complaining about the heat as the two of them trudged away. Mags didn't respond to any of it — he was supposed to be deaf as well as mute, after all. But the Weasel was on occasion a man who liked to hear the sound of his own voice, especially when he had something to complain about.

The Weasel was right about the heat, though. It was almost midnight, and breezes didn't get very far in the tangle of tightly packed buildings in this part of Haven. Paved streets or pounded earth, they all held heat and radiated it back all night. This time of year was about the only time when having your room in a basement or a garret under the eaves was a good thing. If you were up high you at least had a chance of catching a breeze, and if you were in a basement the earth would keep you cooler, even if you did share your space with more than your share of black beetles and rats.

And the rats could be dealt with by keeping a cat, after all.

:Makes me glad I don't fit into a basement,: Dallen remarked. *:I'm surprised with all the heat there aren't more fights.:*

Well, Mags knew the answer to that one. When you were working every waking hour, heat that might make someone with more leisure quarrelsome only debilitated you. *:Prolly around the alehouses,:* he replied. *:Round here, people just wanta get t'sleep.:*

And that was hard enough to do up on the breezy hill. He mopped at the back of his neck as he trotted after a complaining Weasel and was glad that he was going to be there shortly. A good wash under the cold water from the pump, and he'd be ready enough for sleep himself. Well, that was one thing that Haven provided for all its citizens anyway, plenty of water for free. There was a pump on every corner, and buckets too, in case of fire. So many buckets, in fact, that not even here did anyone bother to steal them.

:I believe I am going to start having you open the shop alone some nights,: Nikolas said unexpectedly.

:Wait — what?: he asked, dumbfounded. *:After Lena and Bear —:*

:You made an ethical decision, but it was also a rational one. As Dallen pointed out, for right now, really, the only people that are affected are they themselves. Rational and ethical — that means 'mature' to me. Honestly, if it weren't that you are so far behind most of your peers in all the classes you need to catch up on, I would be considering if I should put you in Whites in a year or so.:

That made him falter in his paces for a moment, and he ran to catch up. Nikolas glanced aside at him, and Mags saw he was laughing silently. *:Oh, don't look so stricken. You'll be a Kirball hero for some time yet. At least two years, you have that much in academics to catch up on. I only wish you were* *as good at Court politics as you are at this sort of thing.:*

Frankly, Mags was just as glad that he wasn't.

:Uh,: he ventured, finally, deeming it a good point to change the subject. *:How mad is Amily at me?:*

:A little less than I and for the same reasons. She's angrier at Lena and Bear, and then, not much.: Nikolas gave him another look, and in the light from a streetlamp, Mags saw him smiling slightly. *:I think everyone will be less angry with them once Bear's father learns of the marriage and puts in his inevitable appearance. I've asked some of my little birds to give me advance warning this time.:*

:To warn Bear?: Mags ventured.

Nikolas snorted. *:Oh, no. I want to see him handle this himself. That alone will tell me if he's made a mature decision.:*

:Why, then?:

:I want to gather an audience. I might even be tempted to sell tickets.:

Even on the Hill it was hot — hot enough that no one could be bothered to put much energy into anything that required physical effort. Even the Weaponsmaster had caved in to the heat and was limiting training to short sessions, sending the class down afterward to swim the river, bank to bank, like running laps around the salle, only a lot more pleasant in this heat. Those who did not know how to swim had learned in short order. Many classes, especially those in the hottest part of the day, had been moved outside, down by the river. Even the courtiers had abandoned the Court, opting to go off to their own country estates or visit those of friends. The Hill was practically deserted except for those who needed to be here to conduct the business of the Kingdom.

The cooks had declared a moratorium on "cooking," switching most of the kitchen work to the early, early morning when things had cooled down. But as hot as it was, no one really wanted to eat anything warm, and with lots of fresh fruits and vegetables, cold meats and bread satisfied just about everyone.

This, far more than the three days of the wedding, felt a lot like a holiday for Mags. Everyone was a little lazy, including the teachers. The good will generated by the wedding still lingered, which meant everyone was inclined to forgive a little laziness.

Lena and Bear had settled into Bear's quarters, but otherwise nothing really changed. They seemed determined to prove that they had made the right decision, and not even those most critical found anything in their behavior or their lessons to complain about. Amily seemed relieved . . . and, somewhat to Mags' bemusement, gave no indication that she was particularly envious or that she was harboring a secret longing to get married herself.

He wasn't sure whether to be relieved or wary. He certainly didn't want to bring it up. He didn't feel in the least as if he was ready for something like that. To be honest, when he looked at some of the other Trainees, he still felt terribly, terribly behind and very young — and in no way ready to go any further with Amily than he had already.

And as for Amily, it seemed to him she was waiting for something — and even she wasn't sure what it was that she was waiting for. Probably not the best reason in the world for getting married, to do so because you didn't know what else to do.

He was flopped down in the grass watching the river and listening to Bard Tharis wax eloquent on the history of King Anders, which seemed to be a specialty of his, and wondering mostly why the weather during that worthy's reign seemed to be entirely composed of snowstorms of monumental proportions, when he heard a familiar Mindvoice in his inner "ear."

:If you want your ticket, my young apprentice, you'd better get it now.:

He blinked a little startled. Ticket? Why would Nikolas be talking about a tick —

:Heads up!: Dallen said excitedly. :Trouble in a Temper is pounding up the Hill at a pace that is rather cruel to his horses, and little does he know what he's in for!:

What? And then it struck him — the memory of what Nikolas had said a fortnight or so ago. :Where're Bear and Lena?: he asked Dallen.

:Waiting at the gate. He won't be let inside, not after that last display of temper, and especially not given what he has with him. And Bear and Lena have some reinforcement — Nikolas didn't warn them, but he did warn someone else.:

By now some of the other Trainees were getting wind of the fact that *something* was up and had begun whispering to each other. A couple of the Herald Trainees must have caught the edges of leaking Mindspeech and were sitting up and staring toward the main gate. Finally the teacher stopped lecturing, looking straight at Mags.

"Trainee Mags. You're the most likely to know —"

"Healer Trainee Bear's Pa is comin' up th' hill, an' I hear he ain't alone, sir," Mags said instantly. "There's reckoning to be trouble." After all, this was a teacher demanding information.

The teacher looked over the class. "I know you have a vested interest in this, Mags, since Bear and Lena are your very good friends. How many of the rest of you do?"

About half the class shot up their hands. The teacher sighed. "There's no point in even continuing then. Fine, I want a three-page paper from each of you on some aspect of the King's reign by tomorrow. I want you to confer with each other *and me* so there are *no* duplicates. Remember, those of you who confer with me first will obviously be able to pick out the easiest and most obvious subjects for your papers. Class dismissed."

The ones who had indicated they didn't really care what happened began a huddled conference. The rest got up and headed for the main gate. Mags was the only one who ran.

Bear and Lena were waiting just outside the gate, and from behind, Mags couldn't read anything other than tension in their postures. He wondered what on earth Bear's father thought he could actually *do* about the marriage. He also wondered just who the man had brought with him . . .

Surely not Bear's ma . . . So far as he was aware, Healer Tyrall did not regard his wife as much of anything other than the vehicle by which he produced Healer-Gifted off-spring. An odd attitude for a Healer, but, then, the marriage had been an arranged one, and according to the little Bear had said, he was never actually unkind to her, merely indifferent. Since she was not Gifted at all . . . and also according to Bear, sweet natured but not very bright . . .

Hmm. Healer married to a gal with nothin' . . . maybe. . . . Thinking about it, he could almost, for just a moment, feel a trickle of sympathy for Healer Tyrall. *Could feel like a racehorse harnessed to a plow horse.* And maybe that was why he had so little sympathy for Bear. After all, *he* had done his duty to his family by marrying the bride they had chosen for him and producing the next generation of Gifted Healers, and by his own stern code, Bear should be doing the same.

Dammit, I hate *being able to see the other side of things!* For, of course, his imagination was already painting the rest of that picture. It wasn't — it couldn't be — all of the story, that Healer Tyrall was overly proud of his rank and position and was a tyrant over his family. He wouldn't be a

183

good Healer if that were all he was — and he wouldn't be holding that position if he weren't a good Healer. Healers, as much as Heralds, were not their own masters. Healers served a greater good. Healers put their own interests second and the needs of those who needed them first. Well, they were supposed to, anyway . . . and he imagined that Healer Tyrall was telling himself that this was exactly what he was doing. And if you came of stock that bred Gifted Healers consistently, well, it was your duty to go and make more little Healers with whatever wife you were given. By that estimation, Bear was betraying his very calling as a Healer.

Well, he was if you took a very, very narrow view of what his duty to his calling and his family was, anyway. It wasn't too hard for Mags to imagine what Bear's father was *thinking,* as opposed to what things looked like from outside his personal point of view.

Even as Mags thought that, the sound of laboring horses grew nearer, and up over the crest of the hill came Healer Tyrall.

And the mercenary company he had hired, about a dozen men, all armed.

Hoo boy.

:I am finding it hard to believe my own eyes. I have never before seen someone as sup-

posedly intelligent as Bear's father so thoroughly deposit a pile of excrement in his own bed, then proceed to trample it thoroughly into all the bedclothes . . . : Dallen was clearly in awe at the epic stupidity he was witnessing. Mags tried to talk to Nikolas, but all he got was a sensation of choking. Whether it was Nikolas who was choking with disbelief, or he wanted to choke the Healer, Mags couldn't quite tell.

The Guard alerted at the sight of armed men, and in no uncertain terms. Before Mags could even blink, they had sounded the alarm, shoved Lena and Bear behind the gate, and dropped the iron portcullis.

Well. So much for doin' things peaceful-like. Fine way to make yer point, Healer, declare war on the King!

Things got a bit chaotic there for a bit. A fully armed Guard company came racing in formation to the gate. Healer Tyrall reined in his horse, which was all too happy to stop, and stared, dumbfounded, at the unfriendly reception.

What? Did he actually not *think about what was gonna happen if he did this?* Mags was thunderstruck. How could the man be so unbelievably *stupid*?

Or maybe he was just so used to being the one in charge that it never occurred to him that he might have had a bad idea here.

Or maybe the heat baked his head so much it drove him crazy, or he's got no brain left. That would be the most charitable guess, though of all of them, it was the least likely.

"In the name of the King, throw your weapons to the ground!" the officer in charge barked, as the Guard trained bows on them all. The mercenaries, being considerably less stupid than the man who had hired them, immediately complied. They were helmed, so you couldn't see their expressions, but Mags wondered what *they* were thinking. He supposed that when Tyrall told them they were to go racing up to the Collegium fully armed, they thought it was perfectly all right. It was possible they had believed him. After all, several of the highborn were permitted to have their own armed escorts at the Palace — though in practice, most didn't bother. Well, if they hadn't known better before, they certainly did now.

From behind the downed portcullis, the officer continued. "What in the name of all the gods is the meaning of this?" he demanded. "How *dare* you bring armed men to the King's gate? I should arrest you for treason and insurrection on the spot!"

Healer Tyrall blinked at the officer for a

moment, as if he didn't understand what had been said to him. Then, as if it had never even occurred to him that the Palace stood here, he shot a dumbfounded glance at it, and for a moment, blanched.

:By the gods . . . I think he completely forgot that the King lives here!: Dallen exclaimed. :All he ever thought was that this is where the Collegia are!:

Mags could scarcely believe it . . . and yet, the man had proven himself completely blind to reality in the past.

:He was so focused on taking Bear away that he completely forgot where the Collegia are . . . : Dallen sounded stunned. :And he thought, if he just rode up with a double handful of armed men, he could snatch Bear up and take him away and no one would stop him.:

But if he had made so monumental a mistake, he was not about to admit it now. He pointed at Bear. "I have come to bring home what is mine," he thundered. "The boy is clearly demented. That scheming little daughter of a traitor probably used her Gift on him to seduce him, just as her father used his to seduce and whore his way into a high position and honors that were not his—"

"Enough!" barked the officer, as Bear went

rigid with rage and Lena did, too.

"No," Bear said, putting one hand on the officer's shoulder, and sounding *far* steadier and more adult than his own father. "Let him speak. Let him vent all the poison he has in him. I want to hear all of it, and I want you all as witnesses."

And speak Healer Tyrall did. He quickly devolved into spittle-spraying, livid rage, and Mags instinctively shielded the people nearest him from any empathic surges that might come from the man. He went on at great length about Lena, and by the time he ran out of words, if anyone had actually believed him, they would have thought her to be a very demoness in disguise, whose only goal was to turn Bear into her sexual slave. Then he went on about Bear, and no one who knew the Trainee would have ever recognized the doltish lout who was supposedly drooling at Lena's feet. But according to Tyrall, he was something less than a halfwit who happened to have a halfwit's savant talent with herbs, and it was his father's duty to rescue him and save his would-be patients *from* him before he killed one of them. From the amount of froth-spewing about Bear's "reckless experimentation" an uninformed listener would have been excused for thinking that Bear was a mass poisoner by this time, inclined to doctor the drinks of the unsuspecting just to see what was going to happen.

As it happened, no one standing here was that uninformed, not even — or especially — the members of the Guard. They knew about Tyrall, and his toady Cuburn, who had actually been sent to the Guard in order to spy on (and potentially disgrace) Bear — and who had been the informant to the foreign assassins who had ultimately kidnapped Amily and put her in deadly danger. They also had been some of the first to adopt Bear's herbal kits, because the Guard was often in dangerous situations without a Healer.

But it was when Tyrall started in on the "licentious fraud of a priest" who apparently had been paid vast sums of money to wed the two, that Bear and Lena's unexpected ally burst out of the portcullis-tower door, roaring with rage.

Before anyone could move, Father Poul had used the shepherd's crook of his order to drag Healer Tyrall out of the saddle. No sooner was the man on the ground, than Father Poul was on him, beating him mercilessly.

"*Venal* am I?" he howled. "*Licentious,* am I? I'll show you venal, you vile disgrace to the Green you wear! The gods know you've got a trouncing coming, the gods know it is overdue, and thanks be to the gods that it's I that's got the glory of delivering it to you!"

It was then that Mags remembered that, besides serving the poor . . . Father Poul's Temple was of a very martial order indeed. In fact, the priests and acolytes were instructed in the offensive use of their crooks twice a day, right after prayers.

He also recalled that nowhere in any of the material that Mags had ever heard, on his visits to the Temple, was there a mention that they should be meek. Or peaceful. Or suffer insults at all.

The mercenaries remained right where they were. It was very clear they did not see themselves as being obligated to save their erstwhile master from the fate he had brought upon himself.

Eventually — but not before Father Poul had reduced the Healer to huddling on the ground and trying to protect his head and neck with his arms — the officer came out the same door and got between them. There was some muttering that Mags couldn't make out, and Father Poul snorted, then turned on his heel and stalked down the Hill. Presumably he was heading back to his Temple. Mags hoped that if he had not worked out all of his rage on Tyrall's body, the walk back down the Hill in the heat would leach the rest of it out of him.

Then the officer grabbed Tyrall by the shoulder and hauled him to his feet. "Healer Tyrall," he proclaimed loudly. "I'm putting you under arrest." He looked at the mercenaries. "You lot are dismissed. You'll be leaving your weapons. Let that be a lesson to you not to listen to an idiot who bids you come riding up to the Palace, fully armed. And you can thank the gods you worship that we are certain your master told you he had permission to bring you up here in an armed state — and that you didn't know any better."

There were some stiff nods and no relaxation of their tense poses. Without a word, they turned and rode away, leaving Tyrall to deal with the situation alone.

Mags wondered if they had been paid in advance. He hoped so. He also hoped they would lodge complaints about Tyrall to the Mercenary Guild, which was responsible for the conduct of all mercenaries and their companies within the Kingdom of Valdemar. The Guild had the authority to go to the King over this — and likely would. Not only had this not ended yet, for Tyrall the punishment had barely begun.

The officer let go of the Healer, who was now ashen-faced where he wasn't black and blue. "As it happens, we had warning that you were going to pull this hare-brained nonsense, and the King already passed down his ruling on what we were to do if you were stupid enough to carry it out. Intentions count for a great deal in this Kingdom and we know you didn't intend treason."

Tyrall's shoulders sagged with relief.

"However, you *did* intend forcible kidnapping. So, the King has directed that your victim be the one to pass judgment on your intentions toward him." The portcullis rose, and Bear stepped out to the other side.

Mags held his breath. He still couldn't see Bear's face from here, and he wondered what Bear was going to say.

Finally, Bear spoke, and his voice was cold. "I don't know this man," he said. "It is true that we share a name, but there are many Tyralls in this Kingdom, and no one I would call Father would ever act in this foolish and treasonable manner. I declare he is of no relation to me. It's of no consequence what he says about me, and as for his insults to my wife, well —"

Bear looked at Lena, who raised her chin. "The Companion isn't concerned with what a donkey says about her. Nor is the eagle in the least bothered about the insults of the foolish cricket. If you listen to dogs barking, and believe what they say, then you have only yourself to blame for getting upset."

Bear nodded. "So, there you have it. I don't care about insults, my wife doesn't care about insults, his actions only bring disgrace on the Healers of his House, and I am not one of them. Let the Healers' Circle decide what to do with him."

And with that, he took Lena's hand, turned on his heel, and the two of them walked stiffly away, leaving Healer Tyrall looking stunned — and as if he had aged a hundred years in that moment.

5

Mags eyed the customer across the counter and behind the barred window with a suspicious expression on his face. Rightly, of course. The man was new to the persona Mags was currently wearing but long familiar to the Weasel and his deaf-mute nephew. He knew better than to present the Weasel with ersatz goods, but Mags was just about certain he was sly enough to try selling imitations to the new man behind the counter.

The customer eyed him back, blandly; he was a cool one, Mags would have to give him that much. But Mags just did not like the color of the item sitting on the counter between them.

"We'll jest be testin' that, then," he said, reaching for the allegedly "gold" button.

"That won't be needful!" the customer bleated. He snatched the button up and fled out the door, exactly as Mags figured he would. The button had been heavy enough for gold, but Mags suspected a lead core. He also suspected the coating was nothing like gold . . . or, at least, had very little gold content. Clearly, the fellow hadn't thought that the Weasel's latest hireling had the intelligence to scrape something across a touchstone and add a little acid.

Well, good. Now he knew not to come to the shop at all unless he had something worthwhile to sell.

Mags was actually in disguise, and he was enjoying himself to the hilt. When Nikolas decided that Mags should be able to man the shop alone, they had discussed having the "nephew" be responsible and had discarded the idea pretty quickly, for all the obvious reasons.

So they had invented a new persona; there was no way that Mags could present himself as old enough to be the Weasel's friend, so it had to be another relative. The obvious choice was the older brother of the deaf-mute — that would account for "family resemblance."

After a few lessons in establishing his new appearance and demeanor from Nikolas' actor friends, he had established a personality and a basic background. People would expect surly — but the Weasel was already surly. So, instead, Mags went for something as close to his own personality as possible. All he had to do was work out "if I wasn't a Trainee, how would I react to all this?"

He imagined himself plucked from the mine, given a couple of baths and semi-decent clothing and regular feeding, then trained up to the duties of the store and aged about six years. So . . . he was as good-natured as the surroundings and circumstances would allow, figuring that whoever the Weasel plucked out of poverty would be so grateful to actually have a job that let him eat regularly, he'd never complain about anything. But he was also tough, young, hot-blooded, and not going to take anything off anyone except for his uncle, and he looked as if he were willing to be absolutely vicious to anyone who even *thought* about cheating the Weasel. As for stealing, well —

His first day, he'd caught someone trying to filch one of the small items from the stuff on the other side of the counter wall. Evidently, the thief either thought he couldn't see him or that it would take him too long to get through the door.

Except he didn't go through the door. He kept a pile of round pebbles at the side of the counter, and he flung one through the bars with enough force to stun the would-be thief. The fellow stumbled and fell to his knees; he wasn't up again before Mags was kneeling on his back, twisting both of his arms into a painful hold.

"Justice" in this part of Haven didn't involve calling the Constables at this time of night, not for people like the Weasel. When you caught a thief, you did what you figured was necessary. And Mags suppressed his own distaste and delivered a vicious beating.

It wasn't nearly as bad as it could have been. Mags made sure to do as little damage as possible, for maximum effect. Anyone else around here who had caught the thief would have half-crippled him.

But the beating sent a clear message: Don't mess with the new man at the counter. And no one did.

This incident would send another clear message: The new man isn't a fool.

People down here didn't need to be taught a lesson twice, and they quickly learned from other peoples' mistakes.

So far, it looked as if Mags' disguise was holding. It didn't take much; as the deaf-mute, he hunched his shoulders and kept his face down, so most of the customers never got a good look at him anyway. As

"Harkon," he stood tall, squared his shoulders, walked with a bit of a swagger, and often glared at other men right in the face as if he suspected every one of them was going to challenge him. A bit of makeup gave him a hint of beard growing in, and some human hair from a wigmaker cleverly pinned with tiny, tiny combs into his own gave him streaks of a much lighter color than his real hair. The streaks were a new trick, one he liked. He often thought it was a pity he wasn't a blond, or at least lighter-haired, like Nikolas. Nikolas could easily change the apparent color of his hair just by combing dirt and grease through it. With hair as dark as Mags had, that wasn't an option.

The actors had tentatively suggested a wig. Wigs . . . were not going to happen. It was far, far too easy for a wig to be pulled off, and they never looked quite right. And they were hot. In weather like this summer, he could not even imagine what it would be like to wear a wig. His poor brain would bake.

But these little bits of hair that were easily pinned in and easily taken out. They worked just fine. His hair was thick, and the pins stayed in well, and when he tied it all back in a tail, there was very little chance they were going to work loose.

He'd even tested the disguise by walking past a couple of his friends in one of the marketplaces during the day, and no one had recognized the young tough with the streaked hair who walked with a bantam-cock's swagger.

So he presided behind the counter of the shop with the authority to buy, and he reveled in the responsibility. It wasn't as if he were *alone,* since he had Dallen in the back of his head the entire time. And it wasn't as if anyone could get at him, not after Nikolas had bolstered the impression that he'd come into more money by reinforcing the wall and door between the "box" (as they called the main room that held all the valuables, the cash, and them) and the rest of the shop. By the time anyone managed to break in, Mags would be long gone, either down the hatch in the floor that led to the basement or up the stair to the attic that led to the roof.

Amily was not entirely happy about this, since once again, he was spending a great deal of his "free" time down here and not up at the Collegium with her, but he was actually spending less time down here now than he had been before. The Weasel was generally only buying in person one night out of every four, instead of every night, so between the deaf-mute and Harkon, Mags was only here half as much as he had been in the past.

It was dangerous to run a pawn shop at night in this area, yes. But he was giving the impression that he was sleeping here, which probably made it a bit less dangerous, since no one was going to lie in wait to ambush him. The shop was stoutly built and had weathered many attempted break-ins. He was in the protected part, which now took up about three quarters of the shop area, where things of real value were kept, and the money was out of reach of anyone but him. There was a stout brick wall with a heavy, barred door in it between him and danger, and his only contact with people came through the window over the counter, which had very formidable bars.

At night when he was ready to close, he made sure that there was no one anywhere around with a simple mental scan of the area. Then, and only then, did he leave the box. He'd pop outside, blow out the outside lamp as fast as he could, and pop back inside again. Then he would lock and bar the door, blow out the inside lamp, and hurry back into the box. Once there, he locked and barred *that* door, and after moving around in a way that would throw a few suggestive shadows, he would blow out *that* lamp.

At that point, no one would be able to figure out what he was doing. People would assume (correctly) that there was a basement, that there was a bed down there, and that was where he slept. And, in fact, he or Nikolas or both had slept down there, now and again. But when he blew out that lamp, he went up, not down. Up into the bit of an attic, and up to the roof. Then it was over the roofs until he came to the bit of hidden stable where Dallen was and the room where he and Nikolas kept their disguises. A thorough wash followed, and he took the streaks out of his hair and changed his clothing. Then Trainee Mags and his Companion would emerge from the inn where they had spent part of the evening with Nikolas' actor friends.

So far no one had ever asked him about why he was allowed to spend one night in four consorting with actors. He'd thought of a few ideas, but he was just as glad that everyone assumed it was something Nikolas wanted him to do.

One thing he had considered was speech lessons. Although he had lost most of the slur and mumble of a thoroughly intimidated slave and had refined his accent, sounding like someone like — oh, Pip, say, or Gennie — took a lot of concentration. It would be perfectly natural to take speech lessons from someone like an actor.

And aside from that, at the moment, he reckoned that his next best answer would be to say that he was getting lessons from them in how to make a girl feel special, and blush.

The blushing part wouldn't be hard. Well, it wouldn't be blushing so much as getting red with embarrassment. He knew that he was backward compared to just about everybody his age when it came to all that stuff. Well, look at Bear! But it seemed harder than any lessons he'd ever had to study for. He just couldn't get his head wrapped around how easy it seemed for other young men to just . . . get romantical with a lady. Asking any of the other fellows for help . . . well, that was out of the question. He was supposed to be the Kirball hero, after all, and either they would think he was making fun of them, or they'd fall about laughing. He certainly couldn't ask *Nikolas,* when the girl in question was his own daughter! Dean Caelen . . . never got his nose out of a book. The Herald that had first rescued him, Jakyr? Oh no. Jakyr had managed to totally mess up his own love life so thoroughly that he scrambled desperately into and out of Haven as fast as he could. He barely stayed long enough to resupply himself and get new uniforms before he was back in the Field, and all in an attempt to avoid the Dean of Bardic, who had once been his lover . . .

No . . . Jakyr was probably the very last person in the whole wide world he would go to for any advice. Assuming he could actually catch Jakyr in Haven long enough to ask for it.

He didn't know any of the Healers well enough to ask them except Bear, and in no way was he going to ask Bear when he himself was still not convinced the whole marriage thing had been a good idea.

And Dallen was no help at all, which scarcely seemed fair when you thought about how he had put Mags inside his own memories so many times in order to teach him how to be a human being and not a feral half-beast. But when he asked Dallen to help him out with Amily, Dallen would only chuckle and say, :That sort of thing is best left for you to discover for yourself.:

Definitely nothing like fair. *I don't* want *to work it out fer myself,* he thought with irritation. *I want instructions, like! I want . . . maps!*

Guidebooks! All this discoverin' for yourself stuff is overrated!

He leaned over the counter with his chin in his hands, pondering the difficulty of feelings. "Feelings" were not something you had a lot of time for back in the mine, and you certainly didn't have any energy to waste on them. The only "feelings" Cole Pieter and his offspring seemed to have for one another was contempt bordering on hatred, which was scarcely a good example to follow.

If he was just going on what was going on inside him, well, it *felt* as though he and Amily belonged together. But how was he to trust that? He could be wrong, and then he'd mess things up just as badly as Jakyr had. If he went by the only stuff he could find in books and the like, there wasn't any of that wild breathless stuff between them that there seemed to be in songs. He just felt good around her, peaceful. He wasn't over the moon or in a daze. Kissing was nice, real nice, and there were certainly a lot of tingly-good-exciting physical things going on when they kissed, but it wasn't as if they both dove into each other the way he'd lost himself in Dallen's eyes when they bonded. And what about that? Was that a problem with him? Was he supposed to feel about her the way he felt about Dallen?

Or was it just a problem with Heralds, that there wasn't, couldn't be, room for anyone in your life other than your Companion? If that was the case, the last thing he wanted to do was lead Amily on!

There wasn't any of the painful stuff of songs and poems and legends, either. He didn't ache inside when he was away from her, he just looked forward to when they'd get together again. He wasn't torn up with jealousy when she talked to other fellows. He didn't worry about her falling for someone else all the time.

And he, at least, didn't seem to feel that *certainty* that Bear and Lena seemed to feel — Bear had said he couldn't imagine being with anyone but Lena, and when he said that, Mags had seen he absolutely meant it. But as for Mags, when he thought about himself and Amily *really* being together, as in, responsible for themselves and all the decisions they would have to make, all kinds of doubts sprang up. Were they old enough? Truly? What if after a while they realized they were only doing this because it seemed to be expected of them? What if either of them *did* meet someone that gave them all those wild and breathless feelings? They didn't always agree on everything now, and he worried that would make trouble later. He had to keep secrets from her now, sometimes, and he *knew* that could make trouble later. She disliked it when her father kept secrets, and he was afraid that somewhere in the back of her mind, she had the idea that her husband wouldn't.

And when you got married or you started sleeping together, weren't there always babies?

That part made him absolutely panic. He didn't know anything about babies. The mine-kiddies always turned up able to take care of themselves — as far as he knew, he was the only one that had ever arrived not able to do that. He couldn't even *imagine* the responsibility of having a baby! He sometimes felt as if he was hardly more than a kiddie himself now, how could he *ever* expect to guide and take care of a baby?

And what was Amily expecting out of him, anyway? What did she have in mind when she thought about being married to someone? What sorts of responsibilities did she expect him to take on? What sorts of things did she expect him to do for her? And what was she looking for? Did she want those breathless, crazy, excited feelings? Was she getting them now? Was she figuring he could somehow conjure them up? Oh, he could probably read her mind and find out . . . which would be wrong, so wrong it wasn't even a temptation, much. But without reading her mind, he was left pretty much in the dark.

Really, truly, seriously unfair of Dallen to leave him floundering like this . . .

Maybe I actually should talk to them actors and get some lessoning in what ladies like. The actors, even the old ones, all gray-haired and going a little soft, still got plenty of ladies. They weren't the ones doing the courting, either. Whatever it was that they knew, Mags dearly wished he had some books about it.

Poetry was no help at all, really, except to make him more certain that he was doing something wrong. The stuff in the poetry just made him feel so awkward he started to stammer. The Herald who taught poetry seemed to think it was all something he called "metaphor" and that all the feelings stuff was just meant to represent something else, which really just did not sound right.

And the one time he'd brought it up to a Healer he didn't know, thinking that with a stranger he'd get something good and honest, he got a lecture on husbandry he could have just as well given back, seeing as he'd practically grown up in a barnyard and shared his "bed" with a lot of kiddies and a few people who weren't kiddies and had no sense that they required privacy for the urges of their bodies. He *knew* all about that part, who was to put what where, and what it all sounded and looked like. And even though at the time it had seemed like a waste of energy to him, now that he thought back on it, well, it did make him want to put *that* part of himself . . .

Well, that wasn't the sort of feelings that the poetry talked about. It was more like Dallen when he was competing with Rolan for a mare.

Which wasn't bad, but . . . that wasn't what you were supposed to have a marriage over. And he did at least know one thing: That was lust, not love. Not that lust was bad, but . . .

Why does this stuff have to be so complicated?

The bell over the door jangled, and one of the regular customers came in — not one of the thieves, but someone who used the shop as a pawnbroker. A carpenter who had been out of work for a while, his tools were the only thing that stood between him and having his family starve. When he couldn't get work, he pawned them and took whatever odd jobs he could get until more work came up. That was how close people around here were to disaster — having to put up the things that gave them a livelihood just to keep food in their mouths.

He came to put down another little payment that would keep his tools from being sold until he could redeem them. Mags nodded at him and opened the drawer that held the individual account books and found the right one. When he opened it, he found a note in it from Nikolas.

Give him his tools. Tell him there was a mistake, and he's redeemed them as of today. Then tell him to check with Father Poul — the Guard was so tickled with the way he beat Bear's father that they raised enough money for an extension to the Temple. There will be work there for him. And I have had a word with Father Poul; if he does good honest work, he'll be kept on to learn from their Master woodworker. The old man's hands aren't up to the job anymore.

Well, that was just like Nikolas; any chance he had to make an honest man's life a little better, he went out of his way to arrange.

"Huh," Mags said, and shrugged. "Note here from the boss, says you're redeemin' yer tools t'day. Some kinda mistake, guess he was overchargin' ye or summat, so ye don' owe past this last payment."

He pulled the couple of copper coins over into the cash drawer, then went to get the carpenter's chest of tools. It was a nice one, but it should be, since such a chest provided a display of the carpenter's skill. Nothing fancy though, no inlay work or carvings.

Well, that was going to change, if he was up to it. A Master woodworker had all sorts of skills, and more skill meant more and better jobs. There must not have been anyone at the Temple with the inclination or ability for the old man to pass on his heritage, for him to be willing to teach someone outside the brotherhood.

Mags unlocked and unbarred the door and handed over the chest. The carpenter took it with a face full of happiness, his hands almost caressing the wood. "Didja hear 'bout that buildin' that's goin' on over at Temple of Rusal?" Mags asked casually. "Puttin' in either a new wing or a second floor, I ferget which, an' they're gonna hire outside th' Temple."

The carpenter paused. "No?" he said a little doubtfully. "You certain 'bout that? I'd'a thought I'd'a heard 'bout it afore this . . ."

"Eh, I wouldn't've heard it if it ain't fer the story that come with it!" With great relish Mags related the tale of the trouncing of

Healer Tyrall, as he himself had heard it from one of the Constables. The tale had grown in the telling.

In fact, the tale had grown to a domestic epic.

Take Bear's father — Healer Tyrall had been painted in the broad strokes of a real villain, something of a monster, really. According to the story, it wasn't that Tyrall wanted Bear home breeding little Healers, it was —

Well, the story went that Bear was some sort of miracle worker with herbs. This, of course, was a very valuable skill so far as ordinary folk were concerned, because you couldn't always get a Healer, but you *could* get hold of a 'pothecary, or, here in Haven, you could go begging up at the Collegium and get herbal physick for nothing. Quite a number of people down here in Haven actually knew Bear because of that. Either they'd gotten medicine directly from him, or they'd benefited from the newly acquired skills of someone he had taught. So people were inclined to believe what Bear's own father did not — that his ability with herbs was a sort of Gift.

Now, according to the story the Constable had told, Healer Tyrall was a venial and greedy man. This was believable indeed, since even down here, people knew about the abduction, how Healer Cuburn had venially and greedily sold information to the assassins about the comings and goings on the Hill, and people knew Cuburn had been Tyrall's man.

So it made sense to them that Tyrall was incensed that Bear was tending to the poor rather than making *him* wealthy by using his skills on the rich.

So they believed the embroidered version, that Tyrall was not only going to break up the lovers, he was going to drag Bear back to a drafty old tower, lock him in, and put him to a sort of slave labor making potions for the highborn to keep them young.

The carpenter listened, rapt. All this was news to him. But he nodded at all the right places and looked angry at all the right places, which encouraged Mags to believe that just about everyone that wasn't actually up on the Hill was going to take this version at face value.

Tyrall certainly had not done himself any favors by thundering through Haven on horseback with a troupe of mercenaries in tow. There were lots of witnesses to that . . . and probably no few people who hadn't been anywhere near but would swear they had seen it and, moreover, had seen Tyrall and his flunkies trample children, kittens, and puppies in his mad race up to the Palace.

At this point, it was Father Poul who became the hero of the story.

According to the story, it was Father Poul who had urged the pair to wed in order to keep Tyrall from exerting paternal force over his son. It was Father Poul who had stood at the gate, crook in hand, and took on not only Tyrall but half of his mercenaries, beating them into submission with nothing more than his crook; and it was Father Poul who had stoutly defended Bear and Lena to the Collegia, speaking on their behalf for candlemarks until his voice was scarcely more than a croak.

Father Poul would likely never recognize himself.

"Anyroad, Guard figgered any'un thet would do all thet must've got god-touched or somethin', plus the Healer-boy helped them out a powerful lot over the past couple years, so they raised the pelf fer some more work on th' Temple," Mags concluded. This last was the only unvarnished truth. The Guard had so much admiration for the crusty old priest that they decided he needed to be rewarded, and since he wouldn't accept a reward for himself, they donated it to an expansion of the Temple of Rusal. Father Poul could scarcely turn *that* down, after all. "Reckon there's gonna be work there."

"I reckon there is, since I ain't heard about it yet, an' that means prolly no one else'll get there afore me," the carpenter said with glee. "Thenkee, Harkon!"

Mags closed and locked the door, dropped the bar across it, went to the window, and made a disparaging noise. "Eh, don't thank me, make some money an' come back 'ere and pick up that set'a wood chisels ol' man Greyer went an' left 'ere when 'e died wi'out payin' it out!" He spat. "I ain't gonna hear the last of that outa the boss until summun buys th' damned things, an' I'm likelier t'get King's Own comin' through that door than summun what does fancy carvin'."

The carpenter laughed. "I might just do thet," he agreed, and he hurried out the door. It was early enough in the evening that the Temple would still be a hive of activity, and unless Mags was very much mistaken, the man was going to present himself and his chest of tools as someone in need of work before the night got much older.

Mags went back to musing. The bell jangled again, but this time it was neither a thief nor a regular customer. Instead, it was a fellow who nodded at Mags, passed by the used clothing and old linens, the heavy items that would take a very determined man indeed to steal, and went browsing among the trinkets and small items meant for ladies. Or at least, what passed for ladies in this part of town. When the choice was go hungry or without a bed or to look for someone willing to buy a few moments of sex, well . . . you survived how you could, around here. And that didn't mean that someone, somewhere, wouldn't want to give you a present, no matter who your legs had been wrapped around last week.

In the mathematics of survival, if there was someone willing to pay for something you had, you sold it, and there was no shame on either side.

Some of the trinkets were, quite frankly, stolen — usually the kerchiefs and scarves of finer quality fabric than was affordable by the folk of these streets and the metal jewelry with paste jewels. Some was not. There were bits of jewelry carved of wood, river shell, bone or common stone that was honest work. Among the ornaments were necklaces he was actually a little proud of that he himself had made, round horsehair braids with a single pretty bead strung on them. He picked out the beads from the broken stuff the Weasel had taken in, things that didn't have a full set to remake into a necklace. These pieces, like the others, were not valuable enough to lock up, but they were good enough to make a girl feel special — and well made enough to make her feel special for a good long time. And just as important, they were new. People down here didn't see much that was new, they couldn't afford it. Give a girl from here a brand new necklace, and she'd feel like Princess Lydia.

Mags was the one who braided those necklaces, a skill he had learned thanks to Dallen. Companion-hair braids were sought-after tokens among the friends of Heralds and Trainees. The first Midwinter he'd been here at the Collegium, he'd despaired of coming up with presents for his friends, and Dallen had gone into his head and patiently taught him how to make the tight, intricate braids to fashion into necklets, bracelets, bookmarks, and even a set of falcon jesses. The same skill worked equally well on horsehair, and since reading while he was in the shop was out of the question, making the necklaces kept him from being bored to death. With a pretty bead strung on them, they looked very nice indeed.

What would make Amily feel special? If there was anyone who had no need of any more Companion-hair anything, it was Amily.

When it came right down to it, there wasn't much he *could* give Amily. She had virtually everything she needed. If she *wanted* anything, she never showed it and had never actually told him.

"Why do they have t'be so complicated?" he sighed, staring at the necklaces, and he didn't realize he had spoken aloud until the potential customer looked up, startled.

"What?" the man said.

Mags sighed again. *"Wimmen,"* he replied.

"You said it, brother," the customer agreed fervently, and they shared a look of complete understanding and universal brotherhood that, in that moment, crossed the barriers of merchant and customer, Trainee and citizen, privileged and poor, boy and man.

They both enjoyed it for a good long moment, and finally Mags was the one who broke the spell.

"Well," he said. "Whasser hair an' eyes?"

"Brown," the customer said. "Why?"

"Carved wood bead, brown cord, like that there carved wood rose. Or mebbe amber. Think I got a amber up there too. Them as gots brown hair allus likes somethin' what goes with their eyes. Blondes, they like somethin' thet stands out, so anythin' on black horsehair. An if'n ye got a redhead, she wants somethin' thet makes 'er 'air look good, so red, like thet there red glass bit." He sighed. "Wisht th' rest uv what they likes was easier to reckon out."

"You an' me both," said the man, as he separated out the amber and brown horsehair necklace, and a red beaded one for good measure, and paid for both. "You an' me both."

Mags set off over the rooftops, but he had a distinctly uneasy feeling as he did so. He couldn't get over the feeling that someone was watching him. More than once he stopped, cautiously dropped his shields, and "looked" for anyone who might be up here — because it *was* possible that a real thief was up here too, had seen a fellow roofrunner, and wanted to be sure he wouldn't be interfered with in his chosen target. But every time he stopped and closed his eyes and searched through all the nearby thoughts for someone whose mind was full of the night, the rooftops, and possibly himself, he found nothing. Nothing but those who were dreaming and those few who were still awake and working. He got flashes of someone laboring over sewing, a potter tending a kiln by night, some people making buttons of wood and river shell, some children carving spoons, someone knitting, spinning, weaving . . . the sensation of working until the worker simply couldn't keep his or her eyes open anymore. Mags knew that feeling, and, oh, how he sympathized. All of these except the potter were indoors, in attic and garret rooms. No one was so much as glancing out an open window

He didn't dare let that feeling of being watched distract him up here. One slip, and he could very well end up in a bad situation. He concentrated on the placement of his hands and feet, on his knowledge of his roof-road, and on where he was going to land next.

It wasn't until he neared the inn where Dallen's stable and the disguise room were that he felt that sensation drop away. He wasn't relieved. He hadn't liked that feeling at all, and he liked still less the idea that his own mind was playing tricks on him.

:You didn' pick up anything, did you?: he asked Dallen, as he slipped down the inn roof and dropped directly down into the courtyard instead of coming in from the alley as he and Nikolas usually did when they

were together.

:Not a thing. You know, it could have been an animal.:

Mags snorted as he unlocked the disguise room. *:An animal? No critter's ever made the hair on the back of m'neck stand up like that afore.:*

But Dallen was quite serious. *:You've never seen some of the things that come out of the Pelagirs. And the closer to human intelligence an animal is, the more likely it is that it would be able to get this far into Valdemar without detection.:*

Well . . . he *had* heard all those stories about the Hawkbrothers. It hadn't been that long ago that there had been a Hawkbrother ambassador or two, making a brief visit under the auspices of Herald Vanyel . . . Was there a chance that one could have slipped across the Border in disguise?

:That's exactly what I mean. We just had a very major event here, the wedding of the Heir. That event might have brought a Hawkbrother here just to see how we've been faring. And some of the Hawkbrothers fly owls. Or it is just possible that one of the Hawkbrother Bondbirds was somehow blown here by a storm, or unusual weather. If they aren't bonded to a particular person, there's no accounting for what one might do.:

Mags carefully removed the streaks in his hair and coiled them into their container. *:Seems pretty unlikely to me. We ain't heard nothin' from them Hawkbrothers for years, so why would they care now? It ain't as if they're blood relatives or nothin'. They got their lands, we got ours, peace between us, so that's all there is. An' I'd think a big old hawk or owl'd find the pickings pretty slim in a town. Crow mebbe, or raven, but they don't fly at night . . .:*

Dallen clearly was not convinced, but he also seemed disinclined to argue the point. *:I'm just saying that it could have been a preternaturally intelligent animal. Or, for all you know, a ghost.:*

The hair went up on the back of Mags' head again. Of all the things he did *not* want to hear about, ghosts were on top of the list. He hated ghost stories. He could never imagine why a ghost would linger, except to get revenge on the living. And how could you stop a ghost? They could walk through walls, they could slip up on you and you would never know it, they could steal your breath while you slept. *:Oh, no. Don't you go puttin' no haunt stories in my head! I wanta sleep t'night!:*

He hastily poured himself a basin full of water and began vigorously washing his face and head, trying to wash away the thought of ghosts. Why, oh, *why* had Dallen said that? He knew how Mags felt!

:Mags, you have to remember that if it is a ghost, it has no connection to you,: Dallen admonished. Dallen knew how he felt about ghosts. *:I have never heard of a ghost hurting anyone in Valdemar. I've never even heard of one that had a reason to hurt someone — revenge — being able to. All they ever seem to do is, well, haunt. I don't think they can hurt you — not like the Karsite demons can.:*

:Oh, thank you, *ye bloody sadist!:* he groaned. All right, there was something he was more afraid of than ghosts. Karsite demons. The first time he'd learned about them in history class, he had scarcely been able to close his eyes that night. *:Now ye got me thinkin' 'bout ghosts* and *demons! I ain't gonna be able t' sleep all night!:*

He pulled on his clothing in a bit of a temper. Dallen *knew* how he felt about these things! And Dallen should bloody well know that trying to reassure him about them was only going to make him think about them more! He stamped his boots into place on his feet with more energy than was strictly necessary and wrenched the door to Dallen's stall open, glaring at him. The Companion gazed back at him, and if

222

he could judge these things, Dallen was not in the least repentant.

"I should put a buckwheat groat under yer saddle," he said, crossly. "I really should. And ride ye all the way up the Hill with it there."

:Oh, come now,: Dallen replied, as he threw the Companion's tack onto him and cinched and buckled it down. *:I've done you a favor.:*

"A *favor*?" he exclaimed, as he mounted, and Dallen headed for the door into the stable. He ducked a little to pass under the top of the doorframe. "A favor? An' just *how* did ye do me a favor, exactly? By makin' sure I'll have nightmares for the next week?"

:First, you can't keep avoiding the subject of spirits and demons if you are going to go out in the field as a Herald, so you might as well get used to the fact that they exist. Second, I kept you from fretting yourself in circles over Amily for almost a quarter candlemark.:

"I'd ruther fret about Amily," he growled.

:Well, I suppose now you'll be fretting about both.: Dallen's logic was inescapable. *:Anyway, we know it's not a demon, and it probably isn't a ghost. So rest easy.:*

"Then I hope at least I don't have nightmares. Sadist."

6

The next three days, Mags was not on shop duty, which pleased him a very great deal. Nikolas didn't get in anything that "needed" the deaf-mute's skills with gemstones, so he didn't ask Mags to come down, and he and his two friends could easily handle the rest of the business that came in the door. Or at least, that was his story. Mags had a feeling that the King's Own had gotten an earful from his daughter about monopolizing what little free time he had. On the one hand, he appreciated it. He could never bring himself to ask Nikolas for any favors for himself, much less tell his mentor that he was feeling strained and stretched and would like him to ease off. But on the other hand, he felt distinctly uneasy about the idea of Amily going to her father with demands that he give Mags less work.

Not that this would have stopped Nikolas from demanding Mags' presence if he actually *had* needed him there. Mags' skill at identifying stones had enhanced the Weasel's reputation, and Nikolas was not about to sacrifice that. But the purpose of going to the shop with Nikolas had always been primarily so that Nikolas could tutor Mags in the art of holding to a persona and disguise, and the mere fact that he was now tending the shop on his own was proof that Nikolas thought he had managed that particular lesson well enough that he didn't need supervision anymore. Or, at least, he didn't need the supervision in the personas of the deaf-mute and the cocky little thug.

All things considered, Mags was just as glad to have his evenings taken only one night out of every four. The sultry heat had begun to ease a bit, so classes were going back to their usual pace, which meant his time was going to get taken up with studies.

Studies he could, and certainly *would,* do with Amily. A bit of combining business with pleasure there, since Amily was a thousand times the scholar that he was and always knew where to look things up. And there was a great advantage to using studying as a reason to spend time with her — he didn't need to think about what to talk about or what to do, when it was obvious that he needed help and she was conscientious enough to make sure he got it rather than trying to coax him into some other, albeit more pleasurable, occupation.

There were more demands on his time coming as well. A few more weeks, and Kirball practice would begin again; that was strenuous enough by anyone's standards, but this fall was going to make some big changes for the Red team and, more particularly, for him. The Guard was not keeping their young recruits here just because they played a good game of ball, and it was time for some of the younger fellows to set out before winter set in, especially if they were going to posts at the Border. They were going to lose all their Foot but Corwin, which was a real pity, and Lord Wess of their Horse. There'd be four new Foot to train up out of the backup players, and there really wasn't anyone outstanding to take the place of Lord Wess unless one of the spring recruits made some drastic improvements, or someone new turned up for the trials when they opened in the fall.

Nor were these the only changes they were facing. Next spring, Pip and Gennie would probably go into Whites and out on their first Circuit, which meant that everyone was looking to him to be team captain next year. And that, in turn, meant Gennie was drilling him in tactics and intended to load a lot more responsibility on him.

In fact, if Amily had intended to get some time with him to herself other than study time and *had* talked to Nikolas about making sure he wasn't down at the shop as much, her plan backfired.

Gennie had decided that she had first call on his time, and what Gennie wanted, Gennie generally got.

And the first chance Gennie got, she made her plans very clear indeed.

The next night after shop duty, while he and Amily had dinner with the usual group, Gennie leaned over the table in the middle of desert. "You and I need another training session," she said bluntly, without giving Amily any chance to object.

"Uh," he began.

"You might as well come on along, Amily," she just said, cheerfully. "Like it or not, Mags is Kirball and Kirball is Mags, and you got both when you decided to set your cap at him."

The others had chuckled, but nodded in a way that pretty much told Amily that this was the truth and there was no arguing around it.

So Amily gave in. With good grace, but it probably wasn't anything like the evening she had hoped for. Poor Amily had to come with them both to an empty classroom, and listen while Gennie and Mags went over things that were probably as boring to her as listening to Bear drone on about herbs was to *him*.

"So, say Corwin's out, 'cause he did something risky and hurt himself; that means you have Tanner, Chet, Potter, and Green as your Foot," Gennie posited. "So, what would *you* do? How would you tell them to run defense?"

Well, I'd been thinkin' *'bout askin' ye fer advice about Amily,* Mags sighed under heavy shield. *But I'm thinkin' now that if ye can't see past the game, an' if ye can't guess Amily might be put out at this, ye prolly ain't the right person t'ask.* Since Gennie was the only other girl he really knew besides Lydia, he really was out of luck on that score. . . .

Gennie finally let him go, and he did get a chance to walk with Amily a little and sit on the bridge and look at the stars. He didn't think she was annoyed at the way that Gennie had appropriated him and his time — or at least, was not *still* annoyed — but she hadn't said a word while he and Gennie nattered on, and she didn't say anything about it now, so . . . well, he just wasn't sure.

Everything was perfectly normal on his

next night at the shop. He had the usual sorts of customers. A few people actually bought things. One old fellow came and redeemed his good suit of clothing and bought a second out of the used clothing bin, which signaled a new level of prosperity for him, and Mags had given him a good price. Thieves brought in small items of the sort he was allowed to buy; some shirts, several fine handkerchiefs, two spoons, five knives, and a carved walking stick. People paid their pawn fees to keep their things from being sold. If anyone had anything interesting to sell in the way of information, *he* wouldn't hear about it — that sort of sale was reserved for Nikolas.

And when he went out on the roof to head for Dallen — he had that feeling of being watched again. This time it came down on him suddenly, rather than creeping up on him, as if whatever it was had been waiting for him.

:Dallen!: he yelped.

:I know, I know . . . I'm checking, and I can't find anyone.:

He did some evasive maneuvers — down a drainpipe, transfer to a second drainpipe, down onto a wall, up onto the roof of a shed, and from there to the side of a roof that wasn't visible from the shop roof —

then hid in the shadows of some chimneys. The feeling did not go away, but he couldn't see anything or anyone, nor could he detect any minds concentrating on him.

He decided to put as much distance between himself and whatever it was as he could. And he definitely did not want to lead it back to Dallen.

This time he deliberately went in the opposite direction to where Dallen was. And at about the same distance from the shop as last time . . . the sense of being watched faded, and he finally felt that he could stop and take a rest. He wasn't winded, but his heart was pounding, and his stomach felt knotted.

He didn't double back to return to his usual route. Instead, he circled around and came at the inn by another path entirely. The feeling did not come back, and he entered the stable feeling uneasy, unhappy, nerves all afire, and a little frustrated. He wondered if he should have searched the nearby roofs for — whatever it was. He still didn't think it was an animal or bird.

Dallen didn't tease him this time, either. :*I can't account for it,*: he said. :*There is nothing that I can use to identify it, whatever it is that is watching you. And all my teasing aside, now I really am wondering if it actually* is *something like a spirit, or a ghost.:*

The prickly sensation on the back of his neck started again, and Mags shivered. *:Why would ye say that?:*

:Because neither you nor I can pinpoint this thing, we can't pick up any actual thoughts, and you are living in a part of town where there is a lot of death. If it is a ghost, I am not sure what to do about it. There's a Gift for speaking with spirits, but none of the other Companions or Heralds at the moment have it.:

Well, that was certainly anything but helpful, or comforting.

However, it finally gave him a direction. He couldn't go report "I had the feeling of being watched" without more than that to offer. But this, at least, was something he *could* go to someone about, and he did. He'd had it happen twice, and he had Dallen's speculation. It wasn't something to concern Nikolas with, at least not yet, but he certainly could ask someone else's advice.

Herald Caelen, the Dean of the Collegium, was always in his office early, and Mags was waiting for him when he arrived, bearing a plate with hot bread, butter, and fruit and a pot of tea.

The Dean of the Collegium was solidly

built, to say the least. In fact, he looked a little as if he had been constructed out of a series of building blocks. If it hadn't been for his graying hair, Mags would have been very tempted to ask him if *he* wanted to play Kirball, he certainly looked fit enough, and with his build, he looked as if he could fend off everything that came at him.

Just now, he also looked a little startled to see Mags. "I see you come bearing my breakfast, youngling," he said as he opened the door to his office, "And I thank you kindly, but the question is, *why* have you come?" His brow creased as he wave Mags inside. "No troubles, I hope . . . ?"

"Not exactly, sir," Mags replied, and closed the door. He took the seat that Caelen waved him to. Finally, now that all the renovations were done, Caelen no longer had to share his office with what seemed like half of the Heraldic Collegium library. As a result, the office was tidy to a fault and looked almost empty. "I come t'you on account of you know what I'm doin' with Nikolas, so you're safest t' ask some things of." Quickly he described that *feeling of being watched,* his and Dallen's inability to find a living person doing the watching, and Dallen's suggestion that it was a ghost. Caelen nodded thoughtfully throughout the explanation, and when Mags was done, he drummed his fingers on his desk for a while, thinking. Mags let him think in peace. In his experience, you didn't get answers out of someone any faster by pelting them with more questions.

"I'm sure Dallen has told you that there is a Gift for speaking with the spirits of the dead that are still lingering on earth," the Dean said, finally. "I'm sure he has also told you that there aren't any Heralds living now who have that particular Gift. It generally doesn't come up for Heralds anyway, it's more an . . . independent sort of thing. They call people like that 'Mediums,' but not too many of them are genuine, and it's a difficult Gift to bear, I am told."

Mags nodded, refusing to feel disappointment yet. Caelen clearly wasn't done speaking.

"Now, I can't tell you whether or not what you sensed was a spirit. I *can* tell you that Dallen is right; it wouldn't be out of the question for the ghost of someone who had recently died to be lingering in that neighborhood." Caelen's sober expression at least told Mags that the Dean was taking him seriously, and at his word. "How often do people die there, as a rule?"

Mags shrugged. It wasn't something he

liked to think about. "Pretty often. Death cart generally has a customer within shoutin' distance of the shop every couple of days."

Caelen nodded. "Out of all of them, I am sure there are a few who aren't aware they have died, or who are afraid to pass on, or would be lingering for some other reason. Did you feel anything other than that you were being watched? Any emotion at all? Anger? Fear?"

Well, at least that was something he could answer. "Nothin' but bein' watched, like."

"Hmm. Well. Actually, that's not so bad. If it is a spirit, at least it isn't angry with you." Caelen drummed his fingers on the desk some more, a look of concentration on his face. "I don't suppose you experienced an intense sensation of cold? Many who have directly encountered spirits have reported that."

In this heat . . . that'd be right welcome . . . In that way his imagination had of picturing something incongruous in the middle of a serious discussion, Mags had a sudden mental picture of someone running about with a gossamer net and a jar, trying to capture ghosts and store them for their cold-producing abilities. "No cold," he said, "but I was movin' pretty brisk. I might not've felt anythin'."

Caelen chewed on his lower lip for a moment. "I don't know," he said, finally. "But what I can do is put the word out to see if there is someone who actually has this particular Gift somewhere within a reasonable distance of Haven, if you like. It might take some time, because there are a great many people who pretend to have it in order to defraud the gullible. And those who do have it sometimes would rather not actually use it, so it might take some persuasion."

But Mags shook his head. "Nothin' attacked me, nor even did anythin' but give me the prickles," he pointed out. "Dallen said it might'a been somethin' out of the Pelagirs too."

Caelen made a face. "Far be it from me to contradict a Companion, but that seems even less likely. The Pelagirs are a long way from here, Mags. Even something that flies would have a difficult time making its way here."

Mags laughed weakly. "Y'know, now I kinda know how that mad feller felt, the one that died? I mean, he was here t'do us harm, but feelin' like somethin' is watchin' ye ain't a good feelin'. 'Twas bad enough fer just that little bit. I'm just glad I could get away from it."

Caelen glanced at him sharply. "Well . . . you were around him. We still don't exactly know what was plaguing him. Maybe whatever it was has somehow attached itself to you, now?"

He shivered. "Hope not." Occasionally the poor man's ravings came back to him in nightmares.

"Well, I hope so too — but that's a possibility we should consider, so if it becomes worse, or it follows you here, I want to know about it immediately." Caelen's expression said without words that he was going to take no argument on the subject.

"Oh, no worries! I'll wake ye up in middle of night if I have to!" Mags promised fervently. "But didn't we figger out that the things was somethin' that was supposed to protect Valdemar? So why would it be pickin' on me now?"

Caelen could only shrug. "I'm sorry, Mags, I am just as much in the dark here as you are.

:It might be . . . not one of ours, but something similar,: Dallen said, thoughtfully. *:They aren't the sharpest swords in the rack.:*

:Who aren't?: he asked.

But Dallen didn't answer, and he knew there was no point in trying to tease an answer out of him. The little information

236

that he, Lena, and Bear had uncovered in the archives had suggested that the "things with eyes" were something set up by Herald Vanyel . . . so perhaps they were a species of invisible creature, and something *like* them had spotted Mags?

So now I have invisible things chasin' after me? Why couldn't he just have a life like — Gennie — where his worst worries would be how long it would take to get into Whites and whether or not they'd win the next Kirball game?

But there was no point in quizzing Dean Caelen any further, since it was clear he was at the end of his knowledge as well.

"Reckon we've got as far as we can, sir," Mags said instead, getting to his feet. "Thenkee."

"Thank *you* for coming to me immediately, Mags," Caelen replied, with a wan smile. "You've got good sense, sense I sometimes wish other people would demonstrate before we end up with problems on our doorstep."

As Mags shut the door to the Dean's office, he wondered about that last remark. Could Caelen have been referring to Lena and Bear?

:He said *other* people,: Dallen said, tartly. :And if you recall, I was the one that advised

237

silence on their part, and I took full responsibility for that. Furthermore, neither Lena nor Bear are his charges.:

:Fair enough. So that means you ain't people?: Mags chuckled. :Good. Means I don' need to share m'pocket pies no more. Them's people-food.:

Dallen's wordless snort of indignation did not need any translation.

The next time Mags climbed out on the roof, he felt the *eyes* on him even before he was fully out of the hatch.

:Ideers?: he asked Dallen, crouching in the shadows, every nerve on fire.

:I . . . can tell where it's coming from, anyway,: Dallen said, hesitantly. :Even if it makes no sense at all. It's coming from above you.:

Above? Reflexively, he glanced up and, predictably, saw nothing at all except the night sky, obscured tonight by clouds, with only a few stars shining.

Of course, it was darker than anyplace other than the inside of the mine. He wouldn't be able to see anything smaller than a horse even if it was practically on top of him.

:Ideers?: he repeated, sharply.

:What you did the last time.:

So he ran, ran in another direction entirely than Dallen's. Sprinted from rooftop to rooftop as fast as he could, just to get rid of that horrible, flesh-creeping feeling of *being watched.*

:It's following you, still above you. But it's slower than you are.:

Well, there went his hope that it was some strange phenomenon, maybe some sort of weather thing, that had nothing to do with anything living. He hadn't thought he could go faster, but he did, and for good measure, he changed direction, time and time again. He was in a better neighborhood, but the houses were even closer together, which made his progress swifter.

:It's stopping. I think you lost — huh.:

:What?: He paused with his hand on a rooftree, panting.

:It's gone.: Dallen sounded baffled. *:Not as in, 'it went away,' but as in 'it just vanished.' It didn't fade, it was as though someone blew out a candle. There one moment, gone the next.:*

Mags swore. He didn't know a lot of oaths, and he didn't use them often, but all of them were screamingly obscene, and at the moment, every one of them felt absolutely appropriate.

■ ■ ■ ■

This time Nikolas was at the shop, and so was one of the most sensitive Empaths at Healer's Collegium. At the usual time, Mags went up through the roof. And just as before, he felt eyes on him.

This time, despite the crawling of his skin, he stayed where he was, waiting for Nikolas and Healer Charis to make their own assessments. After what seemed like forever, Dallen said, *:Right. Come back in.:*

He did, but only as far as the attic. The sense of being watched remained for a moment, then abruptly vanished. Just as Dallen had said the other night; it wasn't as if it faded away, it was as if it had completely vanished. As if a door had opened on it, then closed again.

:Now go back out.:

He did, and waited, and to his intense relief, this time, nothing happened. But right after the relief came puzzlement. Why hadn't it come back a second time? Shouldn't it have reappeared when he did?

He dropped back through the roof and went back down into the shop, where Nikolas and Charis were waiting in the box for him. Nikolas had blown out the lamp at the doorway, closed and locked the front door, and blown out the lamp in the front of the shop. The shop was officially closed for business. Charis was not wearing his Greens; he was dressed in a scruffy, nondescript sleeveless tunic and trews from among Nikolas' disguises. His blond hair had been left alone; it wasn't likely anyone down here would recognize him.

"I got no feelings from it at all," Charis said, before Mags could ask any questions. His normally stoic expression had been replaced by one of extreme puzzlement. "Nothing. No anger, not even interest." He shook his head. "I can't even properly describe it. It was detached, intelligent, yet incurious. Almost as if someone had set a watchdog, yet it was a watchdog trained only to *watch,* and not do anything about what it saw."

Nikolas nodded and ran his fingers through his hair. The shop was very quiet tonight, and Mags could hear the ticking of wood beetles chewing away at the beams, the skittering of a mouse over in the corner. He wondered if they ought to get a shop cat. "That was the same impression I got," Nikolas agreed. "I . . . I don't know what it is. Dallen and Rolan think it might be some sort of . . . not a ghost, but a sort of spirit they either can't, or won't describe. But they don't think it's harmful; they just think that for some reason it got curious about Mags, but not curious enough to follow him for very long. If they're wrong, and it *is* a ghost, Caelen has a new theory based on his own research. He thinks it's someone who hasn't yet realized that he or she is dead, maybe a very young child, who is just watching things to see what happens."

Mags looked at his mentor dubiously. "Y'know, that ain't makin' me feel any better. If anythin', that's creepier."

"Well, Caelen says if that *is* the case, then this sort of ghost fades fairly quickly, and no, we don't know why they do, he just says that they do. So this won't last more than a moon or two more."

"A moon or two." Mags sighed. "Well, I reckon I can put up with it for that long, I guess." The thought of a *dead child* watching him rather made him want to crawl right out of his skin, but he couldn't tell Nikolas that.

Why was it so difficult to figure out what this thing was, anyway? He would have thought, with one of the most skilled Mindspeakers around and one of the best Healers, they'd at least have a guess.

"If ye don' mind, I druther not go over

roofs tonight," he said, finally. "One go-around of bein' stared at is enough fer one night."

The Healer smiled. "I fully understand that, Mags," he said. "I really do. I felt what you felt . . . and that made me very curious. If you don't mind my asking, what is it that makes this so difficult for you?"

Nikolas let them all out of the office, blew out the lantern after lighting a candle stub at it, locked the office door, and led them out the front door. Mags tried to puzzle out what the Healer had meant.

Finally he gave up. "Don't reckon I understand the question, sir," he said respectfully.

Nikolas coughed a little. "I told you that you need to be more direct with Mags, Charis," the King's Own said as he locked up the shop. "He is a very direct sort of fellow."

"An' there's a powerful lot that's difficult fer me, sir," Mags added ruefully. The three of them trudged down the street together, heads down, shoulders hunched, three men going home after a long and tiring day. The street was quite empty tonight; the only activity seemed to be in a few upper-story rooms and in the drink shops — and there was not much of that.

"I mean, why does the prospect of a spirit

243

frighten you," Charis asked after a long moment.

Mags couldn't help himself. He shuddered.

It took him a long time to answer. These were not things he cared to think about.

"I was pretty much a mine-slavey from about the time Cole Pieters reckoned I could pile rocks into a cart an' pull the cart outa the mine," he said. "Now, reckon the *kind* of mine that'd be, an' the kind of man that'd put a bare toddler down there t'work." He paused to let the Healer contemplate that. "Even if he weren't a cruel man, only a greedy one, it weren't like he paid any attention t'makin' things safe. Pretty much all'a kiddies doin' the daytime diggin' were just that. Kiddies. Kiddies gen'rally aren't thinkin' about bein' safe. They don't shore up behind 'em, or if they do, they don't make sure of it. They ain't got the knowing an' the learning that tells 'em when a seam's full'a cracks. They get real hungry, and they're thinkin' of their bellies an' how many sparklies it'll take t' get a extra slice of bread, an' they ain't careful when they're chippin' stuff out, specially if it's big." He paused and let the Healer take all that in. "Reckon ye can see where that's goin', sir. Lots of cave-ins. Lots of people die. Would have been a lot more, 'cept the rock was pretty sound an' didn't need a lot of shorin' up. But this's what generally happened. If the whole roof comes down, it generally kills you on the spot, an' yer lucky."

"Lucky!" Charis exclaimed, shocked.

"Aye. Supervisor hears it, or else he don't, but when he comes down yer way, he don't hear you tappin' no more, an' he checks. Now, if where you was workin' was a good vein, he'll send somebody in there t'clear out."

Mags took a long, deep breath. "Now, if the rockfall didn' kill ye dead, you've been a-lyin' there for however long it took him to check. An' if the shaft you been workin is blocked up now, well. *Maybe* they'll get to you, an' *maybe* they won't, cause if it's blocked up too bad, it'll have t' be a right good seam or vein t' spend the time t'clear out. So yer lyin' there, an' maybe you don't live. An' if ye don't, you're lucky."

This time the Healer didn't utter an exclamation, but Mags could tell he was about to explode with indignation. Of course he was. The very idea that someone young and presumably healthy was *lucky* to die was anathema to a Healer.

"So say it's too blocked up t' get to ye

245

fast. Now, remember, they ain't tryin' t'clear it t' get to *you*. They're clearin' it to get to the stones. And say ye weren't dead in the rockfall, an' ye don't die soon. Ye're lyin' there, in the dark. It's getting harder an' harder t'breathe. Ye mebbe got a lotta rock layin' on ye. Yer bones is prolly broke." He felt the Healer shrinking at the picture he was painting, as well he should. It was horrific, and one that Mags had pictured as his own fate in countless nightmares. Still did, actually, now and again. But he went on, though he was drenched in a cold sweat of fear, because he realized that he wanted, desperately, to have someone *understand,* at long last, understand gut- and bone-deep, the horrible, terror-filled life he and the others had endured, day after day, in that place. He had never spoken much about it, not even to Nikolas and Amily. He wasn't sure why. But here at last was someone who would not only understand it but would feel it. He was a Healer, he was an Empath. He knew what broken bones and suffocation felt like; he'd endured them with his patients. He knew the agony of lacerated flesh and nerve. And he knew fear, the fear you felt when you finally accepted that you were going to die, be snuffed out, and be gone. As hideous as life might be, it was something they all clung to. And not one of them had a hope for anything afterward. Why should they? Such things were promised by men in fine clothing who came, looked past their protruding bones and frightened eyes, and told Cole Pieters what a good thing he was doing, caring for so many orphans. If they could be so mistaken about what was in front of their own eyes, how could anyone believe what they said about gods and heavens and things after death that no one had ever seen?

So Mags went on.

"Like I said, they ain't after *you,* they just wanta clean the stone away so they can be diggin' again. Chances are, ye're gonna die, smothered or bleedin, or all crushed up inside, all alone in the dark. An' that's lucky, 'cause if they drag ye out, you ain't gonna see a Healer. Someone'll haul ye out in the mine cart t'get you outa the way, an' then they'll pitch you out. Ye might die there. An' mebbe it'll be winter an' ye'll fall asleep in the cold. Or mebbe ye won't die at all, mebbe ye'll drag yourself t' under the barn floor, where all of ye sleep, an' mebbe ye'll lie there, and mebbe someone'll bring ye a little food. An mebbe ye'll actually live. Yer bones'll be all twisted up, a'course. But as soon as ye show up fer a meal —" He paused for effect "— *they'll put a pick an' hammer in yer hand an' send ye back in.* Even if they have to take ye in the mine cart an ye crawl into the shaft."

The Healer made a choking noise.

"Now," Mags went on, "figure all them people, them kiddies, that die in there. They're dyin' hard, mostly. Pain. Scared. Fightin' for breath. For the worst, mebbe dying for days. All alone an' no one cares. So you figure what kinda ghosts they'd make." The sweat of fear had soaked through his shirt now, he'd have to leave it to be washed before he could wear it again. The trews too. "Angry, I'd say. Wouldn't you be? Wouldn't you be *mad* that there was people just like you that was alive, and you ain't? So we heard about all sorts of ghosts in the mine. There was one that'd come along, an' no matter how careful you shored up behind you, he'd knock the timbers loose. Or the one that'd work the ceiling behind you, so it all fell in and you was trapped in a pocket and suffocate. There was one that'd find places for water t'come in an' flood the shaft. An' there was plenty, th' ones that'd been brought out t'die, that'd come in the night an' sit on yer chest and suffocate you, or walk through yer dreams an' make ye feel how they died. But those weren't the worst."

"They — weren't?" Charis managed, through his horror.

"No. They weren't. Cause all that woulda happened if Cole Pieters were just a greedy bastard that didn't give two pins 'bout anythin' but money. But Cole Pieters weren't just that. Cole Pieters were the meanest, nastiest, cruelest man I ever seen."

He could practically feel Charis' eyes going wide with shocked surprise.

"I seen him beat kiddies t'death for just about nothin'. I seen him beat 'em senseless, then have 'em dragged down into mine an' the shaft collapsed around 'em. I seen him watch a couple go after each other over half a piece of bread, an' laugh as one of 'em beat in the other's head against a rock. I seen him tie up a kiddie out at the sluices overnight in winter 'cause he wasn't findin' enough glitter, an' the kiddie soaked through wet. He died, naturally. He catch ye doin' anything he could call stealin' an' off'd come an ear, cause ye don't need an ear to work a seam, and maybe it'd fester, and maybe it'd heal. He'd smash your teeth just cause he felt like it." Mags finally ran out of words and stumped along, exhausted by what had come flooding out of him. But he still had one more thing to say. "Now.

You figure what sorts of ghosts *those* kiddies make. Then ask me why I'm feared of ghosts."

He remembered, oh, how he remembered, silently talking to the spirits in the dark. Reminding them that *he* wasn't the one responsible for their deaths. Pointing out he was no different from them — maybe worse off, because he was hungry and they weren't, he was cold or hot, and they weren't, he was exhausted, and they weren't. Begging them to turn their anger on the ones responsible for all the pain — Cole Pieters and his sons. He'd go to sleep thinking at them, or whenever he was startled by an unexpected sound in the mine.

He couldn't remember who had told him and the others about the ghosts of the dead miners. He didn't think it was the Pieters' boys, but it might have been. It wouldn't have been the elaborate story he had just told Nikolas and Charis, of course; the Pieters' boys had about the same imagination as a turnip, and none of that business about dying slowly and painfully would even have occurred to them. But it didn't take much imagination to put together a lot of dead and dying mine-slaveys, ghosts, and some fun scaring the living mine-slaveys together.

Ghost stories were the sorts of things that were whispered in the dark when you were too cold or hungry to sleep, because misery prefers to have company. The ghost stories that the Pieters boys told would have been simple and impersonal. But the stories the kiddies told each other . . . those had names.

"Remember Bat?" "Issie sat on me chest last night!" "I seen Lu at privy, I swear!" Every ghost had a name and a face, and even if the faces looked much alike — dirty, straggling, greasy hair, cheekbones sharp with hunger — it was still the face of someone you'd eaten with, worked with, huddled up with against the cold.

"I'm sorry, Mags," Nikolas whispered, finally. "I had no idea. . . ."

The shape on the other side of him, the Healer Charis, just nodded, dumbly.

:That was well done, Chosen,: Dallen said gently. *:I was hoping we'd be able to get that out of you.:*

He thought about that. *:That why you teased me 'bout it?:*

:Yes. To get you started. You've had that bottled up inside you for far too long, and it needed to be told to someone who would feel it, not merely be horrified, then do his best to forget about it.: Dallen sounded very contrite. *:And now I apologize, because unlike*

Nikolas, I did know, and I prodded at you anyway.:

The sweat of fear was drying, making his shirt itch. Mags scratched at his shoulder absently. *:Ye meant well.:* He pondered it for a moment. *:Reckon was like lettin' pus out of a wound.:*

:Very like.:

"Well," he said aloud, after a long stretch of walking in silence. "Now ye know. So if ye want t'make it up t'me, well, ye can." He scratched his other shoulder. "Figure out if it *is* a ghost. An' get *rid* of it." He sighed. "There probably ain't nobody in Haven that's died as hard as any of the mine-kiddies did, and probably no reason for a ghost t'be that angry, but it doesn't matter to m'gut. Understand?"

Nikolas sighed. "Yes, Mags, we do."

He nodded, as the corner where their inn was came into view. "Good," was all he said.

But it was enough.

7

There were glimpses of eyes in the rock, the cold touch of a clawlike hand. Mags tried not to look, tried not to think about them. But he thought he could see them anyway. He knew who they belonged to, too, but he tried not to think of the name.

Jak. I was Jak.

He could almost, but not quite, hear the name being whispered. He chipped away at the rock in a cold sweat. He knelt in the shaft just as he always did, rock just a few finger lengths from his nose, his knees fitted into smooth hollows that he himself had painstakingly cut out. After all, the Cole boys were only listening for the sounds of rock being cut, and a little work in making smooth places for your legs to fit *now* meant a lot less pain later. His lamp, strapped to his forehead, cast a dim light on the rock face in front of him. One little flame, in that lamp, fed by oil, with a metal reflector behind it. You didn't want the flame to burn too high, it'd burn the skin of your forehead. You turned it as low as you dared.

Except that meant shadows, and in the shadows, were the hints, the glints, of a pair of eyes.

Hungry eyes, the eyes of someone who had scrabbled for life and had it taken away from him anyway.

Jak. I was Jak.

"Leave me be," Mags whispered. "Leave me be, I nivver hurt ye, I nivver took from ye. I nivver shoved ye t'edge of huddle i' th' col'. Leave me be. Go fin' Bon. 'E's th' 'un thet stole yer bread. Go bother Calli. She nobbled yer blanket."

Around him, behind him in the darkness, came the sounds of tapping, and echoes of tapping. He had just begun his half-day down here, but of course, he was hungry already. They were all, always hungry. The porridge of barley and oats that they all got for their breakfast didn't last for very long. Especially not when you were working as hard as you could, chipping away the rock. But he was used to that; in fact, the times when he wasn't hungry were branded in his memory. There weren't more than a handful of them, and most of them were connected with visits from priests, those cursed god-men who promised everything after you were dead.

They must have been branded in Jak's memory too, or at least, whatever memory a ghost had. Maybe that was the problem. Maybe now that Jak was dead he knew what the god-men told was all lies. It was all the same rubbish anyway. Suffer on earth and be rewarded in a heaven Mags didn't believe in, by gods who didn't see fit to do something about misery right now. Sometimes, when he had a moment to think, and something turned his mind toward these gods the priests were so big about, he wanted to hit the priests, hit the gods if they existed. But that took energy, and mostly he didn't have the energy to waste. But Jak, now, Jak had listened to the god-men, and listened to the stupid Cole daughter who read out of holy books at them while they ate, and maybe Jak had believed. And now Jak knew better. Knew it was all lies, that no one had anything for anyone who wasn't important and rich, least of all gods. And now he wanted to be alive again, and he'd do what it took to get alive again.

It didn't work that way, but since everything else Jak had been told was a lie, he had no reason to believe he *couldn't* steal someone else's body.

"Bon stole yer bread," Mags repeated, ruthlessly. "I nivver stole fr'm ye." Mags carefully positioned his chisel and tapped at a likely spot in the seam with his hammer. It was a good broad seam, this one, as wide as the tunnel was tall, which meant there was no problem with spending most of his time hammering out waste rock and getting shouted at for not bringing up any sparklies today. This had been Jak's seam. Was that why Jak was here?

But Jak hadn't died here. Jak had died of eating something bad, up on the surface. Probably those berries. Mags knew they were poison, they all know those plump, dark berries were poison. Jak knew too. But when you were starving and a bully had stolen your bread, maybe those berries were a little too tempting.

Maybe Jak was here because Mags hadn't shared with him.

This was a good seam. Why hadn't Jak managed to bring out enough sparklies to get him extra bread? He should have been able to.

Mags' tapping released a chunk of rock. There was nothing in it that he could see, but it wasn't waste — it would go up to the hammer-mill and the sluices. He set his chisel into a good spot and began tapping again. One more sparkly and he'd get a second slice of barley bread with his broth.

Jak could have done that every day in this seam.

"If ye were hungry, 'twas yer own fau't," he said, under his breath, as the sad eyes watched the back of his head. "Ye hear me? Lookit this seam! Yer own fau't."

That was what Master Cole said all the time. It was easy enough to earn bread, all you had to do was work for it. It was another lie of course, because if you found yourself in a *really* good seam, Cole would switch one of his sons to it. But that was what he told the ghost, lying to it as he and the rest were lied to. Maybe Jak even believed that, seeing Mags pulling out the sparklies now.

There were two sounds in the mine where he was, the tapping and the steady drip of water. They provided a counterpoint to his own tapping and his muttering to the ghost. The rock fractured suddenly and dropped off the face, and there, catching the light was another yellow sparkly; not very big, but Mags' sharp eyes never missed a sparkly. He pulled the rag he kept wrapped around his throat off, folded it a few times and set it on the floor of the tunnel just under the stone. Setting his chisel as delicately as he could, he began flaking bits of rock from the face around the sparkly. A tap, a pause to check his progress, another tap, another pause. It was serious, intense work. One slip of the chisel, and there would be nothing but chips and a beating.

The feeling of eyes on the back of his neck suddenly intensified, and he felt a cold hand touch the middle of his back. He jumped, the chisel slipped, and the stone shattered.

Hoping the Pieters boys hadn't noticed the change in rhythm, he shoved the chips with the rest of the waste for the sluice and went back to cutting the rock face.

But now besides the sweat of terror of the ghost, he was drenched in the cold sweat of fear of a beating. "What'd ye do thet fer?" he whispered harshly. "Ye want me t'die too?"

Yes. . . .

He almost froze. So Jak was after — what? Company? No, he and Jak had barely exchanged a few words, ever. No, it had to be something else. It had to be about what *he* was.

Yer Bad Blood, boy. Yer Bad Blood, and it's damn lucky for you that yer here, an' we can put ye to work an' keep those idle hands busy, or ye'd be dancin' at rope's end already.

He could hear that in his mind, hear what

Cole Pieters said of him. Was that why the ghost was haunting him? Because he was Bad Blood?

Out of the kindness, the pure kindness of my heart, I took ye. No one else wanted ye, not even the godly priests. They all knew what ye were. They all figgered one day ye'd turn on 'em. I'm a bloody saint, I am, fer takin' a chance with you.

Did he deserve this miserable excuse for a life? Did he deserve to be dead?

Or should he just have died with his parents, and all this time the gods had been trying to kill him, and he just wasn't cooperating with them and dying proper-like?

To hell wi' ye, gods! Ye sendin' ghosts t'do yer work now? Tap, pause. Tap, pause. He put his nose as close to the stone as he could and still see, examining the rock minutely.

To hell with gods. To hell with what they wanted. To hell with Jak and his sad story. There were no good stories here. Every kiddy here was unwanted, burdens on their villages, bastards left on doorsteps, kiddies left orphaned — they arrived, more often than not, with tear-streaked faces, and most of the time, their faces remained tear-streaked, day in, day out. There was little enough to be happy about here. Good days meant someone found food in the pigs' buckets before the pigs got their slop. Good days meant you hurt less. Good days meant one of the god-men was going to visit, and you got put into long shirts made of sacks that you pulled on over your rags so it looked like you had clean clothing. The shirts itched, but you weren't allowed to scratch. And you got two slices of bread and better soup, made with peas, and just for that night you didn't sleep hungry. Those were good days, and they didn't happen often.

And the priests, the god-men, would look at the shirts and not at the thin faces, the bony limbs, and tell everyone how lucky they were to have a good master like Cole Pieters, someone who was teaching them a trade, feeding and clothing them. Then there would be a long blather about gods, but not too long, because Pieters wanted them back at the mine. And then the god-man would go have a fine meat dinner with the Pieterses, then go away, and the shirts would be snatched away, and it was all the same again. It was always the same. Nothing ever changed, and no one would come to rescue them.

"Gabble gabble gabble."

He started. That wasn't the whisper of a ghost, and it wasn't any of the kiddies or one of Cole Pieters' sons. It wasn't even words he recognized!

"Gabble gabble gabble!"

He clutched at his chisel and hammer as the mine started to darken and fade around him. What was going on? Was his lamp —

I left the mine —

Everything was dark, and he felt as if he was falling. And the back of his head hurt.

I left the mine. Dallen rescued me. Dallen and . . . and . . .

He felt someone grab him by the hair. He couldn't move, he couldn't fight, he couldn't even open his eyes. Suddenly he was breathing in smoke, thick, sweet . . . he coughed, but that only drove it farther into his lungs. He tried to hold his breath, but eventually he had to breathe anyway, breathe in great, shuddering gulps of the thick, too-sweet air heavy with the smoke. He thought he might throw up, he suddenly had so much vertigo. He heard someone grunt, and felt himself falling sideways.

It was dark. There wasn't much oil in his lamp, and he'd turned it way down. The last one to use it must have taken it off and turned it way up to warm his hands by. You could do that, but it was stupid to. He'd felt when he got the lamp that it was low on oil, but they only got refilled at the beginning of the night shift, and there was no point in asking for more oil So he'd dropped it to the tiniest flame he could and not have it blow out. You didn't need a light to get to the end of the shaft, and if you were working a poor seam, well, you didn't need much light for that, either.

As he knew, this wasn't a good seam. He'd been taken off Jak's old seam as soon as he started bringing out lots of sparklies. Davven was working it now, the suck-up. He could chip away at this thing for candlemarks without needing to see, and save the light for when he worked at the thin vein that held the sparklies. You had to cut away the bad rock before you could get to the good stuff.

He'd noticed on his way out that by his standards, the roof was overdue for a prop, so he brought one in and hammered it in place before going back to work. He arranged himself at the face and began working high, above the seam. He'd work down, in strips, and maybe there'd be something worthwhile when he got to the right rock. He had to bring *something* out or he wouldn't get fed at all.

At least the ghost wasn't in this seam.

But suddenly, he began to cramp. Legs, then arms, knotting up in an instant, and so fiercely that it made him cry out. He expected to hear one of Cole's sons yelling when he did. *"No jibber-jabber!"* But instead, his arms and legs just burned . . . burned . . . felt as if someone had bound them up.

"Gabble gabble gabble!"

His throat burned too. Why did his throat burn? It felt the way it had when he'd inhaled some noxious smoke from when the Pieters boys had been burning a carcass of something that had died and started to rot before they found it. He coughed and whimpered, coughed again.

It was too dark to see, but again, someone grabbed his head by the hair, this time pulling him up. He opened his mouth to protest, and what felt like the wooden mouth of a waterskin was jammed into his teeth. A few drops of liquid dribbled onto his tongue, thirst overcame him, and he sucked at it, greedily, ignoring the musty, odd taste, bitter and sweet at the same time. He drank worse water every day, water murky and gritty with the waste from the mine, water green with algae from the barrels at the mine-head that were never cleaned, water slimy out of the bottles they were given when they went down to work, bottles that were never cleaned either.

The hand let go of his hair, and he fell

back into darkness. Hot darkness. Hot, sticky darkness.

So hot.

Mags worked away at the sluice. It was hot, so hot. In summer, working the sluices was the best job. There was sun and fresh air, and if you got hot you just splashed some water over you, but for some reason, the water was just as hot as the air today, and splashing water over himself didn't make any difference. It was hard work, right enough, swirling the heavy pans of gravel around and around in the running water, and his arms and back ached something terrible. He felt all cramped up again, but at least he wasn't hungry. And it was no worse than mining the seam. It was summer, and this must have been afternoon shift. He couldn't remember. It would be work for long hours, because this was the afternoon shift, and work didn't stop till the sun went down. Well, that wasn't so bad. You didn't really want to go to bed early in the summer, when you could sluice in the sun and let the heat soak into you, especially after a turn in the mine in the cold. Even if the sluice water was as hot as the air right now.

Piles of rock pounded into gravel at the hammer mill were brought here after sorting. Master Cole's daughters and youngest sons did that; a lot of sparklies were pounded out by those hammers, fracturing the rock around them but not the crystals themselves. The kiddies got the gravel when the Pieters siblings were done with it. The sorting house was a pleasanter place by far than the sluices. You were allowed to sit down. The doors and windows stood open to the breeze in summer. There was a fire in there, come winter. The only time the kiddies ever saw a fire was when there were leaves and trash being burned or they took a turn as a kitchen drudge because a drudge had took sick. The sorting house was clean and bright, and the work was just tedious, not back-breaking. But, then, that was to be expected, since the Pieters kids served there . . . and it was rare indeed that anyone else got a turn in the place. Usually old man Cole or his wife or one of the older boys would bend their heads to work there before they let a kiddie in the door. It had happened once to Mags' knowledge, the year that an ague and a flux went through the whole place, carrying off two Pieters kids and several servants, but leaving the mineworkers oddly alone. Maybe even a fever realized what a misery their lives were and figured they had enough punishment.

Or maybe the gods were bastards.

It was so hot today!

Mags stood at the head of the third sluice, with his back to the afternoon sun. Not a good position on a day this hot, but the bigger, tougher fellers got the spots in the shade. He got the pan that had been left by the kiddie on the last shift under the sluice, scooped up enough to cover the bottom from the gravel pile next to him and began swirling the gravel in the running water, watching for the glint of something colored and shiny.

So hot . . . so hot . . . almost as hot as it had been that night, on the roof.

Wait, what roof?

Because he remembered a roof, remembered crouching up there, in a place where no kiddie was allowed to be, but it was night. It was night, and the stars were hidden behind a cloud, and there was that *watching,* the same as the ghost in the shaft, watching him . . . but he ignored it because it had been doing that for days now, and nothing had ever happened. Everyone said it would fade eventually, then go, as the ghost lost its hold on the world.

Everyone said so. Even Dallen.

Dallen? Who's —

He kept his nose on his business, sending

the gravel down the sluice when it was panned out, concentrating on the sweat trickling down his back as a counter to the cramps and numbing of his hands and arms, and the overpowering heat, and watching in that peculiarly unfocused state that let him spot the tiny sparks of color and light that others missed. The little wooden dish at his side filled steadily.

But who's Dallen?

The pain in his back and arms was nearly unbearable. He couldn't remember a time when he'd hurt this bad, not ever. It felt as if someone had tied his arms behind his back and left them there, and they were cramping. Yet, somehow, his hands and arms were doing the job they were supposed to do.

Supposed to do? How could his limbs hurt this badly and still be working, as if the pain belonged to some other body?

Someone had been working his seam last night. Which meant that it might need a support. The cripples that worked the night shift were mostly crazy as well as crippled, and they weren't nearly as particular about safety as he was. He was back in the good seam again, which meant that . . . that ghost might be there. He tried not to think about it, found that he couldn't, and instead just whispered to it in his head, over and over. *I ain't hurt ye. I ain't th' one t'blame. Go haunt th' one thet is.* He didn't dare say anything out loud. The Pieters boys were working nearby and might hear him. He knew they were certainly listening to make sure he kept working. That was why Davven got pulled off this shaft. He'd only worked enough to ensure he got double bread, then slacked off.

He fetched a timber, but that left him able to carry only his chisel and hammer, He crawled in, found as he had expected that the roof needed shoring, and hammered his timber in place. Then he went to work.

It was a nightmare. His hands chipped away at the stone, but they felt numb, as numb as if he'd immersed them in cold water, or slept on them wrong and they'd fallen asleep. His arms screamed at him, and his back —

Finally he couldn't take it anymore, and the chisel dropped from his fingers as he moaned and his eyes closed. Or had they been closed all along? He couldn't feel rock under him, it was wood, and it was moving. He wasn't kneeling, he was lying on his side. And then came *that voice* again.

"Gabble gabble! GABBLE!"

Hands in his hair, and this time as his head was pulled up, he was able to get his eyes open a crack. Dim light filtered through canvas felt like staring at the sun. There was someone between him and the canvas.

Canvas? *Wood?*

Someone did something behind his back, and his arms stopped hurting, his back stopped hurting. He felt first one hand, then the other, pulled around in front of him, as if they'd been tied behind his back. A finger and thumb pressing hard at the hinges of his jaw forced his mouth open. The neck of the waterskin was shoved between his teeth, and he was suddenly aware of that burning thirst. But this time it wasn't water, it was a kind of soup or broth, salty and meaty, but with the same bittersweet aftertaste that the water had had. His head felt thick, as if someone had stuffed him into a helmet that was too small.

Helmet?

He drank, because otherwise he'd choke. He was let fall again, and this time he actually *felt* something take over him, pulling him back into the mine, and had time to think *drug* before . . .

He knelt to his work in the mine, but he could hear Pieters' sons talking, working away in their seams, and they were scared.

Absolutely terrified.

"I ain't never seen anythin' like it," said Melak, the third son and Jarrik's junior. "I mean, I heerd the stories, but seein' one — it ain't right. It was hot-mad and tryin' and tryin' t'get in, and every way it got stopped, it just tried a new one. Smart. Things like that got no right to be as smart as a man."

"Ain't just that it's smart, neither," Jarrik grumbled. "It's got the luck of a devil. Tyndale shot at it, an' did nothin' but miss."

"It scares me. What's it want?" There was real fear in Melak's voice, something Mags was not accustomed to hearing. "Why won't it go away?"

"It wants somethin' here, I guess," Jarrik replied. "Somethin' or someone. Either way, Pa ain't letting it on the property. He swears he's keepin' it off."

"But how?" Melak almost wailed the words. "Ye can't shoot it, ye can't fence it out, and ye can't stop it! We don' know what it wants! What if it wants to get in here and kill one of us?"

"Why would it —" Jarrik stopped.

"You know why," Melak said flatly. "You *know* why. It's more'n half a spirit, too! It could even be —"

"Don't say it!" Jarrik retorted harshly. "Don't even *think* it. Let Pa handle it. Let

Pa handle it and leave well enough alone!"

Standing there in the dark, listening them talk about something they feared so much they wouldn't even put a name to it, Mags shivered. When had this — monster, or whatever it was — turned up and started besieging the mine? Days ago?

Now a horde of little things began to make sense. The sluices had been left without a Pieters supervising them, and half the older boys were not at the mine for the past couple of days. The girls had scarcely been seen out-of-doors and had quickly scuttled back to the Big House when they did come out. The cooks had been less attentive at the giving out of the food, and a fair amount of cabbage and scraps had been joining the broth in the bowls rather than being husbanded in the pot.

At least half the workmen hadn't been visible over the last three days, either.

This thing they were talking about . . . what was it? A demon?

You know what it is.

The Pieters boys had their own store of tales that they told, pretending to tell them to each other but really doing it to scare the kiddies working the seams. Most of the stories were about awful things down here in the mines. There were the ghosts of anyone that had died down here, and Mags knew of some few. These ghosts went about looking for someone who was the exact age they had been when they died — and when they found him, they would tear him apart trying to figure out a way into his body. Like Jak. Jak, who had been lurking, trying to figure out if Mags was the right size, the right age, the right person to take over.

You know it isn't that.

There were the Knockers, twisted up little dwarfs no taller than your knee, but monstrous strong. They would wait until everyone was preoccupied and then just snatch a kiddie, grabbing him in his seam before he could utter a sound, bashing his head in with his own hammer, then dragging off the body to eat.

You know it isn't that, either.

There were the Whisps, ghostlights that would lead you into dangerous parts of the mine, then drop a rockfall on you. They'd do it by putting you to sleep, then getting you to walk in your sleep to where they were going to kill you.

Wake up, Mags, you know what it is!

There were the Horrors, which got into your head and made you crazy, like the night-shift cripples. When the Horrors got you, all you saw were black things coming at you, all claws and red eyes, and you'd drive your head against the wall of the shaft to try to get them out, or you'd make a cave-in yourself to try to stop them, or if they managed to bring you above the ground, you'd throw yourself down the well to be rid of them.

But every one of those was a monster *in* the mine. What about out of it? What was roaming about out there that was so scary the Pieters boys wouldn't name it, wouldn't describe it, and didn't have any bragging ideas on how to get rid of it?

Suddenly, he didn't want to leave at the end of the shift.

But you didn't have to be afraid. Remember!

No, he was afraid that whatever *it* was, it would be up there. Waiting. Watching. The Pieters boys said it was looking for someone. Some sort of devil. Mags didn't believe in gods, but he believed, most fervently, in devils.

And if a devil had come here, there was likely only one person it had come for. Well, two, maybe, except the boys were saying that Cole Pieters was driving the thing off himself, so it hadn't come for Master Cole.

All right, then. It had to be coming for Mags. Because Mags was Bad Blood. It would grab him and drink his blood to make itself stronger. And then it would carry him away to torment him forever.

It isn't a devil. It isn't a demon.

It's coming for you, but not to torment you.

He shook his head violently. It was as if there were some other part of him, talking to him. Some part of him that remembered something important, but what was it?

Drugged. You're being drugged. Every time they give you something to drink or something to eat, you're being drugged. That smoke — it was probably a drug too.

Wait — what?

The mineshaft *had* gone away for a moment. There had been — someone. And that voice saying things he couldn't understand.

He shook his head again. This was all wrong, his head was all messed up. Maybe he'd gotten some taint in his soup, a bit of bad mushroom. It had to have been some sort of fit, this other part of him talking to him, talking nonsense.

At least his arms had stopped hurting.

Then he thought about that devil out there, and he was terrified all over again. It was coming for him, it was coming for him, just as it had come for him on the roof.

Like the thing on the roof! That's what happened! Remember! Fight this and remember!

His heart raced, and he was sweating. And

it was so *hot*! The mine had never been so hot. He couldn't figure it out. Why was the mine so hot? It was always the same temperature. It had never been hot before.

He was held in a strange paralysis of fear; he couldn't lift his chisel, and no one was coming to check to see why he wasn't working.

If anything, that was even stranger than the gabbling voice. The Pieters boys had ears like owls; they heard *everything,* and, most especially, they were listening for what wasn't happening — the steady tap-tap-tapping coming from ten different shafts. So why weren't they checking on him?

He realized at that moment that there was no sound of the others chipping away at the rock either. In fact, there was no sound at all. Just the terrible heat and silence. And in that heat and silence, his lantern went out.

Now it was heat, and silence, and darkness.

And he was lying on his side.

How could he be lying on his side?

The surface underneath him was wood, and moving, vibrating, and swaying from side to side. There was cloth over him. He was sweating buckets now, his clothing was soaked through and —

Clothing?

He was wearing real clothes, just as the Pieters boys did, not rags. He could feel them on his skin, even if he couldn't move his arms or legs or open his eyes.

Where had he gotten clothing?

He wanted to scream, but he couldn't.

His thoughts seemed to be struggling through thick mud. It was so hard to put them together.

This couldn't be the mine. And it felt too real to be some sort of fever dream. Or if it was a fever-dream, it was so impossible that he must be dying of it.

But what if it wasn't a fever dream? What if this was real, and it was the mine that was the dream?

He was in clothing, soaked in sweat. He was terrified. His head hurt. He was lying on his side. He couldn't open his eyes, or move anything.

Think!

It was hot, stifling hot.

He wasn't hungry . . .

That realization lanced through him like being struck by lightning. *I'm not hungry.* At the mine, the only time you weren't hungry was when you'd had some lucky accident. Maybe you somehow found a patch of cattails or cress or poke or goose grass no one else had gotten to, and you gobbled it all up there on the spot. Maybe the cooks had had an accident with the ovens and a *lot* of bread was burned and intended for the pigs, but you got to it first. And you remembered those times, because they shined out in your mind. But he didn't remember a windfall like that recent enough to make him full now, and of all of the parts of him that hurt, his stomach wasn't one of them. His stomach was entirely happy.

That only made him more frightened. If he wasn't at the mine, where was he? Why was he here — and where was *here* anyway? The surface he was on was moving, shaking a little —

He strained his ears, and he could hear the sounds of wheels, and hooves. Was he in a wagon or a cart?

But *why*?

He tried to remember . . . but the only thing he could think of was . . . a roof. Or, rather, a rooftop.

That only frightened him more. He shouldn't be able to remember a rooftop. Why would he have been on a rooftop? Particularly a rooftop like the one in his mind, surrounded by more of the same, under a cloudy night sky.

And his head felt so . . . *wrong.*

Why? Why did it feel as if there was part

277

of him, inside his head, that was either missing or, like his uncooperative limbs, not working?

And why couldn't he move?

That rooftop — had he fallen from it? Was he now lying in a state of paralysis, being taken somewhere? Had he broken his neck? But if he had, why wasn't he dead? If he had, why could he *feel* his arms and legs, but not move them?

What had he been doing up there in the first place?

The surface he was lying on gave a great jolt, confirming that it was a wagon. But he didn't roll, or otherwise move. He was wedged in this position, on his side, curled like a child. He could feel it, even if he couldn't move.

And it was so *hot . . .*

His stomach might be happy, but his throat was parched, dry, his tongue felt swollen. His mouth and throat felt on fire with the need for a drink. Without even thinking about it, he managed a moan.

The wagon or cart he was in stopped moving. He heard someone dropping to the ground, then footsteps. The cart tilted a little.

There was a sound of cloth being whipped away, and a brief breath of cooler air. He fought to open his eyes and succeeded, only to find himself in the dark.

A hand groped over his face and buried itself in his hair.

He was hauled up by the hair. There was someone there, who ruthlessly jammed a thumb and forefinger into the hinges of his jaw to force his mouth open. The wooden spout of a waterskin was shoved in between his teeth, and bittersweet water trickled over his tongue.

He drank, because the burning of his mouth and throat would not allow anything else. He drank, because some instinct told him that if he didn't, it would be forced down his throat in some very unpleasant manner.

But he didn't drink fast. He didn't gulp at the water, the way he vaguely recalled doing earlier. He drank sparingly, only as much as would ease the burning thirst, and the person feeding him didn't seem to notice that he wasn't sucking the water down as fast as he could.

Maybe because it was dark. Or maybe the person was so impatient, in so much of a hurry to get this over with, that he wasn't paying attention.

There was a drug in the water, he was certain of it. Water shouldn't taste like that.

Was he sick? Was that why he was being drugged?

But sick or injured, none of this made any *sense.* Cole Pieters would never have wasted real clothing on a mine-slavey, much less sent one away to be treated for injury or illness. What had happened to him? Who had him, and where were they taking him, and why?

He wasn't dropped down, he was lowered back, even if it was by the hair, and curled back up in that fetal coil. He felt boxes and bags all around him, arranged into that shape to hold him there.

This time the person didn't cover him up again. He felt the cart shift with the other person's weight, then heard him drop down to the ground, go around to the front of the cart again, and heard him climb back up.

"Gabble gabble?"

"Gabble." A snort. *"Gabble gabble gabble."*

"Gabble."

The cart began to move again.

Mags felt his head reeling. Had he lost all ability to understand speech? There was not a single word there that he recognized!

But then, it didn't matter, as he found himself back in the mine, crouched in the mineshaft, hands wrapped numbly around his tools and waiting for the devil to come for him.

8

The devil had found him. The horrible thing was coming for him, the devil that Cole Pieters had sworn was his due. It had just popped up, in the middle of the yard, just as they were all heading out of the mine.

Mags hid, hid in the place he knew the best.

The mine.

They were all terrified, even the Pieterses, so it looked as though claiming he was a saint for taking in all the mine kiddies wasn't doing any good. The devil had already torn one boy apart, mistaking him for Mags, so maybe the thing wasn't real good at figuring out who his victim actually was supposed to be. But then again, the other boy had been right next to Mags, so maybe the devil had just missed him and gotten Davven by accident.

Or maybe the devil was here for a lot of them and would get around to him, sooner or later. A devil probably wouldn't care if he got a few extra on his way to the one he wanted. Maybe the devil was just here to kill everyone. Depending on why it was here — if one of the crazy cripples had gone to hell and sent it back, well everyone was going to be dead. Even if they *liked* the mine-kiddies, the crazies all figured they were better off dead than here, and they said so, often.

Mags didn't know and didn't particularly care. He ran, and so did everyone else who saw the thing, which must have confused the devil even further about which of them to chase. After all, all the mine-kiddies pretty much looked alike, matted mops of dirty no-color hair on top of stick-thin, sexless bodies in rags. Once they began to run, it would be even harder to tell them apart.

You couldn't really make out what it was. It was sort of a smoke-shape, and sort of a shimmer in the air, and sort of a black thing like a kind of burned-up skeleton in the middle of all that. It kind of changed within the smoke, first one thing and then another, and only bits of it visible at any one time. But you could sure make out what it was doing. Mags had seen it shred that boy it had pounced on, just tear off arms and legs and — well at that point, he'd been too busy running to look back.

Mags left it chasing after two of the Pieters boys, hoping it would catch them and be sated. Or at least catch them and give them what they had coming. But he was pretty sure it had marked him as a target; he could *feel* it, and he ran for the mine. His first thought was to hide in a place where the devil would be at a disadvantage and he would not. By the time he got past the mine head, he had a plan — not much of one, but at least it was some kind of a plan.

His arms and legs were aching, his back was aching, and his side was aching when he finished working his way through the labyrinth of shafts to the latrine tunnel. He ducked inside and kept running, keeping to the edge of the shaft. Most people didn't bother going all the way to the end to relieve themselves, so it stank hardly at all by the time he got to the back of it where the seam of sparklies had died out in tough granite. He had to crouch after a while, as the shaft narrowed and started to peter out. Then he went to his hands and knees.

By that point the tunnel was only high enough to crawl along, which was what he was counting on. There was a lot of fallen rock here, and that made it painful to crawl, but it would be a lot more painful to get caught by the devil.

If the devil hunted by smell, the latrine-stink might confuse it. If the devil hunted by sight, well, he had an answer for that too.

He stopped where he had a timber shoring up the roof, but a good amount of rock that had either been shoveled in or fallen down all around him. Carefully, moving more quietly than a mouse, he built up a wall between him and the rest of the tunnel. He could hear lots of screaming off in the distance; as long as he heard that, he had time to build his wall. Maybe in the dark it would look to the devil like the back of the shaft. Placing the rocks stone by stone, he had wedged the final one in when he heard someone come screaming down into the mine. Then he blew out his head lantern and waited, trying not to breathe.

Wait, where did the lantern come from?

He brushed the irrelevant thought away. There were much more important things to think about now, like living. There were lots of screams in the mine now, echoing through the tunnels. He couldn't tell if it was more than one person, but he thought it might be. And he thought he could hear the devil now, too, making a kind of growling deep in its throat and muttering to itself.

"Gabble gabble," it said, then answered itself in a second voice. *"Gabble gabble."*

He ached all over, ached not just with the aches of working all day and the aches of running for his life, but with cold. Where before he'd been hot, now he was cold, cold enough to shiver. He clenched his teeth to keep the devil from hearing them chattering with cold.

Shivering, terrified, he huddled in on himself, arms wrapped around his legs, eyes clenched tightly closed, and listened to the devil mutter to itself. It sounded like it was having an entire conversation right outside the latrine tunnel.

And his head felt so wrong, as if someone had stuffed it with rags. Or cut pieces out of the inside of it. What was the matter with his head? Why did it feel so wrong, as if something was missing?

He was shivering so hard now that he couldn't sit, he had to lie down, which wasn't going to help *at all* because the rock would be so cold. . . .

But the rock wasn't cold, or at least, it wasn't any colder than the air was . . .

. . . because it wasn't rock.

It was wood.

And it was moving.

It wasn't a devil that was muttering somewhere beyond his head. It was two men, having a conversation, and he couldn't understand a single word.

He was lying on his side in a curl, shivering with cold. His head ached so badly, but now, for the first time, when he tried to move his arms and legs, he could, just a little. That was when his mind cleared a little, and he realized that his last clear memory was of being on that rooftop.

A rooftop in a city.

Haven. The city was called *Haven.*

He remembered being up there, looking around himself. He was about to go . . . somewhere. Somewhere important. And then, once he got to the important place, he would go home, only "home" wasn't the mine, and he didn't belong to Cole Pieters anymore.

Something up there was watching him in the memory, and he was studiously ignoring whatever it was, because it had been watching him for a long time now, and nothing had come of it. Everyone said that eventually it would go away, that it wasn't dangerous, and nothing was going to happen. Except this time, something did.

Whatever it was that was up there in the darkness, whatever it was that had only been watching him until that moment, had . . .

287

done something. Something unexpected, catching him completely by surprise. And then there was blackness, and he found himself back in the mine.

How had he gotten to a city from the mine in the first place? And where was this place that he knew was home, even though he couldn't even remember what it was?

Little by little, fragments of memories came back. He clung to them fiercely.

That bittersweet taste in the soup and the water . . . that had to be a drug. And the smoke — that must have been how they'd gotten the drug into him the first time, after they hit him in the head. He was pretty sure he'd been hit in the head; it felt as if someone had nearly cracked his skull open. He'd been burning hot for what seemed like forever but had probably only been days, but now he was cold. What did that mean? Had he been dreaming himself in the mine for weeks? Was it winter now? Or had he been burning with fever, and now the fever had broken?

Maybe all it meant was that the weather had changed . . . the weather had been due to change to colder. Everyone in Haven had been complaining that it hadn't. He remembered that, too, even though he couldn't remember who the *everyone* was.

He couldn't understand a word the two men were saying, and that sent him into a panic. Had he lost his ability to understand speech?

Had he had that same thought before?

Was he going insane?

He huddled in on himself more, and despite his effort to keep quiet, his teeth started to chatter.

The wagon stopped.

Oh, no . . .

Of all things, he wanted to hang onto this clarity. He didn't want them to drug him again! He squeezed his eyes shut, held as still as he could, breathing evenly as if he were still unconscious, but allowed his teeth to chatter.

This time he heard two sets of footsteps coming around to the back of the wagon, two men grunted as they pulled themselves up into the rear, and the wagon moved under their weight.

And that was when he suddenly realized, with a touch of hysteria, that he *desperately* needed to urinate.

He felt boxes and bales being moved around him, and kept still and limp. But he was not expecting it when he felt rough hands hauling him upright.

The men gabbled at each other in a

grumbling sort of way as he debated — should he stay limp? Or should he act like . . . like a sleepwalker?

He had about a fifty percent chance of guessing wrong; he guessed, and acted like a sleepwalker . . . half-cooperating as they manhandled him down out of the wagon. He almost wept when he realized this was what they were expecting.

He cracked his eyelids slightly. Sleepwalkers sometimes opened their eyes, so he didn't think it would matter, and it would keep him from hurting himself if he could see where he was going.

Wherever he was, it looked nothing like the land around the mine. It *did* look like early fall. He could smell the leaves turning, and they were going colors, here and there. The trees were more sparse than they were around the mine, the ground seemed harder, barer. It was definitely hillier. He thought it was very early morning, the sunlight had that thin quality to it.

The men walked him over to a clump of bushes and . . .

It took all of his control to keep from reacting as one of them, with a grunt of disgust, pulled his trews down and took out his . . .

But the desperate need took over, and he

let loose, even though it was someone else doing the directing and all. His knees nearly gave with relief when the man pulled his trews back up, roughly, making it crystal clear that he would rather have been doing *anything* else.

That's why they're feeding me soup. So they don't have to worry about getting me to squat.

He let them half carry him back to the wagon, arrange him in a curl, but this time on his other side. His teeth were still chattering; the men didn't seem cold, but his clothing wasn't very heavy, and it was clammy and damp with sweat. Their clothing was a lot heavier than his, and it looked a little odd to him, something like a padded leather jacket over baggy trews wrapped at the ankles with thin strips of more leather.

They hauled him up, dropped him into what was evidently "his" spot, and curled him on his side. He was almost grateful when one of them tossed a heavy blanket that smelled of horse over him before they piled the bales and boxes around him and tossed a canvas over the top of it all.

Now he opened his eyes completely. He still couldn't move, much, so he concentrated on trying to remember, instead.

My name is Mags. That was easy, he already knew that.

The last thing I remember is being ambushed on a rooftop, in a city called Haven.

Why was he on the rooftop in the first place?

There was a man . . . Nikolas. He could see Nikolas in his head — nondescript, unmemorable, and yet somehow he knew that this "Nikolas" was a very important man. He was doing work for Nikolas. Work that . . . was also important.

He got another flash of memory, of a shop of some sort. A shop that sold. . . .

No, a shop that mostly *bought.*

Pawnshop.

His mind supplied the name.

All right, he was there at that shop, in Haven . . . why? Doing work, but — what kind? And the clothing he was wearing now . . . it was all wrong. It felt wrong. He only wore this to do that work for Nikolas. It wasn't his usual clothing.

All right then, what *was* his usual clothing? He tried to picture it, imagined himself getting dressed in the dark, and when he came out into the light he would be wearing —

Trainee Grays!

And with those two words, everything he had not been able to remember, everything he was, came flooding back.

He knew now that his dream of a devil was just made up out of fear and old nightmares. What the "devil" really was, in that conversation that he *had* recalled correctly, the thing that had been frightening the life out of the Pieters boys, hadn't been a bad thing at all. It had been Dallen, a Companion, and they had been frightened, not because Dallen was evil, but because the coming of a Companion meant that their entire mining operation, based as it was on slavery, cruelty, exploitation, and murder, was going to be exposed. They had known that there was no way that the Companion had come for one of them. Every single one of them was complicit in how the mine-kiddies were mistreated and abused, and no Companion would come for someone who would sit back and allow that sort of thing to happen. That meant that Dallen had to be there for one of the mine-kiddies . . . and eventually, no matter what threats held him silent before, as soon as the kid knew he was safe, the truth would come out. Or else, if he remained silent and terrified, they would work a Truth Spell on him, or have a Healer look into his mind and find out.

When that happened — as, indeed, it had, when the truth had come out of Mags — they would be in more trouble than they could possibly imagine.

No wonder they had been petrified. No wonder they had tried to shoot Dallen . . .

Not that they'd ever had any chance of actually hurting the Companion. All things considered, it was unlikely that any of the boys would have been able to hit a barn, much less a Companion as agile and clever as Dallen. None of them were marksmen, though they liked to think that they were. They were never given the leisure to practice, for one thing. Cole Pieters made sure his boys were no good with anything that might be used as a weapon, other than the crudest implements of club and ax. The mine-kiddies were better marksmen with rocks than the Pieters boys were with any weapon.

But despite their father's orders, probably they hadn't been shooting to hurt — because the penalty for harming a Companion was life in penal servitude, and not even their father's threats would convince them to risk that — but to drive Dallen away. A stupid idea, since a Companion on Search couldn't be driven away from his Chosen with a drakken, but the Pieters boys were all very stupid. Sly, but stupid.

And then, when Herald Jakyr had turned up, summoned by Dallen's frantic demands to *his* Companion, it was too late. Not even Cole Pieters would dare harm a Herald. Jakyr — that was probably where his mind had gotten the name *Jak* from. He'd never known a "Jak" in the mine that was near to his own age, near enough to have haunted him.

Oh, it all came back to him now.

And so did the memories connected with that rooftop. Or at least he *thought* he knew what had happened, because whatever had occurred, it had been very fast indeed, and he didn't have any actual *memory* of when he'd been taken down, much less what had done it.

But he remembered going up on the roof, as always. He'd been minding the shop alone. Dallen was at the inn. Everything had been completely normal, other than the fact that the sky was overcast and there was fog coming up off the river. He'd felt that "watching" sensation, just like always. He had paused to take his bearings before a lightning run across the rooftops to get away from it as quickly as he could, because it was still giving him the crawlies to feel those unseen eyes on him.

And then, out of nowhere, he felt . . . something. Whether it was that the watcher had alerted these two men, or that the watcher had, itself, somehow moved to strike him unconscious, he didn't know. There had just been that flash of knowledge, the certainty that *something changed,* and then nothing.

Dallen! Dallen must be frantic by now!

He dropped all his shields — because Dallen must be pretty far away at this point, and he was going to need all the reach he could get —

That is, he tried to drop all his shields. But it was as if he didn't have shields to drop. Or the shields weren't his.

Or his Mindspeech had somehow been cut away.

It felt like a blow to the gut. It left him gasping, literally gasping, as if someone had ripped out his innards, and he was in too much shock to feel pain. And he must have made enough sound that the men at the front of the wagon heard him. The wagon stopped again, and as Mags felt rising panic, he heard the footsteps coming around, felt the man get into the wagon, felt the hand in his hair.

Then it was as he remembered from his nightmares, and the waterskin was forced into his mouth, and all he could manage to do was keep his eyes shut and to drink as little as possible. He was afraid to let too much of the liquid dribble out of his mouth. It was broad daylight, and his captors would see and force more down his throat. Obviously they wanted him for *something,* but without Mindspeech, he hadn't a clue as to what that would be. Or *could* be.

He only knew for sure that he had to stay lucid, somehow. Had to keep his awareness of who and what he was.

The man finally let him back down into his cavity, and wave after wave of vertigo swept over him, until finally feverish delirium took him.

But now, he knew what that was. And he clung on tightly to his knowledge of himself. *My name is Mags. I'm a Herald Trainee. My Companion is Dallen . . .*

He wouldn't think about what not having Mindspeech would mean. He did know, at least, that there were Heralds with very little, very weak Gifts. It was the Companion that made the Herald, and surely he could keep right on doing what Nikolas was training him for even if his Mindspeech was gone forever. He'd just have to be cleverer than before.

And all right, even if he couldn't do *that,* the main job of a Herald was to see that the Kingdom's laws were known and obeyed, and you didn't need a Gift to do that. All you needed, when it came right down to it, was for people to *think* you had a Gift. He could do that.

In his feverish state he saw himself tricking people with some of the sharpster moves he had been learning from Nikolas and some of Nikolas' slightly disreputable friends. "Cold reading," was what one of the actors had called it, a fellow who had eked out his small pay from small parts by telling fortunes. If you threw enough hints out, people would tell you with their reactions if you were close to the truth, and you could soon have them convinced you could read their minds or were talking to spirits or could see the future. He claimed you didn't actually *need* the Truth Spell if you were good enough at cold reading. He could do cold reading. He'd been doing some of it on the shop customers. He could imagine himself somewhere on Circuit, in the field, being persuasive, coaxing, being . . .

He found that he was surrounded by a small group of people in rustic garments. They were angry, very angry . . .

This is a drug dream. Now he knew what that other voice inside him was. It was the part of him that still hung on to reality. Even if this felt, looked, sounded, even *smelled* like reality.

". . . stole it, I tell ye!" growled one old man, who seemed to be the leader of one side. "Stole it right out o' my pasture, she did!"

They were all crowded into what looked like the common room of a tavern. Dark, smoky wooden walls. Smells of food and beer. He was sitting at a table, the others clustered around him.

The be-aproned woman who led the opposite group snarled at him. "I no more stole it than I'm the Queen of Valdemar! *He* let it stray, it ate half my cabbages, and I'm keeping it in payment for my loss!"

She turned to the man next to her, as Mags concentrated on trying to catch all the *tells* Sieran had shown him. "Haber! You be my witness! Tell the Herald!"

The man turned to Mags, a hangdog expression on his face. *"Gabble gabble,"* he said, and waved his hands apologetically. *"Gabble, gabble gabble gabble. Gabble."*

The angry man stamped his foot and snarled. *"Gabble!"* he spat.

It's them . . . Mags managed to think through the fog and the confusion, and through the intensely *real* feeling that all this had. *It's them. The ones driving the wagon. They're talking.*

299

He couldn't quite break free of the hallucination, but part of him, at least, now knew it was a fever dream and nothing real. So when it all started to go wrong, and the crowd turned on him, he made it all stop, made it all go back to the beginning. He'd learned how to do that with his nightmares, thanks to the Healers. He still had the nightmares, but at least now he could control them.

". . . stole it, I tell ye!" growled the old man, who was complaining to Mags about a disputed goat. "Stole it right out o' my pasture, she did!"

He paid more attention to the old man this time, a wizened old goat in linen shirt and breeches and a leather apron. The old man was afraid, underneath all that bluster he was afraid of the woman. In fact, everyone was at least a little afraid of the woman. Why were they afraid?

He interrupted her when she began her response. "You're lying," he said flatly, and that was when her face stretched out and grew a set of terrible jaws, bat-wings burst out of the back of her shirt, and she reached for him with awful claws.

But again, he managed to remember, *this is drugs. This is a fever dream.* He managed to wrest control away, and send it all back to the beginning again.

". . . stole it, I tell ye!" growled the old man, whose eyes were bleak and blank. "Stole it right out o' my pasture, she did!" Mags knew what was in his mind without needing Mindspeech. He didn't expect to win, but he wasn't going to give up without a fight. He couldn't afford to. He was going to starve without that goat.

But Mags was ready this time, and the moment the woman began to change, the knife was in his hand one moment and in her throat the next, and she fell over, black blood pouring out of her throat, face caught halfway between woman and monster, as all of her neighbors stared.

Then Mags wasn't looking down at a dead woman. He was looking up at a live one. She smiled at him, and he felt transfixed with utter delight, his entire being suffused with a golden glow of happiness and well being. *"Gabble gabble gooo,"* she crooned at him. *"Gabble Meric good boy gabble."* She picked him up, and he giggled giddily. She was half his world, and he adored her so much, the source of food and warmth and comfort! *"Gabble goo goo goo,"* she whispered in his ear as she cuddled him against her breast. Her breast! The source of all things wonderful!

But he wasn't hungry right now, so he stuck his thumb in his mouth and sucked on that until she pulled it out and gave him his bappy to suck instead. He loved his bappy, a cool stone with a hole in it, just exactly the right size to pop in his mouth and ease his gums when they hurt. It sometimes annoyed him that he couldn't swallow it, it was so smooth and nice, but it was fastened quite thoroughly to a big piece of cloth that prevented him from doing so. He nestled against the Breast, the wonderful, bountiful Breast, and sucked his bappy, and fell asleep, listening to Her whisper to him. *"Gabble gabble Meric gabble . . ."*

He slept then, both in the drugged dream and probably in reality, because when he next was aware of anything at all, it was that the wagon was swaying quite a lot, it was dark, too dark to see, and he was cramping again. But he clamped his mouth shut on his moans. He didn't want his captors to realize he was awake. Eventually, he knew, they would decide it was time to drug him, and then it would be back to the hallucinations again —

Can I make them think I'm getting weaker, so the drug has more of a hold over me?

He thought maybe he could. When they got him out to take care of his bladder, he could be a little rubber-kneed. There might be other things he could do. Now that he knew what was going on, maybe he could —

The wagon stopped. He tried not to brace himself. *Stay quiet, stay limp,* he repeated to himself, over and over, just as in the mine he had repeated over and over to the ghosts to leave him alone.

And that made him think of something else entirely. What if that watching thing was somehow with them now? How would he know? Without Mindspeech he couldn't sense the thing! He felt panic churning in his gut, although enough of the drug held him still that muscles that should have been rigid with fear were just cramped and painful. It was just adding insult to injury that the drug that kept him paralyzed did nothing about the pain or the cramps. He was so caught in his tangle of fear and hurt that he didn't even realize the men were in the wagon with him until they hauled him up and out.

He didn't have to fake being weak-kneed; his muscles really were so cramped that they were not cooperating with his captors. He kept his eyes shut this time until they were done with him.

But they must have realized what being curled up was doing to him — finally.

Instead of putting him back, they hauled him with his arms draped over their shoulders some distance from where they had taken him, and laid him down, stretched out, on a blanket that was now spread out over something softish. Leaves, or pine needles, maybe. They extended all his limbs as he feigned unconsciousness. He didn't have to pretend that he couldn't move. He still couldn't, and he fought down another round of panic as he wondered if he really *was* paralyzed as well as without Mindspeech.

But . . . no. He remembered bits from Bear's chattering. People who were paralyzed couldn't feel their limbs, either, and he certainly felt his. It was just the drug. In fact, one of his hands and both of his feet were practically on fire now . . . they'd been "asleep" from pressure and now were "waking up." And his right ankle just ached from having been bent at a bad angle for so long.

He heard the sound of a fire being started with flint and tinder. After a while, he cracked one of his eyes open, just a little.

It was sunset. He couldn't see exactly where he was, but it looked like a forest, a thicker forest than the last time they'd stopped. More pines, fewer trees with leaves.

He cracked the other eye and edged his

head over by the tiniest possible increments.

Both men were engrossed in doing something over the fire, with their backs to him. Cooking, he thought. Well, that made sense, soup would go bad pretty quickly; they were obviously taking great care with him for some reason, and they wouldn't want to poison him with bad soup, so they would have to stop to make fresh fairly often.

They were talking quietly, so quietly he couldn't hear anything but a murmur.

He still couldn't imagine what they wanted with him.

One of the men got up, moving with smooth grace, then came over and stared down at him, and he tried to keep his breathing even and quiet. After a moment, the man went away, then came back again, and threw the horse-smelling blanket over him, then went back to the fire.

Disorienting waves of vertigo engulfed him as the pain and cramps eased and his limbs relaxed under the warmth of the blanket. Obviously the drug wasn't done with him yet.

Mags closed his eyes, fought off the dizziness the only way he knew how, by concentrating on everything else around him.

Sound first, that was easiest. Near at hand, the fire crackling, the two men muttering occasionally. The sound of muffled metal on metal in a regular, slow pattern. Someone was stirring food in a pot. Someone who actually knew how to cook. Mags remembered dimly, from when he worked in the Pieters' kitchen, how the cooks would end up with pots full of half-burned and ruined food because they didn't bother to set someone to stir it. Fat sizzling in the fire and the flare-ups that followed.

Farther away, the sounds of tearing and chewing. He knew those sounds, it was a horse eating grass. A horse? More than one? The stamp of a hoof. Another. Then two snorts, just slightly apart in time. Two horses, then. No harness jingling. So, they were definitely here for the night.

Under the cover of the blanket and between waves of dizziness he tried wiggling fingers or curling toes, but nothing happened. Back to listening, then.

Leaves moving in a slight breeze, and a moment later, that same breeze cooled his forehead. The sound of something small moving through the underbrush. A couple of birds he couldn't identify in the middle distance, and far, far off, the faint honks of a flock of geese.

No sounds whatsoever that were man-made except those of his captors.

That disposed of sound. Smell?

Nearest, the stink of his own sweat. No surprise, given how he'd sweated his clothing until it was soaked. Under that, the faint smell of crushed pine needles. The fire gave off a slightly different aroma than he was used to. Meat cooking, both the sharp scent of meat cooking directly over the fire and the more mellow aroma of meat cooking in water. So they were making their own dinner as well as his soup. And there was a baking-bread smell, although, again, it wasn't the sweet scent he was used to. From the direction of the horses came the smell of torn grass. All around, the faint and bitter smell of leaves turning.

Finally, the last of his aches melted under the warmth of the blanket. He couldn't help it; his body felt comfortable for the first time since he'd been put in the wagon, and even though he tried to fight it, between the remains of the drug and his relaxing body, he dozed. But it wasn't restful, because there was a great and terrible gulf of loss between him and any real rest.

He couldn't hear Dallen. He couldn't hear Dallen. He was all alone in his head for the first time since he'd been Chosen, and only once in all his life had he felt so completely alone, abandoned, and in despair. That was when he had decided that he didn't deserve Dallen and had tried to give up being Chosen.

It hadn't worked, of course. But now —

It felt like a bitter betrayal. Not by Dallen! By his own body, perhaps. But he'd been *promised,* faithfully, that he would never be alone again. And now he was. And it was horrible.

He wept, silently, until he was so exhausted all there was left was sleep.

When he woke again, it was to snores; his eyes were sore, and his face itched from the tears dried on it. He itched all over, from the dried sweat. They hadn't drugged him — he cautiously cracked an eye and turned his head a little to look toward the fire.

One man was curled up on his side, a lump under a blanket. The other sat with his back to Mags, poking at the fire with a stick.

It was startlingly quiet. Overhead, the stars were spread across the sky like a dusting of heavy pollen, or seeds spilled from a giant basket onto the black earth, too many and too thick to count.

With infinite care, Mags tried to move his right index finger.

It moved!

He almost cried all over again.

He tried all the fingers, one at a time, then tried the left hand, and moved on to his foot. He could move! But he wasn't going to press his luck by trying to move his arms or legs. That might alert his captor, and that was the very last thing he wanted to do right now. Now he knew approximately how long it would take for the drug to wear off, and —

Before he could finish that thought, the man at the fire straightened and tossed the stick he had been using to poke at the fire into the coals. Then he reached over and shook his fellow awake.

Time for the second watch, then.

But it seemed that it was time for more than that, as the first one reached down and picked up something next to him, and as Mags hastily closed his eyes again, he recognized with dismay the shape of the waterskin.

— *no* — he thought.

But his captors had their own plans. And there was no help for it.

All he could do was, as before, try to drink as little as possible. And then wait for the dreams to carry him away again, and cling to his knowledge of who and what he was as he was tossed around like a leaf on a storm wind, and with about as much control over his fate.

9

They had stopped giving him the drug in his food, and now it was only in his water. He must have convinced them that he was weakening, and that they didn't have to drug him so heavily anymore.

Or, maybe, they were running low, and they were trying to stretch out what they had.

The point was that his moments of clarity were longer, and he was able to move now at the end of them. In fact, he was in his curled position, secretly flexing his muscles to exercise them, when the wagon stopped.

He froze, not daring to move at all, lest he be heard.

"Where are you going, and what are you carrying?" asked a harsh voice that sent chills of fear all down his spine. Fear, because even though he understood the language, it was *not* one that he wanted to hear.

This was Karsite.

"That is none of your concern," replied one of the now-familiar male voices, heavily accented and thick with arrogance. It was an arrogance that Mags remembered only too well from the so-called "merchant-princes." *"Behold this seal, dog, and know the will of your masters. We are to go where we will and answer only to them."*

There was a long pause. Then, *"It appears real,"* the first man said, grudgingly.

"That is because it is real, hound," the second replied, voice laden with contempt. *"Go back to your meddling in the lives of the small and weak. We have important work to do and no time to waste satisfying your pitiful curiosity."*

Well . . . this was worse than he thought. As he listened to the sounds of a fairly large troop of men marching away, he felt his heart plummeting. If he'd had any doubt before, it was erased now; these were the same sorts of assassins who had been systematically trying to destroy Valdemar at the behest of Karse. They must still be holding to their contract with Karse to have a token that enabled them to be rude to the captain of a troop of Karsite regulars with impunity. So not only was he somewhere on the Karsite side of the Border, he was in the hands of people who could order Karsite soldiers around.

So very bad. Really, the only thing worse would be to be in the middle of being tortured for information.

Which . . . could happen at any point.

Because right now, for whatever reason, they were taking care of him. But if they lost the protection of that token — or if they insulted someone badly enough that he decided to ignore it — the Karsites would find *him.*

At least I'm not wearing Grays. And at least there's nothing on me that says I'm from Valdemar . . .

Not that such thin protection would last long if they were all tossed into a Karsite prison, because eventually the drug would wear off, and they'd start to question him, and if his story didn't match that of his captors . . . or they noticed his accent . . .

He started to sweat.

Maybe if that happens, I'd better pretend to be insane.

Mags could not look up at the canvas throw over his head without craning his head to the side in a way that got painful before very long, but then, there wasn't much to see, just the cloth lit from behind by whatever light was coming in through the canvas cover of the wagon. The two men babbled at each other in urgent voices as the wagon swayed and rolled over uneven ground, and the bed slanted first one way and then another. He'd thought the road they were on was rough, but now he knew he had been quite mistaken. Mags was pretty sure what they were doing, and it was exactly what he would do under the same circumstances. They might have sounded arrogant when they addressed the captain of that Karsite troop, but he reckoned now that they were not as sure of their status in Karse as they had pretended to be. So they had left the main road and taken to something less traveled.

That wasn't their only problem. He could hear thunder in the distance. They were about to get hit by a storm, and they were on what was a very bad road. That could spell a lot of trouble.

Evidently that occurred to them, too. They stopped the wagon as a peal of thunder growled for a very long time, and the light inside the wagon faded so much that he could barely make out the shapes of the things penning him in. This was going to be bad, and they knew it. But they hadn't pulled off the road, so they weren't stopping — which might, or might not, be a good plan. He didn't know a lot about driving wagons, but he did know that trying to drive horses in a storm was going to give them an enormous amount of trouble. He figured they weren't going to take any chances on him waking up during the storm, so they were going to drug him now.

Dammit! Under cover of a storm, of course, would give him the best possible chance at escape. Even if they pulled off the road, he would have a chance of overpowering them and getting away.

But there wasn't anything he could do about it — except that, as they poured the drugged water into him, to let as much as he could dribble out one side of his mouth, counting on it being so dark they wouldn't notice.

Only one of them came around to the back and got in. By the little lurches the wagon was making, the horses were nervous and the driver didn't dare leave them unattended. Mags let about half the water leak out of the side of his mouth, and evidently the man feeding it to him didn't see it. He even held the last mouthful and spit it out once he'd been laid down again.

But being stopped had meant that they hadn't fed him the soup, either, so since his stomach was completely empty, the drug hit him fast. All he could take note of when he passed into a dream of being huddled with the other mine-kiddies in their pit under the barn floor during a thunderstorm was that he still hadn't been curled back up in his cavity, and the fellow was doing a lot of moving things on the other side of the wagon.

This time, he came awake all at once, as an enormous *boom* nearby made the horses scream. The wagon lurched and swayed wildly. And *he* was in complete darkness.

He didn't panic, because for once, on waking, he knew exactly where he was. Except — he wasn't curled up. He was stretched out, and he felt wood pinning him in on all sides. Not coffin-tight, but he hadn't a lot of room to move, either, except at his head and his feet. The blanket had been laid over him. A moment later, as another bolt of lightning hit nearby with a simultaneous crash of thunder, the wagon rocked and bucked, and he felt boxes and bales hit the side of whatever it was he was in. If he'd been in his usual position, by now he probably would have had every bone in his body broken by stuff falling on him. He didn't think he was in a coffin, because why would they have a coffin with them? That would be just daft — no one transported bodies in coffins for very far except the very rich, who could afford to have the bodies of their loved ones preserved. A coffin in a common wagon would just attract attention. But they had probably unpacked some sort of equipment from this box and stuffed him in it to protect him, knowing what was going to happen as they continued down these terrible roads in a storm.

I guess I'm worth quite a bit if they're taking that kind of care of me.

They might have thought the storm would blow itself out or that they could get to the other side of it, and by the time they realized how wrong they were, it was too late and too dark to stop.

He couldn't move — yet — but he sensed he had a fair amount of room in this thing, whatever it was. And if ever he was going to get a chance to escape . . . yes, he might be able to manage it, even now.

As the wagon lurched and rolled, and rain sluiced over the top and sides, as lightning struck and thunder boomed, he worked his fingers and toes until life came back into his limbs. Once he could feel fingers and toes moving normally, he flexed his muscles until they all came back to life. Then he tried simply lifting the top of the box.

No good. Something had it fastened down tight. He didn't dare pound at it, not now, not when he was within an arm's length of his captors. He tried to remember what he had seen of the wagon itself. It wasn't much like a solid wooden gypsy or minstrel caravan or a prosperous trader's wagon; it was more like a farmer's wagon, except with a round, tentlike canvas top held up by hoops of wood over it all. Had there been a drop-down flap at the back? Or — could his luck be good enough that there was no back to it at all?

He decided that it didn't matter. His plan involved getting out the back, and that was what he was going to have to do, even if it meant smashing through whatever was blocking him.

So, when the wagon was lurching and wallowing down a hill, he used his weight to slide the box he was in to the front of the wagon, and when it was going up, he did the same, only moving to the back. He hoped that he was shoving the rest of the cargo out of the way, but it was impossible to tell from inside. He *was* sliding farther each time. And his captors were too busy fighting their panicked horses to pay much attention to what was going on behind them.

And then it happened.

Another bolt of lightning smashed into the ground so near to them that he *felt* it, felt the shock, felt the hair stand up all over his body, smelled the sharp scent of the lightning itself and the scorched smell of the earth. Thunder hammered them. The horses screamed, and the wagon lurched forward into a downhill run that sent everything in the wagon bouncing and flying, including him and his box. He braced himself inside it, getting bone-bruising jounces as the box danced all over the floor of the wagon, but knowing from the impacts on the top that however bad it was in the box, it was much worse outside it.

Fueled by hysterical strength, the horses lurched up the next hill. A huge bounce gave him the moment he needed, and he shifted as much of his weight to the foot of the box as he could. The box went skidding toward the back of the wagon. And this time . . . he felt it teeter on the edge, balancing there for one precarious moment.

And then the wagon lurched again, and the box went flying into the storm and the night. It hit the ground, knocking all the breath out of him, then began rolling and bouncing down a steep slope.

Desperately, he splayed out his limbs and braced himself inside.

The slope was certainly steep enough, and he had enough momentum, that it just kept tumbling. The blanket they had wrapped him in tangled up around him and cushioned the blows a little, but not much. It felt as if he were being beaten; it was almost impossible to keep entirely braced.

And then, sickeningly, he felt — falling. And the thought flashed through his mind that the end of the fall would be at the bottom of some horrible chasm.

But the fall ended, quickly, in a splash.

And water immediately started pouring in the seams of the box.

Now he began frantically kicking and pounding at the sides of the box; he had no idea which was the top, and all he could think of was drowning, trapped in this thing, as icy water soaked him, and his kicks and flailing blows splashed water about wildly.

But then he felt the box settle, only half full of water.

His relief was short-lived, however. A moment later, he felt it shift with the pressure of the water rushing around it, and he knew in a moment it could be swept into deeper water, where he would almost certainly drown. But with that brief respite of relief, he knew he had to concentrate his efforts on the one place where he could get the most impact from his blows.

Not the sides of the box, but the foot.

He wriggled until he got his arms stretched up and braced against the head of the box, and began to kick downward with all his strength.

After his legs started to hurt, fear gave him new strength. And as the box shifted in the current again, he finally felt the wood give.

More hysterical blows later, as the box shifted into slightly deeper water, and he was having trouble keeping his head above it, he felt the bottom pop out. He eeled out faster than he would have believed, somehow having the presence of mind to bring his blanket with him, and not a moment too soon. As he scrambled for the bank, he could see clearly in the nearly continuous flashes of lightning, the box ripped away from the rocks it had landed among and spun away into the darkness. He clutched the corner of the blanket between his teeth and scrabbled desperately with hands and feet through water that pulled at him, until he finally managed to fling himself onto the bank, panting and half-dead.

All he wanted to do was lie there and not move. But he knew he didn't dare. First, the water was rising; he could feel it climbing higher on his legs. Second, he thought he could hear shouting somewhere above. And third, he knew that if he did remain lying there, the wet and the cold would get him, and he would very probably die of the cold if the water didn't carry him off first. Somehow he managed to get to his feet, wrap the blanket around himself, and stagger off along the shore of the raging stream.

He had no real idea of what direction to go in. He had no idea where in Karse he was. He didn't know where the wagon was, either, except that he was pretty sure he was still on the same side of the water as it was. All he could do was try to put as much distance between himself and his captors as he could.

So he went upstream, away from where the box was spinning away on the current, because with luck, they would go in the opposite direction, assuming he was being carried away by the water.

He staggered on long past the point of exhaustion, long past the time when his limbs burned with fatigue and his mind blurred. There was only the fight to keep putting one foot in front of the other and keep that wool blanket clutched around himself. The only light he had to see by was the lightning, which showed no sign of abating.

So as long as there was light to see by, he forced himself to move on, stumbling over fallen branches and rocks, finally grasping at tree trunks to help move himself along. His lungs burned, his sides ached, his legs and feet were a torment. The rain pounded his hair flat, and only the fact that the blanket was wool was keeping him from freezing to death. And even so, it was so heavy with the added weight of the water that it was a terrible temptation to let it fall off his shoulders and leave it behind.

Finally, just when he thought he was going to just drop down where he stood — and in fact, was swaying with fatigue — a bolt of lightning revealed the entire face of the hill above him. And he thought he saw —

Another bolt flashed across the sky as he peered at the spot.

It looked like a sort of cave, under the roots of an enormous tree.

It was the best he was going to get at this point.

He staggered up the slope, groping toward the promise of shelter. When he finally reached it and clawed his way in through dangling roots and vines, he found a musty-smelling — but dry — den, full of blown-in leaves. There was also a sort of animal smell, but it was old, and at this point he would have happily shared the space with whatever creature had made it home. Or snakes. Or mice or bugs or any other thing. He didn't so much crawl in as fall in, wind himself tightly in his precious blanket, and plummet into the first undrugged sleep he'd had since the ordeal started.

His belly woke him, growling like an unsated animal.

He was sorry he was awake, once he opened his eyes and moved a little. Every muscle in his entire body was whimpering in protest when he moved the least little bit. His stomach felt as if it was gnawing on his backbone. It growled even as he thought that.

Shut up, stomach.

The first thing he *wanted* to do was to try and reach Dallen, but the moment he woke, he knew from the feeling in his head that his Mindspeech was still gone.

And he couldn't help it. Despair hit him like a rock, a despair so black and deep that it took him over like that storm. He cried, then. Cried until his nose was clogged, his eyes were sore, and his voice had turned into a hoarse croak. Was Dallen even *alive*? Dallen would have come rushing to his rescue the moment things fell apart, and these bastards had to know about Companions by now, what they were, how important they were. How a Companion would go through fire and hell itself to get to his Chosen. So had they waited? Had they stayed just long enough to ambush and murder?

Gods, I swear by my life, if you let that happen, I will track you all down to your lofty homes and kill you.

His thought actually wasn't that coherent. It was more like a simple wail of anguish and the vague threat of mayhem in the heavens if Dallen was gone.

That started the sobs all over again, until he was so exhausted by grief that all he could do was lie there and watch the sun move on the other side of the roots and vines. He wished in that moment that he had the strength to crawl to the water he could hear rushing by out there, fling himself in, and drown.

It was his own exhaustion that saved him, but it was the stubborn will to live that had kept him going in the mine that dragged him out of his grief. A stubborn will to live that presented him with logic instead of emotion.

They can't have killed him. He wouldn't have come alone.

And he knew at once that was true. Of course he wouldn't have. He was Dallen. Dallen, who had as much experience with these bastards as Mags did and knew to expect the unexpected from them. Dallen would *never* have just rushed after Mags, not without help.

If it was the hit on the head that took your Mindspeech, he might have "lost" you right away anyway.

That was possibly true . . . he still wasn't entirely certain how his bond with Dallen worked . . . but it did stand to reason that if he couldn't sense Dallen, then Dallen couldn't sense him, either.

You don't know that your Mindspeech is gone forever until you see a Mindhealer.

That was true, too.

And it was all enough to get him to crawl, aching and weary, to the vines, part them a little, and look cautiously out.

Cautiously, because it occurred to him that it would be just his luck to find himself staring at the backs — or worse, the faces — of his kidnappers.

But there was nothing to be seen out there but the dangerously high waters of that stream — not so much a stream as a small river, raging at both banks and full of big branches and debris — the steeply sloping bank covered in vines, and the nearly identical bank on the other side.

He crawled carefully out into the sunlight. At least the rain had done him one favor. He wasn't filthy and stinking anymore. In fact, he and the blanket were remarkably clean. He pulled the still-damp blanket out after him, spread it out in the sunlight, and considered his options.

There was one thing he remembered about Karse. It was south of Valdemar. So if he went north, it stood to reason that eventually he'd get across the Border. He wished he had some idea of how long his captors had held him, but by the look of things around him, it was really autumn now. He had been correct, although some trees were still green, many had begun to turn, so there had already been one good frost. That was both good and bad. Good, because as he remembered from his scrounging when he was a mine-slavey, next to all the young plants of spring, fall was the time of the most abundant wild food. He probably should avoid berries unless he actually recognized them, but there would be nuts and seeds, for sure. But fall was bad, because winter was coming, and the only thing he had between himself and winter's cold was a single blanket.

I did all right with as much in the mine, he reminded himself. *As long as I find myself shelter every night, I'll do all right.*

He was woefully lacking in everything else, though. Short of navigating by the sun, he had no idea how to keep himself going in the right direction. He hadn't yet taken any of the wilderness survival classes at the Collegium, nor the classes in how to find directions, nor the ones where you memorized detailed maps. He didn't have a knife, a bow, or any other sort of weapon.

Well, time to fix that.

All his crying had at least done one thing; his stomach was so upset now he wasn't the least bit hungry. Thirsty, though . . .

He made his way with some difficulty down to the river, clambered over the rocks, and scooped up handfuls of the icy water, splashing some over his sore eyes after he'd drunk. He looked with longing at the flashing silver forms farther away. He had more chance of flying home than he did of catching those fish. Even if he'd had fishing line and a hook, he didn't know *how* to fish.

But he filled his pocket with river pebbles that were as close to round as he could get, and then experimentally pulled up some of the smaller tendrils of vine. After he stripped the leaves away, he found to his relief that the stems shredded into tough, flexible threads. He could work with this.

A candlemark or so later, his skills at weaving horsehair had yielded him a sling, a stick with a formidable, triangle-shaped rock bound into the fork at one end, and a few arm-lengths of cord. He used part of the cord to bind his blanket around his body and then formed a kind of sling out of it at the back by knotting opposite corners over his chest. Now his hands were free, he had a way to carry things, and he had two weapons, both of which he knew how to use, and use well.

Fortunately, the stream was coming from the direction he wanted to be going — north. He tried not to think too hard about what he would have to do if he was forced to leave his source of water.

Deal with that when it happened.

As he walked, he turned over rocks ahead of him. Almost at once he was rewarded with a redbug, a little crustacean that had pinchers on the front and a most delicious tail. Those had been great prizes back at the mine, and he refused to think about how good it would taste tossed in a fire for a moment. He didn't have a fire, and he'd eaten them raw before. He pounced, and a moment later he was sucking out the meat and the guts, then cracking the claws between his teeth to get the little meat that was in them as well.

He had to stop at noon, afraid he would lose his bearings with the sun overhead, but by then he had caught and eaten a half dozen more redbugs and a handful of cress. His stomach was less than pleased with this meager fare, but he'd lived on less at the mine, and he kept telling himself as much. He was on sharp lookout for cattails. If he could find cattails, he could sleep with a full stomach.

While he waited for the sun to move on, he scanned the bank above him, looking for anything that looked like one of the nut-bearing trees he was familiar with — or, indeed, anything else that might be of use.

Then, while he was at it, he looked for the signs of humans.

Not that he was going to approach any Karsites — but if he got a chance, he'd steal from them.

In order, what he needed as much as food were something to use for a knife, something to carry water, and a way to make and carry fire. He could do without fire for a while;

there were a lot of things he could and would eat raw, and the blanket and a little shelter would keep him warm at night for now. He could do without carrying water as long as he didn't stray from the river.

But he was already feeling the lack of a knife. He knew in theory he could make a knife by fracturing a flint rock — but what did flint look like? He had no idea.

While he waited, he caught and ate a few more redbugs. Each one helped ease the hunger pains in his stomach. And he made some more cord from the ubiquitous vines. He tried tasting the leaves to see if they were edible, but, sadly, they were too bitter to choke down.

He resolved to stop as soon as he saw any place that would serve as shelter for the night. It would be much better to stop early and *have* shelter; he could use the extra time to hunt for more food. At least when it came to food, he was not as completely in the dark as someone who had grown up in a city would be.

But right now, he would cheerfully have murdered someone for a knife, a fire-starter, a little iron pot, and a waterskin.

As he worked his way along the riverside, he took anything he saw that looked potentially useful. A few more stones for his sling.

Some clamshells, and he wished that he knew how to find live clams. He hesitated over the skeletal remains of a very large fish and finally took some of the rib bones. About midafternoon, he spotted another cave, a real one this time, and that decided him. It was time to stop and make camp.

It wasn't so much a cave as a washed out area beneath a rock overhang — not sheltered enough for an animal to make a den, but the fact that the dirt in the back was dry proved it would keep off another storm. He left everything he had gathered in the cave and went down to the river to forage for food in good earnest.

The redbugs were thick here. He actually managed to eat enough to fill his stomach. There was still plenty of light, so he marked the overhang with his blanket spread out and went up the slope, checking back to make sure he could see it as he went.

And just as he was about to turn back, his diligence was rewarded with a hickory tree.

It was the squirrels that told him it was there; they had been busily foraging among the leaves for the nuts, and chattered at him angrily for disturbing them. He went to his hands and knees as soon as he realized what he had found, and by the time he was weary, the front of his shirt bulged with his bounty.

Careful not to lose a single one, he made his way back down to his shelter, cached the nuts, and gathered more of the vines. This time he knotted the strands into a very fine-meshed net bag to hold the nuts; by the time it was finished, it was almost dark. He went down to the river for a final drink, then came back, secured all of his treasures behind him, wrapped up in his blanket, and lay down as far in the rear of the shelter as he could get.

It was a good thing he took that precaution too.

Some time during the night, another storm rolled in. This one wasn't as intense or nearly as long as the first, but it did have a great deal of lightning, and it woke him up out of a sound sleep.

It was just as cold as the other storm, too. He wondered, as he watched the river rage below him, if this sort of weather was normal for autumn here. Dallen would have known, probably. The mere thought made him ache for the sound of Dallen's Mind-voice in the back of his head.

But the place he was in now looked as if it had been washed out. That argued for the river coming all the way up here at least now and again. So these sorts of storms probably were the norm.

On the other hand, the hillsides hadn't been scoured bare, so floods probably weren't usual. He did resolve to keep an eye on the water level from now on, however, because a storm he wouldn't even see a *hint* of upstream could send a torrent racing toward him.

Finally, exhaustion and a full stomach sent him back into sleep again, despite the lightning and thunder.

By the third day, and a happy accident, he realized he *had* his knife. In reaching back into the blanket-pouch for cattail root, he cut himself on one of the clamshells. He had cursed at first, then, suddenly realizing what had happened, he had actually laughed aloud. He made a point of collecting every shell big enough to be useful after that, especially the broken ones. With a knife, he could cut strips from his shirt hem to use to make a better pocket for his sling. With a knife, he could peel the cattail roots and not have to chew the root, bark and all, and spit out what he couldn't eat. With a knife, he could sharpen sticks to a good point for crude spears.

He was very, very glad he had those crude spears when he heard voices on the afternoon of the fourth day.

They were speaking Karsite, and they were coming from somewhere above him.

He had already found his shelter for the night; or, rather, he had dug it for himself. He had found an enormous, downed tree, and he had patiently enlarged a hollow under it and lined it with dead leaves. He had just finished peeling his dinner of cattail roots and was about to go down to the water to see if he could augment them with redbugs, when he heard the voices.

"Make camp here," ordered one. *"You and you, go down to the river and bring up enough water to hold us through the night. You and you, dig the latrine pit. I don't want anyone out of camp after dark. Nobody goes outside the perimeter."*

Quickly, he gathered everything up and tucked himself back in under the log, pulling the weeds up and toward him to conceal the opening. Just in time, too. Shortly, a couple of men in identical brown tunics came blundering down the hill, hung all over with what looked like waterskins, like pods hanging off a tree. He peered longingly at them. Oh, what he would have given for a chance to snatch one!

No such luck. It was broad daylight, and there were two of them. Even if he'd had the skills of a thief in a tale, that would have been suicidal.

They filled their skins in the river, complaining about the cold and wet, and lumbered back up the slope, grumbling loudly the entire time about how heavy the water weighed. Evidently their captain heard them. *"Quit your bellyaching and move, or I'll make you march with them all day tomorrow!"*

After that, no one came down to the river, and from upslope came the sounds of men making camp. Or at least, that was what Mags assumed the sounds meant. Wood chopping, digging, hammering, the voice barking orders, the sound of a couple of mules — mules and not horses, as he heard one of them bray, startlingly loud in the absence of other animal sounds. The men were sent back down for water again, which made sense now that he knew about the mules, since the mules would need as much water as a couple of men. They had probably used up a goodly share of the water from the first run setting up a watering trough for the mules and taking care of cooking and washing needs. This would be the water that would hold them through the night. Then, as the sun began to set and the valley filled with shadows, there was the sound of at least one fire, the smell of woodsmoke and cooking, and men talking. It was impossible to hear what they were saying over the rushing river below him, but the cooking smells nearly drove Mags mad. It seemed a punishment designed specifically to torment him, to be cramped in his damp little cave, chewing on a raw cattail root, while above him were men warming themselves at a crackling fire and eating cooked food.

He reminded himself of all the times he'd smelled the good dinners the Pieters were eating while he and the other kiddies huddled over their watery soup and single piece of bread. And he *had* food. He'd filled up on redbugs before he stopped, and he still had lots of hickory nuts and cattail roots. He muffled a nut in his blanket, cracked it between two stones, and ate it slowly, reminding himself to enjoy the rich taste. He peeled and ate another root, then another nut. He concentrated on how good they tasted, the rich taste of the nut, the slightly sweet crunch of the root, and how much more satisfying they were than soup that had barely one sad shred of cabbage in every four spoonfuls. It helped; in fact, it helped tremendously.

He didn't dare sleep, however. Despite the officer's order that no one was to leave the camp after dark, he didn't dare take the chance that someone would, anyway. So instead of sleeping, he dozed as lightly as he could, listening for the sound of clumsy footfalls coming down the hill over the sound of the river.

He was startled awake by the blat of an inexpertly sounded horn at dawn, and he spent the next couple of candlemarks listening intently. Four men came blundering down the slope this time, laden with waterskins. Halfway up, he heard someone curse. Someone else said, *"Leave it. It's probably bust in the fall."*

His heart leaped. Was there a chance, was there even a chance —

He maintained his silent vigil, however. *If* it was a waterskin that the man had dropped, it might very well have broken in the fall, and he had no way of mending it. Or the captain might send someone down after it anyway. Or it might not have been a waterskin after all.

So he peeled a root and ate it, slowly, taking tiny bites. Peeled another and ate it. Ignored the smell of hot food as best he could, although the smell of cooking meat was extremely hard to take. Listened as hard as he could and watched through his curtain of weeds.

Finally he heard what he had been hoping

337

for: the jingle of harness, the rattle of wheels on rock, and the tramp of feet. And all of it going downstream, away from him.

Had this been the same group that had stopped his kidnappers?

He was pretty certain they were just patrolling, not looking for him specifically. His kidnappers had kept him carefully concealed, after all, so unless for some reason he'd been taken on the orders of someone high up in the chain of Karsite authority, no one in Karse knew he was here. So these fellows might be looking for interlopers, bandits, and troublemakers, but not specifically him.

He'd been very, very careful about the traces he had left behind. He'd tossed everything he couldn't eat into the river to be carried away and scattered. When he pulled up cattails, he was generally using the fibrous leaves to make twisted cordage while he walked, the redbug shells from the bugs he ate vanished into the river immediately, and so did the cattail peelings. There was nothing in the places where he'd slept to show that it hadn't been an animal that had denned there. He didn't leave tool marks on anything, because he didn't have tools. He'd walked on rock to avoid leaving human footprints.

He didn't think they'd find any trace of him.

And even if they did, *they* were not the ones hunting him. They had come from the opposite direction of his kidnappers. He just had to hope his kidnappers didn't meet up with them.

He hoped, even if they did find something, they would assume he was a native Karsite, a hunter or a vagabond. It wasn't as if they had any way of telling the nationality of whoever had left some broken nutshells.

He waited a good long time before moving out of his shelter, and when he did, it was cautiously. With a careful eye uphill, just in case someone came back, he crept down to the river until he found the spot where the men had been filling their skins. He looked upslope. Their path was painfully obvious, with torn up weeds, bare patches where they had dug their feet into the soil, and everything trampled. Slowly, telling himself not to hope, he worked his way up the slope, examining their path for a couple of arm lengths past the trampled area, looking for whatever they had dropped.

And his heart leaped when he spotted it — a round, brown shape caught in the middle of a scraggly bush, hidden from above by the leaves but visible from below. They'd have had to get down here to spot it. No wonder they hadn't wanted to go back.

Scarcely daring to believe his luck, he worked his way into the thorny tangle, suffering his fair share of scratches on the way in before his hand closed around it. And he shed a bit of blood on the way out, too. But when he drew it out, he could have shouted for joy.

Not a waterskin, but a water gourd, which was probably why they hadn't bothered to go after it. Gourds were easily grown, easily replaced, and cheap. This one wasn't broken, and the stopper was still rammed securely in the neck. It was obvious what had happened — the carrying-strap had snapped. A Sun-In-Glory had been inked with a stamp onto the side, meaning it was Karsite army issue and not someone's personal property — probably part of the equipage for the mules. Another reason why they wouldn't care. If they had lost someone's personal waterskin, there would have been words at the very least, but losing a bit of the army equipment was unlikely to generate any repercussions.

A water bottle! He had a water bottle!

That was the second of his needs taken care of!

Emboldened by his luck, he climbed up to the camp. Who knew? They might have left something else behind. When you have plenty of equipment, you can think about leaving things that are broken.

They had at least piled their trash in a tidy heap, which showed good discipline — but when he took a stick and poked through the remains of the fire in the fire pit — there were still coals!

Something about *coals* twinged something in his memory. What was it?

Was there a way to carry coals with you to start a fire when you didn't have a fire-starter? Yes! That was it!

While he waited for his mind to relax enough for the information to come to the surface, he built the coals back up a little. As long as he had a fire, there was no reason not to roast some cattail roots. And while he waited for them to bake, he turned over the trash pile and found treasures.

Half a knife blade. A real knife blade! It looked as if some idiot had been using it to try to pry something apart and had snapped it in half. He could make himself a wooden handle, and he'd have a short, but usable, knife. Two broken water gourds, one snapped off at the neck and one cracked across the bottom. An assortment of broken or worn pieces of leather; from the looks of things, the men had been put to work mending some of their gear and the mule harness. Some torn, stained, burned cloth. In short, between last night and now, he had been *given* virtually everything he had asked for.

That was when his memory finally let the information about carrying fire float to the surface.

He hunted for damp moss, and when he found it, he carefully lined one of the half gourds with it, the one that had the crack across the bottom. Then he scooped up one of the best coals with a clamshell and rolled it into the gourd, then covered it with hot ashes and more moss. He made a carrying net with bits of cordage and fitted it to the gourd, then did the same for the intact water gourd. He wrapped the leather and cloth around the knife blade and smaller bits, stowed all of that in the other broken gourd, then tucked that in the back of his blanket sling with his other sparse gear. Last of all, he *really* put out the fire, tidied the trash pile, ate his roasted roots, then made his way down to the river again, carefully making sure to step in the same places the

Karsites had.

That night, he had the first cooked meal he had enjoyed since the drugged soup.

The fire that he made was tiny, and he made certain to build it under the shelter of the overhanging rock he camped beneath to disperse the smoke. He ringed it with his sling pebbles, and when they were hot enough, he teased them away from the flames and used a clamshell to scoop them up and drop them into the other broken gourd, which was now full of water and redbugs. While the redbugs steeped in hot water, cooking slowly, and his cattail roots roasted in the fire, he whittled down a split piece of branch into a handle for his new knife, fitted it to the blade, and bound the whole tightly with his vine cord.

"Redbugs" were actually green or greenish brown when alive; they turned red when cooked. Cooking them in the barely simmering water heated by the stones was the best way because it didn't take very long to cook that tiny amount of meat, and the more you cooked it the tougher it got.

Mind, he'd have eaten leather, and enjoyed it, at this point.

He sighed with satisfaction as he ate his bugs and his roots, drank the slightly gritty, bug-flavored water, then banked the fire for the night. Now he had everything he needed as soon as he was forced to stop following the river. Cookpot, water carrier, fire, and a knife.

He was one step closer to home.

He slept very well that night.

10

It was a good thing that he'd found the Karsite camp when he had, because by afternoon of the very next day, the river took an abrupt turn to the west, and when he climbed the slope and a tree above it to see where it was going, it appeared to be heading straight west for as far as he could see.

He got down out of the tree and had to sit for a moment, as he found himself completely overcome with panic.

All this time, he'd been following this watercourse, and it had been a reliable source for water, food, and shelter. Now he would have to leave it. And now he would be completely at the mercy of the Karsite lands.

And, of course, he was increasing his chance of running into Karsites themselves.

He told himself to stay calm, but it didn't help. He was scared. This wasn't something he'd ever done before. All of his ability to survive depended on things he had learned at the mine, where he'd had a reliable source of water and learned how to catch slow-moving things he found in the ponds and pick wild, growing things he could rely on. He didn't really know what the Karsite lands would or could offer. He was pretty sure he would be a terrible hunter. Once away from the river he had no idea how he was going to find water. He wasn't sure he was ready to hunt for shelter away from the riverbank, which provided a lot of over-hangs. Aside from the cattails, hickory nuts, cress, and redbugs, there hadn't been much of anything he had recognized as food.

And he had no idea how to find his way if the trees got too thick to see the sun.

Nor did he have any notion of what animals out here were dangerous. Were there wolves? Bears?

He wouldn't have worried if he'd still had Mindspeech, or, at least, not so much. He'd have been able to sense animals before they got close, and he would *hear* peoples' thoughts in plenty of time to get out of sight. Now . . . he was half blind, and the thought made his mouth dry with fear.

But there was no hope for it. He had no idea where in Karse he was, except that it couldn't have been more than a fortnight by wagon south of the Valdemar Border, because he was pretty sure he hadn't been unconscious for much more than that. He could walk at about half the speed of a wagon, and he wasn't confined to roads. So by that reckoning, he didn't have much more than half a moon before he'd be home and safe. Or, at least, he'd be reasonably close to the Border.

But if he went wandering off his northward path, there was no telling where he'd end up or how long it would take him. He *had* to get across before the snows began. He didn't think he could survive too many winter nights with just a blanket.

He took a last, longing look at the river, which had become a sort of friend. Then he turned his back on it and headed northward.

As the sound of the waters faded away, he reminded himself to always go downhill if he could. He would have the best chance of finding more water in the low spots. Water must be his first concern now; you could go quite some time without food, but no more than three days without water.

If he hadn't found that gourd . . .

Head north . . . try to stay downhill.

And now he discovered yet another "try to stay . . ." because the mine-kiddies had scoured the immediate area of the mine so thoroughly that it was — he suddenly saw — nothing at all like a wild forest. There was a *lot* of undergrowth. And he was trying not to leave traces of his passing.

His estimate of how long it was going to take to get to the Border shot alarmingly skyward.

No hope for it. I just have to take it one step at a time. Literally.

Keeping the sun at his right, he began picking his way across the forest floor.

It was hard not to feel both frustrated and discouraged. There had to be a hundred things around him that he could use to help him, if only he knew what they were. He didn't dare touch the mushrooms he passed. He *did* find an oak tree and gathered a lot of nuts, but until he found more water than what he was carrying, he had no way to get the bitter taste out of them. He could hear squirrels scolding him, but he couldn't see them to try to get a shot off with his sling. He had to stop when the sun was overhead, so he checked on his coal (it was still glowing) and climbed a tree to try to scout out his path.

He couldn't get high enough to actually see anything without the tree swaying alarmingly, so he climbed back down and had a sparse meal of cattail roots.

By midafternoon he hadn't come across any sort of shelter or water, and he was beginning to feel unease. Should he count on finding water in the morning and try to make some sort of crude shelter now? Or should he try to find water and hope there was shelter nearby?

The distant growl of thunder decided him.

This time the storm was relatively slow moving. It didn't arrive until after nightfall. He had managed to find an evergreen tree with flat, frond-like "needles," and had stacked cut branches three layers deep on a lean-to frame lashed between two trees. He'd piled more of the branches on the ground beneath it to keep him — hopefully — up out of the water and mud. He got his little fire started in what he hoped was the most sheltered part of the lean-to, and by the time the storm arrived, he had cracked and roughly ground up two handfuls of acorns, which were now tied up in bags of that burned and stained cloth he had salvaged, waiting for the rain to wash the bitterness out of them. He'd eaten two roasted cattail roots and was wrapped in his blanket, just waiting for the storm to hit.

When it did, he was glad that fear had invested his preparations. Some people would probably have thought that he was using up too much cordage on lashing down his shelter. Some people might have told him that three layers of branches were too much.

They'd all have been dead wrong.

There were leaks, but the only bad one was providential — he put his watergourd right underneath it and let it fill before poking at the branches cautiously until it somehow went away. His fire remained, burning bravely, although it gave out no warmth at all. He was very glad for the layer of green boughs on the ground.

It was cold. Although there were no major leaks on him, a mist of fine rain came at him through the open side of the lean-to.

He told himself all the ways he was lucky. He had water to wash out the acorn meal, so he had food for tomorrow. He had basic shelter, so he wasn't going to get soaked and freeze. His fire was safe. *Nothing* was going to be out hunting in this weather. Bears, wolves, or whatever — they were doing the same thing that he was, crouching down in their shelters and trying to get some sleep.

He did sleep, though he didn't dare sleep much because he had to keep feeding his little fire bits of things to keep it alive.

Finally, at some point during the night,

the storm moved out, although as far as he could tell, the sky remained overcast.

There wasn't anything he could do about "not leaving traces" now; he planned on taking the shelter down, and had carefully used his cordage in such a fashion that he could salvage it all, but there was going to be a ravaged tree and a pile of cut branches when he was done.

On the other hand, it wasn't as if he'd seen any signs of humans here. There hadn't even been anything like a trail to follow.

With the storm gone, the sounds of the forest began. Slowly at first, and mostly the steady dripping of water through the trees. But after a while he heard other things. Small rustlings in the underbrush and through the leaves. Noises up in the trees above his head. The sound of something larger, farther away . . . it sounded as if it had hooves, there was a sort of subtle *thump* to its footfalls. It was moving off, though, so nothing to worry about, and if it *was* a deer, then that meant there weren't any wolves or bears or whatevers nearby.

Insects. Lots of insects still. Some crickets. Lots of crackles and scuttles right under him, which probably would have been disturbing to someone who hadn't spent most of his life sleeping in filthy, used, vermin-ridden straw every night. He hadn't heard any of those insect noises by the river, but then the sound of the water had probably drowned it all out.

He nodded off, and woke, fitfully, remembering to feed his little fire and enduring the empty ache that the silence in his head produced. Again and again, he agonized over the thought that his Mindspeech had been obliterated by whatever those assassins had done to him. It almost didn't matter that he'd still be able to be a Herald without it — because what really mattered was not having Dallen with him anymore. Or, at least, not in the same way.

But people go blind, and carry on. And deaf. It would be horrible, but —

Would it be so "horrible" to just be . . . ordinary?

Because ordinary people didn't have Companions, never had that incredible surety of never being alone again. Ordinary people carried on, fell in love, muddled through, had their lives, even did incredible, heroic things . . .

So maybe you shouldn't feel so bad about just being ordinary now.

On that unsettling thought, he slept again, and when he woke, just in time to blow his fire back to life before it died, it was dawn.

■ ■ ■ ■

These were either extremely tall hills, or else very short mountains. The land wasn't particularly prosperous either, from the look of it, which probably accounted for why he hadn't seen any signs of people. The forest was thick down here in the valleys but quickly thinned out on the slopes, and you could see the stony bones of the land poking out through the thin soil near the top. Not good farming land, although he wondered what he would find if he ran into another stream and sifted through the gravel. These hills might well hold metals or sparklies.

Again, another reason why he probably wasn't seeing signs of people. Mines concentrated a lot of people on a small piece of property, and they needed to be on roads. Miners didn't do much besides their jobs, which were backbreaking and difficult and didn't leave them a lot of energy to waste.

So you wouldn't likely find miners out roaming the forest for fun.

Assuming their masters would even allow them to get off the property in the first place. No telling how mines were run in Karse. Miners *might* be better off than in

Valdemar, but given what he knew about Karse, probably not. In his limited experience, there weren't a lot of happy mining collectives, where everyone shared and shared alike and no one was worked into exhaustion for the sake of a few rocks, even in Valdemar.

The rain had indeed leached all of the bitter out of his acorn meal, and he munched that for a change from the cattail roots. Meanwhile, he kept his eyes on the ground, watching for greens, even as he kept the sun at his right shoulder.

And he was, at last, rewarded; in a patch of sun, dandelions grew thickly. He stopped then and there, sharpened a fallen branch for a digging stick, and took the time to get as many of the roots as he could. It was too bad that at this time of year the leaves were too bitter to eat, but now he had lunch, and maybe dinner too.

And then, just as he was about to stop because the sun was almost overhead, a glint of something shiny and red among the leaves ahead made him dart forward —

And nearly trip over the tangle of thin, prickly blackberry vines.

The vines were thin, the foliage sparser than the ones he was used to. Possibly it was the thin soil. But there were berries hiding under those leaves, berries that nothing had wanted to fight the thorns for, and he ignored scratches to get on hands and knees, eating two for every one he harvested. He tucked the berries into a pouch of much cleaner cloth — the cloth that had held his acorn meal until he ate it all and had hung out in the rain all night. It was worth every scratch; the tart-sweetness of the berries nearly brought tears to his eyes, and he chewed the seeds carefully to get all the benefit out of them. He lost track of time as he foraged, getting food and drink in one, saving his precious water. It was only when he realized that the sun was well and truly over his left shoulder that he came to his senses and knew he'd been at this for well over a candlemark. Probably two.

And now he was faced with a dilemma: find a place to make a shelter here and keep foraging until the berries were gone, or move on and try to find water?

The berries were food and drink together. He wouldn't have to search for water if he stayed here.

But they would also attract other creatures. And he wouldn't see the things that came for the berries at night until it was too late. Bears wouldn't care about a few little blackberry thorns.

He had no more cattail, but he did have dandelion root, acorn meal, and enough berries for another meal. He thought about hiding in a flimsy little shelter while a bear snuffled about outside. It was fall; bears wanted to eat to bulk up to sleep through the winter, and he wouldn't be able to do much against a bear.

Move on.

With a sigh of regret, he gathered and stored a last handful, then took his scratched self out of the patch.

The woods of this valley were quiet; the trees were tall, but there was nothing but trunk down here near the ground. The undergrowth wasn't as thick, except in places where the sun got past the leaf canopy, or places where saplings had managed to become trees. It was a lot easier making his way through here, but he had to be very careful to keep track of the sun. One more providential find of wood sorrel added to his provender, and at long last, the faint sound of trickling water rewarded his pauses to listen. It took him off his self-appointed path, going to the east, but he tracked it to its source in the side of the hill. It was either a very tiny spring or a seep, but there was enough there to refill his bottle and fill his cooking gourd, and he made a bit of a basin to collect more by damming the outflow with rocks in case the dripping ran dry in the night. Then, finally, he had a bit of luck as he hunted up and down that spot of steep hillside; he located a good place to spend the night. Not a cave, but a solid rock overhang, a place to build his fire out of danger of another storm and maybe get some shelter for himself. And, more to the point, it was a solid bit of stone and earth at his back, with nothing nearby to attract animals.

By sunset he had a porridge of acorn meal and dandelion root cooking, was slowly munching his trefoil-shaped leaves and stems of sour sorrel, with his slightly squashed berries laid out to finish his meal. He listened carefully to the birds he could hear singing all around him, knowing they would be his first warning of anything coming that he couldn't see. But as the little valley he was in darkened with shadow, they remained tranquil.

He finished his sorrel, ate his lukewarm porridge straight from the pot, taking out the cooking stones and sucking them clean, then cleaning out every bit that was left in the gourd with his finger. He wished wistfully for salt. Or maybe some wild leek or onion. But . . . well, at least it was food, and he made sure to get every morsel. Only when he was sure he'd gotten the tiniest bit did he take the cooking gourd to the spring in the growing dusk and rinse it.

He sat drowsing on his blanket, his back to the rock, after finishing his berries. He was tired, but not yet tired enough to actually sleep. Loneliness, a hundred fears, a thousand doubts plagued him and had to be put down one by one before he'd be able to rest. After a while what sorted through his mind to the top was that last thought he'd had before he slept.

Would it be so very hard to be *ordinary*?

It wasn't as if he would ever be completely ordinary. He was still a Herald, no matter what happened; he would always have Dallen, and he would always have that special job to do that only Heralds could do. So maybe he should stop thinking of himself as somehow crippled without Dallen actively in his head.

He'd managed to get himself free without Dallen's advice. He'd managed to survive this long in the wilderness, even though he hadn't actually had the classes in doing so. It had been hard, but . . . the only horrible things were the fears, the doubts, and the loneliness. And most people had that sort of loneliness. It was only Heralds who didn't — maybe some of the Healers, who had Mindspeaking or Empathy.

Bear's "ordinary." So's Amily.

They didn't seem miserable to him. Bear was *really* happy now, and since her operation, so was Amily.

Aye, but they can't miss what they never had . . . can they?

Well . . . maybe. Maybe not. Maybe he ought to turn things around and try to look at it from their point of view. After all, they lived at the Collegium . . . and surely Bear, at least, after enduring all the scorn his father had heaped on his unGifted son, must at times long desperately for some form of Gift, even the slightest, if only to prove to his father that he was just as good as the rest of his brothers.

And Amily . . . her father was the King's Own. She'd grown up among Heralds. There must have been times when she would have done *anything* to have a Gift and be Chosen. Maybe . . . well, likely . . . there still were.

But neither of them were bitter. Neither of them — at least as far as he knew — spent most of their time fretting after something they didn't have.

I want it back! howled part of him, the part

of him that felt crippled and bereft without Dallen right with him.

But if he couldn't get it back?

He wrestled with that problem, stared that possibility right in the face, so to speak, and reminded himself that just because he didn't *want* something to happen, that didn't mean it *wouldn't.* Slowly, reluctantly, he came to the understanding that there was only one possible answer to that question.

Then . . . I don't get it back. I live with that. I do my best. And I figure out how to make everything work without it.

Because every moment he wasted in fruitless railing and longing was going to be a moment he could be using to make things work, and every moment he wasted that way would be one less moment when he could be working toward being happy and enjoying what he had.

That didn't mean he wasn't going to cry over it; he would. He knew he would. He was on the verge of it now. But he was *not,* by all the gods that were, going to let it ruin his life and the lives of everyone around him. Just as he would learn how to make things work if he were blinded, or lost a hand or a foot or anything else, he would learn how to make this work.

He wouldn't *like* it. There was no reason

why he should. And he wouldn't stop trying to get it back, either.

But in the meantime, just as he wasn't going to curl up in a ball and wail helplessly and die because he was stuck in the howling wilderness without equipment or food or proper training, he wasn't going to do the same because he'd lost his Mindspeech.

Fought my way through everything Cole Pieters threw at me. Fought my way through bein' called a traitor. Gonna fight my way through this. I got Dallen, I got Amily, I got friends. I got a place I need to get back to. I got —

Suddenly, the birds all stopped their go-to-bed sounds.

All at once.

A cold, frightened silence descended like a curtain over the dark forest; reflexively, Mags started to smother his fire. Then he thought better of it. Fire was a weapon. And if there was something out there nasty enough to make *everything* freeze in terror, he was going to need all the weapons he could get his hands on.

Fortunately, he had everything he needed at hand to make a new one. Things that lurked in the dark and hunted in the dark generally didn't like light, or fire. It was possible that fire wielded as a weapon would even keep a bear or a wolf at bay.

He had his club; he also had another stout branch he had foraged to make a second. The dried grasses and pine needles he'd gathered to make up a bed, he now pulled by the handfuls out from under his blanket, and bound to the end of that branch, tightly, to make a torch. Then, with stone-ended club in one hand and unlit torch in the other, he waited, eyes straining fruitlessly to see what was out there in the darkness, what was moving among the trees.

He took slow, quiet breaths, listening as hard as he could. The silence was so intense he could actually hear the trickle of water from the tiny spring. Whatever was out there, it wasn't something that made noises pushing through the undergrowth.

A strange, eerie cold crept over him. He shivered as an icy touch seemed to run down his spine. It wasn't just imagination either; the temperature here really had plummeted in just a few heartbeats, because now his breath steamed out into the dark blue dusk in clouds.

He couldn't wait any longer. He thrust the end of his torch into his tiny fire, and as soon as it caught, he held it up like a barrier between himself and whatever it was that was in the growing dark.

He might not have Mindspeech, but evidently it didn't take Mindspeech to sense what was out there, because he could *feel* uncanny eyes on him. And it knew he was here too; it had known even without the torch or his little fire. It had sensed him and come a-hunting.

It was waiting for something.

It was like that *thing* that had been watching him — more inimical, more savage, but very like it.

Demon?

He'd read enough about the wars with Karse to know that the priests could call up demons — or, at least, what the Chroniclers called demons. The descriptions varied, and more than one had said that the things were only partly visible at best, but one thing they all agreed on. The Karsite demons were vicious and fully capable of ripping either a man's body or his mind to ribbons.

He squeezed himself into the smallest possible space he could, with as much rock around him as he could get.

Was this why the Karsite captain had told his men that he didn't want anyone venturing out of camp at night?

Was this why they had obeyed him without a murmur?

Did these things prowl the land at night,

on the watch for the unwary, acting as some form of control to keep people within their homes after dark? That would certainly cut down on rebellion . . . and bandits.

There was definitely something out there, something he couldn't *quite* see, something that was just a ripple in the darkness. It hovered in the air, moving slowly, back and forth, in front of his shelter. Like a cat prowling back and forth in front of something that it has cornered but isn't quite sure is prey. The ripple moved back and forth, and he moved the torch to follow it.

The force of its regard was like a blast of icy air. He wanted to shake his head violently, but didn't dare take his eyes off it. It felt as if he *should* be sensing something from it, yet was not. There *should* be something pressing against shields that were no longer there, but he couldn't actually feel anything.

Finally, it made a sound, a snarl that sounded exactly like the air being ripped into two. Evidently, it was frustrated too . . .

It still couldn't seem to make up its mind whether to attack or leave him alone. The temptation to shout at it was almost overwhelming, but he resisted. He didn't want to do *anything* that might trigger an attack.

The snarls stopped. That horrid silence

descended again.

But only for a moment.

The air was split with the most unearthly, ghastly, terror-inducing howl that Mags had ever heard in his life. It turned his bones to water; it made him want to curl up and hide his head in his arms, it knotted his gut with fear and paralyzed his thoughts. The first howl was followed by a second, which was, somehow, even worse. From paralysis, his mind sprang into mindless, gibbering panic, and only the fact that *it* was between him and any path to escape kept him pinned here. If he'd had even the slightest chance of getting past it, he'd have bolted into the darkness.

Silence again.

He shivered, but the torch seemed to be keeping it at bay for now, frail barrier that it was.

Another snarl.

The darker it got, oddly enough, the easier it was to see it — or, at least, see that odd patch where it was. It wasn't so much formless as it was a sort of series of suggestions . . . not-quite shapes that hinted at limbs, a head.

Those hints were as horrid as the howl had been; some were spidery, some were vaguely suggestive of a snake, some were . . .

unholy meldings of a fistful of knives with a limb.

It was the change in those suggestions of shape that warned him, the momentary drawing back — it lashed out at him, and he countered by thrusting the torch at it.

It howled again, this time with pain, and went for him.

He was in a fight for his life, and knew it. With torch and club he blocked and parried, struck back when he could, and tried above all to keep from being driven out of the scant shelter he had.

The thing screamed, howled, and yowled in pain. He managed to strike it several times, and the feel of club or torch on flesh was solid enough. But it struck him just as many times, and its talons were razor-keen and icy as blades taken from a frozen river. They left behind a burning ache that slowed him a little for every strike, left slash wounds that, oddly, did not bleed.

And worse than that, a strange lethargy was coming over him, emanating from those wounds.

He fought it, but his vision was starting to blur, and he felt himself sagging back against the rock. He could barely hold the torch up . . .

He saw the thing retreating a little to lick

at its own wounds; saw a glimpse of a hell-red eye for a moment as it glared at him. Then it retreated further into whatever half-life it lived in, and he felt that it was watching him.

Waiting.

And why not? He was growing numb. He had to drop the club to hold the torch in both hands. In a moment, he would drop that, too, and then the dimming of the world would go to black, and he would . . .

He felt the torch falling from his fingers and heard it rolling away.

And as he, too, toppled over, he thought he heard a voice. It was shouting something garbled, and the thing turned to face away from him. There was a feline yowl, and the thing screamed angrily, but also in pain.

"In the name of the Sun, creature of the nether realms, and of the Light and Life, I banish thee!"

But by then the cold and the blackness had claimed him.

11

Cold . . . the last time he had been this cold, he had nearly frozen to death in that blizzard. But that had been mere insensate winter, which had no real interest in whether he lived or died. It didn't care what happened to him any more than the stars did. If he'd died, it wouldn't rejoice, and since he'd lived, that didn't matter to winter's icy blasts either.

This cold had a terrifying life of its own, and it *wanted* him dead. It wanted far more than that, too, but it knew it would not get that — it knew that once he was dead, he would escape its reach, so there was a frustration there as well, behind the urgent need to kill him. It was determined that he would not escape. The mere possibility that he might escape sent it into a rage.

It wasn't so much an entity as a force, a hatred for everything that lived, for every positive, *good* thing in the world. It would have liked to crush them all beneath its icy weight until there was nothing left in the world but cold, and dark, and despair.

It couldn't get that, so it would settle for crushing him now, pulling the life out of him and enjoying his terror and grief until he finally escaped the thing into — well, wherever it was he would go that took him out of the possibility of pursuit.

Oh, that is not going to happen, ye bastard. Not today. I ain't gonna die fer you.

He felt his will harden against it, mustered up a burst of strength from somewhere, and somehow thrust the thing away. It was a strange sensation, since he didn't seem to have a body, exactly, and neither did it.

If I did have, I'd give ye such a shot in the good bits!

It moved to envelop him.

He eluded it.

"That's right, outlander . . ."

Encouraged by that voice somewhere past the darkness, he thrust back again, harder this time. And with the memory of how he had fought against those assassins behind it. That seemed to help!

"Do you accept the Blessing of the Sun?"

He didn't even hesitate at that. Of course he accepted the blessing of the sun! Light, life, warmth — he needed *all* of those and needed them now! He could feel the ice in his veins spreading out from the wounds the Entity's creature had made, a cold poison that was intended to make him give up and die and let the thing add what was left of his life force to its power.

But he wouldn't give up. And if something wanted to give him blessings, by the gods both small and big, he would take them!

As if he had opened a door with that thought, light blazed up around him, heat rushed into him and joined with him, filling him with strength. He sensed that he was only going to get one try at this, and as the Entity tried to engulf him again, oblivious to his new source of strength, he allowed it to surround him, a cloud of evil miasma enveloping him, trying to freeze and choke off life and breath.

He waited a moment for it to feel as if it had won. That moment of triumph would be its moment of weakness, when it dropped its guard.

He felt that surge of pleasure.

Then he exploded inside it like the sun bursting up over the horizon.

The howl that erupted from the wounded Thing was worse than anything its creature that had attacked him in the forest had produced. But it was mercifully brief, as the

Entity evaporated into light.

He could feel he had a body again — a heavy, weary, slightly sick feeling body. But alive, and not being poisoned anymore.

And Mags opened his eyes, conscious of a strange weight on his chest, to find a pair of exceedingly blue, slit-pupiled eyes in a furry red face staring at him as the huge cat they belonged to nearly touched noses with him. It peered deeply into his eyes, and he was conscious of something that was far more than human searching for something within him

The cat pulled its head back as soon as his eyes were open. Mags was immediately aware of three things, and three things only.

The first was that he was lying on his back inside some sort of cave and was blessedly warm again. Every bit of that deadly chill seemed to have been driven from his poor, abused body.

The second was that the cat was extremely heavy, in fact, the largest feline he had ever seen in his life.

The third was that he felt as if he had been sliced to ribbons . . . he felt the wounds as *present,* but not the pain yet. But in a moment, he knew that the pain would start, and when it did, he was going to start screaming, and he was not sure he would be able to stop —

As if that thought had awakened the agony to its duty, the awful pain started at that very moment, and his mouth opened —

"That will be all, I think," said a voice that sounded very irritated, and a hand touched his forehead, and he plunged back down into blackness.

It hadn't been a *bad* blackness, that darkness that had followed the touch of finger to forehead. Not like the drug dreams he'd had, and certainly nothing like the place where the Cold Entity lurked. In fact, it had been a very, very pleasant blackness, a warm and fuzzy sort of blackness, a place of comfort and vaguely happy lassitude not unlike all those times he'd floated in and out of sleep in the Infirmary at the Collegium when he'd been badly hurt. He had the distinct sense that he was being cared for by someone who had no intention of hurting or imprisoning him and that he was safe, and the best thing he could do at the moment was to be calm and sleep and heal.

When he woke again, it was with a clear head — though he tested, and his Mind-speech still wasn't back — to find that he was, indeed, in a cave. Above him was the rough rock ceiling, craggy and uneven, with light reflecting irregularly from it. He was lying on something extremely soft and comfortable and was covered with some fine, heavy fur blankets, because he could feel the fur soft against his chin. There was something else on him, weighing down his legs, in fact, and he tilted his head up to see that the cat was holding him down. It raised its head, gave him what he would have *sworn* was a look filled with smugness, then stood up, stretched, yawned, and sauntered off.

That was when he understood he was lying on a bed made up on the floor of the cave. The rough rock wall was within touching distance to his right. To his left there was a cut floor not unlike the Pieters' mine. He appeared to be in a little chamber cut into the rock, with a passage leading out to where the light was. There was nothing else in the chamber but him, though he had to admit that the absence of any sort of a door was something of a comfort.

He heard footsteps, and a moment later a figure in the passage cast a shadow over him.

"Trouble not to untruths speak," said a slightly irritated-sounding voice. "Demon-rider of the North, I know you are."

He blinked. "Um, excuse me?" he replied. "I wasn't riding that thing, it was trying to eat me. Or something."

373

The figure came farther into the chamber, dropped down a three-legged stool, and sat down on it with the air of someone who was being put to a great deal of trouble. The cat came back in and made a noise that sounded like admonishment. The man snorted.

"Pardon it seems I must beg," he replied, with faint sarcasm. "Reaylis is to saying thing you ride is to being like him, not demon."

Mags put his hand up to his head, feeling a bit bewildered and very foggy. "Uh . . . right." Reaylis . . . was the cat? Well, why not? Valdemar had talking horses, why shouldn't Karse have talking cats? "Uh . . . why did you help me? Not that I'm ungrateful! But —"

"Explanation long, time for eating, then sleeping." The man shoved a bowl at him and put a cup down beside the bed. Both were pottery as rough as the cave walls. The bowl held some sort of fish stew, and since he hadn't been given a spoon, Mags drank it straight from the bowl. The mug held nothing more sinister than water. The man snatched up both as soon as he was finished, and before Mags could say anything at all, stabbed a forefinger at his head, and the next thing Mags knew —

He was waking up again.

He was hungry, and he needed to use the privy. There was no sign of the cat this time and no sounds from outside the chamber. He decided to try to move.

He regretted the decision a little, because all those wounds he thought he had felt really did exist. They weren't *raw* wounds, though; the pain was more ache than anything else, though when he pulled back the sleeve of the oversized shirt he was wearing, there were neat, clean bandages running all the way up his arm, so he couldn't exactly look at his injuries.

It seemed the shirt was the only garment he was wearing, but it was so big it came down past his knees. The cat appeared as he was getting unsteadily to his feet. It looked at him with keen intelligence, meowed once, and walked away with its tail in the air. It had very odd markings, like nothing he had ever seen before: reddish-brown face, ears, tail and paws, the rest cream colored. There was a suggestion of stripes in the red parts.

Clearly, the cat wanted him to follow, so he did. It led him through a larger chamber that looked as if it served a lot of purposes and toward what looked to be a tunnel out to daylight.

That was exactly what the opening proved to be, and the cat directed his footsteps to a nicely constructed latrine, which he gratefully used. The area around the cave — or mine — mouth was well tended; there were a couple of benches, a small herb garden, a larger vegetable garden. Someone had left a basket of mixed vegetables on the bench. Mags eyed it, decided it wasn't too heavy for his weakened state, and picked it up, taking it back inside. In the main chamber was an actual fireplace — it looked as if it had been built making use of a natural fissure leading to the surface, or perhaps an air-channel that had been cut — and an area that looked as if it was used as a kitchen. Mags washed the vegetables, then began peeling and cutting them up, thriftily saving the greens and peels together, in case his unknown host had a use for them that he couldn't figure out.

The floor was uneven but smooth. The walls and ceiling were rougher. There was a dresser with shelves holding a few dishes, pots and pans, and implements on one side of the fire and a second holding some bags, boxes, and sealed or stoppered pots on the other. There was a small table with two benches just in front of the fire, a little table or stand near the entrance to "his" chamber with a big pottery basin on it. That was the extent of the furnishings.

There was a pot over the banked fire, keeping warm; Mags gave it a good stir. There was a bowl soaking in a pan of water; he cleaned it. And about then was when he ran out of energy, and he made his way back to "his" chamber to lie down.

He dozed a little and was awakened by his rescuer, who nudged his shoulder with a toe, since both hands were full. He sat up, and the man handed him a bowl and a mug again.

"Reaylis says I am to be thanking you for help," the man said, and sniffed. "So I am thanking you."

"You rescued me, you patched me up, you're feeding me," Mags pointed out. "I thank *you,* sir, and taking care of a few dishes and vegetables is scarcely going to repay what you did for me."

The man hmphed. "Well. Correct thinking," he said, sounding mollified. "You move. Come out. Sit in the sunshine. The Sun will give you His blessing." He went to a chest in the shadows past the foot of the bed that Mags had not seen, and rummaged, "Here. Pants."

He dropped a pair of worn linen trews on the foot of the bed.

Huh. The sun again. All right, this guy must be pretty religious. Again, vague memories of classes reminded him that the Karsites worshiped the Sun. *If it'll make him happy, I don't mind sitting in the sun. 'Specially after being so cold.*

He wondered if he ought to try saying something in Karsite, but his Karsite wasn't any better than the priest's Valdemaran. He suspected that the only reason he had understood what the Karsite captain had been saying to his captors was the pure accident of them using words he actually knew.

The man helped him to his feet and then led the way out. Mags paused just long enough to pull on the trews, then followed. As soon as they got into the main room, which was now lit by a variety of lamps and candles, Mags got a good look at him.

He wore long robes, which looked too big on him, of a faded red. They'd been belted up to a bit below his knees, making them more practical for wandering around in a forest. The sleeves had been tied up too, by the simple expedient of running a cord through both sleeves across his back and gathering them up that way.

He wasn't old though; he looked to be in his late teens or early twenties. Much too young to sound as grumpy as he did.

His blond hair was long and braided into a single tail down his back. He had a square, severe-looking face, a mouth that looked as if it never smiled, and blue, deep-set eyes. His hands were big, and it was obvious he was used to doing a lot of hard work, for the fingers were callused and his forearms well muscled.

Mags moved slowly and carefully; it felt as if he might tear something open if he moved in a hurry. "My name is Mags," he said, as they went down the tunnel to the outside. He noticed something he had not on his way out the first time: a door right where the tunnel joined the main chamber that swung outward. It would be very difficult in the confined space of the tunnel to get enough leverage to wrench it open, and almost impossible to batter it down. At some point someone had set metal brackets into both the door and the stone wall of the chamber to allow a stout bar to be dropped into them, holding the door in place.

"Franse," said the man, shortly, over his shoulder. "Brother Franse."

Mags had not been sure what time of day it had been when he had awakened, but now he was pretty certain it was afternoon. One of the benches had been situated in such a way that it caught the sun. Mags was very happy to sit down on it.

Franse went to work in the herb garden, pinching off a leaf here, a stem there, obviously collecting just enough for a particular dish or dishes. The garden itself looked as if it had been harvested recently, and Franse was just taking fresh herbs while they were still growing, before the frost killed them all.

"If you don't mind my asking," Mags said diffidently into the silence, "what was it that attacked me?"

"Demon," Franse replied, and he added something that sounded like curse words. "Sun-forsaken black-robes are to be sending, send every dark, the night to take. To be like wolves, like dogs, to be in their homes keeping people. To be making people like — baaaaaa!" He put his hands to his head like ears and bleated like a sheep.

So the thing hadn't been after him specifically. He sighed with relief, and let the sun soak into him. It felt awfully good, actually, more so than he would have expected; in fact, the sun felt a lot like being bathed in a soothing salve.

The cat strolled onto the path from around some bushes at the end of the garden, tail high. It really was as big as he remembered; its head would easily come as high as his knee. It was a very handsome cat, with its striking cream and red markings. It paraded toward them, looking very self-satisfied, paused long enough to give Franse's hip a rub, then sauntered over to Mags. It regarded him for a moment. Its blue eyes seemed to stare into him.

"Hello . . ." He tried to think of the cat's name. ". . . Reaylis?"

That got a short huff of purr, and the cat got to its feet, then continued its leisurely stroll into the mouth of the tunnel.

"Was this a mine?" he asked Franse, who straightened from his work, put his selected handful of herb bits into the basket at his side, and got up. At Franse's puzzled look, he mimed digging and pointed at the tunnel.

"Aye. So Old Harald said." Franse moved over to the vegetable side of the garden.

"Old Harald?" It seemed as if Franse treasured words more than gold, he was so stingy with them.

"Red-robe as was here before me." Franse carefully examined his vegetables before selecting them. "Master of me. This you are liking?" He held up a bunch of beets. They looked beautiful. Then again, after days of nothing but broth followed by days of only what he could scavenge, anything would look beautiful. He was ready to bite into them raw.

"Um. Yes, thank you." Mags paused, trying to think of something to say, but this time Franse actually initiated a question.

"You can being to arrow?" he asked, miming using a bow. "I am to be finding —" he mimed using a sling "— with you, you can to being to arrow?"

"Yes," Mags said simply, then added, "I can shoot a bow and use the sling. But I am better with a bow."

The man sighed. "Shooting. Shooting. Good. You will to be shooting damn rabbits that are to be eating —" he waved his arm at the expanse of his garden.

Mags mouth watered at the thought of meat for the first time in days. "Would it be safe for me to sit out here in the dusk? I mean, if you have these demon things prowling around, I'd rather not risk it, but dusk and dawn is when rabbits generally forage."

Franse might not be able to speak Valdemaran well, but it seemed he understood pretty much everything Mags said.

He made a dome with his hands and looked to Mags.

"Safe? Sheltered?" He tried to think of

one of the words from the old Chronicles that had mentioned magic. "Protected, shielded, warded?"

"Ah!" Franse nodded. "Warded is garden. Safe it is. To be not moving, you." Franse got up and took his basket down into the former mine. When he returned, it was with a light bow and a quiver full of hunting arrows. Mags checked both over. The fletching on the arrows could stand being renewed, but the bow had been stored unstrung, and someone had been regularly conditioning the string. It was safe enough to shoot without snapping either the string or the bow and, almost as important, both light enough that he could pull an arrow quickly without tearing open his wounds and strong enough that an arrow from it would kill a rabbit within the small confines of the garden.

"If rabbit —" Franse mimed a rabbit running away "— out of garden, you *stay,*" Franse cautioned gruffly, then went back into the cave. "No walk, you. No run, you." He came out again with a crude wheelbarrow and a rake, going out past where the bushes started to rake up leaves, stuff them into net bags and load them on the wheelbarrow. Mags stayed where he was. The cat came out, jumped up on the bench beside him, and curled up in the sun for a nap.

After a couple of trips it was obvious that Franse was bringing the leaves in to pile them on top of some of the plants still in his garden. Mags had seen the gardeners at the Palace do that with some of the flower-beds, so he assumed that this protected them against the cold.

He started to get up to help, but Franse waved him brusquely back. The second time he tried, Franse glared at him.

"Not Healer am I," he said crossly. "Not to be hurt my work. Not to be hurt the Sun's work."

Well, that seemed to settle it.

Mags wished rather desperately that his Mindspeech were working. Franse seemed to know he was a Trainee, and from Valdemar, and Franse himself was a Karsite priest, yet why wasn't he trussed up and waiting to be turned over to the Karsite authorities? Why, in fact, had Franse just given him a weapon and ordered him to shoot rabbits, when he could probably use the thing to hurt Franse, or even kill him?

Franse didn't seem to think much of other Karsite priests either. Mags knew that there were priests of many sorts that went off to be hermits, and given Franse's apparent misanthropy, he seemed to be the sort of fellow who would do that; but if that was the case, why rescue anyone, much less someone he knew was an enemy of Karse?

This was all terribly puzzling, and Mags was left to sit there on a bench in the sun and try to sort it out without a lot of clues to go on. So he sat with an arrow nocked loosely to the bow as Franse moved out of sight with his barrow. Evidently the leaves weren't all he was going after today.

Then a little bit of movement under the leaves of the bushes ringing the garden caught his eye.

Cautiously, a rabbit eased partly into sight. It looked around, nose quivering. Mags knew better than to move; rabbits had excellent vision all around their heads, and his best chance at a shot would be if it put its head down behind something to eat. He'd practiced this sort of thing on the target range. If he could see any part of it, he'd know where the chest was, and the chest was his target.

It eased a little more into sight, stretching its neck out. There was something in particular that it wanted, but it was not sure it was safe to get it yet.

Then it sat up tall on its hind legs and took a good look around in all directions. Mags remained very still. There wasn't any

385

sort of breeze, so there was nothing to carry his scent to it. Out of the corner of his eye, he saw the cat watching it, also not moving.

Satisfied, the rabbit dropped back down to all fours and hopped slowly into the garden, moving with great caution.

Then came the moment Mags had been waiting for. The rabbit put his head behind a huge, green leaf.

Mags was pleased to find his aim was still good.

He started to get up, but the cat jumped down, stood in front of him, and *glared* at him for a moment. Startled, he remained where he was. The cat sauntered over to the garden and ducked behind the leafy vegetable. A moment later it came out again, head high, with the rabbit's neck in its mouth. It carried the rabbit, arrow and all, right to Mags, then dropped it at his feet and darted off again.

He had just pulled out the arrow and cleaned it when the cat returned with a small, sharp knife (held by the handle) in its teeth.

This time it stood there looking at him with the knife in its mouth until he took it. It sat down and watched him expectantly.

Well, what else was there to do?

He skinned the rabbit and cleaned it,

bundling the meat in the skin to keep it clean and keep the bugs away, and then offered the cat the offal and the head, which Reaylis cheerfully accepted and ate. Well, it ate the offal; it took the head and sauntered off with it. Mags wasn't sure what it was going to do with the head. Save it for later, like a dog? Find a sharpened stake just outside the garden and impale it there as a warning to other rabbits? Given what he had seen from this cat already, he would not be in the least surprised to find a row of staked vermin skulls out there on the other side of the hedge surrounding the garden.

Just as he was considering these possibilities, Franse returned with a wheelbarrow full of acorns. His eyes lit up as he spotted the bundle of fur on the bench beside Mags.

"Ha! Triumph!" he crowed. "Good hunter you are! Ha!" He took the bundle and went into the cave, coming out only a moment later. "Tearing hurts you were not?" he asked, in a voice that was almost accusing.

"The cat did all the work," Mags said. Franse nodded as if this was something to be expected. "He took the head away, too," Mags added.

Franse shrugged. "Reaylis does what Reaylis will do," he replied. "Food is to being soon. With meat!"

The priest trundled the barrow full of acorns into the cave. Mags waited to see if another rabbit would appear, but by the time Franse came back and signaled that he was to come back inside, nothing had turned up but the cat.

The priest waved him in the direction of the little chamber where his bed was, and he wondered with a twinge if he had usurped the poor fellow's bed. And if so, how was he to make amends?

Franse came in with the usual bowl and mug, but there was a look of intense satisfaction on his face as he handed both to Mags, who was sitting cross-legged on the fur blanket. Mags' mouth watered as he smelled the savory meat in the bowl; it was some sort of beet soup or stew, nothing like anything he'd ever had before, and his stomach registered its approval with a loud growl.

The priest actually grinned a little, then went out and came back with a bowl and a mug for himself. "Now, shoot you, we like men can eat!" he said happily.

Mags blinked. "Not a good hunter, are you?" he ventured.

Franse sucked the meat off the section of ribs he was holding, licked them dry, and grimaced. "No good hunter, I," he admitted. "Only Reaylis hunter is."

Well, then, that was what he could do to make amends. "Do you know how to dry meat?" he asked cautiously. "Or smoke it?"

"Aye, aye, I am to being dry fish and vegetables and in smoke hang," the priest assured him, and bit into the leg with strong, white teeth. "Reaylis brings not enough to smoke."

Well, the bow and arrows would be good for small game. Mags wasn't about to try for anything bigger than a goose with it, though. He decided to broach the subject of the sleeping arrangements. "I hope I didn't take your bed . . ." he began, tentatively.

"Eh?" The priest looked startled.

"Now that I am getting better, I can sleep by the fire," Mags elaborated. "If this is where you sleep, I can sleep by the fire."

The cat sauntered in just as he said that, and cat and priest exchanged a long look. Understanding came over the priest's face. "Ah! No, is —" he looked at the cat again. "Is *old* bed. I am to be having bed of Old Harald."

Oh, well that was all right, then. Mags felt very much better about the arrangement. He had to wonder, though, if Franse was such a bad hunter, who had shot the enormous bears that had provided the furs for the bed? Had it been Old Harald?

Well, he's a priest, maybe people give him things. Or he gets them from the temple. Or they belonged to his former Master.

Franse offered the cat the other leg from his bowl, but the cat wasn't interested. "Is not to be liking —" Franse fished a bit of beet from his bowl and held it up.

"Beets," Mags supplied.

"Ah! Reaylis not liking beets," Franse explained, and he demolished the last quarter with relish.

Mags was very, very conscious that he had a considerable debt to discharge here, before he could even think about trying to get back to Valdemar. He was also conscious that he faced a danger he hadn't even been aware of when he'd escaped — because he didn't think he'd be able to face off one of those demons again, and he *knew* he was unlikely to be rescued by someone like Franse a second time. But first things first: Discharge the debt.

He slowly became aware as he finished his meal that the pain of his wounds was increasing, and Franse must have seen that in his face. The priest hastily slurped the last of his broth, collected their crockery, and hurried out, coming back with a pot that smelled very familiar. Mags was certain that several of Bear's salves and balms smelled exactly like that. The man gestured to Mags to take off his shirt, which Mags did, a bit self-consciously, only to be surprised at the fact that his entire torso was wrapped in bandages, as well as both arms. How had the priest managed all that alone?

Franse unwrapped his chest and back first, and Mags tried not to wince at the extent of the lacerations. Neat lines of stitches showed that some of them had been bad enough to require sewing up. But they were healing, and quickly, and there was no sign of infection. It appeared that all the lacerations were on his chest and shoulders. This man might not call himself a Healer, but he was certainly every bit as good as Bear, and maybe better.

Franse handed him the pot and mimed him spreading the creamy yellow salve inside the pot on his chest wounds. Franse dipped his fingers in the pot and worked on Mags' shoulders while Mags took care of the rest. When his chest was rebandaged, they took care of his arms. Franse mimed, face going a little red, that he was going to have to take care of his legs himself. "Must to being make morning eat," he muttered, and hurried out.

It gave him a very strange, slightly shuddery feeling to work on his own wounds this way, to see the damage under his hands. It wasn't bad on his calves, but his thighs had some tears that could have killed him if they'd gone deeper.

Good thing he'd been able to keep it somewhat away with that torch.

When the priest came back, Mags handed him the pot, and he handed Mags another mug. "To be make sleep," he explained, at Mags inquiring look. Mags hesitated, but only a moment. After all, Franse had had ample opportunity to do whatever he wanted by this point. If the priest had wanted him dead, the simplest thing to do would simply have been to let the demon do it. And if he'd wanted Mags incapacitated, he could have tied him up. He drank the bitter stuff down and got into the bed again, feeling the salve killing the pain in his wounds and the medicine in the tea starting to work on him.

He deliberately was not allowing himself to dwell on how far he was from home, how hard it would be to get there. Right now he couldn't even move outside the garden, so right now the very best thing he could do would be to let the medicine make him sleep and do whatever he could to heal his wounds. Worry about leaving once he had the ability to leave.

He drifted off to sleep hearing Franse in the main room, droning away aloud. Prayers, he assumed. After all, the man was a priest . . .

He woke to the sound of something that sounded a lot more joyful than the droning of last night, a song that lifted his heart and put a smile on his lips without him being able to understand a word. Franse was evidently a good singer as well as a very devout fellow; whatever this morning hymn was saying, he was putting a lot of feeling into it. His voice was a rich tenor, and the song made Mags think of the songs on Midwinter Eve in Valdemar.

Mags got up and went out into the main room, where he found a crude basin ready for him on a little table right by the doorway, something that looked like soap, and a rough towel, as well as the pot of salve and a roll of new, clean bandages. That was what told him that it was all for his use.

He felt much better after a good wash; the stuff wasn't soap, but it was a root that cleansed in much the same way as soap did. He rebandaged his arms and legs and left his chest to do last, and Franse arrived from outside in good time to do the actual bandaging.

Franse took the basin away or, rather, started to, and that was when Mags noticed that he was . . . well . . . just a little clumsy. He tripped several times in the rough floor, saving himself each time with a muttered curse. He went out to dump out the water in the basin, and when he came back, he started to put the basin down just a little short of the shelf it was supposed to fit on. Mags was close enough to make a lurch for it and save it — and that was when he understood why Franse was not, and would never be, any sort of a hunter.

"You don't see very well, do you?" he asked, breaking the silence.

Franse shrugged.

Mags thought about this. "There are things," he said, slowly. "Round pieces of glass. They can be put on your face in front of your eyes so you can see better." He made circles with his thumbs and forefingers and mimed Bear's lenses.

Franse gave him a look full of skepticism. "How?" he asked, squinting at Mags doubtfully.

"Like . . . like jewelry!" Mags replied. "Wire or wood around the lenses, wire behind the ears or leather tied so —" He mimed that as well. Did the Karsites have long-vision tubes? He thought they might. "You know the tubes? Generals have them, that can make far things look near?"

But Franse shook his head. "Not for the seeing of generals, me," he replied without rancor. "Not Old Harald, not me. We are low — low — no great ones come to us." he brought his hand down to the floor.

"Humble," Mags offered.

"Aye." Franse sighed. "Humble. Such things . . ." He shook his head.

His attitude suggested that while he understood what Mags was telling him, that there was some object that would allow him to see clearly, he didn't think someone like him would ever be allowed to have it.

"My friend has such a thing," Mags said, because suddenly he realized how he might get himself safely back home. If Franse could be persuaded to come with him, in return for a pair of spectacles, he could go in the disguise of Franse's servant or helper. He already knew how to play at being a deaf-mute. He would never have to say a word. Franse could do all of the talking; surely people would give them food, or there would be food and shelter at the temples . . .

Why, they might even be able to get

donkeys or even horses and get to the Border in no time!

"Aye?" Franse looked glum. "A demon-horse rider not *humble* is . . ."

"He's not a d— not a Herald," Mags corrected. "He's a Healer, but he does all of his healing as you do, with herbs and salves. No —" he closed his eyes as Healers often did to concentrate, held out his hands flat, and wiggled the fingers to suggest the Gift working. "Only herbs, knives, needles, salves, bandages."

"Aye?" Interest returned. "And he such a thing is given?"

"So he can see well to make his medicines," Mags explained. "It is not easy to make such a thing in Valdemar, but it is not difficult either. A humble man could have such a thing."

"But I am not a Healer of the North." Franse's face fell again.

"But I must get home safely," Mags said, very quietly.

Franse gave him a sharp glance, but he said nothing. Instead, he turned to the fire and ladled out big bowls full of acorn-and-berry porridge for both of them. Finally, Franse produced spoons. Mags was relieved; he was beginning to think Franse didn't possess such a thing. But it appeared that he had two at least, besides the big one in the pot, all three carved of wood and dark with age and use.

He helped with the cleaning of the place as best he could, moving stiffly and carefully to keep from hurting himself. He discovered that Franse had some pretty clever solutions to not being able to see well — keeping the medicinal and culinary herbs in two separate cave-chambers, for instance. Franse had a broom, and unlike Franse, Mags could actually see where the dirt and dust-balls were. When he was done, the floor was cleaner than it had been in a long time. To his great disappointment, he got tired *very* quickly. But he did manage to get another rabbit, this one just outside the garden, and two squirrels from trees that overhung it. The cat fetched all three like a dog. They ate very well that night, then sat quietly at the fire. Franse wove rope by feel; Mags carved a spoon. He could certainly understand why Franse only had two. Carving a spoon wasn't that hard, but when you lived alone, the last thing you wanted to do was to cut your hand. Even if you were as good with herbs and the like as Franse, having to do things one-handed could make things very difficult.

Franse was awkward as company as well

as physically, and it wasn't just because his Valdemaran was pretty scant and mostly limited to telling Mags what to do. More and more, Mags got the feeling that Franse was a hermit not only because he had served with a hermit, but by virtue of his very nature. He liked silence. He liked doing things alone. He just wasn't very good with people, and he was extremely shy. Although . . . that might have been because he was so self-conscious about not being able to see.

In fact, unless Mags was very much mistaken, he probably had more and longer conversations with the cat than he had ever had with people, including his former master.

And then there was the cat . . .

Now, Mags didn't know anything at all about Vkandis Sunlord. He didn't think too many Valdemarans did, unless there were some followers of this god who, for whatever reason, had gone across the Border to set up in Valdemar. But he did know this: Not once had he *ever* heard about a Karsite priest *helping* a Herald or a Herald Trainee. Karsite priests were usual right in the front lines, sending curses and other nastiness at the Valdemaran troops. Not once had he ever heard of a Karsite priest invoking the blessings of Vkandis on a Valdemaran. Yet Franse had done all that. And Mags had the distinct impression it had been at the direction — even the urging — of that cat.

The cat, if he understood Franse correctly, was something like a Companion, but he'd never heard of mobs of cats accompanying the Sunpriests into battle against Valdemar, and something *that* odd would certainly be noticed.

Vkandis had helped, had blessed, him, a Herald. He'd felt that himself. He'd *felt* a warm force, a great and powerful force, joining with him to drive off the chill poison of the demon's claw marks. Something *that* odd had never happened before to his knowledge; he was certain if it ever had, the smallest child in Valdemar would be aware of it.

There was something in this equation that he was missing, and he wished desperately for Mindspeech so he could ask directly.

But at the moment it was looking as if he might as well wish for a gryphon to fly him home. He was just as likely to get the one as the other.

12

Franse did not bring up the subject of eye lenses again. Then again, Mags was in no shape to travel yet. His second morning in the priest's home was much like the first, although he did exert himself to hunt squirrels outside the garden with Franse's nodded permission. He had to lie down and sleep, or at least rest, right after the noon meal, which was convenient for Franse, since he did some sort of prayer or ceremony he was somewhat secretive about at that same time.

A lot of the awkwardness of the previous night was gone. Franse was warming to him (and he to Franse!) a lot faster than he would have thought. He decided that some of the priest's apparent misanthropy was nothing more than shyness. Some was acute embarrassment over his own clumsiness. The more time Mags spent with him, however, the more a latent hunger for company seemed to awaken in him.

And that cat . . . was abetting that.

The third day proved that.

After a long staring session with the cat just after breakfast, Franse abruptly announced that he was going to show Mags where there were birds to hunt for meat, and the two of them had ended up at a secluded pond Mags would never have guessed was there. Not only did Mags manage to bag several ducks and a goose, but Franse was able to teach him how to fish, so they returned to the cave with not only dinner but provisions to smoke and dry for the winter.

The cat highly approved of the bird guts and heads, and the guts, heads, and tails of the fish. Franse was happy with the feathers and promptly used all of the body feathers to restuff a flat pillow. Mags saved the flight feathers to redo the fletching on the arrows, grateful that this was a basic skill every Trainee learned early.

This put the young priest in a very good mood, though mostly that consisted of smiling at Mags shyly, motioning at the duck in their stew, and saying "Is good!" a lot, with Mags nodding in agreement.

He was beginning to think about trying to broach the idea of him leaving as soon as the larder was full of meat and fish. With two people fishing, that part would go pretty fast, and the small animals and waterfowl around here seemed to be utterly unaware that a human could actually kill them. Probably because with his bad eyesight, Franse would have to be within a horse length of them to hit them. The expedition to the pond had gone well, Mags' wounds were sealed, and he was feeling more energetic — and he couldn't put this off for too much longer. Trying to get through these mountains in winter would be a nightmare.

He still wasn't sure how he was going to avoid the demons . . . but maybe Franse had some sort of talisman or could make some object holy to Vkandis that would protect him.

Or maybe — he could go back to his first idea. Franse could seal up the cave for a few days or a fortnight and come with him. That would make things both easier *and* faster, if he would.

He caught the cat and Franse staring at each other again during dinner and sighed, knowing what they were doing. Mindspeaking. Things would be so much easier if he could Mindspeak again! They both turned to look at him. "What is?" Franse asked, looking concerned.

"Oh . . . I used to be able to do that," he said without thinking. At Franse's puzzled look, he added, "Head-talk," and pointed from Franse to Reaylis and back.

"So?" Franse looked startled and went into another of those staring sessions with the cat. Then he looked back at Mags. "Reaylis saying is, you are —" he waved his hand in the air between them, miming a wall. "He tries head-talk, nothing."

Mags looked back at them, intensely frustrated. How could he explain that he had been kidnapped, drugged, and hauled into Karse against his will, and he didn't know if it was a hit on the head, the drugs, or something else entirely that had stolen his Mindspeech?

"I got hurt. Before demon," he said, finally, and mimed someone hitting him on the back of the head. It was as good an explanation as any, and what was Franse going to be able to do about it, anyway? He was like Bear, he didn't have a Healing Gift, and Mags had no idea if the drugs had been gone from him long enough that they shouldn't be affecting his Mindspeech or not. If they weren't, it wasn't something Franse could fix, and if it was the drugs, without knowing what drugs they were in the first place, how could Franse counter them?

Franse's face in the candlelight grew very thoughtful, but he said nothing. They both finished the meal with a great deal of content, all things considered. They even had a sweet afterward: crab apples baked all day in a little honey on the hearth. It was wonderful to have something sweet, but he really missed breads. The closest thing that Franse could manage was acorn flour, which wasn't really even close.

"Do you ever help people on a farm or village around here?" he asked, as they both chased the last tiny bits of honey out of their bowls with their fingers. You didn't waste food in Franse's house, table manners be damned.

He shook his head. "Was village near. Gone." His face closed in. "Black-robes."

Those were the Karsite priests he had cursed before, and this was the second time he had demonstrated contempt, even hatred for those who should have been his brothers. There was something going on here that was very important for Nikolas to know; the problem was . . . how was he to get it out of Franse? Franse would probably tell him, but how could he ask the right questions?

"Can you tell me about the black-robes?"

he urged, but Franse only looked frustrated and spread his hands. "No —" and he mimed speaking with one hand.

Mags sighed. "You don't have the words." *Dammit. I think I really, really need to know everything about this. And he'd tell me if he could. But I can't understand him.*

Franse only sighed. "Sleep," he suggested.

Mags nodded. Maybe sleep would improve things.

Maybe when he woke up, his Mindspeech would be back.

Maybe a gryphon *would* appear to carry him to Valdemar . . .

As he climbed into his bed, another thought occurred to him. If Vkandis had helped him in the fight with the demon, maybe Vkandis approved of him finding out what was going on.

So before he drank his mug of medicinal tea and pulled the fur blankets up over himself, he thought, very, very hard. *Vkandis Sunlord, if ye want something heard, I'll be yer messenger, but yer gonna haveta help me hear it m'self.*

There was a heavy weight on his chest. A terribly heavy weight on his chest. It felt like a warm bag full of apples. Or bricks wrapped in fur. Or —

He opened his eyes. It was dark, very dark, and Franse had long since put out the lanterns and the candles in the main chamber. He shouldn't have been able to see. But he could. The heavy weight on his chest was the cat, and every hair on it was glowing, faintly. Its eyes were glowing too, a deep, luminous blue, just like a Companion's eyes. Just like Dallen's eyes.

The cat stared hard into his face, pupils dilated to pinpricks. He stared back and found himself falling into those blue, blue eyes, just as he had fallen into Dallen's eyes when he had first been Chosen . . .

But this time was different. This time, it wasn't as if he were joining something. This time it was as if he were being examined, rather as a Healer would examine him to find out what was wrong. He felt as if he were being prodded, poked, turned around about and even upside down and shaken a little, then put back on his feet. It wasn't *unpleasant,* but it was entirely disconcerting. Behind the entity doing the prodding and poking, he sensed something very much larger, warmer, interested in a detached fashion. He sensed a question from the first entity, a response from the second, though he couldn't tell what the question and answer were.

Then came the distinct feeling that the first creature was poised, like a hunter with a spear, about to make a single, decisive strike.

And a moment later — it did.

There was a moment of absolutely blinding sensation — not *pain,* though it was something like pain. Something absolutely overwhelming.

:There, that should do the trick, I think. Can you hear me, Horse-Boy?:

His eyes flew open again; he had not known they were closed. That had been a mind-voice!

:Of course it was a mind-voice,: the cat said, sounding amused. *:It was my mind-voice. I fixed you.:*

He stared at the cat, aghast, amazed, and very nearly delirious with joy. *:You fixed me! Reaylis! You fixed me!:*

The cat purred. *:Naturally. You called on the Sunlord and offered yourself as a go-between. In order for you to do that, I had to fix your Mindspeech. So I did.:* The cat licked his whiskers. *:Mind you, I'd have done it before if I'd known you were actually broken and not just headblind, with or without Vkandis telling me to.:*

He blinked. *:Uh . . . why?:*

The cat purred again. *:Because I'm a* cat, *silly. Cats do what cats will do, and neither man nor god can do anything about it. That's why Vkandis made us His instruments. He has an interesting sense of humor, does the Sunlord. Now, I want you to sleep and let that heal. It's raw right now. It won't be good to use until morning, and even then we will have to go slowly and carefully, just as with your physical wounds. Tearing mental channels open is bad.:*

He wanted desperately to try to call Dallen. He also knew that if a *cat* told him not to do something, it was probably a good idea not to do it.

:All ri—: he began.

:There's a good Horse-Boy.: And the next thing he knew, there was sunlight reflecting off the rock from the tunnel and the smell of hickory-and-acorn porridge cooking.

The cat was nowhere in sight. He *wanted* to leap to his feet and run out into the main room, he *wanted* to try calling Dallen. He *wanted* to do a lot of things.

But he'd been hurt and healed so many times by this point that he knew how stupid it would be to do any of them just yet. Calling Dallen would be dangerous. Leaping up and running into the next room would hurt him. So, one step at a time.

He got up, put on his trews, and walked gingerly out into the main room. Franse looked up at his footstep.

:Reaylis says —: Mags heard tentatively in his mind. Franse's mind-voice was not unlike Franse himself: clean, strong, simple on the surface, complex beneath, shy.

:Reaylis is right,: he replied with relief. *:Now we can finally talk!:*

The talking was slow, with pauses for Mags to rest when he began to get an odd ache just behind the point between his eyebrows. They ate while they talked, and as Dallen had often pointed out, this was not at all bad, being able to eat and have a conversation at the same time without being in the least impolite.

:We begin with you, De—: Franse glanced at the cat, who had appeared as if summoned. *:Pardon. Reaylis says I must call you Horse-Boy from now on. Or Mags. He prefers Horse-Boy.:* The young priest grinned, shyly. *:I think I prefer Mags. So, we begin with you. Why are you here, how do you come to Karse, and why is your Horse not with you?:*

Mags grinned back ruefully. *:Don't ask for much, do ye?:* He had a long drink of tea and thought. *:Shortest story I can. Yer leaders hired some sorta folks we never seen* *afore t'muck up things in Valdemar. From some place farther away than we ever heard of.:*

Franse considered this, then nodded. *:I did not know of this until now, but it was not important to us, so there is no reason why I should have known. Reaylis knew of this, tells me it is true, and that he cannot penetrate the fog that is about them. So we can tell you nothing of them.:*

Mags sighed. Well, damn. *:I got no idea how or why, but they seemta recognize me. They tried takin' me a while back, an' nothin' came of it. They tried again, and this time they nobbled me. Whacked me up aside the head an' drugged me. When I woke up, m'Mindspeech was gone, an' I was in a wagon.:* He described briefly how he had tricked them, how he had gotten away, and how his mind-voice still hadn't come back. *:Then that demon came after me, and you and Reaylis got rid of it.:*

Franse nodded slowly through all of this. *:These Gifts — all but Healing — they are anathema here. Children who have them are put to the fires. Only Healing and magic are permitted. The only reason that I escaped was because of Old Harald and Reaylis. They stole me from my parents before the black-robes came to the village and made it appear*

410

that I had gone out through a window and a demon had taken me. The demons take many who are caught outside their walls after dark.: He glanced down at the cat. :Suncats are the holiest creatures of Vkandis, so it says in our Holy Writings. And yet I am sure if the black-robes caught sight of so much as a hair of Reaylis' tail —:

:I would be a pretty fur collar,: the cat put in, wrapping his tail around his feet, neatly. :They give lip service to the concept of the Suncats, but if they could catch any of us, we would be quite, quite dead.: The cat yawned. :It is a good thing that we are cats, and easier to hide than horses.:

Mags had to chuckle at that.

:So I am in hiding, and Reaylis is in hiding,: Franse continued. :There was a village near here that I did some healing for, and sometimes performed the offices of priest. I pretended that I was itinerant, a priest without a home temple; there are many such red-robes, for there are many more villages that are poor and cannot support a temple than there are priests to tend them, and so long as we don't interfere in any way with what the black-robes want, they ignore us. But the village produced too many Gifted children. The black-robes declared it cursed. They took the people away, burned the village to the ground, and sowed

411

the ground with salt.:

Franse must have been watching on the day that happened; Mags got furtive glimpses of the scene through his mind's eye. The terrified villagers, the children herded into barred carts, the adults tied together at the waist and tied to the back of the carts. The flames racing through the tightly clustered houses. The carts moving away, the people forced to follow, stumbling and weeping or numb with shock. The black-robes moving among the smoking ashes, literally spreading salt over the ground so nothing would grow there.

Part of Mags wanted to yell at Franse, *Why didn't you do something?* But really, what could he have done? He was one very young man and a cat. There had been at least five of those black-robe priests and a troop of armed men.

And, possibly, demons. What could one man and a cat have done against all of that? Could he have stopped them? No.

So he kept his thoughts tightly to himself.

Besides, Franse *had* helped him, when he had no reason to. Franse had saved him from another demon, Franse had tended his wounds and fed him. He should be feeling grateful to Franse — and he was! — not sitting in judgment on him.

But that made him think of something that caused him some alarm. *:That demon you chased off — is it gonna go back to its master and —:*

:It wouldn't dare,: said Reaylis, and switched his tail angrily. *:We have driven such things off before, Franse and I. It knows the taste of the Sunlord's lash, and it will not risk such again.:*

Well, Mags reckoned they knew their business better than he did. He took comfort in the fact that they'd driven demons off before. If no black-robes had come to complain about it until now, likely they wouldn't turn up this time either.

Suddenly he found himself yawning, his head feeling too heavy for his neck, and aching.

"Bed, you," Franse said aloud. "Maybe hunt, maybe not, sleep now."

Scarcely able to keep his eyes open, Mags could only nod, get up from the table, and stumble to the little chamber, where he was asleep as soon as he pulled a blanket over himself. For the first time since this ordeal had begun, he went to sleep without feeling that part of him was dead.

He woke to the smell of frying fish; for a moment he was confused as to his surroundings. Franse had never fried anything before; his mostly vegetarian diet didn't give him any fat to fry in.

Then he remembered: the ducks and the geese. Franse was no fool, and he was quite a good cook. He must be harvesting the goose and duck fat as the birds hot-smoked in the little smokehouse he had made for the fish that he *was* able to catch. And Franse must have decided that the occasion warranted a little celebration in the way of using some of that precious fat.

He knuckled the last of the sleep out of his eyes and came back into the main room. Reaylis was watching the proceedings avidly. Franse looked up briefly and waved him over.

"Know you calling Horse wish. Is needing more —" Franse gestured.

"Energy," Mags supplied.

"Aye. So — this —" He gestured at the fried fish. They looked wonderful, crisp and brown and delicious. "You, me, Reaylis. Reaylis and I help."

Franse was quite a good cook, and he did not waste a single morsel of that precious fat either; he tossed sliced vegetables in what was left until they were coated and lightly fried them, too, moving them constantly to keep them from sticking to the bottom of the pan. With a sprinkling of salt, everything was perfect, and Mags thought that this was a meal he would remember for a very long time.

When they were done — Reaylis shared the fish, eschewed the vegetables — and the cleanup was complete, Reaylis hopped up on the table between them. The cat looked deeply into Mags' eyes, and for the first time since Mags had awakened for dinner, the cat's mind touched his. *:We can only do this once, at least for now,:* the cat admonished, his blue eyes narrowing in concentration. *:For one thing, we want to do it while there is still daylight so the demons don't sense it. And if it starts to hurt you, we are going to stop. There will be other days, if you don't hurt yourself, and you'll get better and stronger every day. But if you hurt yourself, the damage might be irreparable.:*

Mags thought about how he'd been feeling since he'd awakened without Mindspeech and shuddered. No matter how much he had told himself he was resigned to being ordinary . . . in his heart, he knew he hadn't been, and he would never be. He needed this, and he was not going to risk losing it again. He took a very deep breath, and nodded.

:All right,: he agreed. *:So, what do I do? I've*

415

worked with other people afore, but not like this.:

:You do the reaching. That is all you need do; Franse and I are used to working together, and when Old Harald was alive, we worked with him as well. It will be as if you are reaching for something that is too high for you, and Franse and I are lifting you. You'll sense it, so don't be startled.:

Mags looked to Franse, who nodded. "All right," he said aloud, and he closed his eyes.

Somewhere out there was Dallen. Actually . . . once again, he could just barely sense Dallen, like a sound right on the edge of audibility. Dallen was definitely out there. Mags just couldn't *quite* hear what he was "saying," as if someone were calling far in the distance, but all you could make out was that it was a human voice, and not something else, making a sound.

He "reached," straining. He felt, as Reaylis had told him he would, the other two, "lifting" him, somehow putting him a little closer to Dallen, making that voice a little clearer.

Now, with great excitement, he realized that he could get some of the sense of what Dallen was calling.

Dallen was weary and in despair. He was calling only because he was driven to, not in any expectation of an answer. It sounded like someone who had been shouting the same thing, over and over, into the wind for days. And the single thing he kept calling was Mags' name.

:Dallen!: he "shouted," or tried to. *:Dallen! It's me! I'm here! I'm in Karse!:*

There was a startled, incredulous pause. Faint, faint and far, but he felt the emotions. *:Mags!:*

:Dallen!: he replied, joyfully. *:I'm in Karse! Karse!:*

But he felt the strain; felt the ache starting behind his eyes. Then it was worse than an ache, it was a burn, and Franse and Reaylis immediately pulled their support away, and the sense of *Dallen* receded until it wasn't a voice anymore, it was just that vague presence, faintly, in the back of his mind. He felt a moment of despair himself, he wanted *so* badly to really talk to Dallen — but the pain in his head warned him not to try.

As did Reaylis' teeth firmly set in his finger. There was warning there; he knew that if he tried again, Reaylis would put a very quick end to the attempt with a hard bite.

With an unhappy, strangled sob, he let go of the contact and let it fade into the barest, dimmest awareness that Dallen was out there, somewhere. Reaylis let go of his finger, evidently satisfied that he understood the warning.

He opened his eyes. Franse patted his shoulder awkwardly, gingerly. Reaylis still sat like a statue of a cat, eyes tightly closed. Then the cat shook himself all over like a dog and opened his eyes again.

:*I was able to reach your Horse long enough to make a contact thread with him. He will follow it to me, and here. Now* no more *for you today,*: the cat said sternly. :*And maybe not tomorrow. Things were starting to rip in that thick skull of yours. That makes more dangers than one, you know. Injuries to the parts of your mind that are responsible for Mindspeech are like any other injury except that what they "bleed" is not blood. But it can still be sensed. And you do not want anything that can sense such things to be attracted, now, do you?*:

Mags got a sudden, rather disconcerting and frightening flash of something he really did not *want* to see clearly following a sort of "blood trail." No . . . no, he didn't want that.

He started to stand and found himself swaying a little with fatigue, and the pain in his head blossomed into a throb that seemed to go right through his skull. It must have shown on his face; Franse hastened to support him and aided him to his bed, went off and came back with another one of those herbal concoctions of his. Mags was rather more grateful for the very dim light in his chamber right now; light seemed to be stabbing right from his eyes into his skull. He drank down the potion in three gulps and wound himself in the fur blankets, putting his head on the pillow and waiting for the pain to subside. Franse just patted him on the shoulder again and let him be.

But he wasn't unhappy — far from it! He felt as if he would happily have endured ten times the pain without Franse's drugs just for that faint contact. And to have that sensation of at last having Dallen back *with* him again — oh, that was worth anything!

Dallen was coming. The cat had implied as much. Dallen was coming for him, and he was sure of the Companion's ability to cross the Border, elude demons, and find him. It couldn't be long — a few days, maybe a fortnight, and it would all be over at last.

He was going home.

The next morning, his head still ached — it was rather like the way his body had ached after the first time he'd been riding, however, and Franse and Reaylis both decided that he hadn't done any permanent damage to himself. They examined him minutely over breakfast, although you would never have known what they were doing if you had only been watching what was going on. It would have looked like nothing more than two men stolidly working their way through bowls of acorn porridge in silence, while a cat washed himself on the hearth.

:You are fine. But no more reaching that far for now,: Franse said sternly. *:At least a day before the next attempt, and probably two.:*

His body ached too, and he felt a little feverish. Again, this was a bit like the way he'd felt the first time he'd been riding and all those muscles that had never been used before protested that they'd been stretched, torn, and fearfully abused. But when the cat accompanied him out into the garden to stand vigil over the vegetables while Franse went fishing, he ventured a question or two.

He took his usual place on the left-side bench. The cat leaped up beside him. Once again, Mags marveled at the size of him. Reaylis really was huge, and the reddish-brown mask, ears, paws, and tail were not only striking, the combination was remarkably handsome. *:I think I still feel Dallen,:* he said, hoping he wasn't deluding himself.

The cat stretched and yawned, showing

teeth and tongue. *:You do. Stop prodding it and leave it alone. You're like a child with a bitten cheek or a missing tooth, you can't seem to stop sticking your tongue into the wound.:*

He grimaced, because that was exactly what he was doing. And he knew it.

:Patience. Would I catch a mouse if I kept prodding at the hole? Of course not.: The end of Reaylis' tail flicked. *:He's coming. I am sure that he is getting plenty of help; he would not try to do this alone. He has to work out how to get here, how to get across the Border, how to keep the demons from seeing him. He'll know all this better than I will. I do not know what resources he has, nor do I know what powers he may have. I sense that your Horses are somewhat more limited than Suncats, but, then, there are a great many more of them than there are of us. But nothing will keep him from you now, any more than anything would keep me from Franse.:* The cat turned his head a little, and he glanced at Mags out of the corner of his eye. *:And you are completely missing that blasted rabbit over by the kale. You might have had your breakfast, but I have not.:*

Mags took the hint, and the shot. One rabbit later, and one sated cat, the rabbit quarters were in the pot of vegetables stewing on the hearth, and Mags and Reaylis were back on the garden bench. Reaylis was washing himself with great thoroughness and apparent concentration that was belied by the fact that he was talking to Mags at the same time.

:I know that you have many, many questions, and I am far more prepared and equipped to answer them than Franse is. Keep what you say short,: the cat advised, eyes half-closed as he worked on his paws. :Let me do all the work. And if you would rather say things aloud, do. I'll get the sense from your mind.:

Mags thought about all the things he wanted to know. Things that were important for Nikolas to know. He tried to figure out how to frame his questions about what was going on with the Karsite religion, with the demon-summoning black-robes, with all of the complicated situation — into something very short and very simple. What would give him the most information for the fewest mental words?

Finally he sighed. :What the hell is goin' on with yer priests? Why're they so bad?:

The cat paused. :What always happens when religion goes to the bad?: the cat replied, and resumed his grooming. :Power. The love of power overcomes the love of the *gods. Priests stop listening for the voice in their hearts and souls — which is very, very hard to hear even at the best of times — and start to listen only to what they wish to hear or to the voice of their own selfish desires. Priests begin to believe that they, and not the gods, are the real authorities. Priests confine broad truths into narrow doctrines, because more rules mean that they have more power. Priests mistake their own prejudice for conscience and mistake what they personally fear for what should universally be feared. Priests look inward to their own small souls and try to impress that smallness on the world, when they should be looking at the greatness of the universe and trying to impress that upon their souls. Priests forget they owe everything to their gods and begin to think the world owes everything to them . . . .* : the cat stopped, and shook his head. : *Power is a poison. Priests should know better than to indulge in it. But once they do, you stop having those who wish to serve becoming priests, and you start see-ing those who wish to* be *served becoming priests, and the rot sets in. It started to hap-pen long ago here as humans reckon time.* :

Mags thought about asking why the Sun-lord had allowed this to happen but thought better of the idea. After all, not that long ago, he hadn't been altogether certain that gods existed at all, and now, well, maybe it would be a bad notion to draw their attention too closely.

The cat was far from done with the subject, however. *:Once there were the black-robes, the red-robes, and the white-robes. The black-robes were few, and their mandate was to control the demons in order to protect the people of Karse from their depredations, not command them. The red-robes tended to the everyday needs of the people, and the white-robes were made up of outsiders who had been called to the Sunlord's service or those who went to serve the Sunlord in foreign lands. Go-betweens, if you will, charged with keeping the peace — bridges from the people of the Sunlord to the outside and back again. But then the black-robes began commanding demons; little things at first, hunting down a bandit tribe here, repelling an attempt at an invasion there . . . it all must have seemed to be in the best of causes and for the best of intentions. But they got used to being called on to use the power. They got used to being deferred to because they had the power. And then one day, a black-robe said to himself, "Why shouldn't I be the Son of the Sun? I'm able, I am powerful, I am intelligent." And he commanded his demons to make it appear that Vkandis had chosen him.:*

Mags' head hurt, so instead of thinking the question, he asked the next one out loud. "Didn't anybody say anything?"

:Of course they did. Especially the Gifted among the red-robes, who had the power of Mindspeech, and the white-robes, who were pointing out that this was not the way things were done. In fact, they conspired among themselves and very nearly overthrew him. But his demons were too powerful, the Gifted red-robes were slain, the white-robes fled, and that was when Gifts were declared anathema.:

Mags felt his jaw dropping open a little.

:And that was when the Suncats began coming only to Gifted red-robes, helping them to hide themselves, seeking out and hiding those like Franse. I have been helping the red-robes who live in this place for quite some time. Six red-robes have come and gone, in fact, and Franse is the seventh.:

Mags got his mouth and his brain working again. "Does Franse know all this?"

Reaylis finished his washing and arranged himself in a dignified pose. *:Of course not. It will be a long time before the people realize that they are oppressed, that their rulers are evil, and that they must rise up and overthrow them. We are here merely to keep the spark alive. They must be the ones to blow it into a fire to burn away the rot. Gods do not sweep* *in and fix things. You are not children to be saved. You must save yourselves.:*

"Then why are you tellin' me? Unless you think Valdemar should —"

:No, and your King would be the first to tell you that Valdemar should keep itself to itself unless the people of Karse ask for help.:

Well, that seemed definitive enough.

:You need to know, because your King needs to know that Karse must be left alone and why this is so. The temptation to save these people will be great, but they must save themselves. The key to their prison is within their grasp, but only they can use it.: Reaylis shook himself all over again. *:You must tell them, Horse-Boy, you and your Horse. Oh, it will be perfectly all right if you help a few here, some refugees there, if they come to you for help . . . but to make a formal war of it? No. No, to make war for the sake of imposing what you think is right upon someone else is never going to end in anything but agony. And you must tell them that, make them understand, so they do not even think of making the attempt.:*

"I will," he promised, though as soon as he did so, the temptation to go back on the promise was incredible. After all, what had the people in that little village done to deserve suffering?

They didn't get up on their hind legs and drive the bastards out of their village, that's what, came the reluctant answer.

It was a hard truth, but unless someone was so vastly outnumbered and overpowered — like, say, the slaveys in Cole Pieters' mine — they always had the power in their hands to take back their freedom. That was the choice: to lie down and be abused, or stand up and refuse to be abused and throw the abusers out. Lying down and taking it never worked anyway; you might suffer and die if you fought, but you were going to suffer and die regardless, and at least the suffering and dying part would be shorter if you fought.

:*So you see.*: The cat nodded. :*It's not punishment for allowing this to happen. It's the consequence of allowing this to happen. It's the consequence of cowardice, of apathy, of giving up. The two things are very different.*:

Mags sighed. He still didn't like it. He could see it, but he still didn't like it. He actually agreed with it. But he didn't like it.

:*So see to it that it doesn't happen to your people, Horse-Boy. Now, let's work on getting those shields of yours working again.*:

13

Three days later, and the ache in his head was still a dull throb, so Franse and Reaylis were still forbidding another attempt to reach Dallen. So, early in the morning, even before the sun had come up over the mountains and down into the valley, Mags was shivering down by the pond, bow in hand, and severely puzzled.

There were no waterfowl at all, nor any sign of them.

Though the sky above was a cloudless blue and sun gilded the tops of the mountains on all sides, here in the valley, it was deeply shaded and a thick dew lay over everything. It was chilly, and a faint mist hung just above the surface of the water.

He had come up on the pond as silently as always, and there had been no sounds of birds taking off as if he'd flushed them. But the pond was utterly still and empty; not only were there no ducks or geese out in the open water, there were no little coots, no waders, not even birds in the reeds, rushes, and cattails. It was as if something had frightened *everything* off before he got there, which made no sense. A fox or a wolf might flush a few birds at the verge, but they'd only go to the deeper water where they knew they were safe. A goshawk might take down one, and perhaps even flush the whole flock, but there would be signs of the successful hunt — like a goshawk with a fat crop and a half-eaten carcass — and a goshawk wouldn't have disturbed the smaller birds. In fact, the smaller birds would be scolding it right now, noisily.

What could this mean —

"Not to be moving, Northerner," said a harsh, heavily accented voice behind him. And something sharp pricked through his shirt to his skin, before withdrawing.

He froze.

"Good. I am to be having a large sword, and there are twenty men with crossbows," said the voice, sounding extremely satisfied. "You will to be dropping your bow. And you will to be turning."

He did so. Slowly.

The voice belonged to a man who could have been Franse's cousin: big, very blond, very strong, and dressed in brown leather with riveted plate mail over it. He barked an order, and half a dozen men pushed their way through the cattails and rushes at the edge of the pond, heading for him. They were dressed in much the same way, except without the plate mail.

Mags was surrounded. These men must have infiltrated the area in the early morning or even before dawn; that was why there were no birds.

He thought about fighting them and trying to run, and thought better of it. Granted, he knew the area much better than they did, but there were far too many for him to fight off effectively.

The last thing he wanted to do right now was to fight, end up with another blow to the head, and lose his Mindspeech again.

And they'd called him "Northerner," which suggested that they knew he was from Valdemar, or at least guessed it, but didn't know he was a Herald. He could be anyone or anything. So he submitted tamely while they bound his hands behind his back, roughed him up a little, and then bound his arms to his body, leaving just a sort of leash of rope by which they could pull him. He didn't fight any of it, and he didn't ask any questions either.

For one thing, he was pretty sure that asking questions was going to get him hit some more. For another, he was also pretty sure that they wouldn't answer him.

He *did* let down his shields a very, very little bit, but he snapped them back up again as something exceedingly cold and exceedingly *nasty* brushed against his mind. It had a very familiar feeling to it, and after a moment he understood what it was.

It felt like that Karsite demon.

Now he felt terror; he clamped down his shields so tight that not even the slightest thought would escape; as he stumbled along in the wake of the Karsite who held his leash, he felt cold sweat breaking out all over his body. He was just glad that he wasn't wearing *anything* that was identifiable as belonging to a Trainee. Somehow they already knew he was a Northerner, but maybe he could get away with . . . well he would have to think of a story, and fast.

His mind raced as he stumbled along; he was paying very little attention to where he was going or even to his captors.

Why would a Valdemaran be in Karse anyway?

He couldn't feign being feebleminded, and he couldn't feign being a deaf-mute. He'd had a bow and clearly knew how to use it, and he'd responded to the orders of the Karsite soldier.

Well, what if he wasn't a Valdemaran, as such . . .

Who crossed borders all the time? Traders . . . entertainers . . . all right, he could pass as either of those. Or rather, something like an apprentice trader. He could grade gemstones in his sleep. Or if the Karsites didn't, for some reason, forbid entertainers, he could easily pass himself off as a rope dancer. In either case, he could say he was with his family, and they'd all been attacked in the night — that would certainly be plausible enough and account for his wounds. And the cat had said that the demons pretty much roamed the night at will to keep people penned in their houses after dark.

But how had they found him in the first place?

The Mindspeech. It has to have been the Mindspeech. Maybe it was that connection to Dallen that had somehow alerted the demons . . .

He was jerked out of his preoccupation by a sharp tug on the rope; he looked up and realized that the group had reached Franse's cave, and there was an even larger group of men together with a trio of black-robe priests there. The armed men were evidently ransacking the cave; they were hauling everything that had been inside out into the light, and what was too heavy to take out in one piece, they were breaking up and dragging out the bits.

He could hear the sound of axes on wood from inside, and even as the group he was with halted, someone hauled out part of one of the dressers and dumped it on the pile of discarded and wrecked furniture.

He tried not to wince.

Franse! The cat!

He felt sick.

He hung his head and looked around as covertly as he could for some sign of Franse and Reaylis, full of dread, and sure after what the cat had told him that he would see their bodies, or blood and evidence of a struggle. But as he peered around, allowing himself to shiver in fear, he didn't see anything at all that would have told him that his friends were even in the cave when the soldiers arrived.

Did they have a back way out to escape? He found himself praying that they did.

The three black-robes certainly appeared extremely displeased, which would argue for Franse and the cat having escaped their clutches. So if it was Mindspeech that had somehow betrayed them . . . maybe Mags could convince them that it wasn't *his* Mindspeech . . .

But he swiftly revised his idea of what to tell them after one look at them. They didn't look like the sort who would allow entertainers into their country, and he very much doubted that they let anything other than select traders in, either.

However, he might be able to use his gem-sorting ability after all . . .

And even better, there would be enough of the truth in this story that if they had some sort of variation on the Truth Spell, he might be able to pass it.

I worked at a mine in the North. That was true enough. *I'm a damn good gem sorter.* That was true too. *I was kidnapped.* And that was true.

Now, if they asked *why* he was kidnapped . . . *I don't know, I don't know who it was that grabbed me or why, but maybe they were gonna rob a mine and they wanted somebody to sort out the good stuff.* The first part was true, and the "but maybe" part might allow him to slip the rest of that in without making it come up as a lie. And it would sound plausible. He hoped.

The Karsites were snarling among themselves, and they were talking too fast for him to understand what they were saying.

The black-robes were *definitely* angry, and eventually, when no one brought out any more signs of Franse and Reaylis than another couple of sets of oversized and worn red robes, one of them left the other two and stalked over to him and his captors.

The priest grabbed him by the collar and shook him. The man was bigger than Mags and quite strong, and Mags didn't have to feign cringing.

The Karsite priest shot out a rapid string of syllables and looked at the one in charge of the group that had taken Mags.

"Where the Cursed One is?" the man demanded.

Mags shook his head violently and tried to look scared and stupid. The "scared" part was easy enough to manage. "I don't know!" he wailed. "He sent me out to hunt this morning! I don't know!"

The man babbled back at the black-robe . . . that was when Mags realized why he had been able to understand the men who had stopped his kidnappers and why he couldn't understand *this* lot. These people were speaking about three times faster than the ones who had interrogated the assassins, probably because the troop of soldiers, or at least their leader, had recognized the assassins as foreigners.

Mags braced himself for further interrogation, but the black-robe just looked disgusted and barked an order. Mags found himself shoved roughly aside with a handful of guards, while the black-robes barked orders, and small groups of armed men peeled off to search in every possible direction.

Mags kept his head down and shivered. He didn't have to pretend fear; he could, very dimly, sense the inimical cold of demons, and they were *inside* the mine. Somehow they had managed to break through whatever Franse had used to guard the place.

Or else plain old humans got in, and then they could follow.

If such things could feel anything at all like comfort, they were feeling it now, in the dark, away from the sunlight. There was no sense of restlessness. They liked it in there, particularly now that everything Franse and Reaylis owned had been removed.

Mags broke out in a cold sweat all over again. Were the black-robes going to bother to question him at all? Or were they just going to shove him into the cave and let the demons handle him?

He was afraid to draw attention to himself but afraid to *not* draw attention to himself.

He didn't want to bring down their wrath on his head, but he didn't want them to consider him disposable, either.

He remained where he was, trussed up like a bird for the spit, while the men who had been sent out to search returned in groups of two and four, empty-handed. By this time, the sun was high overhead, and he was beginning to hope that Franse and the cat had managed to escape. He was pretty sure that if they got far enough away, the cat would be able to ensure their safety. Hadn't Reaylis hinted that there were more Suncats than just him? He could probably guide Franse to another Suncat, another Gifted red-robe who could hide them.

Of course, that leaves me pretty much hung out to dry . . .

But he couldn't blame Franse for that, any more than he could fault Franse for not helping the village that had been destroyed. Franse couldn't even see well enough to shoot a rabbit — how was he going to defend himself? He couldn't, of course. All he could do was run.

He sat on the ground where they had left him, just inside the garden, which had been thoroughly trampled. They'd stuck him in the cabbages; he managed to get himself marginally comfortable, sagged forward, and plotted out a story for himself, using as much real detail as he could. He didn't know if there were mines on the southern Border that Karse shared with Valdemar, but he'd bet the Karsites didn't know, either. He closed his eyes, strengthened his shields and added all the little details he could think of — especially how he had gotten kidnapped. He built up the picture of his life in his mind, and the picture of the person he should be. Stolid, unimaginative, someone who just wanted to go home. Someone who was completely bewildered by everything that had happened to him until now.

Now and again he looked up through his hair, and nothing much had changed. The black-robes had taken the one bench that had survived from inside and the two outside; they were directing the couple of soldiers that were left in sifting through Franse's wrecked belongings, and they were fuming. The sun coming straight down through the trees told him that they had been there for several candlemarks. He forced his muscles to relax as they tried to cramp up on him, and he wondered just what the Karsites were going to do with him. What did they *think* he was? He was pretty certain that if they had any inkling that he was a Trainee, the end would have been swift . . .

Unless, of course, they intended to take him to a city and make a spectacle of his execution . . .

He broke out in a sweat all over again. He could picture that far, far too easily. From what he understood, it would be the sort of thing they would do, too. Somehow he had to convince them that he'd make a very poor show . . . though how he would do that, he had no idea. Maybe instead he could convince them that his skill with gems was too valuable to lose?

He should definitely try to convince them he was terrified. That wouldn't be at all difficult, since he actually was.

More and more of the men sent to search for Franse and Reaylis came back empty-handed. The black-robes became angrier and angrier. This would be a very, very bad time to draw attention to himself, so he did his best not to.

Then, just when he was certain things could not possibly be any worse — of course, they became worse.

Much, much worse.

The sound of horses interrupted another snarling match between the officer in charge of the armed men, and the chief black-robe.

Both of them looked up; they clearly knew who was coming, and neither of them looked happy about it.

Mags didn't recognize anything about the men who rode in and dismounted until one of them opened his mouth.

Then he recognized the voice. It was one of his kidnappers — so, presumably, the other man was the second.

It was the first time he'd gotten a good look at either of them.

They certainly had the look of being part of the same tribe, if not the same family. Both of them were taller than Mags, about as tall as Stone had been. Both sported a healthy tan, but nothing that would make them stand out in Valdemar, although their black hair did put them starkly at odds with all the blond and light-brown Karsites. Still, there were plenty of black-haired people in Valdemar as well. He couldn't see the color of their eyes from here, only that they were dark, not light, and deep-set beneath heavy brows. Both were clean-shaven. The speaker's hair was clipped closely to his head, like a newly sheared sheep, and the other wore his hair pulled back in a tail. Their garments were virtually identical to the Karsite tunics and trousers, and they wore riveted leather armor over it all. They were well muscled and clearly fighting men.

Both of them had light swords and very long daggers. The swords seemed to have a slight curve to them.

The first man spoke slowly, enunciating every word carefully, so Mags had no trouble following him. He stared at the black-robe as if the man were something he had just scraped off his boot. *"You will turn this boy over to us. He is ours,"* the assassin ordered, with his customary arrogance.

The black-robe stared for a moment, then exploded into incoherent rage. Clearly he was not accustomed to being addressed this way.

Mags had never seen anyone so angry in his life. The man grew purple in the face. He screamed at the assassin, spittle flying, as the assassin stood there coldly with his arms crossed over his chest. The other two black-robes were angry, but not nearly so furious as their chief. Mags huddled over his bound hands and arms, only cautiously taking peeks covertly through his hair. Right now would be a really, really bad time to attract attention.

When the chief black-robe had reduced himself to impotent spluttering, the first assassin held out his hand behind him, and the second reached into the front of his tunic, extracted a folded paper, and set it into the waiting hand. The first one handed it to the black-robe.

The black-robe seized it and tore it up.

Or, to be more precise, he *attempted* to tear it up. Grunting with effort and struggling with what looked like a simple piece of parchment or vellum, he couldn't manage the tiniest rip. That only made him fume more. And when he tried to wad it up and throw it at the assassin's feet, not only would it not allow itself to be wadded, when he tried to throw it down anyway it wafted back to the assassin's hand, and the assassin presented it all over again, with a smug smirk.

Mags felt his mouth go dry. *The hell?*

The other two black-robes behind their leader were just as startled by this and grew pale, and all the armed men stepped back involuntarily, even their captain. It was perhaps an unlikely reaction to something so outwardly harmless — but what kind of magic (and it *had* to be magic!) could make a fragile piece of paper act as if it were stronger than steel and fly like a feather?

The chief black-robe was the only one who was not impressed. He spat out some words, but he snatched the paper out of the assassin's hand and opened it. His face contorted into such a scowl it scarcely looked human as he read the paper. When he spoke again, looking up at the first assassin, his words dripped vitriol, and there was the promise of future mayhem behind them.

"We will challenge each other one day when you are not hiding behind the robes of the Son of the Sun." Both of the black-robe's fists were clenched, and now his fury was mingled with frustration. A dangerous combination.

The assassin continued to smirk and shrugged. *"When our task is complete, we shall be gone. You may seek us out if you dare. Your little pets will find a warm welcome, and I should enjoy covering my books with your skin. In the meantime, I will take my property."* He pointed with his chin at Mags.

The black-robe turned his back on the assassin; Mags assumed that he *thought* he was expressing utter contempt, though what he looked like was a spoiled child who wasn't getting his way for once.

Well, now wouldn't be the time to tell him.

But he gestured vaguely in Mags' direction, as if to say *"Take it, I don't need it,"* and stalked into Franse's former home, shouting at the top of his lungs, his voice echoing out through the tunnel entrance.

The other two black-robes followed him

in, leaving Mags, his captors, and the assassins alone together.

A most uncomfortable silence hung over them all.

The man holding Mags' rope dropped it abruptly, as if saying, *"You take it! I don't want it!"*

The assassin just looked at the Karsite.

Now Mags couldn't see the man's expression very well from the position his head was in. But as the assassin handed the paper back to the second one, Mags actually heard his captor gulp, audibly.

That more or less suggested whatever look the assassin had been giving the Karsite, it had been enough to frighten and intimidate a hardened soldier. One who served black-robe priests who controlled demons.

It was also true that while the Karsite soldiers had been exuding an air of *don't make me kill you,* the assassins had an aura of something else altogether. Something more like *I just might kill you if I can't think of anything better to do.*

The assassin continued to watch Mags' captor. Mags could see the Karsite actually starting to shiver. Then the soldier carefully bent down, not taking his eyes off the assassin, and picked up the end of the rope. He tugged on it, and Mags clambered clumsily to his feet. It was a good thing his hands were tied in front of him, or he'd never have been able to get up.

He tugged on it again and led Mags to the assassin. The assassin held out his hand, and the man put the end of the rope in it. Then the seemingly hardened, tough soldier actually *skittered* away as fast as he could, never taking his eyes off the assassin and never turning his back.

"Good." The assassin raked the remaining soldiers with a cold glare. *"We will be going. Follow, and you die. Tell your master that if he sends his little dogs after us, I will be picking my teeth with their bones."*

He led Mags over to the horses, but he didn't move all that quickly, which at least meant Mags wasn't falling over his own feet trying to keep up. He did fasten the end of Mags' rope to the back of the horse's harness — which was when Mags saw that both horses were still in wagon-harness and the men were riding them bareback. They must have just unhitched them and left the wagon somewhere in order to travel faster. How had they found out that the black-robes had found Mags in the first place?

Had it been that unseen watcher?

It was as reasonable an explanation as any. He was afraid when they kicked their

445

horses into a walk that they would go too fast for him to keep up — that they would punish him for escaping by dragging or half-dragging him all the way back to where they had left the wagon.

But they didn't. They kept the horses to a reasonable slow walk. If he hadn't been trussed up and in the hands of enemies, it might even have been a pleasure, since the woods were cool and they were picking an easy trail for him. He might even have felt some relief, if he hadn't been so completely uncertain as to their motives; after all, he'd been taken out of the hands of people who absolutely *would* kill him, and who had means of telling when or if he used Mind-speech. Now he was in the hands of people who had at least taken some care of him and might not be able to tell . . . well, unless he used it on them. Ice and Stone — or their guardians, whatever they were — had certainly been able to tell when that happened.

There was no obvious path away from the cave for quite some distance, as Mags had already discovered. In fact, it wasn't until they passed by the remains of a village — scorched chimneys sticking up out of barren earth where nothing grew — that they finally came upon the remains of a road.

Mags recognized it immediately; this must be the village that Franse had seen burned to the ground. He wondered what had happened to the villagers. He was afraid to even speculate.

Mags averted his eyes. The assassins seemed indifferent to the signs of tragedy all around them. It might just have been another part of the forest.

Because the road formed a break in the tree canopy, the undergrowth was much heavier on either side of the road than it was deeper under the trees. Strangely enough, the wildlife didn't seem to take too much notice of them. Maybe because it had been so long since anything saw a human being that the birds and animals had mostly lost their fear.

They walked about half the afternoon before they came to the spot where the wagon had been left, and Mags would never have known it was there if they hadn't stopped, dismounted, tied the horses to a tree, and gone to what looked like a thicker part of growth at the roadside and begun pulling away greenery. He was astonished. So astonished, he found himself making mental notes.

They had picked a spot where the undergrowth was set back a bit from the roadside;

perhaps this had once been a wider spot in the road. They had fitted the wagon into that spot. Then, somehow, they had found and cut branches from bushes or trees that had not withered in all the time they had been gone. It looked as if what they had taken had mostly been evergreens, which meant they must have combed a good part of the forest around here to find them. He could not tell where they had cut the branches from, which meant they also must have been very careful in their pruning, either taking the entire thing off at the root, or selecting branches from the side away from the road.

There had been some ivy vines here, and they had parked the wagon in a way as to make the best use of them without cutting or breaking them. But the real genius lay in what he only saw after they finished pulling out the branches and pulling off the vines.

The basis for the covering was a net that covered the entire wagon and was stretched between two trees as well as thrown over the top of the wagon itself.

It was a brilliant idea; it certainly would take up next to no room in the wagon storage, and you could easily weave vegetation into it. Working backward, he could see that they had first draped the net over the wagon, tied it up, then made use of the ivy vines, carefully disentangling them from the tree, the undergrowth, and each other and draping them over the net at irregular intervals. Many had been long enough, once untangled, to toss right over the top of the wagon, and they caught and held on the net. An hour or so, and their own natural growth turned their leaves toward the sun, making them look as if they had grown there in the first place. Then the men had tucked the branches in all over the net to fill in the look of a small thicket, complete to the dried grass and dead weeds that looked as if they had grown there at the base.

It wasn't just a big lump of vegetation. It blended in to the rest of the thick undergrowth on that side of the road. It just looked as if here it was a trifle thicker, but not at all unnatural.

The two men scattered the cut branches, and while one came to get the horses, the other untied the end of Mags' rope from the harness. He held the rope in one hand and looked at Mags meditatively.

"I can hit you on the head again, and we can load you into the wagon," he said. "Or you can get in on your own. Which is it to be?"

He spoke Valdemaran with absolutely no

accent, which astonished Mags so much that his jaw dropped. For a moment, all he could do was stare at the man. But when the assassin started to move, he came to his senses.

"I'll get in," he said hastily.

The man allowed him to lead the way, trussed up as he was. After a moment of study, Mags put his rump against the back of the wagon, jumped backward up onto the back, swung his legs over, and inched his way inside, scooting himself along on his rump and heels and wedging himself in to his captor's satisfaction.

"Now that you have seen that it is much preferable to be with us than with those sun-dogs, I expect you to behave yourself," his captor said sternly, as the jangling of harness up front told Mags that the other man was putting the horses to the wagon, and they were probably going to be away from here soon. His eyes were very hard and very cold. The look in them warned that if there were further trouble, Mags would not like the result. "If they had known what you are, we would have arrived to find you with a slit throat. If they ever catch their other quarry and he tells them what you are, which he will, they will be looking for all of us, and not even the written shield of the head dog will protect us. So I advise you to be very quiet. We have been mandated to bring you home, boy, but that mandate does not include getting ourselves killed in the process. It takes twenty-five years to train to where we are now, and that is an expense in time and effort the Shadao does not like wasting. We will not hesitate to throw you to the sun-dogs if it becomes a question of you or us, and the Shadao will favor our decision."

Mags nodded vigorously to show that he understood; his mouth was too dry with fear to say anything.

"Good. I see we understand one another." The assassin pulled down the canvas flaps of the back and tied them closed, leaving Mags in the half-gloom of the interior. After a while, one of the men clicked to the horses, and the wagon started moving.

Mags sagged against a bag of what felt like oats and wiggled until he was marginally comfortable — although he was anything but comfortable inside. He shook with fear and reaction. He was still in terrible danger, and that little speech had left him with far more questions than answers.

Unlike the first set of — well, what would you call them? *Saboteurs,* he supposed. Well, unlike them, this pair spoke flawless

Valdemaran. So they must have been carefully prepared so that they didn't stand out at all once they got into Haven. Like Ice and Stone, they were consummate professionals. Mags was beginning to suspect that catching Ice and Stone had been largely a matter of luck and the right set of circumstances; if *that* pair's primary goal had been to get Mags rather than to disrupt the leadership of Valdemar . . .

I'd'a been in a wagon heading south months ago . . .

Instead, Ice and Stone had been faced with divided goals, and as a result, they'd failed both missions.

Clearly these two had a single mission. Get Mags. Like an arrow loosed by an expert marksman, they'd been sent to the target, and they would hit it.

We have been mandated to bring you home, boy.

So they did want him alive. But not at the expense of their own lives, so if Franse was caught, and the Karsites caught up with these two, they would probably pretend they'd had no idea he was a Trainee and slit his throat themselves to prove it.

Mags had no doubt that they were right; if Franse was caught, he'd have no choice but to tell the truth, and given everything he'd seen about the Karsite black-robes so far, Mags was not entirely sure that being dead would guarantee silence.

Poor Franse. He devoutly hoped his friend was well away, and not just for his own sake.

That chief black-robe was . . . terrifying. That was all on his own. Everyone, including the other two black-robes, had been afraid of him, and Mags was as certain as he had ever been of anything that it was for a very good reason.

Now he was angry. He'd lost his primary quarry. He'd been deprived of the only thing he had managed to capture. And worst of all, he'd been shown up by the two assassins in front of his underlings.

He was going to make life pure hell for them from now on, so that they remembered very clearly that while the assassins might be bad, *they* were elsewhere, and *he* was right here with their leashes in his hand.

And if he caught Franse, what he would do to the young priest did not bear thinking about for very long.

Because he had been shown up in front of his underlings, if they learned from Franse that Mags was a Trainee . . . well, a man like that black-robe would take *no* chance on the quarry escaping a second time or being protected by the assassin pair. He would come with not twenty men, but two hundred. He would come with much, much better magicians.

And he would come by night, when their demons were free to move and at their strongest.

So although the assassins had faced down the Karsite priest and his underlings once, even Mags' captors knew, arrogance aside, they would have no chance in a face-off a second time.

Aye. They'll toss me out like rotten fish. Then claim I controlled 'em, or suchlike.

Hideous as it was, his captor was right. His best chance of survival — unless he could escape again — lay with them.

14

They didn't stop moving all night. Mags figured they were trying to get plenty of distance between themselves and the Karsite hunting party. They also moved on decent roads, which puzzled him for a moment, until he realized they could make much better time that way and that it would be harder to tell which way they had gone. By the direction of the sun through the canvas, he figured that instead of going south, they were actually going north and a little east. That made sense too, if they assumed the Karsites would think they would be going south.

The upside of this was that they didn't drug him. The downside was that they didn't untie him either. They solved the problem of giving him food and drink by coming back there and feeding him a few bites of some odd food that seemed to be composed of dried meat and berries pounded together, and giving him drinks out of the waterskin.

Bites? It was more like slivers. The stuff was so hard he had to suck on it. It was good though, better than he would have expected if he'd been given the description.

He tried to concentrate on trivialities like that and not on his predicament. Before sunset, he had not wanted to try letting down his shields, in case his captors *were* sensitive to Mindspeech. Considering how cautious they were, Mags would expect — if he were in their place — that their victim would try something of the sort as soon as he could. If he *didn't* use Mindspeech right away, he might lull them into thinking he didn't actually have it, that he had some other Gift, or that his Gift was too weak to be of any consequence.

He didn't think they actually knew that much about him. They hadn't addressed him by name, for one thing. He didn't think they had personally gotten anywhere near the Collegia, because that had been one of the big mistakes that Ice and Stone had made that eventually led to them being unmasked and found, and these people never repeated their mistakes.

Without hanging around the Collegia, or having close contact with someone or an actual informant at the Collegia (and *that* wasn't going to happen after the last round!), there would be no real way for them to find out exactly what his Gift was. That sort of thing wasn't bandied about outside the Collegia or the Circles, and it actually wasn't even bandied about *in* those venues. You would generally say if you were asked, or if it was relevant to something you were doing (like Kirball), but otherwise the subject didn't tend to come up outside of training classes.

Thinking about that just gave him another source of puzzlement. If he wasn't being hauled away somewhere unknown because of his Gift, what *was* the reason?

Well . . . I do seem to look like someone a lot of these people know . . .

Was that the answer?

But why?

An incredibly wild idea occurred to him. *Is there a chance they want me to take this person's place?*

Oh, that would be insane! How could he *possibly* do that and get away with it? He didn't even speak their language, there was not a chance in a million he could fool anyone for any length of time!

And how would they plan to coerce him into doing it, anyway?

Then he went cold all over, because he knew very well how they could coerce him. All they had to do was threaten Valdemar and the people he loved. *Do this, and we drop the Karsite contract. Do this, or we kill the girl, her father, the Healer, the singer, the Horse.*

And he would. He would do it.

What other possible choice could he make? He was a Herald. In the choice between his own wishes and the welfare of Valdemar, there was no choice.

With that nightmare scenario galloping through his mind, along with possibility after possibility of *who* they could want him to impersonate — or rather, what sort of person, since obviously, even if he knew *who* it was he wouldn't recognize *what* he was — somehow sheer emotional and physical exhaustion caught up with him, and the even rocking of the wagon over good, sound roads in the darkness lulled him to sleep.

He woke immediately when shifting weight in the wagon warned him that one of his captors was on the way back to him. When his eyes opened, it was obvious that it was day again, though from the dim light it couldn't be long past dawn. It was the second man rather than the first, the one who generally didn't say much. This close, Mags thought the second man might be a bit older than the first one; maybe five years or so. The man held the waterskin to his mouth — it was still plain water, to his relief. Then he shaved off some more slivers from the food brick and fed them to Mags slowly.

He tried asking a question or two — simple ones like "What's your name?" and "What is that food?" but the man just shook his head sternly and said nothing. It was very clear that what he wanted from Mags was silence.

Well, then, that was what the assassin was going to get. Right now, the best thing Mags could do was cooperate.

When Mags elected not to ask any more questions, the man seemed to approve. He stowed the water and food brick, then unlocked and rummaged in a box.

What he came up with was not exactly encouraging, however. It was two sets of heavy leather manacles with chains holding them together and a pair of locks.

He locked the manacles around Mags' wrists as Mags' heart sank, and he did the same with his ankles. These things were going to be even harder to get off than the rope. He had thought he *might* be able to untie his wrists if he contorted himself enough to pick away at the knot with his teeth, and once his wrists were free, he figured he could wiggle out of the torso ropes.

But then the man unbound his arms and untied his wrists, leaving him in relative freedom.

Of course, his arms immediately began to protest having been bound for so long, but he didn't care. At least now he could change his position in here.

The man thriftily coiled up the rope and stowed it away. Then he went back up to the front of the wagon. Taking the key to the lock with him, of course.

The chain between the manacles on his wrists was quite long, and at first Mags thought that was a mistake — but he soon realized that not only did so much chain give him decent freedom of movement, it also rattled loudly every time he moved. No good trying to rummage through the stuff back here in the wagon, then — not when the sound of the chain rattling too much was sure to bring a head poking through the canvas flaps at the front.

Well . . . at least he could move.

He used his relative freedom to make an area more comfortable for himself, in no small part because he wanted something to think about besides all the nightmare scenarios his imagination could conjure up. As soon as the chain started rattling, sure enough, a head poked in through the canvas. But when his captor realized what he was doing, the head retreated again, although the kidnapper continued to check on him from time to time to make sure he wasn't up to any mischief. Mags had, of course, already found out that any box that might have something in it he could use to escape with, had been locked.

By the time he had finished, a couple of candlemarks later, he felt the wagon leaving the main road, and almost immediately it lurched to one side, throwing him right into the padded hollow he'd created for himself, using the rolled up net as a kind of coiled, wreath-shaped base. Grimly he set himself to hanging on. This road had to be at least as dubious as the one that had led to his escape. He might even have taken the chance on going out the back again, manacles and all, except that this was broad daylight, it was not raining, and the chain between his ankles was pretty short.

After about another candlemark of lurching and bumping that made him grateful he wasn't still tied up like a bundle of wood to be tossed all over the interior of the wagon, he felt the wagon stop.

He sat up. Were they *stopped,* stopped? Or had they encountered a blockage? And if they had encountered a blockage, or even a hazard, could he possibly use the chance to escape again?

He felt the wagon move as first one, then the other man left the driving box.

But his hopes were dashed when he saw their shadows cast on the canvas by the sun coming around to the rear.

The canvas at the rear was untied, and the first assassin stood at the back, beckoning to him. In one hand was a small crossbow.

"Come out, and take care of your needs," the man said brusquely. "Then we will eat and drink."

With clanking and clattering, he clambered awkwardly out of the back of the wagon and followed the man's directions. It appeared that they were on a steep mountain path just wide enough for the wagon. There was a much wider spot here, and they'd pulled the wagon off to the side into it. The horses looked exhausted, as well they might, since they had been traveling all night. The second man was unharnessing them, so it appeared they were going to be here for a little while, anyway.

Taking care of his business over the edge of the cliff wasn't the easiest thing under the watchful eye and crossbow of his captor . . .

It appeared that the wide spot in the road wasn't the only reason for making a pause here. When he came around between the wagon and the cliff face, he discovered the second man filling up a pan from a thread-like spring, and at the first man's nod, he made use of the trickle of water himself, cleaning hands first, and then face and neck, then getting a drink. The water was icy cold and made his teeth chatter, but it felt better to be a little cleaner.

The second man had already started a fire and was making . . .

Mags saw with a sinking feeling, that he was making some sort of herbal concoction.

"Sit," the first man ordered.

Obediently, he sat down next to the fire.

"It is time for you to learn who you truly are," the first man said solemnly, taking him entirely by surprise, because this was certainly not what he had expected the man to say. "You were born in the North, but your blood is of the South. Your home, your people, are in a land the Northerners do not even have on their maps." The man peered at him intently. "You know this to be true. You have *felt* it. You have felt your blood calling to you from your homeland!"

Mags stared at him, unable to think of anything coherent to say.

"Look at me!" the man continued, and gestured at his partner. "Look at Levor! Then look in the mirror! Our eyes are your eyes! Our hair is your hair! The very shape of nose, chin, brow — yours!"

Mags had to fight to keep his jaw from dropping.

"This is why we took you from those pallid Northerners," the man continued, as Levor nodded solemnly. "The Shadao has been searching for you — or for your parents — since before you were born. Never would we have thought they would have traveled so far, but when our people came here, following the old trail through the signs and shadows, and the sun-dogs offered us a contract, it was thought, *why not?* So we sent the disposable, the expendable, for gold is gold, and it is difficult and costly to search so far from home. And lo! The expendable died, but in the dying, they found you!"

The man paused, evidently expecting some sort of response out of Mags.

"Uh . . . the ambassadors?" he hazarded.

The man laughed. "Not those fools! They could not even see what was beneath their very noses! No, it was the hunter-killer that came with them. *He* saw you, and though he was half mad, he knew you for what you were!"

The memory hit him like a club.

Mags motioned to the others to put their heads together with him. Carefully, Mags thought his directions into the heads of the Guardsmen as hard as he could, staring into their eyes. All four of them nodded slowly. The redhead pointed at Mags, and mouthed the word "bait." Relieved, Mags nodded.

:Tell them the weapons might be poisoned,: *Dallen said.*

Gulping, Mags did so. The big man looked angry, the red-head narrowed his eyes, the third shrugged, and the fourth smiled grimly.

Mags looked at the fourth curiously. The man stared back at him, hard. Slowly, Mags sensed a thin mental voice. It won't be the first time we've handled cowards of that sort, boy. You just see to it that you don't get scratched.

Mags nodded.

:All right. We are getting something in place. Stand up carefully and wait for my signal.:

They got to their feet, one at a time, so

465

slowly and carefully that even their clothing didn't whisper. And they waited in the semi-darkness, Mags feeling ready to scream with the tension, as a tuneless humming threaded its way toward them from the back of the room.

Finally —

:Now. But don't charge him. Walk out until he can just see five of you, but not who you are. And let him hear your footsteps.:

Mags relayed that. And at his signal, they moved forward, soft footfalls muffled by the shelves and boxes all around them. They rounded the last shelf to find the strange man on his feet, waiting for them, a knife balanced on the tip of one finger.

:Now you step into the light, Mags.:

Mags did so, his hand clutched to his sword hilt.

The man stared at him.

"Not YOU!" he screamed. "YOU are not supposed to be here!"

The memory was burned into his memory. He couldn't have forgotten it if he'd wanted to.

So was another.

He read the posting in the Guard reports with a dry mouth. "The two dead were a woman and a man in foreign garb. The woman told us that no one could understand their speech, and they communicated mostly by

466

signs. Their clothing was rich; presumably because of this, the brigands hoped to puzzle out whence they came and demand a ransom. With them was their child, a small boy of perhaps two or three years of age.

There was nothing else of value that could be pointed to as theirs except their clothing. Lacking any other clue, I placed the child with the townsfolk to be dealt with as an orphan without resources. We buried the captives within the chamber that had been their prison."

Anticipation turned to disappointment. Was that all there was?

Another memory, this time from the Kirball game where Amily had nearly been snatched.

Mags started for Amily, as Dallen laid back his ears and backed away from the man who was trying to seize his bridle. But wait — there was Ice! Ice on one side of him, Stone on the other! But why were they here, instead of focusing on Amily? Weren't they — wasn't it Amily they wanted?

But he felt it now, felt their concentration on him, felt a chill of real fear lance through him . . .

Instinctively, Mags ducked under Ice so that the man rolled over his back and landed on the ground. Mags got a startled glimpse of something in his hand that glittered, reflexively *kicked it away, spun, and ran toward Amily.*

:They're 'ere!: *he mind-shouted.* :They're 'ere and they're after both of us!:

Mags sensed Ice coming at him from the side. This time, instead of dropping and rolling, he abruptly changed directions, heading for the piled supplies for the stables. He vaulted over a stack of hay bales and switched directions again. Ice followed him — out of the corner of his eye he saw that Ice was wearing a Guard uniform. Stone probably was, too.

They had known him. And their reaction had been to abruptly change their plans from one target to two. That was, ultimately, the only reason why they had failed in the end. They had seen him within their grasp, and instead of protecting the prize they already had, they had rushed after another quarry. Him.

And a last memory . . . this one very recent.

"You gotta deal with your past, Mags, you have to. If you don't, it'll just keep coming back to haunt you, and one day it'll do something to you that you can't get out of."

Bear probably had no idea how prophetic his words were going to be. Because right now Mags' past evidently *had* caught up with him, and he *couldn't* get out of it. It literally had him in shackles.

"Now you begin to see," the kidnapper said with supreme satisfaction. It was an extremely smug satisfaction, too . . . and a sense that he had been certain all along that once Mags was exposed to "the truth," he would fall tamely into line. "You are one of us, boy. And we will help you to see that."

For the first time in Mags' presence, the other one — Levor — nodded. "Kan-li is correct." He smiled. If it was meant to reassure, it did the opposite, since the smile sent chills down Mags' back. "We will awaken you to your true self. The Shadao has sent his talisman with us for you. We shall give you its spirit, and you will understand your proper place among your people. Then there will be no more need for such as this —" he gestured at the manacles.

Talisman? Like the ones that Ice and Stone had worn? The ones that had *murdered* them, crushed their minds out of existence, when it knew they had been captured?

Somewhere in the valley down below them, a bird began to sing happily. Considering how Mags felt right now . . . he'd have cheerfully changed places with that bird, even knowing a hawk was about to eat it. Because what they were suggesting was worse than quick death.

"We have brought the herbs of remembrance with us," Levor continued. "I prepare them now. We shall give them to you, and you will remember. Then we shall prepare you and endow you with the talisman of the Shadao. Its spirit will infuse you, and you will embrace your people and your destiny again. Then we shall steal swift horses and ride away from here, back to our clan."

He felt overcome with nausea, and terror sat in a hard lump in his stomach.

They're gonna drug me, then . . . do some kinda magic, and that thing *will take over and . . .*

Absolute despair crushed him like an overwhelming wave of blackness. There was no way out of this. There was no one to rescue him . . .

But —

There was one thing left he *could* do, and that bird, which sounded exactly like one he listened to every morning at the Collegium, reminded him of that. He had a duty to fulfill, and he could bargain with them to do just that. There might be nothing else he could do, but at least, he could bargain. He would lose . . . he, or at least the Mags he knew . . . would be utterly obliterated. But he *could* win something. Something important.

"You gotta know I ain't gonna put up with this," he said, roughly, losing some of the cultured tone of his speech under the stress. "I'm gonna fight you, and that *spirit* of yours, and I don't care if it kills me. I don't care what you say about you bein' my people. I don't know nothin' about this Shadao or any of these people, and I don't care spit about 'em."

Levor looked slightly shocked, although that might only have been because Mags had talked back to them. Both the kidnappers looked like people who were not used to being talked back to or having their authority challenged. Kan-li merely nodded, as the little fire crackled and the pot simmered.

"Mebbe I'll die. Or mebbe you'll win. I reckon the odds are even." He took a deep breath. "But there's somethin' I *do* care 'bout, right now, right this minute. I care 'bout the people that saved me. And that ain't you. So. I'll make ya a deal." He swallowed, and he tasted tears. He didn't want to die, and this would be a kind of death. But he was a Herald of Valdemar, and there was so much that was more important than one little life. "Ye don't need the sun-dogs

471

no more. Ye got me. Ye can all go home. Call off yer contract with the sun-dogs. Tell 'em they can stuff it up where their sun don't reach, an' call everybody ye got here back. Promise never t'go after th' Nor— Valdemar an' the rulers of Valdemar ever again. Promise me thet, pledge it, an' I won't fight ye. I'll drink yer stuff, an' ye kin do what ye want with yer talisman, an' ye won't haveta hold me down or knock me out."

Kan-li smiled, very slowly. It was the first genuine smile that Mags had seen from him. "So speaks an honorable *man.* We understand your feelings of obligation. We will accept your bargain. Behold."

He held out his hand, and Levor reached into his tunic and brought out the folded parchment. Kan-li took it, muttered a few words over it, and tore it quite simply in two, without any fanfare.

Then he shoved the two halves under the simmering pot, where they went up in a few heartbeats, leaving behind nothing but ashes.

Mags sagged with defeat. "All right," he said. "You got it. Bargain made."

Kan-li nodded. "Bargain made. But forgive me if I do not remove the manacles. I believe in surety. And I do not yet know the extent of your honor."

Mags nodded. He hadn't expected any-thing else.

"It will take some time for the herbs to steep," Kan-li continued. "Perhaps you would prefer to wait in the wagon."

Since that sounded more like an order than a request, Mags nodded again. Wearily, he got to his feet and shuffled over to the wagon, clambering back into it and falling into his nest.

Once there, he felt tears leaking out of his eyes, but he could not be bothered to wipe them away. He could *not* resign himself to this, and yet, at the same time, he knew he had no choice. So . . . really, all he wanted to do now was to get it over with. Take the drugs, put on the damn talisman, and be done with it. Waiting wasn't going to make things any better.

:Mags:

He didn't even have the strength to sob, really. It all seemed to have run out of him when he agreed to this . . . thing. And yet, he would not have undone his bargain if he had been offered the chance. He couldn't. Not and still remain Mags. All he could do was accept, and cry.

:MAGS!:

He'd ignored the first little whisper of Mindvoice because it was so weak, so tenuous — and because it wasn't Dallen. Not that he wanted it to be Dallen. He really wanted Dallen safe, in Valdemar, and away from him. Dallen couldn't save him, and —

: . . . Mags . . . I know you can hear me. Stop wallowing in misery and answer.:

— that, however, was impossible to ignore.

As was the distinct sensation of claws prickling in his mind, as a sort of warning that they would soon be unsheathed if he didn't behave himself.

: . . . Reaylis?:

:Finally. Now, don't say anything, just listen.:

In the midst of misery, he felt a flash of happiness. At least Reaylis was free, and if he was free, so was Franse.

There was a long pause. For a moment he began to think that the voice in his mind had just been a figment of his imagination.

:Idiot. Their talismans are listening.:

. . . Oh. Now *he* felt like an idiot.

But what on earth could Reaylis, or Reaylis and Franse together, do? He was still chained to this devil's bargain . . .

:Shut up. Dallen is with us. We're going to get you free.:

. . . but . . .

:Agree to the drugs, but ask them to go down to the valley first before they give them to you.:

He couldn't see how that would make a difference, but . . . he could profess a concern that he'd start having visions and wander off the side of the cliff. They shouldn't have a problem with that. How long could it take to get down to the valley, anyway? Not long enough to make much of a problem for them.

:*Good. Now, I see you promised only not to fight their drugs or that specific talisman. Excellent. You won't be breaking your promise.*:

Kind of moot, since he still didn't see how one young man, a cat, and a Companion were going to be able to free him anyway. Especially not drugged.

:*I want you to take the damned things and have the damned visions so you can get to the bottom of this mystery about your past, idiot.*:

There was a very long pause. He wondered for a moment if that was all there was going to be.

But no.

:*Your friend the Healer is right. It's going to keep coming back on you until you deal with it, and right now you need some clues so you can start.*:

He didn't want to hope only to have his hopes dashed. But it did sound as if Reaylis and the others had actually thought this through.

:I am not even going to dignify that with a reply.:

The offended hauteur of that actually teased a faint smile out of him.

:Better. Now, I am not going to tell you what we plan.:

Of course not! If the talismans could listen, they might be able to get it out of his mind.

:Just get down to the valley, take the drugs, get as much as you can out of the visions. I'm finished.:

And . . . that seemed to be that.

He waited for a while to see if there would be anything else — or if his kidnappers *might* be aware he had been getting messages from the Suncat. But all he heard out there were occasional murmurs and the weary sighs of the horses. Finally he scooted to the back of the wagon and put his head out.

"Uh —" He coughed, but he'd already gotten their full attention when he started moving. "Iffen ye don' mind . . . afore ye give me that stuff, can we move t'the valley? I don' wanta be tied up like afore, an' I don' wanta fall off th' rim, neither."

Kan-li looked at his partner, who shrugged. "It is possible. It would be safer.

Also, we could more easily ward our camp in the valley."

The two of them switched to their own tongue and discussed it for a few more moments.

"More grass for the horses," Mags suggested during a pause.

That seemed to decide them. It looked as if Levor had permitted the fire to die down under the pot anyway; he lidded it up, strapped the lid down with a piece of buckled leather, and carefully carried it to the wagon, where he wedged it in.

There was the usual sort of business of harnessing up the horses, but they didn't turn to go back down the trail as Mags had thought they would. Instead, they went forward. They must know this road . . . had they traveled it before? Or had they been scouting the region?

Maybe it was something as simple as memorizing a really good map.

They went very slowly and very carefully, with Levor poking his head into the wagon every so often to make sure the pot hadn't spilled. Mags held himself in place, feeling the tension mount. Because even with the prospect of rescue at hand . . . he still didn't want to do this. He didn't care for drugs at the best of times, and at the worst . . . he *really* didn't care for drugs. He had far too many bad memories and nightmares in his past, and he wasn't looking forward to revisiting them.

And anyway, he couldn't have been more than three when his parents had been killed. How was a three-year-old going to know anything? Unless these drugs were supposed to open him up to that talisman. He was horribly afraid that was the case. Maybe with the drugs they wouldn't even need to put the talisman on him, it would reach out and take him.

And he *had* agreed to accept that. Could he accept it and still remain himself? Could he accept it and still remain loyal to Valdemar?

He didn't know, and he didn't want to have to find out the answer the hard way.

But he didn't have a choice. The only thing he could do was to trust to his friends, trust to his own training, and hold onto himself for dear life.

15

By late in the afternoon, they had reached the valley floor. It was clearly a better place for a camp. Although the valley wasn't particularly wide, there was a nice stretch of meadow full of knee-high grass and even a little stream running along one side of the valley. Both of Mags' kidnappers looked upon this with approval.

They quickly made another, much superior camp, tethered the horses within reach of the grass and the stream, and consulted with each other at great length in their own language. They actually pitched a tent, dug a latrine, got some boxes and other things out of the wagon and tethered canvas over the lot, and looked as if they planned to settle in for a few days. Meanwhile, Mags made himself comfortable in the wagon. He had the feeling they were going to decide that he needed to drink this stuff as soon as possible.

Finally Levor got the pot out of the wagon and set it down by the fire. He began straining the liquid through cloth into a bowl; when he had filled the bowl, he brought it to Mags.

Mags looked at the stuff dubiously; it looked like swamp water and smelled about the same. But when he looked up at Kan-li, it was pretty clear from the kidnapper's posture that if he didn't drink it down, the kidnapper was perfectly prepared to "help him" and hold him down and pour it down his throat.

So he drank it. It tasted as awful as it smelled, and it sat uneasily in his stomach. So uneasily that he wondered if he was going to vomit it all up again.

But just as he thought that . . .

He thought he might just have hallucinations or the sort of view that a baby would have of his parents. But that wasn't what he got at all.

What he got was very much like standing under a colossal waterfall of images, feelings, fragments, sounds, as if someone had shattered lives and was pouring the bits over him.

It was completely disorienting, completely overwhelming.

None of it was coherent. It was all pouring straight into him. He understood, somewhere underneath his panic, that these were visions, not hallucinations and not memories. Or not *his* memories.

At least it was all limited to his past, and not to anyone else's. A few dozen lives, not thousands. But fragments just kept rushing at him, and he couldn't sort them out. A baby's birth (his?). A couple and their infant fleeing on fast horses. Kidnapping attempts — a *lot* of them. Killing, lots of killing. Fighting. More running. Something stolen. Glimpses of a trading caravan. Glimpses of Karsite priests and a city the size of Haven, centered with an enormous building that was not a palace. Another caravan. Storms, inns, sheltering in the wilderness, guesting in temples . . .

None of it made any sense, and the more he tried to sort it out, the more kept coming at him. It felt as if he were drowning in images, feelings, sensations . . . he felt battered and beaten by it all. It was exactly like being in a hailstorm, and the hailstones kept getting bigger, hitting him harder . . .

Or a sandstorm, and the images and memories were eating away at him.

The more he tried to stand his ground, the quicker he was being eroded. His life was joining the storm.

Finally he just . . . let go. Let go and let everything flood over him. He didn't try to sort through it, he didn't try to make any sense of it. He just collapsed on himself and let it roll over him.

And the moment he let go, it stopped pounding him, and it was as if he were in the center of a flood but was managing to keep afloat on top of it.

He just clung tightly to his sense of who he was and what was worth living for. The more he did that, the less the flood affected him, until he felt as if he were something like a chip being tossed on the waves of a raging torrent instead of a rock being eroded by a sandstorm.

He clung to himself even more tightly then; and finally, after what seemed like an eternity, it dawned on him to *shield.*

Maybe he was missing something by doing this, but at least he wasn't getting eroded bit by bit.

He made his shield "slick" on the outside, and now everything was just slipping over him. He was still at the heart of a vision-storm, but it wasn't battering him.

There was no way to sense time, no reference at all. He was utterly divorced from his body. At least with the first lot of drugs these people had fed him, he might have been lost in nightmares and hallucinations, but he had an anchor with his body, which got hungry and thirsty, and fought its way clear of the drugs on a regular basis. He couldn't sense his body at all now. He had no idea what was happening to it in this kaleidoscope of utter chaos.

But once he shielded, he could at least still sense Dallen's faint presence, and he hung onto that. As long as he had that, he wouldn't go completely mad. As long as he had that, he was himself, Mags, and not Meric.

Or rather, he was Meric, but he was mostly Mags . . . there were things he *did* want to remember when this was over, things that belonged to Meric and only Meric. Things about his mother, his father.

Meric. That had been what his mother called him, the mother that had died shielding him.

He sensed these things off in the maelstrom, but he didn't go fighting after them. That would only have opened him up to erosion again.

He concentrated on remembering everything good about being Mags. He went over every move in every Kirball game he had ever played. He concentrated on what it felt like to become a single entity with Dallen.

He tried to remember every song that Lena had performed for him. He tallied all that Bear had taught him — healing, history, and plain, honest friendship.

And he thought about Amily.

Amily and Dallen were like twin supports for him, keeping him steady, helping him to hold on. They were remarkably alike in so many ways . . . brave, steadfast, loyal . . . curiously vulnerable, surprisingly strong. He finally understood, or at least, he thought he did, what Amily wanted.

She wanted to be herself. Not her father's daughter. Not the cripple. Just herself. But that was by far not the only thing she wanted. She wanted the same for everyone — that was why she didn't press him on anything. She wanted him to make up his own mind about things, without persuasion, much less coercion. To be *himself.* Maybe the reason she understood that so well was because she had been regarded as everything *but* herself for so very long by so many people. She knew what it was like to be tucked under a label and have no one look past that label.

But Mags had looked beyond the obvious, and he had seen the quiet, clever girl for all she was and could be. That was one reason why she loved him.

And she had, consistently, looked past *his* labels.

That was one reason why he loved her.

Oh, yes . . . that was part of Mags, too. He loved Amily. He hadn't recognized it as "love" until this moment because it was such a quiet version of that emotion — and in that, it was the twin to hers. But it was love, all the same. And it was very like the love he and Dallen shared, though he rather had the notion *that* was more like brothers.

That's what they don't have, these men . . . and they would never think I would, either.

That must be why he was able to ride out this flood when others would be overwhelmed and lost in it, even losing their very selves to it. Mags understood then that it was not because he was able to hold onto himself that he was surviving this. It was because he was able to hold onto others.

And holding to that, holding to the warmth, the friendships, the loves . . . holding to all those things outside himself that made life worth living . . . that was how he weathered the storm, floated on the torrent; and finally, as the tempest of memories and images, visions and sensations, began to ebb, he drifted safely into shore, dropped lightly onto the sands of morning, still himself.

■ ■ ■ ■

He didn't open his eyes. Quite frankly, he was completely exhausted. This might have been the most difficult and physically demanding night of his entire life.

He could hear Kan-li and Levor speaking, but now he found he could make out fragments of what they were saying. Kan-li was asking his underling how long Mags would remain unconscious.

Levor professed that he had no idea. Kan-li was not happy about this, but he didn't argue. Instead, he changed the subject to whether or not one of them should remain here with Mags while the other went to steal some faster horses.

:Mags.:

It was Reaylis. Mags kept himself from starting, and possibly making a noise, just in time.

:They're a bit distracted, and they and their talismans are far enough away from you that you won't alert them. It's safe for you to speak now. Are you all right?:

He considered that. *:Mostly,:* he replied.

:I expect you feel as though you've been running up a mountain with Dallen on your shoulders,: came the unexpectedly sympa-

thetic reply. *:I don't know if you know your maps of this part of the world all that well, but you are not horribly far from White Foal Pass, and there are a fair number of Heralds and Guard in this part of the world. Dallen has managed to summon a goodly number to your side of the pass. It would make war break out again if they crossed the Border, but if we can get you to them —:*

:Aye,: he replied, and then he nearly *did* jump out of his skin as a cold nose and equally cold . . . something . . . thrust into his hands, then a weight landed on his chest. His eyes snapped open, and once again, he was looking to Reaylis' blue eyes. The cat had just slipped a very thin, very sharp little blade into his hands.

:Hide that in your boot,: the cat said. And between that moment and the next, Reaylis was gone, slipping between the canvas and the body of the wagon. Mags slid the blade down his ankle just in time. Kan-li unfastened the canvas flaps, looked in, and caught him awake.

"The day renews," Kan-li said, and he looked at Mags with his head tilted ever so slightly.

"The day renews," Mags replied automatically, then realized he had answered the kidnapper in his own language.

Kan-li nodded with satisfaction. "Good. It has begun, and the life of our people has taken root in your soul. There will be another drink of the herbs in the afternoon, all things permitting, and perhaps a third tomorrow. Then, the talisman."

Mags just gazed at him, allowing all of his exhaustion to show.

"Perhaps food and drink, then sleep?" he replied, sagging a little sideways in an exaggerated version of how he really felt.

Slowly, Kan-li nodded. He went out, and came back with a full waterskin and a wooden bowl of soup — at least this time the soup was real soup, with meat and other things in it, and not just broth.

There were seasonings to it as well that his tongue didn't recognize but that his *memory* did. It was extremely disconcerting, because he still felt exactly like himself, and yet he had all these . . . bits . . . that were not supposed to be part of him, that had become part of him.

:That was the whole point, idiot,: the Suncat said acerbically.

Kan-li returned, took the bowl, and helped him out of the wagon. To his chagrin, he was extremely wobbly, but at least it didn't take much to exaggerate his weakness. It took Kan-li's aid to get to the area they had marked out for a latrine, but at least by the time he got there, his gait had steadied, and Kan-li did not linger but only waited at a distance for Mags to finish and walk back to the wagon on his own. Once he saw Mags could manage alone, he stayed by the fire. He was watchful, though, and it was clear that if Mags made any sort of move that Kan-li didn't like . . .

Mags got in unassisted and crawled to his nest.

He curled up in it in a position where he could easily reach his boot and the manacles, lying on his side the way he'd been forced to lie when they'd captured him. He closed his eyes and feigned sleep.

:He's coming to check on you right now.:

He heard the canvas move a very little. He kept his eyes closed and breathed deeply.

:He's gone. Start cutting on your bonds now. I'll warn you if they come back so you can stop.:

The knife was very sharp, and Mags worked diligently at the manacles on his ankles, cutting them *almost* all the way through, and just leaving a little tag of leather he could readily snap. He had to stop three times as his captors looked in on him, but Reaylis gave him plenty of warning.

:How are you feeling?: Reaylis asked after the third check.

He took stock of himself. *:Not bad.:*

:Can you fight? You won't be fighting very long, I expect, but you might need to fight. Franse certainly can't.:

He took a deep breath and felt a hot, smoldering anger inside himself that he hadn't expected. These kidnappers and assassins had fully expected that embedding all this *stuff* about his supposed people would make him turn toward them.

In fact, it was having the opposite effect. And he had no idea why.

He only knew that every bit of him rebelled, utterly, against their culture, their beliefs, and their way of life, even though he couldn't consciously remember anything about it. He just had the utter conviction that it was all just *wrong.*

And he knew then that this must have been how his father and mother had felt. Only this complete sense of revulsion could have made them flee so very far, across so many foreign lands.

And he was *not* going to allow these people to win.

He was going to find out what he needed to know to make them fear Valdemar and Valdemarans so much it would be hundreds of years before their kind would even *think* about coming there again — and leave them with a lesson so indelible that never again would they dare take a contract to destroy the Kingdom.

He went to work on his wrist manacles. *:I can fight,:* he said grimly. *:And I want to go home.:*

It was a good thing that knife was so sharp, and he was very patient. He was literally cutting the leather one fiber at a time. He narrowed his concentration down to *feeling* how the blade was biting into the leather, adjusting it minutely until he felt a fiber part, listening to the faint creaks and snaps as he worked his way through it.

By the time he had the wrist-cuffs down to the same little stub of leather, the sun was far past noon, and the wagon was entirely in shadow. Evidently they had decided to let him sleep rather than give him that second dose of herbs. Perhaps they thought he was in such a weakened state that the second dose would not be needed until tomorrow.

:Mags! Plans have changed! Snap your cuffs now, and be ready to get to the back of the wagon and jump!: Mags started, and he slipped the knife into his boot. The tone of Reaylis' Mindvoice was beyond urgent, and

Mags didn't question him. Especially not since, at that moment, he heard shouting erupt outside, and the voices were Karsite.

Damn! He snapped the cuffs, but he gathered up the chain from the wrist cuffs, using the cuffs themselves as a handle for the loop of chain. He might need a weapon after all and that tiny knife, sharp as it was, was not going to do the job. Then he gathered himself under cover of all the noise going on out there, and moved to the back of the wagon.

He peered out through the canvas. The sun was just going down. The camp was ringed by Karsite soldiers, but fortunately they all seemed to have axes, clubs, and swords at the ready, not bows. The three black-robe priests were standing next to the fire, and the chief of them was having a shouting match with Kan-li.

Kan-li's hands were starting to glow a sullen orange in an alarming fashion, and Mags could see a chain with an amulet dangling from one of them.

Had he changed his mind about further doses of their herbs, given how long Mags had been sleeping?

Or was the amulet also some sort of weapon?

Remembering the insensate entity that

had seemed to inhabit the ones that Ice and Stone wore, Mags could well imagine that it was.

Now the Karsite priest's hands were also starting to glow, an ugly red, as his face turned that extraordinary shade of purple again. The other two were making gestures as the sun dropped below the horizon, gestures that Mags suspected had something to do with demon summoning. Levor was backing up and reaching for a weapon at his belt. It wasn't a sword; at this distance, Mags couldn't see what it was.

The priest lunged for Kan-li's throat, hands glowing the color of old blood.

:NOW!: shouted Dallen and Reaylis together into Mags' mind, as a white shape burst out of the forest nearest the wagon and hurtled toward Mags. Mags balanced on the back of the wagon, preparing to jump. Clinging to the saddle was Franse, with Reaylis somehow balanced on his shoulders, both hands buried desperately in Dallen's mane and his eyes squeezed shut.

Calling on every bit of his Kirball-field skill, and replicating a trick he and Dallen had practiced over and over, Mags launched himself at Dallen's back at exactly the same time that Dallen skidded to a halt beside the wagon, turned on a single hoof, and hurtled back toward the forest. Mags landed just behind the saddle, and grabbed for the cantle with his left hand, rather than grabbing for the belt around Franse's waist. Poor Franse was going to have a hard enough time staying on without *him* pulling the young priest about, whereas Mags could probably hang upside down under Dallen's belly and be all right.

Most of the soldiers were watching the fight unfold between their black-robes and the kidnappers. The other two black-robes now stood in a ring of dark, smoky shapes that were beginning to resemble the thing Mags had fought. The chief black-robe was struggling against Kan-li, who had tossed the chain of the amulet around his neck and was trying to strangle him with it. The few Karsites who'd seen Dallen burst out of the forest and were assuming he was going to charge across the clearing were caught off-guard when he reversed and leaped back the way he had come. They had begun moving to cut him off, but now he was racing away from them too quickly for them to switch from swords to bows.

There was only one man between them and the forest, a common Karsite soldier who was coming for them with upraised sword. He had a bushy, blond beard, and his mouth was open in a yell. Dallen cut left, and Mags spun the chain in his right hand three times and smashed at the man's head as if he was sending a Kirball into the goal. The man went down in a spray of blood as Franse winced and whimpered. Poor Franse; he'd probably gotten splattered. The soldier had been wearing an open helm, and the chain hadn't left much of his face.

:Hang on, Mags,: Dallen said grimly as they raced into the trees, then came out again on a road that wound through the darkening valley. Dallen's hooves pounded on the clean, hard surface, and the sound echoed off the walls of the valley. *:The black-robes are calling their demons now the sun is down, and it's even odds whether they'll go after the kidnappers or us.:*

:We'll just see about that,: Reaylis responded, Mindvoice tight with fury. *:Come on, Franse! Snap to!:*

The Suncat uttered an eerie wail, setting every hair on end. It went on and on, and Mags noticed with a start that the Suncat began to glow too. But not with the sullen red glow of the black-robes' hands nor the unsettling orange of the kidnappers' — this was a true sun yellow, pure and clean.

And *increasingly* bright.

Well, they weren't going to make it hard for their pursuers to find them . . .

:That's not an issue,: Dalen snapped. :We're making for White Foal by the fastest route, and that's the road, and they know it. Our only hope is to outdistance the humans and fend off the demons.:

Franse was hunched down in the saddle, and although Mags couldn't see his face, he had the impression the young priest's eyes were still squeezed tightly closed. But Franse wasn't frozen with fear now. He was . . . doing something. Working with Reaylis, somehow. Maybe feeding that sun glow?

:How far are we?: he asked Dallen.

:Half a candlemark, at my speed. They figured to throw off the Karsites by heading in the least likely direction.:

Well . . . half a candlemark could be an eternity. But Companions were faster than any horse and had more endurance than any ten horses. So it would be the demons that would be the —

He caught movement out of the corner of his eye, a shadowy thing coming out of the darkness beyond Reaylis' glow, and reflexively slashed at it with the chain.

The demon howled and careened away, back into the darkness. Mags felt a rush of elation. So he could actually *hurt* these things!

:*Sun and iron,*: said Dallen. :*Franse and Reaylis are supplying the sun.*:

Indeed, by this time Reaylis was glowing so brightly they were actually illuminating the road as brightly as if they were carrying a bonfire with them.

Mags got the sudden urge to "join" with Franse and Reaylis in something like the way he was already joined with Dallen. He didn't even question the impulse, he just held out a mental "hand" and felt it grasped, and through that connection came a warming, pure strength.

Another demon howled up from behind them; Mags sensed it was wailing from the pain of the light and that only a greater pain was coercing it to come at them. But it couldn't hold up to Mags smashing the chain through it; it actually fell apart as the chain went through it, a disconcerting and somewhat grisly sight. Bits and ichor flew everywhere. The ichor that landed on all of them melted away in the light from the Sun-cat. It burned with cold where it touched Mags' skin, but the sensation faded immediately.

:*Of course. We accepted the Blessing of the Sun,*: Dallen said absently. :*Or you did for both of us.:*

:You are the Sword of the Sunlord. We are the Shield,: Franse added, then another demon roared in from the side, and Mags fended it off. This one was bigger and stronger; he spun the chain in a figure eight to fend off the claws until he got an opening to slash sideways through the body; and like the others, it exploded into goo and bits.

Not so much Sword as Flail, he thought absently, grateful now that the Weaponsmaster trained them to use anything that came to hand. Him, in particular, given what he was doing for Nikolas.

:UP!: shouted Dallen, and without even glancing upward, he swung the chain in a circle over his head, causing an explosion of demon parts as the creature dove straight into the chain.

Another came up from behind at the same time and actually snared its claws in Dallen's tail. It howled with pain, and smoke sizzled up from the place where it was caught, until Mags silenced it with a horizontal slash across its middle.

Dallen raced on through the darkness as Mags intercepted demon after demon with either his chain or his fist. The fisted hand took some nasty slashes, but although the cuts burned for a little, it was nothing like the first time he'd fought a demon. There was none of that sense of being poisoned.

He was losing blood, though . . . and he could feel his arms getting tired and sore.

We can't keep this up forever.

The Suncat's light was dimming too. He and Franse were getting tired, too.

The demons understood this all too well. They started coming not singly but in twos and threes. Mags was forced to keep the chain in constant motion, weaving a web of protection all around them, but now the demons were able to get through it with a slash or a cut. Mostly, they didn't connect, but sometimes they did.

There was a glow ahead. Up there, on the road, a light. Torches!

Was it the Guard? Or had the Karsites left an ambush when they came to confront Kan-li and Levor?

:Karsites,: said Dallen.

His heart plummeted. It fell even more when the torchlight glinted off the points of the two or three dozen spears that were pointed in their direction. The Karsites had taken up the standard defense against a cavalry charge — three ranks of spears, butts set against the ground, points pointed at the horse. Mags was so transfixed with horror that a demon got through with a slash to his bicep before he drove it away.

:Hang on!: Dallen shouted, and he put on a burst of speed that made Mags drop the chain and hold to the cantle of the saddle with both hands.

Mags barely had the chance to register Karsite uniforms in the torchlight, when Dallen made an incredible leap, vaulted right over the waiting spearmen, then barreled through the troops behind the spearmen, ramming horses and men with scant regard for either, using everything he and Mags had learned on the Kirball field. His actions took the Karsites completely by surprise; they must have been expecting that once Dallen saw them, he'd either stop or try to turn and run. They certainly had not expected him to leap over their spears, then ram his way through the rest of the troops. Then again . . . while they knew about Companions, they clearly didn't know what one could do. And Dallen was a superb athlete among Companions.

In moments, Dallen was on the open road again. Mags dared a glance back, seeing the milling soldiers trying to reorganize themselves. They just had not prepared for this.

They certainly didn't expect what was following their quarry, either.

The following wave of demons hit the

bewildered troops, a tide of black and shadowy shapes full of razor claws and needle teeth. Someone tried to fight back, reflexively, and the screaming started.

The demons clearly didn't care who they tore into, and when the first rank of soldiers attacked by instinct, they turned their wrath on something that wasn't running away. The Karsites were unprotected by priests. And the black-robes responsible for sending the damned things hadn't seen fit to leave them with any protection, either. To the demons, these were just easier targets, much preferable to chasing something that hurt them with Sun and Iron. They were perfectly happy — if demons could be happy — to turn their attention to the soldiers.

Mags turned his face away and shut his ears to it as Dallen galloped toward the Border, the road ahead illuminated gently by the golden glow of Vkandis.

And in the distance was the faint glow of more torches.

Theirs, this time.

It was a flawless autumn day. It would be a little colder in Haven, and according to Dallen, the leaves were in full turn. Mags was sorry he was missing it, but the messages of welcome and relief that had come down to him partly made up for that.

It felt as if he had been away a year, though it hadn't been more than a moon or so. The Healers here had not wanted to let him go back up until they were absolutely certain that the drugs he'd been fed were all out of his system, his mind was sound, and his wounds were not going to suddenly do something uncanny.

Evidently that was a problem with demon wounds when you didn't have a Suncat around. Franse and Reaylis had more or less promised to slip across the border every couple of weeks from now on to make sure that there was no one on the Valdemaran side suffering from them, and the Healers had more-or-less promised to bring anyone that *was* so afflicted here.

There was no sign of trouble from the road to White Foal Pass. Even Reaylis could not say whether the kidnappers had died at the hands of the black-robes or vice versa, but given that they had faced not only three Demon Summoners, but an entire troop of Karsite soldiers, Mags thought that for once they might have met their match. Neither he nor any of the other Heralds could sense that curious *presence* that their talismans lent them.

It was moot, anyway. If they had survived,

whatever happened next was going to depend on the decision of their leader, this "Shadao," and by then . . . well, Mags was not going to be sitting around idle for the next several months.

He took a deep breath of the leaf-scented air, stretched, and headed for the tent where the glass grinder was working on the last touches to Franse's lenses. But Franse beat him by emerging from the tent before he got there, followed by Reaylis, tail held high.

"Leather, huh?" Mags examined the lenses strapped around Franse's head with a critical eye. Unlike Bear's lenses, which were held in place with wire, or a set he had seen that had been set into a wooden frame, these had been sewn into a sort of leather half-mask that buckled at the back. The leather-maker who'd made the frame had had the amusing conceit of using a leather that matched the dark, brownish-red of the Suncat's face, so that when the two of them turned to look at Mags, he saw two masked faces with big eyes looking at him.

"It is making more sense in forest," the young priest said, and shrugged. "I am glad making of lenses is over. 'Is clearer or smaller? Is clearer, or smaller?' I am hearing that even in dreams." But he grinned, and Mags grinned back.

There had been no more interference the rest of the way to the Border, where they had been met by an entire Guard company, five Heralds, two Healers, and a Valdemaran red-robe priest of Vkandis who had a tiny temple on the Valdemar side of the Border and protected this part of it from the demons. He didn't have a Suncat, and he greeted the sight of Reaylis with disbelief and awe that pleased Franse and that Reaylis accepted as nothing less than his due.

After all, he *was* a cat.

It had taken about a week to round up a lens maker and grind lenses for Franse, and meanwhile the two of them had recovered from exhaustion and wounds.

Now Franse was returning to Karse, something that had surprised everyone but Dallen and Mags. After what Reaylis had said to him, Mags was not at all surprised to hear that Franse's sense of duty to his people was sending him home again.

Well, not *exactly* "home."

"I cannot return to cave, is nothing to return to," Franse had said philosophically. "Anyway, is no one there is needing us. Here . . . is need." Then he grinned. "Also, is supplying whatever I need, your Guard. If home is ruined again, no worry, just to be filling out Valdemar requisition! Ha!"

And now that he had a safe harbor over the Border to retreat to at need — not to mention the ability to *see* what he was doing — there was nothing to hold him back from helping wherever he could.

"I'm going to miss you, but I'm glad you're going back," Mags said, sincerely.

Franse clapped him on the back. "Now that skinny little Northerner has given me eyes and courage?" He laughed. "Rabbits, beware! But you — you have task ahead of you as well, my friend. Harder than mine."

"Different. Not harder." Mags already knew he had a puzzle to unravel . . . not to mention a lot to deal with. He had some vague ideas, but right now he needed to talk to wiser heads than his. Not to mention find a way to sort through that tumble of memory-fragments that, for the moment, were just sealed away in a part of his mind until he found a way to deal with them. But the past could not be ignored any longer.

Franse nodded. "Well. You and I both part tomorrow. What of tonight?"

Mags slowly grinned. "You ain't been to the inn here yet, have you?"

"I have been too busy with pieces of glass and discussions with my fellow priest. And sleeping and healing. Why?" Franse and Reaylis both tilted their heads to the side, looking oddly alike.

"Because they make the best rabbit stew you ever tasted," Mags said with satisfaction.

:Oh, DO lead on!: said Reaylis before Franse could answer, licking his chops. *:And take notes, Franse. Take notes. You can see, and that means you can hunt. From now on, I expect to be fed properly. As is, of course, my due.:*

"Of course," Franse replied aloud. "Just as soon as claw punctures on shoulders finish to heal."

ABOUT THE AUTHOR

Mercedes Lackey is a full-time writer and has published numerous novels and works of short fiction, including the best-selling Heralds of Valdemar series. She is also a professional lyricist and a licensed wild bird rehabilitator. She lives in Oklahoma with her husband and collaborator, artist Larry Dixon, and their flock of parrots.

The employees of Thorndike Press hope you have enjoyed this Large Print book. All our Thorndike, Wheeler, and Kennebec Large Print titles are designed for easy reading, and all our books are made to last. Other Thorndike Press Large Print books are available at your library, through selected bookstores, or directly from us.

For information about titles, please call:
  (800) 223-1244

or visit our Web site at:
  http://gale.cengage.com/thorndike

To share your comments, please write:
  Publisher
  Thorndike Press
  10 Water St., Suite 310
  Waterville, ME 04901